GOOD INTENTIONS

THE ROAD TO HELL
BOOK 1

BRENDA K DAVIES

This book is dedicated to all those who love to lose themselves in stories and dream, you make the world a far more interesting place to be.

GLOSSARY OF TERMS

Adhene demon <ad-heen>- Mischievous elf-like demon.
Craetons <Cray-tons> - Lucifer's followers.
Madagan <Mad-a-ghan>- A beast from Hell. Resembles a boar with a giant tusk in the center of forehead. Mottled red and black skin, plumes of smoke from a blowhole in top of head. Extended, round skulls, cloven hooves.
Palitons <Pal-ah-tons> - Kobal's followers.
Revenirs <Rev-eh-ners> - Mummy-like skeletons. Debilitating cry. Suck life from victims with "kiss".
The Wall - Blocks off all of Washington, Oregon, California, Arizona, New Mexico, Texas, Louisiana, Mississippi, Alabama, Georgia, Florida, South Carolina, North Carolina, Virginia, Maryland, Delaware, New Jersey, Connecticut, Rhode Island, Massachusetts, Vermont, New Hampshire, and Maine. Blocks parts of Nevada, New York, Pennsylvania, and Arkansas. Similar wall blocks off parts of Europe.
Varcolac demon <Var-ko-lack>- Born from the fires of Hell. Only one can exist at a time. When that one dies another rises from the Fires of Creation. Fastest and most brutal of all the

demons. They are the only kind that can create and open natural gateways within Hell as well as close them. They control the hellhounds.

Demon Words

Mah Kush-la ˈmɑː <kush-la> - My Heart.
Mjéod <myod> - Mead or a demon drink.

Glossary of Symbols

Humans took some of them and turned them into what became known as the Elder Futhark, also known as runes.

Eiaz <e-az> **-** (Tilted Z) - Speed, heightened senses, and protection.
Risaz <ree-saz**> -** (Straight line with a triangle attached to the middle) - Force of destruction.
Sowa <sow-ah> - (Backwards E with sword piercing the center) - Blade of fire.
Zenak <zen-ach> - (Three wavy lines) - Eternal fire and life.
Ziwa <zee-wah> - (Two V's with a line connecting the top, like fangs) - Guardian of the hellhounds. Mark is considered gift of strength, endurance, and virility. Considered a blessing and a curse as well as marks bearer as having a piece of the hell-hound's soul within them.

PROLOGUE

River

I was nine when the first of the fighter planes flew over thirteen years ago. I remember tilting my head back to stare at them as they moved over us in a V formation. Excitement buzzed through me, but I felt no fear. They had been a more common sight before the military base closed last year; despite that status, they still occasionally flew over our town.

When the planes vanished from view, I turned my attention back to the game of hopscotch I was playing with my friend, Lisa. I was about to beat her, and I wanted to finish before Mother woke from her nap and called me away. Lisa stared at the sky for a minute more before turning her attention back to me. She bent to pick up the rock on the ground as four more planes flew over us in a tight formation. They left white streaks in the sky as their engines roared over us.

The rock Lisa had picked up slid from her fingers and clattered onto the asphalt. Together, we watched as the second wave of them disappeared from view. I don't know why the initial wave hadn't bothered me, but the second wave caused a cold sweat to trickle down my neck.

Following the noise of the planes, the world around us took on an unusual hush for a Saturday afternoon in July. Normally there were shouts from kids playing up and down the street. The rumble of cars driving down the highway, heading toward the beach, was a near constant background noise now that tourist season was in full swing.

Turning my attention back to Lisa, I waited for her to pick her rock up again and continue, but she remained staring at the sky. The planes had unnerved me, but what did I really know? At that point in my young life, my biggest problem was napping in the house a hundred feet away from me. I hoped their noise hadn't woken Mother; grouchy was a permanent state for her, but when she was woken from a nap, she could be a real bear.

I glanced over at my one-year-old brother, Gage. My heart melted at the sight of his disheveled blond hair sticking up in spikes and his warm brown eyes staring at the sky. He lifted a fist and waved at the planes fading from view. His coloring was completely different from my raven hair and violet eyes, due to our different fathers. Mine had taken off before I was born; Gage's father had at least stuck around to see his birth before leaving our mother in the dust.

Turning his attention away from the sky, Gage held his arms toward me before shoving a hand into his mouth. Unable to resist him, I walked over and lifted him off the ground. I cradled his warm body in my arms. I always brought him with me during Mother's naps so he wouldn't wake her, and because I couldn't stand him being alone in the house while she slept. I'd been alone so many times before he'd come along that I refused to let him be too.

Gage wrapped his chubby arms around my neck, pressing his sweaty body against mine. Lisa wiped the sweat from her brow and brushed aside the strands of brown hair sticking to her face. Waves of heat wafted from the cooking asphalt, but I barely felt it. I'd always preferred summer to winter and tolerated the heat better than most others.

Six more planes swept overhead, leaving a loud, reverberating boom in their wake as they sped by. Car alarms up and down the street blared loudly. Horns honking in quick succession, and headlights flashing had all the dogs in the neighborhood barking. The relatively peaceful day had become chaotic in the blink of an eye.

Along the road, doors opened and beeps sounded as people turned off their alarms. Shouts for the dogs to be quiet could be heard over the noise of the vehicles. Some people ran out of their homes and toward the squealing cars to try and turn off the alarms that wouldn't be silenced.

Gage's arm tightened around my neck to the point of near choking. I didn't try to pull him away; instead I held him closer when he began to shake. Then just as rapidly as the rush of noise had erupted on the street, everything went completely still. Even the dogs, sensing something was off, became almost simultaneously silent. The few birds that had been chirping stopped their song; they seemed to be holding their breath with the rest of the world.

I remember Lisa stepping closer to me. Years later, I can still feel her warm arm against mine in a moment of much needed solidarity. "What's going on, River?" she asked me.

"I don't know."

Then, from inside some of the nearby homes, screams and cries erupted, breaking the near silence. Exchanging a look with Lisa, we turned as one and ran toward her house. We clambered up the steps, jostling against each other in our rush to see what was going on. We'd scarcely entered the cool shadows of her screened-in porch when I heard the sobs of her mother.

We both froze, uncertain of what to do. Tears streaked Gage's cheeks and wet my shirt when he buried his face in my neck. He may have only been a baby, but he still sensed something was completely wrong.

Instinctively knowing we would be shut out of whatever was going on if we alerted them to our presence, it had to be grown-up stuff after all, we'd edged carefully over to the windows, looking in on the living room. Peering in the windows, I spotted Lisa's mom on the couch, her head in her hands as she wept openly. Lisa's father stood before the TV, the remote dangling from his fingertips as he gaped at the screen.

My eyes were drawn to the TV; my brow creased in curious wonder at the mushroom cloud I saw rising from the earth. A black cloud of rolling fire and smoke covered the entire horizon on the screen.

Beneath the cloud, words ran across the bottom of the screen. *The U.S. is under attack. Nuclear bomb dropped on Kansas. Possible terrorist attack. Possible attack from China or Russia. Numerous areas of reported violence erupting.*

"It's World War III," Lisa's father said as the remote fell from his hand and her mother sobbed harder.

My heart raced in my chest, and my throat went dry as I struggled to grasp what was going on. I knew something awful had happened, but I still couldn't understand what. How could I? I was a child. My time on this earth had been spent trying to avoid my mother as much as possible. It had also been filled with taking care of my brother, friends, TV, books, school, and the endless days of summer, that until then, I'd been so looking forward to.

I hugged Gage as I vowed to do anything I could to keep him safe from whatever was about to unfold.

Standing there with Lisa, I may not have completely understood what was happening, but I knew nothing would ever be the same again. The only world I'd ever known was now entirely different.

The cries and shouts in the neighborhood increased in intensity when more planes flew overhead with a loud whoosh that rattled the glass in the windows before us and set off some of the alarms again. Turning, I glanced back at the street to find some people running back and forth, hugging each other before running toward another house. Some got in their cars and drove away with a squeal of tires. Much like a chicken with its head cut off, they were unsure of where to go or what to do.

What could anyone possibly do? Were we next for the bombs? The hair on my nape rose.

I turned back to the TV and watched as the cloud continued to rise. More words flashed by on the bottom of the screen, but I barely saw them. I became so focused on the TV, I never heard my mother enter the porch until one of her hands fell on my shoulder.

Tilting my head back to look at her, I realized it must be worse than I ever could have imagined if *she* was touching *me*. It was the first time she'd touched me in a comforting way in years. It would be the last, that wasn't by accident or in anger, for all the years following.

"What is happening?" Lisa inquired in a tremulous whisper.

"The end," Mother replied.

I wouldn't know how right she was until years later.

CHAPTER ONE

River

Gathering the bundle of fish I'd caught, I lifted them off the ground and grabbed my pole. I'd eaten so much fish over the years, I kept expecting to sprout gills one day. Gills were a better option than starvation though. Despite the vast quantities of fish I'd caught over the years, I still hated the vacant stare of death in their eyes and the fact I'd been the one to cause it. I avoided looking into their eyes as I swung them over my back and gathered the rest of my equipment.

Turning back to the ocean flowing through the canal, I stared across the deep blue water swirling with rapid currents. On the other side was a rocky shoreline and pathway that practically mirrored the shore where I stood. More fishermen and women stood on the rocks or waded down into the water. I couldn't make out any of their features, but it didn't matter anyway; I'd probably never meet any of them. Below me and across the way, there were more people walking the rocks, plucking crabs from between them, and tossing the clawing creatures into baskets.

The crisp, briny smell of the ocean tickled my nostrils as I inhaled the familiar, well-loved scent. I brushed away the strands of black hair the breeze tugged from my ponytail and blew across my eyes. The power of the sea, the life flowing through it called to me, making me feel strangely more alive and yet all alone as I watched the sun dancing across its surface. Above me, seagulls and herons cawed and circled before plunging into the water.

An older man with gray hair and a kind smile waved to me before gesturing at the stripers hanging heavily against my back. "Nice catch today, River," he commented.

"Thanks, Mr. Wix," I replied and shifted the weight of the three fish I'd caught. Now that it was mid-May, the bigger stripers were finally starting to come through the canal again. The most we were allowed to pull from the ocean was three a week, so as not to deplete the fish population now that they'd once again become Cape Cod's main food supply. Mostly, I only caught one at a time so they wouldn't go bad but today was a special day and I had plans for these three. "Good luck to you."

He wiped the sweat from his forehead. "I think I'm going to need it," he muttered.

I knew how he felt. It had taken me years to become as good at fishing as I was, and I most certainly hadn't done it alone. After the bombs, it had fallen on my shoulders to keep my family fed. Gage was still breast-feeding, thankfully, but my mother and I were on our own.

One day, with my stomach grumbling and my head spinning from lack of food, I had decided to take my small, freshwater pole here. On my first cast, I managed to hook myself in my right eyebrow. After cutting the line, I placed a new hook on the line and successfully cast the hook into the water. I'd barely had time to breathe before the pole was snatched from my hands by the strong current, which had probably been for the best because if I had miraculously managed to catch something, it would have snapped my pole like a toothpick.

I had returned to my neighborhood, desolate and starving as I shuffled down the street at sunset. My eyebrow throbbed from the hook still stuck in it; I'd had no success in getting it out on my own. One of my neighbors, Mr. Anderson, had spotted me walking down the street, sniffling as I tried not to cry. He'd taken me into his garage, pulled the hook from my eyebrow with a set of pliers, and placed a piece of ice over it.

I'd sat on a stool, with the ice over my eye, and stared at all of the poles and lures hanging from the hooks and pegs on his back wall. Many on the Cape enjoyed fishing, but he had reveled in making his own hooks, lures, and poles. To him, it had been better than actually fishing; to me it had been a stark reminder of my recent failure.

"Seems we've got some things to teach you, young miss," he'd said after I'd told him my story and how my mother and I hadn't eaten in two days. He'd sent me home with a small-mouth bass to eat, and instructions to return early in the morning so I could start learning how to fish. He told me if I was late, he wouldn't offer again.

I showed up a half hour early and ready to go. He taught me how to catch fresh water fish for a few years before determining I was old enough and strong enough to handle saltwater fishing. He'd also patiently taught me how to bend the hooks and create lures, with a vise and a pair of pliers, in his garage. When I was ready for them, he'd given me a couple of his poles and taught me how to care for them.

He'd allowed me to use his materials in exchange for giving him a fish every once in a while. When we ran low on supplies to create our fishing gear, we would scavenge for metal and other scraps we could find from junkyards and abandoned homes.

On my fifteenth birthday, he'd gotten together with some of our other neighbors to scrape up enough supplies for me so I would be able to have my own workspace. To this day, it was the kindest thing anyone had ever done for my family and me, and I'd openly wept over the gifts.

I may have been sixty years younger than him, but I quickly became his adopted daughter, or perhaps I'd become his replacement for the grandchildren he'd lost. They were living in Kansas with his son when the bombs were dropped, and they had been his only remaining family.

Whatever I was to him, we had both needed each other, and when he passed away in his sleep the following year, I'd spent the next six months crying every time I went out to fish. I still thought of him often and couldn't help but think of him now as I stood in his favorite fishing spot, but instead of tears, I smiled as I stared out at the water.

Turning away from Mr. Wix, I started climbing the boulders, careful to avoid the people set up around me. The canal was one of the best places to go for the saltwater stripers; unfortunately, everyone in the area knew it. The rocks were clustered with fishermen and women looking to feed their families.

At least we were a coastal community; from what I'd heard, the inland towns of Massachusetts were worse off than us, but then we never knew what was true and what wasn't. Rumors swirled like the wind around here.

I glanced up at the Bourne Bridge, arching gracefully over the canal. At one time we'd been allowed to travel freely over the bridge, but after the war finally ended, barricades had been established on the bridge to stop the crush of people trying to move onto the Cape after the bombs had fallen.

What had once been a thriving tourist community, now

depended on being able to feed its own by shutting out the rest of the world.

After the bombs, the Cape had experienced an influx of people looking to get as far from the radiation fallout as possible. There hadn't been enough homes for them, or resources, and the homicide and robbery rate skyrocketed overnight. People killed each other for a loaf of bread before it had been determined that the ocean hadn't been affected by the radiation from the bombs, and it was still safe to fish from its waters.

The terror and insanity of those first six months was something I could never forget. I would lay in my bed with Gage in my arms, praying no one would break into our house, kill us, and then claim our house as their own, as was becoming the frequent practice. All through the night, the screams of others would resonate through the air, fires would erupt, and sobs were heard.

The only protection we'd had against the roving groups of thieves and murderers were the residents from our neighborhood who would patrol every night, looking to keep as many people safe as they could. Still, they weren't able to save everyone.

Eventually, the small military presence we had here at the time, what remained of the police force on the Cape, and most of the residents got together to start removing anyone who hadn't been a resident before the bombs. Afterward, they'd shut off the Bourne and Sagamore bridges.

Now, soldiers guarded the bridges against people coming over. Military boats patrolled the canal and surrounding ocean to keep out anyone who might try to cross over that way. The supplies we had here were shared and bartered amongst the towns on the Cape and with those across the canal as well as they could be, but it was essential that the natural resources weren't depleted beyond their ability to replenish themselves.

I turned away from the bridge and my mind away from those early, awful memories. Things were far better now, and today was a day mostly of celebration, not one of melancholy, I decided.

Finally breaking free of the rocks, I straightened and adjusted my catch when I reached the asphalt pathway running the length of the canal. When I was a kid, the pathway had been well maintained, the grass cut, and the asphalt smooth. It had been a popular place for tourists to walk, bike, and run while watching the water and birds.

Now, I kept my eyes on the pathway to avoid the potholes and broken chunks of pavement upheaved over the years by the weather and foot traffic. I kept one hand on the strap holding the stripers against my back while the other swung free. The nearly knee-high grass tickled the back of my free hand when I cut across it to the railroad tracks beyond. I followed the tracks for over a mile before slipping into the woods.

There were places to fish closer to home, but none of them yielded as large of fish as the ones caught from the canal. Besides, I liked to walk along the glistening ocean waters and pretend things were the way they used to be before the war.

The pathway beneath my feet was well worn by some of my neighbors and myself. Around me, birds chirped in the trees whose leaves had recently bloomed again. I watched the play of shadows over the ground before me as the branches swayed with the breeze. Over my head, a squirrel screeched and leapt from one branch to another. It chased after another squirrel, its tail raised as the other ran away from it.

A sense of peace stole through my body. Some of my first memories were of being soothed by nature, and I'd always felt a strong affinity to the earth and all of the living things on it. It was a balm to my soul, one that strangely energized and revitalized me. But then, I had some pretty strange ways.

Unable to resist, I rested my fingers against the trunk of a red maple with leaves the size of my hand. I sighed when I felt the pulse of life flowing through the tree and into the earth where its roots ran deep. My fingertips tingled, and a smile tugged at my mouth as I swore I felt the worms turning over within the dirt.

I didn't know if others could feel this thrum of life or not; I had never asked. I had enough personal oddities that only those closest to me knew about. I didn't need to add another one to the pile.

It may not be an oddity. This could be something everyone experiences. I tried to convince myself of this, and it could be true as I was sure I didn't know *every*thing about my friends and family, but for some reason, I doubted they felt this too.

Reluctantly, I tore my fingers away from the rough bark. A strange sense of loss filled me, but I continued onward. I couldn't stand around touching trees all day. Even those who loved and accepted me might toss me into the nearest holding cell they could find if I never moved away from a tree again.

I wouldn't blame them if they did either.

CHAPTER TWO

River

The pathway opened up to reveal the backside of my neighborhood. Stepping onto the street, I made my way down the road toward the small, gray, Cape-style house at the end of the block. I was almost to the door when I heard footsteps behind me. Glancing over my shoulder, I smiled when I spotted Lisa running toward me.

Her oak-leaf-colored eyes were alight with happiness as she arrived at my side. "There you are!" she gushed. "I've been waiting for you for *hours*."

I glanced at the early morning sun hovering over the trees. It had probably been more like minutes. Lisa wasn't exactly known as an early riser and had a tendency to exaggerate; *she* should have been a fisherman. Her light-brown hair, pulled into a ponytail, bounced against the back of her neck when she fell into step beside me. She tugged up the sleeve of her faded red T-shirt when it slipped off one of her shoulders to reveal her collarbone. The knees of her pants had holes in them from the time she spent in the large community garden in the center of our neighborhood.

"You haven't been up for an hour, much less waiting for me for *hours*," I replied with a laugh.

She grinned at me and did an odd little half skip. "You're right," she admitted.

Walking by our neighbors' homes, I noted the sagging porches, the faded shingled siding, and broken shutters on most of them. Vines encircled the porch railing of the house on my right. The vines had started taking over most of the porch last year and were slowly weighing it down. There was little time for anyone to do home repairs anymore, and many didn't have a way of obtaining the things they would need for some of the repairs.

Money as currency was almost a thing of the past. I'd heard some still used gold and silver to obtain certain things, but paper and coin currency was gone, and I didn't know anyone who would choose gold over a meal or clothing. All that mattered anymore was survival. Food was the main currency; it was exchanged and bartered for on a daily basis.

"Where's Asante?" I inquired of Lisa.

Asante was a Guard in the community and Lisa's boyfriend for the last year and a half. Two months ago, she'd moved out of her parents' house and into one on the next street over to live with him.

"With everything going on today, he had to go into work early," she replied. "You know how crazy and hectic things get on Volunteer Day."

"I do," I said and shifted the weight of the fish on my back. May fifteenth may have become the most looked forward to day of the year on the Cape since the war had devastated the nation.

"You are going today, right?" Lisa inquired.

I nodded and slid the fish off my back. "Wouldn't miss it." Few in town would, my mother most likely being one of them.

Walking by the fences surrounding the community garden, I glanced inside at the man and woman already weeding the plot set up on almost three acres of land. The houses that had once stood on the land had caught fire one night nine years ago. The owners who had survived the fire had moved into the empty homes of those who had died over the years or been killed during the turbulent times following the war. The small gardens everyone had been growing behind their homes had been moved here. They'd been combined and expanded on with the land left behind by the fires. Almost everyone in the neighborhood worked in the garden, but some spent more time in it than others.

The neighborhood I remembered from my early childhood was far larger and far different than the closed-in streets that had once existed. Due to the burned down houses, the neighborhood had grown to include homes I'd never been able to see from here before. I knew everyone on these roads and most of the people in town. Before, I'd barely known anyone beyond my street and school. The whole neighborhood working together over the years was what had kept us all alive.

At the next house, Lisa followed me up the steps and inside. When the screen door creaked shut behind us, the owner of the house, Mrs. Loud, glanced up from the paper she'd been reading and smiled at me. The town still put out a monthly paper of events that was passed around the residents, as there were never enough copies for everyone to have their own.

Pushing her glasses onto her head, Mrs. Loud folded the paper and pushed it aside. "Good catch, Ms. Dawson," she said to me.

I unhooked the largest fish and placed it on the counter

she'd built between the living room and kitchen of her home. "Lucky catch. Can I get some salve?" I inquired.

Mrs. Loud took the fish and placed it into the small cooler behind the counter. The rolling blackouts made it difficult to keep things well refrigerated, but the fish wouldn't stay in there for long, and there was ice inside to help keep it cool when the next blackout occurred.

"Bailey still has a rash?" she inquired of my youngest brother as she slid the top of the cooler closed.

"Yes, but it's getting better."

She pulled the green tin of homemade salve from the shelf. I didn't know who made the stuff, it wasn't anyone in our neighborhood, but it worked miracles on Bailey's diaper rash. It was also great for the cuts my hands often received from fishing and from making the lures and hooks.

"That's good." Mrs. Loud put the little green tin in front of me. "Anything else?"

A pair of new shoes would have been fantastic. I looked down at the hole in the top of my shoes and stuck my big toe through it. I wiggled it back and forth as I debated her question. I could probably get another couple of weeks out of the shoes if I had to and Gage really could use a new pair of pants. He was growing so fast it was almost impossible to keep him clothed.

"I could use some new pants for Gage," I finally said.

"Another growth spurt?" Mrs. Loud asked. "He's going to be taller than everyone in town."

"He is," I agreed.

Beside me, Lisa picked up one of the shell necklaces on the counter and ran it between her fingers. Not many people traded for the necklaces, but they were pretty, and they helped to keep Josie, the young widow woman down the street busy. I lifted my hand to the pink and white shells around my neck. None of them were bigger than a nickel, but they were all polished until they shone. Josie had given it to me a few months ago when I'd stopped by with some fish for her.

"I'll add a couple of inches onto his last measurement and have the pants made up for you within the next couple of days," Mrs. Loud said.

"Thanks, Mrs. Loud. I'll see you later today."

"Wouldn't miss it."

I nudged Lisa toward the door. She looked up at me and blinked, pulled from her thoughts by my prodding. Releasing the necklace, Lisa gave Mrs. Loud a smile before we returned outside again. She walked with me down the street toward the small Cape house I shared with my mother and two brothers.

"I should get to work," Lisa said and waved toward the garden. "I'll see you in a couple of hours."

"Sounds good."

She smiled at me, glanced at my sagging, blue house, and squeezed my arm. Feeling as if I were carrying a hundred fish on my shoulder instead of two, I walked up the cracked walkway to the faded gray door with my shoulders hunched. I stopped myself from knocking on the door before entering; it was my home, but it had never felt like such to me.

CHAPTER THREE

River

Twisting the knob, I pushed the door open and stepped into the shadowed interior of the house. From the room on my left, I could hear the drone of the TV. I stepped into the room to find my mother in her customary spot in the armchair. Tufts of yellow stuffing poked through the worn brown fabric. She had to sit on two pillows as the springs had busted out of the seat years ago.

Her blonde hair waved around her face. A face that had once been pretty, but the bitterness of her soul had made it impossible for me to see any prettiness in her. Dark circles and bags lined her watery blue eyes. She was smaller than I was at five foot two with a slender build. I was almost five-nine with an athletic build honed by years of walking, fishing, and working outside.

Her mouth was always pursed, and in my twenty-two years, I'd rarely seen her smile. There may have been a few smiles before my stepfather, Gage's dad, had taken off after Gage's birth; there had been less after.

I'm not sure if she knew who Bailey's father was, I certainly didn't, nor had I ever known my own father. The only thing I'd ever been told about my father was that he was a bastard she'd met while in high school and he'd been passing through town. I didn't know his name. He'd left her when he found out she was pregnant and had never been heard from again. I'd once seen a picture of him—there was no denying my resemblance to the man—but she didn't know I'd ever seen it.

She called him the prick, and throughout most of my life, she'd referred to me as a bastard, useless, or the evil being who had ruined her life, which was fine by me. I didn't think much of her either. I would think even less of her than I did, but she had at least succeeded in creating Gage and Bailey, and they were the lights in my life.

My mother glanced at me before focusing on the TV again. Despite her hair being a stringy, unwashed mess around her face and her near constant frown, she looked untouched by the years with her smooth, wrinkle-free skin.

"Did you eat?" I asked her.

She didn't bother to acknowledge me as she listened to the news anchor drone on. She could sit there for days listening to these reports and being completely useless. I had no idea how she could tolerate it as only two TV channels came through anymore, both of which were news stations that reported from close to the wall and said the same things over and over again.

After the war, the government had taken control of all utilities and media, dealing out electricity and news amongst the surviving states and towns. Bills no longer came, taxes had ceased, but somehow the government kept some things running. It may not be smooth, but it worked, for now.

Looking at the man on the screen, I saw the wall in the distance over his shoulders. He was positioned in front of one of the better built sections of the wall, instead of one of the more haphazardly tossed together parts constructed of whatever debris could be found to create it at the time.

I'd come to realize most of the news reports came from the better-built sections of concrete stretching high into the sky. Probably to make everyone think everything was completely under control.

I tried to believe that, but I didn't understand why the wall had been built in the first place. What was in the middle of our country they were so afraid of us seeing, or were they afraid of it reaching us? Had the nuclear attacks created hideous monsters on the other side? The frightening possibility might not be too far off.

I'd never seen the wall in person and probably never would. It had been constructed all the way around the country, separating the states that had survived the attack from those that had been lost. What had once been fifty states was now only twenty-three states, plus Alaska and Hawaii. Parts of Nevada, New York, Pennsylvania, and Arkansas were on our side of the wall, with the rest of the surviving outer states, but the interior states had all been lost to the war and bombs.

I'd heard the swirling questions as to why the invaders had attacked the middle of the country and not New York City, Washington D.C., Boston, or Atlanta. Why hadn't they gone for more populated and political areas of power when they'd attacked us? But then, they had also taken out the main source of our food supply with the attack.

They hadn't wiped out our government and military in one swoop, but they had taken a good chunk of our population and many had starved to death in the chaotic months following the bombs. Some probably still did starve to death in some areas. In some ways, their attack on the Midwest states had been the cruelest option.

Gage walked in from the kitchen. His dark blond hair stood

up in tussled disarray, and his brown eyes were focused on me. The bottom of the linen pants he wore, which I'd purchased only three months ago, hung to the midpoint of his shin. I'd made the right choice going for pants for him instead of a new pair of shoes for me.

He grinned as he nodded toward the fish slung over my shoulder. "Good catch, Pittah."

I smiled at the name he'd called me ever since he'd learned how to speak and hadn't been able to pronounce my name correctly. "Thanks."

I walked past him and into the kitchen. Opening up the small ice chest, I dumped the fish inside. Like Mrs. Loud, we had extra ice in there in preparation for the blackouts, but sometimes the blackouts lasted days and nothing helped to ward off spoiling then. Gage would have this fish filleted and ready to cook before it could spoil and the other one would be going to Volunteer Day with us.

Gage had once insisted he should be the one doing the fishing and me the cooking. He'd given up after two days when the only fish he could catch, I burned to a crisp, and not on purpose.

"Did she eat?" I asked him and waved my hand at the living room.

"Naw, she's been watching that TV like a zombie."

I rolled my eyes and pulled the tin of ointment from the pouch of my faded green windbreaker. My finger got caught in one of the holes on the outside of my pouch. I'd have to take the time to stitch it again tonight, before the hole became too big. I placed the tin on the counter.

"Mrs. Loud is going to make you some new pants," I told him.

Gage glanced at the bottom of his pants. "They're fine. You need new shoes."

"They're not fine. You look like you're going wading, and I can make it a couple more weeks with the shoes I've got. Where's Bailey?"

I'd just gotten his name out when I heard a giggle from one of the kitchen cabinets. I glanced at Gage who smiled back at me. "I have no idea where he is," Gage said.

Another giggle followed his statement. "I wonder where he could be," I said, playing along with Gage.

"I don't know. Maybe he's run away," Gage replied.

"I hope not. I sure would miss him."

Bailey's laughter grew louder before becoming muffled. The image of him with his pudgy hands over his mouth, trying to stifle his laughter, burst into my mind. Taking a deep breath, I rested my hands on the counter as the clear picture of Bailey hiding beneath the sink in only his diaper grew stronger in my mind before fading away.

Gage rested his hand on my shoulder, drawing me back to the "real world." His mouth compressed as his eyes surveyed me. "You okay?" he demanded.

"Fine," I croaked out.

"Vision?"

"Sort of," I murmured and opened the cabinet next to the sink to remove a glass.

Turning the water on, Gage took the glass from me and filled it before handing it back. "What did you see?"

"Where Bailey is hiding."

"Not much of a secret," he replied flippantly, but I heard the undercurrent of tension in his tone.

He hated it when the "weird occurrences," as he liked to call them, took me over. *I* hated it when they took me over, but I tried not to let him see that. The older Gage got though, the more he saw through my 'it doesn't bother me' façade. Neither of us knew what caused the strange happenings or why.

For the most part, they were innocuous, but once, when I'd been exceptionally pissed off at my mother, the curtains in my room had caught on fire. To this day, I still wasn't *sure* it was me who had started it, but I couldn't rid myself of the sinking suspicion it had been my fault. I was touching them at the time after all.

Gage had helped me douse the flames and dispose of the curtains, but we'd both been rattled by what had happened and never spoke of it again.

I also didn't know why a couple of times golden-white sparks had danced across my fingertips and hands. I repeatedly told myself it had only been static electricity. I may be the queen of denial, but I had no idea what else it could have been, and trying to figure it out only made my head hurt. Besides, that had only happened a few times, and there was no reason why it couldn't have been some strange electrical phenomenon. Thankfully, it had never drawn the attention of anyone else when it happened, so I'd somehow managed to keep one oddity to myself.

The visions, and glimpses of things I had no way of knowing about, happened more often and were more difficult to keep from Gage. The only other person who knew about them was Lisa, but she knew nothing of the curtain incident. I saw no reason to freak her out over it.

These strange occurrences were a few more of the things I assumed I'd inherited from my father; the man had left more than his child behind when he'd abandoned my mother. I sometimes wished I knew how to contact him, not because I would like a father in my life, but because I wanted to know if anything like this had ever happened to him.

There were times I felt completely alone in the world. A freak living in a world that had become pretty damn freaky on that long ago July day.

"I don't know where to look for Bailey," I said, forcing the words out and giving Gage a smile as I returned to playing the game. "We'll have to go into town without him then."

Gage's brown eyes were still troubled, but he didn't question me further. It was risky for us to talk of such things. If someone ever overheard...

I shuddered at the possibilities. Today would be the day, if something were to happen, but I knew I had nothing to worry about from Gage and Lisa, so I would be safe. I glanced at the living room doorway, but the only sound I heard out there was the continuous update from the news.

"Guess I'll get to play on the swings all by myself today," Gage said loud enough that Bailey could hear him.

The laughter from beneath the sink stopped. My smile was genuine now as I finished off my water. "Maybe we could find him," I suggested.

"Do we really want to try? It doesn't seem like he wants to see us."

There was complete silence from under the sink before the door creaked open a little. I pretended not to notice it, but out of the corner of my eye, I saw one of Bailey's blue eyes press against the crack.

"We might as well try, but if we can't find him, we'll have to leave without him. Bailey!" I called. "Bailey!"

The door closed again and another giggle sounded. I bit my inner lip to keep from laughing as we went through the kitchen, opening and closing the cabinet doors. Gage opened the closet door in the hall before closing it again. We were halfway through the charade when I saw the cabinet open again and Bailey's eye peeping out.

Growing tired of waiting, I thought.

Bending down, I pretended to search the cabinets on either side of him before closing the doors. "Only one place left to look," I said loudly. Bailey's laughter increased, and I cracked the door open and poked my head inside. He was exactly as I had pictured, tucked beneath the sink in only his diaper. "There you are!"

Bailey squealed with laughter when I grabbed hold of his plump belly and pulled him from beneath the sink. "Here I am!" he cried and threw his arms around my neck. "You're a bad searcher."

"I am," I agreed and placed him on the counter.

His blond hair hung in disheveled ringlets around his flushed, round cheeks. He was only two and a half, but like Gage and me, he was tall and his legs hung down over the counter to kick against the silverware drawer. I poked his round belly before checking his cloth diaper. My nose wrinkled at the potent aroma wafting from it.

"You stink," I told him and kissed the tip of his nose.

He giggled then laughed when Gage handed him a small piece of bread. "Eat this, B," he told him. Bailey held the bread as I gathered a towel and spread it out on the counter. "What are we feeding this kid?" Gage asked when I pulled the diaper off.

"I don't know, but we're going to have to stop," I replied and Bailey giggled again. He may be the worst smelling kid on the face of the planet, but he was also the happiest.

I would have given anything to be able to toss the diaper out, but we couldn't afford to waste anything. I dropped it into the can Gage held out for me. I really hoped Bailey would get the hang of toilet training soon, but so far, he'd been stubborn about it.

"I'll take it outside to hose it off," Gage offered.

"Thanks."

"I stink!" Bailey declared proudly.

"You do," I confirmed as I cleaned him up and pinned a

clean diaper on him. "Now we're going to get you ready for town."

"Town!" he shouted gleefully.

I lifted him off the counter as the lights went out. Heaving a sigh, I listened to the last, fading words of the news broadcast. Gage's smile vanished when he stepped back through the door. His gaze went straight to the now-hushed living room.

"Crap," he muttered.

Seconds later, I heard the shuffling sounds of my mother's feet. Bailey's smile faded away; his arms slid around my neck as he pressed closer. His warm body helped to ease the chill creeping down my spine. After all my years with our mother, I should be used to her, but I could live another fifty years and never be quite prepared for the woman who appeared in the kitchen.

Her blue eyes slid over us, but never really seemed to see us as she approached the sink. I cradled Bailey closer and stepped away from her. "We're going to Volunteer Day," I said to her.

She didn't respond as she retrieved a glass and filled it with water. Her eyes flitted over me before focusing on Gage. She wasn't overly fond of any of us, but there was no doubt I was the one she cared for the least.

"Make sure you take your brother's diapers with you," she told Gage.

Like we ever forget. I held back the words. I was a guest within these walls, an interloper, and there were more than a few times when I'd been kicked out on the street. I'd spent those times with Lisa's parents, but after a week or two, I was asked back as Gage would refuse to cook for her or do anything around the house. Unlike me, he didn't care if she ate or not. Possible starvation, and the fact she didn't like taking care of her children, had always allowed me back into the house.

I couldn't risk being thrown out again. She may be a small,

frail woman with stooped shoulders and bones that stuck out, but she could cause a lot of damage to my brothers without me here to take the brunt of her vile words.

Over the years, my hair had been pulled, and I'd been slapped in the face more times than I could count. I'd been beaten so badly I couldn't sit for a week, and once kicked in the stomach, but her main weapon was her mouth, and she wielded it like a pro. I had more practice at fending her off than my brothers did and I tried to keep them from the worst of her degradation.

"We won't forget the diapers," Gage promised.

She opened the cooler and snickered at the fish inside. "Striper again."

"I'll grill them," Gage said, his eyes flickering to me as he tried to placate her antagonism toward me. "Something different tonight."

My mother's eyes landed briefly on me. Her upper lip curled as she looked me up and down. Turning his head away, Bailey rested his cheek against mine. "You're such a waste," she sneered. "Evil. The spawn of Satan."

I'd heard it before; I was sure I'd hear it many more times before I was able to break free of this woman. Something I hoped to be able to do one day, but though she despised me, she was my mother, and I couldn't abandon her here to die, even if I could somehow walk out the door with Gage and Bailey. She may not love them, but she would fight me for them and possibly have me thrown in jail if I tried to take them. While my brothers were here, so was I.

"Garbage, just like your father," she spat.

I kept my mouth closed while she shuffled back out the door. My shoulders sagged and I inhaled an unsteady breath. I hated that she still rattled me, that I hadn't better hardened myself against her. Maybe one day.

"I'll gather Bailey's clothes after I take a shower," I said to Gage.

His troubled eyes met mine before he gave a brief bow of his head. I handed him Bailey and slipped from the room.

CHAPTER FOUR

River

The center of town was abuzz with the excitement of the day. There was little for anyone to be excited about these days, but the yearly Volunteer Day was one of those things. Mingling with the people of the town were some of the soldiers who guarded the bridge and helped to maintain order in the town. The police force had been absorbed into the Guard branch of the military that some people joined when they were eighteen. Most of those who joined the Guard remained in their towns and with their families, unlike the volunteers.

I spotted Asante amid the bustling crowd. He stood with a group of Guards who watched the crowd with blank expressions. Asante had grown up in a house down the road from us and had enlisted six years ago, the day he'd turned eighteen. He'd done his grueling, three-month training at the nearby military base that had been reopened after the war. Many who enlisted didn't get through the training, but he had flown through it with flying colors and returned to living in the neighborhood when it was over.

Making my way through the crowd, I stopped before him.

"Santa," Bailey, unable to pronounce Asante's name, greeted.

Asante smiled down at him, his sable brown eyes twinkling with amusement. Beads of sweat dotted the top of his freshly shaven head as the sun played over his mocha-colored skin. Bailey stuck his hand in his mouth and grinned back at him.

"Hey, B," Asante greeted Bailey. "River, how you been?"

"Same stuff, different day," I told him. "You know how it goes."

"I do. How many volunteers do you think we'll have today?"

I frowned as I pondered his question. Normally, ten to thirty kids volunteered every year, but lately there had been more growing suspicions and horror stories about what resided on the other side of the wall. The rumors had cropped up once every few years since the war had ended, and when they did, the number of volunteers decreased.

It didn't matter. I already had a pretty good idea of how many there would be. "Eight, what do you think?" I asked.

"I'm going with eleven."

"You're more optimistic than me."

He turned his attention away from me as the large, covered truck rumbled by us. All around us, people stopped to stare at the camouflage-colored military vehicle. It was a clear sign the soldiers from the wall had arrived. Every year, on May fifteenth, the government sent back some of the soldiers who guarded the wall to every town on the Cape.

This day was the only time we saw vehicles as big as the ones that came to collect the volunteers. The Guards had some vehicles to transport them back and forth to their assignments, but they were mostly pickup trucks, some vans, and cars. For the rest of us, gas had become so sparse and regulated that feet and bicycles were the main mode of transportation.

"Our yearly visit," Gage murmured from beside me. "One of these times, I'd like to see a volunteer we know return."

I adjusted my hold on Bailey as the truck parked in the center of what had once been the high school football field. One year after the first bombs fell, we had returned to school. I'd stumbled through another couple of years of schooling before realizing I couldn't keep up anymore, and there was no reason to. Many of the things we'd learned in the past weren't as relevant anymore. People now taught medicine, gardening, sewing, fishing, construction, carpentry, and anything else necessary to survive. I missed learning and wished I had the chance to read more often, as we still did have a small library, but there just wasn't any time for such things anymore.

Though my schooling had ended earlier than I'd hoped, at least I had learned what started the war when I'd returned to school. We'd been told Russia was behind the attack. They'd grouped together with North Korea and China to launch an invasion that had decimated our country, but ultimately failed.

There had been a similar attack in Europe and Asia that had been more successful. Many Middle Eastern countries had fallen to them before parts of Germany, France, Norway, and Sweden also succumbed. Now, like us, those countries were scattered and trying to rebuild behind a wall, but they were surviving.

We'd never seen the invaders here. They'd never come at us from the sea or across the land from the center of the country. The war that had been waged in the Midwest was something we had little idea about; the news stations hadn't been running during the war, and the people who went to fight never returned.

When the government started recruiting people to build

the wall a couple of months after the war started, people had gone, but none of them had returned either. Letters from those fighters, builders, and past volunteers made their way back every year, so we knew some of them were still alive.

Going to the wall was associated with death by some. Others believed it an adventure, a promise of better things for themselves and their families. It was usually the younger people who considered it an adventure, which was one of the reasons why I suspected the government started taking volunteers at sixteen.

I'd never considered volunteering, not with Gage and Bailey to care for. That didn't mean I wasn't as curious as everyone else about what went on at the wall and what became of the volunteers who left here and had yet to return. I wasn't sure if it was the curiosity or the promises given that drove most of the volunteers to step forward.

It didn't matter, the volunteers would keep enrolling and the government would keep coming for them. I watched as a woman with her hair pulled into a severe bun climbed down from the driver's seat. Gray had started to streak her dark blonde hair. Lines had formed under her eyes and around her mouth. She stopped and stood at the front of the truck with her hands folded before her.

Lisa arrived beside me and handed me a caramel apple. I smiled as I took it; I hadn't had one since last year, and they were one of my favorite treats. Somewhere in the distance, a guitar began to play and then the beat of drums sounded. It was the one day of the year when a celebratory air actually permeated the town again.

Perhaps it should be sad, some members of our town would be leaving today to never return, but it had become a day of excitement and new beginnings. The government brought in supplies, and letters from loved ones at the wall were handed out. Treats we didn't have all year were concocted to say goodbye to the people who would be leaving us today. After the volunteers stepped forward, dancing would commence until they left at sundown.

I took a bite of the apple as Lisa walked over to kiss Asante's cheek. They spoke in hushed whispers while I allowed Bailey to take a lick of the caramel coating. He nibbled at the apple before I took another bite and gave it to Gage.

"Mine!" Bailey shouted and grabbed for the apple. "Mine!"

"I can't wait for him to outgrow this stage," Gage muttered as he reluctantly handed the apple back into Bailey's clapping hands. Bailey smiled happily and dove into the caramel once more. Sticky goo smeared his face and stuck in his hair when he finally came up for air again.

"I'm not getting it back, am I?" Lisa asked when she reappeared at my side.

"I'll get you another one," I told her.

She waved her hand dismissively. "I think he's getting more joy out of it than I would. So how many volunteers are we thinking?"

"I said eight, Asante guessed eleven," I replied.

"I'm thinking twelve," she said.

"Nine," Gage guessed.

Bailey rested one of his sticky hands against my cheek and giggled. "Thanks," I said. I pulled his hand away and kissed his tiny fingers. He returned his attention to the caramel.

"I should be going. Have fun today," Asante said. He kissed Lisa's cheek before walking away. His shoulders were rigid in his forest green uniform shirt. Guard was spelled across the back of the shirt in gold letters.

"Let's see what goodies we have this year!" Lisa declared.

Gage practically skipped ahead of us as we worked our way through the crowd while waiting for the volunteering to begin. The scents of frying fish, vegetables, and cooking sweets caused my stomach to rumble. The snap and crackle of the fires and the animated tones of the voices surrounding us added to the excitement of the day. The red and yellow tulips lining the outside of the field were in full bloom; their sweet aroma was barely discernible over the numerous foods filling the air.

The dunk tank in the back had become a big draw. Gage stepped forward to take his chance at knocking the kid into the water; on his second throw, he hit the bull's-eye. The kid tumbled into the water with a big splash.

A cheer went through the crowd. A young girl stood on her toes to kiss Gage's cheek. The fierce blush burning my brother's face made me laugh out loud. He threw back his shoulders and ran a hand through his hair, causing it to stand more on end. I had to bite my cheek to stifle my laughter, but Lisa wasn't quite so discreet.

Gage shot her a look before stepping away from the girl now digging her toe into the ground and turning the color of a lobster. Gage hurried into the crowd.

"Who was she?" I asked when we caught up to him.

"A girl." He pretended to search the crowd as he tossed his answer back at me.

"Does this girl have a name?"

"Cherry."

"Seriously?" Lisa blurted.

Gage glowered at her. "You're seriously annoying."

Lisa grinned at him. "I don't have siblings to pick on so I get River's."

"Whatever," he replied with a roll of his eyes.

"Do you like her?" I asked Gage.

He shrugged, but his skin was becoming more flushed and now his neck had begun to look like he had a sunburn. I had to bite my lip to keep from laughing again. "I barely know her," he mumbled.

I thrust Bailey into his arms. "Remember birth control."

"I uh... I..." he sputtered.

"I know you're only fourteen, but the time will come, and when it does, remember the diaper from this morning."

"I stink!" Bailey declared and Gage winced.

Gage's mouth shut when Bailey placed a sticky, caramel-coated hand against his cheek. I grabbed a napkin from a nearby table and wiped at the caramel coating he'd left on my cheek.

Then again, if Gage were anything like me, I wouldn't have to worry about him having sex for years to come. However, I still wasn't going to take any chances. Gage was cute and extremely responsible, but accidents could happen, and he wasn't as tied down as I was right now.

Most guys weren't exactly clamoring to date a girl with a deadbeat mom and two brothers to raise, but Gage could break free of that and do something more with his life. I'd never allow him to volunteer, I couldn't handle not being able to see him again, but with his kind and prideful nature, he'd make a great Guard.

I may not have much of a dating life, but I wouldn't have changed one thing. My brothers were my world. Besides, I'd had little time for the boys who had been interested in me and the few dates I'd been on had been awkward. I knew fishing and changing diapers; I was the least sexy conversationalist in the world.

Not to mention, I'd always kept myself at a distance from men. What if I accidentally had golden-white sparks dance over my hands, or caught his clothes on fire, or had a vision in front of him? I couldn't risk any of those things; it would be far too dangerous if someone were to find out about me. At the end of all my first—and last—dates, I'd found myself on my doorstep watching as the boys and men all but ran away from me. I'd usually end up biting my lip to keep from laughing out loud at their hasty retreats.

Walking through the crowd, we passed the band as the open grilling pit drew us onward. "Hello!" Mrs. Loud greeted us with a smile and a wave as she lifted one of the large stripers and flipped it over. I wasn't sure, but it looked like the one I'd brought her earlier today. Next to the fish, some mussels, crabs, and lobsters were also on the grill. "What would you kids like?"

"I'll take some lobster," I replied and held out one of the plates on the table.

For the past month, everyone had been gathering special supplies for this day. There was no trading for food today. People volunteered to bring the supplies, others volunteered to help cook and run the games. Mrs. Loud handed me a lobster tail before turning and dishing out food to the others. We walked over to a clear patch of grass on the football field and settled in to eat.

When we were done, I gathered the plates and brought them back to the grilling pit. Two large tubs, one of warm water and soap, and one of just warm water had been set up at the end of the table containing the plates and silverware. I washed everything, rinsed it in the tub of warm water, dried them, and stacked them neatly back on the table.

"It was delicious, Mrs. Loud," I told her.

Preoccupied with dishing out more food, she didn't look at me when she replied, "Thank you, dear."

I was almost back to the others when a flyer was thrust into my hand. A hollow feeling filled my stomach, but I looked down at the paper and read the words on it. *We are looking for someone who has unusual abilities. This person may be able to see things they shouldn't, have telekinesis, or perhaps possess other abilities beyond the normal human scope. If you know of someone like this, or possess such abilities, please come speak with us. Age does not matter. You will be rewarded. We require your help!*

I stopped feeling the warmth of the May afternoon as my blood ran cold and my legs wobbled. I glanced at the Guard who had handed me the paper, but she had already turned away. Besides, it didn't matter; the Guards weren't the ones searching for a human with abilities. The government was.

CHAPTER FIVE

River

My gaze drifted past the Guard to the woman still standing by the truck. An older gentleman with gray hair cut close against his skull now stood beside her. The style of his hair emphasized his high cheekbones, square jaw, and compressed lips. These older military personnel were the ones who had been members of the military before the war started and the only ones who came back for Volunteer Day.

Keeping the paper, I walked back to where Lisa and Gage sat on the lawn. They each had a flier in hand. When I approached, they lowered their fliers quickly and tried to hide them. They gave up and brought them out again when they spotted the matching flier in my hand.

"It's the same one as last year," I whispered when I settled onto the lawn.

"Why are they looking for people like this?" Gage demanded.

"Shh," I whispered. My gaze darted around, but there were few people near us. "I don't know." I glanced at the two people standing near the truck again. "Do you think the rumors of experiments are true?"

Lisa leaned closer to us. "I think most of the rumors are true. None of us know what goes on over the wall. I don't trust those news broadcasts for one minute. We only know what they tell us, and I believe most of it is a lie. And why did they start handing these fliers out four years ago? The volunteering has been going on for eleven years now. What happened four years ago that made *this* start?"

"I don't know," I muttered as I glanced at the flier again. "Maybe I should talk to them."

"Don't even think about it," Lisa said firmly. "Nothing good is going to come out of whatever it is they're looking for. Mark my words on that one."

"What if they find out?" I looked pointedly between her and Gage. "I could be putting you both at risk."

"I'm willing to take the risk." Lisa pulled the flyer from my hand and crumpled it into a ball. She snatched Gage's next and crushed it with hers. "Stay away from whatever this is."

I had to agree with her on many things, but the idea of something happening to any of them petrified me.

I didn't have much time to think about that as the man who had been standing by the truck stepped forward and lifted his hand into the air. Some conversations continued to swirl around us but they died off when more people realized he was about to speak. With the sunlight beating down on the man, the metals on the chest of his blue uniform shone. I didn't know what they used for material for their clothing, but it was of far better quality than anything any of us wore.

"Good afternoon, ladies and gentlemen," he said in a clear, booming voice. "I am Colonel Ulrich MacIntyre and I'm so happy to see all of you here today for the volunteering. I so enjoy coming to these seaside communities, and who doesn't love a good lobster?" Polite chuckles followed this statement. "Now, could we have all of the sixteen-year-olds in the community come forward?"

Finally finished with licking the caramel off his apple, Bailey toddled over to me and settled in my lap. Gage handed me his glass of water and a cloth to wipe off Bailey's fingers and face with. From amongst the crowd, people made their way toward the trucks and the pair of military personnel.

The teens lined up beside the colonel with their parents behind them. My mother hadn't bothered to come on the day I'd stood up there, but Lisa's mother had stood behind me throughout the experience.

I finished cleaning Bailey off and settled him in my lap as a heavy air of expectancy descended over the crowd. There were at least fifty teenagers up there waiting to declare their fates. I didn't envy them; it had been such a simple choice for me, but it wasn't for many others.

Clearing his throat, the colonel drew everyone's attention back to him. "Volunteering is a sacred duty only few are brave enough to undertake. All volunteers will leave their homes and families behind for a life spent protecting the wall and the many who reside outside of its borders."

Lisa shot me a pointed look. *'From what?'* she mouthed.

We'd all heard this speech before, but that had always been the question. What was on the other side of the wall? The rumors were anything from animals and humans deformed by radiation, to brand new creations as a result of the radiation, to Russian, North Korean, and Chinese fighters who hadn't been beaten like we'd been informed, and still waged war on the other side.

It was a question I was dying to know the answer to, but we were too far from the wall to ever know. The closest section of the wall to us was over three hundred miles away. My feet definitely weren't going to make the trek.

We'd heard stories that howling screams, ghostly calls, and other strange sounds could sometimes be heard in the towns residing closest to the wall. Sometimes those who were allowed to cross the bridges onto the Cape, or enter the ports in order to trade with us, said the towns closest to the wall lived in fear of what was on the other side. It was whispered those people would have fled if there had been a guarantee they would be able to find someplace else to live.

I tried to believe they were only campfire tales, meant to scare people away from the wall, but I couldn't shake the belief that at least some of it had to be true.

"The volunteers will be well compensated for their bravery with a home, clothing, and food behind the wall," the man continued. "They will never again have to wonder where their next meal will come from. Not only that, but their parents or guardians will receive a stipend of food from the Guards for the rest of their lives to help offset their needs."

This was the reason most people volunteered. It wasn't so much the promise of something new, better clothing, and steady shelter that made them step forward, but the ability to help take care of their family too.

"All volunteers will receive training and be taught how to take care of themselves and how to protect others," the colonel continued.

Again, we were told this, but we had no way of knowing what happened after the volunteers were taken away. Letters were sent home from past volunteers and families were allowed to send mail to the front, but the letters arriving here never revealed any info about what went on at the wall.

"All volunteers take pride in what they do as they help to rebuild our great nation. They are amongst the many celebrated heroes of this majestic land. Now, as you all know, all first year volunteers are sixteen years of age. If you are not sixteen, please return to where you were seated. You will have your chance soon." No one moved from where they stood lined up beside him. "If you have not come forward yet, please do."

The only mandatory attendance for today was for the sixteen-year-olds in town. I didn't know why they were all required to stand up there, if they weren't going to volunteer. Maybe the government felt it would embarrass some of those who didn't volunteer into doing so, or maybe they thought people would look down on those who didn't volunteer. Either way, they were wrong. Standing up there, I hadn't felt embarrassed, ashamed, or looked down upon when I hadn't stepped forward. I'd only wanted to return to Gage in the crowd.

"Now," the man stepped forward and turned to face the kids. "Who amongst you is brave enough to face a whole new world and to protect and serve your great nation?"

Lisa leaned over to whisper in my ear. "Volunteers *must* be down this year in the other towns. He's really pouring it on thick."

I nodded my agreement as the man walked in front of the people gathered before him. "Please step forward if you are willing to become one of the great many who have kept this country alive."

There was a shuffling within the group, and then five boys and two girls stepped forward. My gaze focused on a small girl at the end. Her hands were folded together before her, and her head was bowed. A willowy woman with two twin boys, one on each hip, stood behind her. I couldn't tear my gaze away from the young girl as I waited for her to do what I *knew* she was going to do.

With a dejected look at her mother, the young girl took a step forward. The woman gave an awkward lurch forward as she tried to grab hold of her daughter's shoulder and pull her back. The young girl brushed away her mother's grasping hand.

Tears streaked the woman's cheeks; she glanced between her daughter and the others standing forward from the group. The kids were all trying to look so proud with their tilted chins, thrown back shoulders, and gazes fixed on something in the distance. On most of them, their shaking hands, trembling lower lips, and misty eyes belied their brave front.

"Eight," Lisa said. "River's right again."

"I don't know why any of us ever guess against her," Gage said.

I smiled wanly at him as I held Bailey closer against my chest.

"Let's give a round of applause for these brave men and women!" the colonel announced proudly.

Cheers ran through the crowd while the families grouped back together. They hugged each other close as tears were shed.

"If anyone else, who is of age to volunteer and is under the age of twenty, would like to volunteer, you may do so now!" the colonel declared.

It was rare anyone volunteered after the age of sixteen, but some did because of unforeseen events or maybe to escape the island. I'd only ever seen two do so, and no one moved forward now to join the teens who had volunteered today.

With the volunteers established, the cover on the back of the truck was pulled away to reveal the bags of mail, clothing, and other supplies stashed in the back. With no set postal service anymore and no real means of distant travel, letters only came and went to the wall on this day each year. Families with children who had volunteered in the past, rushed forward to collect the letters from their loved ones and to hand over the bags of letters they had written over the year. Everyone else waited to receive and divide the rest of the supplies until all those letters were delivered.

Cheers and laughter rang out as the families happily gathered their letters. Sometimes, along with the letters came the news someone had been lost. While I watched, I saw ten families being led away from the crowd and toward the high school by the military woman.

"That's not good," Gage muttered.

"No, it's not," I agreed.

"That's more than five times the amount of deaths from last year," Lisa said.

"From *any* year," I replied.

"Some of those rumors about things amping up at the wall must be true." Gage glanced at the wadded up fliers near his hand, shoving them roughly aside before rising to his feet. "Come on, let's go dance or something."

I placed Bailey on the ground and rose to my feet. Keeping hold of his hand, I led him through the crowd already beginning to celebrate once again. Glancing over my shoulder, my gaze fell on the last young girl who had volunteered. I'd seen days ago she would do so, I somehow knew her name was Carrie, but the thing I didn't understand was why I felt like I'd be seeing her again.

I didn't get impressions or visions or whatever they were about myself. I was too old to volunteer, and I knew neither Gage nor Lisa would ever betray me, but I knew something wasn't right.

CHAPTER SIX

River

It was late afternoon when we made our way back home. Bailey was asleep on my shoulder, his arms draped around my neck and his little breaths blowing against my cheek. The sweet scent of caramel clinging to his skin filled my nostrils. Damp with sweat, his hair stuck to my cheek. I kissed his head, my heart swelling with love when he released a small snore.

At our street, Lisa broke away with a wave to go to her and Asante's small house. We walked in silence to our house and up the stairs to the door. No lights were on within, and I didn't hear the drone of the news. Gage and I exchanged a resigned look when we realized the blackout was still in effect. Our mother would probably be in a worse mood now that she hadn't had her TV to watch all day.

"I should cook the other fish before it goes bad," he said.

"Yeah," I agreed as he opened the door.

The screen door creaked closed behind us when we entered the house. Gage strode down the hall, and I started to turn to the right to put Bailey to bed when I saw Gage freeze beside the island in the kitchen. His head was down and turned to the side, his arms at his sides. He lurched forward and grabbed something from the counter.

I stopped, curious to see what had caught his attention. He spun toward me, his mouth gaping open and a piece of paper in his hand. "River—"

Whatever he'd been about to say was cut off by the squeak of the screen door opening behind me. A tendril of alarm coiled within me; I didn't need any extra senses to know something was completely wrong. I kept hoping, if I didn't turn around, I wouldn't have to see what was making Gage's mouth open and close like that and his eyes bug from his head.

No matter how much I didn't want to look, I knew I had to face what was waiting for me. Taking a deep breath, I turned to find the middle-aged man and woman who had arrived for the volunteering standing in the doorway. Behind them stood my mother and a handful of Guards.

I placed a protective hand against Bailey's back as my chin rose. My heart sank when I belatedly realized Gage had been holding a flier in his hand.

My mother rarely left the house, but there had been no electricity all day today. With nothing to do here, the volunteering must have drawn her out. Or perhaps the military had decided to do a door-to-door search this year in order to uncover this someone different they were looking for.

Either way, I knew my mother had been the one to sell me out. She may not know the extent of what I could do, but it had always been present in me. The foolish child I'd once been, the one who had still held out some hope she could come to love me, had told her about some of the visions I'd had before. I'd been too young to realize the love I was seeking by telling her my secrets would never be given. She would never love me the way a mother should love her daughter.

As I'd gotten older, and realized I better distance myself from this woman, I'd tried to keep it from her, but it was already too late by then.

Over time, I'd learned that she hated me, but I hadn't known how much until *now*. She'd relied on me, but she'd found another way to take care of her family by getting rid of me. Something she'd probably been wishing she could do since the day I was born.

The silence stretched on endlessly; Bailey shifted in my arms. Burrowing closer against my neck, he let out a contented sound that caused tears to flood my eyes. I hadn't given birth to him, but I loved him as if he were my own. Gage and I had been the ones to raise and take care of him, and I knew before any words were exchanged, I would never see either of them again.

"River Dawson?" the colonel inquired.

"That's her," my mother confirmed when I stayed mute.

My nostrils flared, and I strove to remain calm with Bailey in my arms. "I'm twenty-two," I said. "Too old to volunteer."

"That's not why we're here," the colonel replied.

"I'm *not* volunteering."

"Doesn't matter, not with this."

I glanced at my mother; I didn't ask her why she'd done this because I already knew the answer, but I wanted to choke the woman.

"It does matter!" Gage said angrily. "*No* one is taken to the wall against their will."

"These are different circumstances," the colonel replied.

"What circumstances?" Gage demanded.

"It's been brought to our attention your sister has certain abilities."

Gage gave a snort of disbelief, but before he could speak

again, my mother did. "She does. I've seen them myself. She's scared me since she was a child. She has the Devil's eyes."

My teeth grated together at this statement, one I'd heard countless times over the years. My eyes weren't a normal color, but violet wasn't exactly something I would associate with being demonic. However, her words had perked the attention of the military man and woman; their eyebrows rose, and they exchanged a pointed look with each other. Something about their expressions caused my blood to run cold.

For the first time, real panic hit me as I looked back and forth between the military personnel and the Guards beyond. I would never be able to shove past them to escape. *Maybe* I had somehow managed to set those curtains on fire all those years ago, but I had no idea how it worked or what would happen if I tried to set something on fire now. I couldn't take the chance of anything happening to Bailey.

"The only thing about me that frightened you was I was yours and you were supposed to take care of me!" I snapped at my mother.

"She sees things she's not supposed to! I know she does," my mother accused. "She told me so herself!"

Right then, I would have given anything to go back and kick six-year-old me in the throat.

"She's a lunatic; everyone around here knows that. If not for my brother and me, she wouldn't eat. She barely moves out of that chair." I thrust a finger at the torn and stained recliner in the living room.

Bailey squirmed in my arms; I rubbed my hand across his back in order to calm him. "It does not matter, miss," the military woman replied. "You will come with us."

"I am the main food supply and caregiver to my siblings." My tone remained calm, but my heart raced and sweat dampened my palms. All I wanted was to turn and bolt out of here, or set my mother on fire. If it wouldn't confirm to them I was different, I may have done it, if I could figure out how to do it.

I'd never hated her before. I'd never had any respect for her, and I'd disliked her, but I'd never *hated* her. Now hatred festered inside of me like rotten fish, and if I had a chance at getting to her, I would have beaten her to within an inch of her life.

The man's eyes flicked to Bailey before going to Gage who strode forward to stand behind my shoulder. "That's true!" Gage declared. "That woman has nothing to do with us. Without River, we would have died years ago."

"Because your sister will be coming with us, food will be supplied to you from now on," the colonel replied.

I could feel Gage's growing agitation as he shifted behind me. I risked a glance at him. His hands were fisted at his sides, a vein in his forehead throbbed, and a thin layer of sweat coated his flushed face.

"She'll throw us out on the street!" Gage retorted and thrust a finger at our mother.

"As per the rules of volunteers' families and the agreement with your mother, you will be taken care of."

The blood pumping through my veins felt like ice. I found it increasingly difficult to breathe as the realization sank in that I had no choice. I glanced toward the back door. Even if I could get away and make it out of this house, there was nowhere for me to go, nowhere for me to hide. We were on an *island* for crying out loud.

And what of Bailey and Gage? I couldn't leave them behind with my mother. I couldn't take them with me, and if I could somehow manage to escape with them, running and hiding was no way for them to live.

I turned back toward the crowd in the doorway before looking at my mother's smug smile. The colonel turned in the doorway and waved some of the Guards forward. I gasped when Asante stepped through the door.

His sable eyes were sad when they met mine. "I'm sorry, River. I didn't know this was going to happen when they ordered us to do the door to door inquiry," he said.

"It's okay, Asante. I know. I'll go willingly—"

"No!" Gage shouted. The ragged tone of his voice caused tears to burn my throat.

Shifting my hold on Bailey, I seized hold of Gage's arm when he took an angry step forward. His muscles bulged beneath my grip as he glared at the people across from us. If I let him go, I knew he would launch at them, and I didn't want to think about what would happen then.

He couldn't be locked away; there would be no one to care for Bailey, and I couldn't stand to see Gage hurt in any way. Bailey lifted his head from my neck, and blinked sleepily at the group gathered across from us before shoving his hand into his mouth.

"There's no choice here," I hissed at Gage. "I have *no* choice." Turning back to the group, I focused on my mother. "I'll come with you willingly, *if* you agree all she gets out of this is only enough food for her to survive. I want my brothers to be taken care of by someone else, and *they* will receive whatever other compensation you promised her."

"That's not the deal!" my mother shouted.

Bailey jumped, his body trembling against mine as he removed his hand and cuddled closer against me. "River," he murmured.

"It's okay," I told him and patted his back.

"Miss, you really have no choice here," the colonel said in a gruff tone.

"I know I don't." I finally looked at him again. "But I will either walk calmly out of here, or I will kick and scream and throw myself in ways that will be guaranteed to draw a crowd. There are already rumors running rampant about the wall, about the increased deaths and what *really* goes on there. Would you prefer the people here to see you drag a cared for member of this community, who helps provide food to everyone, takes care of her brothers, never volunteered, and is twenty-two years old, from her house? You know it will only cause the unrest to increase."

The colonel and the woman exchanged a look again.

"It won't help you next year on Volunteer Day. We may be a remote community, but gossip always spreads," I pressed.

"We will make sure your brothers are taken care of," the man replied.

"Away from *her*."

Gage trembled in my grasp as he looked at me with tears shimmering in his brown eyes. *Don't cry, don't cry, don't cry!* I told myself fiercely. If I lost it now, I would turn into a blubbering mess they would have to carry from here anyway and that would do nothing to ensure my brothers avoided my mother's clutches.

"Away from her," the man promised.

"I'll take them. They can live with me and Lisa," Asante offered. "If that is permissible?" he asked of the colonel.

The colonel and woman studied me. "Would this be agreeable to you?" the colonel inquired.

Asante's warm brown eyes were misty with tears when I looked to him. I bit my bottom lip to keep a sob suppressed. I'd never considered the possibility of losing my brothers; my future without them was a bleak pit of misery I couldn't face, but if I couldn't be here for them, then I trusted Asante and Lisa to keep them safe and protected. They would do far better than our mother. Unable to trust myself to speak, I gave a terse nod.

"They will be kept safe and your friend will receive enough rations to keep them well-fed," the colonel said to me.

I blinked back the tears filling my eyes as my shoulders sagged.

"That's not part of the deal!" my mother thundered.

"Take her outside," the colonel ordered brusquely.

My mother thrashed against the two men who clasped her arms, but they easily succeeded in removing her from the house. Turning to Gage, I tried to hand Bailey over to him, but his arms locked around my neck. "No!" he yelled in my ear.

Tears choked my chest and throat. I turned my face into his neck, inhaling deeply of his caramel, baby scent. I'd never forget it, never forget the warmth and chubbiness of his tiny body or the happy giggles he emitted with such ease.

Please don't let this take away his laughter, I pleaded as I struggled not to lock my arms around him and refuse to let go.

"It's okay, B," I murmured as the first tear slid down my face. "It's okay. You have to go with Gage now."

"No!" he shouted again.

His hold on me cut off my air supply, causing me to cough. "Gage," I choked out. "Help me, please."

Gage remained unmoving, his eyes hollow and filled with tears as he stared at the two of us. Finally, he stepped forward and took hold of Bailey's arms, prying them from my neck.

"No!" Bailey wailed, his feet kicking in the air, his face flushed as Gage pulled him away. His tiny hands grabbed for me, tears streaked his face. "River!"

I couldn't hold back my tears as I stepped forward to embrace them both.

"I love you, Pittah" Gage whispered hoarsely.

I'd assumed my brother long past those words and crying; to hear and see those things now was nearly my complete undoing. "I love you too. I'll be back," I vowed. I brushed the hair back from Gage's face as Bailey squirmed in his arms.

"No one comes back from the wall," Gage replied in a monotone that made me shiver. "If that's where they're taking you."

"*I* will come back," I vowed. I kissed Gage on the cheek before kissing Bailey's forehead. "I love you, Stink Bug."

He tried to grab me again, but I managed to sidestep his tiny fingers. I forced myself to move further away from them before I couldn't. Thrusting my shoulders back, I wiped the tears from my eyes and strode toward the doorway.

I stopped before Asante. "Thank you."

"Lisa and I will keep them safe no matter what it takes," he vowed. "And away from your mother."

I bit my bottom lip to stop a fresh wave of tears. "Tell Lisa I said bye and I love her."

"I will."

"Let's go," the colonel said and took hold of my elbow.

Bailey's loud wails followed me down the stairs, shredding my heart as we walked across the front yard. The lump in my throat threatened to strangle me as we approached the waiting truck. The camouflage cover had been replaced on the truck, but the newest volunteers had their heads poked out the back of the vehicle to watch us.

I'd expected them to lead me to where the volunteers sat in the back; instead, they walked me toward the cab. I didn't see my mother anywhere, something I was unbelievably grateful for, but more than a few of my neighbors had been drawn out by the government vehicle and curiosity.

The woman opened the passenger door for me and gestured for me to climb inside. Taking a deep breath, I gathered my courage as I stared into the unlit cab. I couldn't embarrass myself by trying to run away from here now. I may be able to lose these two, but they'd have every Guard on the Cape hunting for me, and I had no idea what they would do with my brothers if I broke our agreement now.

My legs barely supported me when I climbed up the two steps and into the truck. I'd just settled in when I spotted Lisa running down the road toward us. Asante stepped forward to intercept her before she could reach the vehicle. I turned my head away from Lisa's frantic gestures as her cries rang down the street. Tears slid down to fall on my hands folded in my lap.

The colonel settled in beside me and started the truck.

"Where am I going?" I inquired in a hitching voice.

"To the wall."

"Why? What is it you want from me?"

"You'll learn what you need to know as it becomes necessary."

With those cryptic words, he shifted the truck into drive and hit the gas. I'd been determined not to look back, but I found my gaze going to the driver's side mirror when we got to the end of the street. In its reflection, I could see Asante, Lisa, Gage, and Bailey. Asante stood beside Lisa, who now held Bailey. He had his arms extended toward the truck while tears streaked his face. Gage was further ahead of them, bent over with his hands on his knees as if he'd chased after us.

I didn't care what it took. I *would* see them again.

CHAPTER SEVEN

River

The further away from home the colonel drove, the more I realized how different things were in this area compared to my hometown. Farms and livestock stretched out as far as the eye could see with houses dotting the landscape. Some of the houses sagged from years of wear and appeared to be abandoned. Others were in better repair and had a few people wandering around outside them.

Those people stopped what they were doing to watch the passing trucks driving down the road. Before we'd driven over the bridge and off the Cape, we'd been joined by fourteen other trucks carrying volunteers, one from each of the towns on Cape Cod. Along the way, five more trucks had joined us from nearby towns on the other side of the bridge.

"Do you send a truck to each town in the state on this day?" I'd inquired when the other trucks first joined us.

"No," the colonel had answered. "We send twenty trucks out at a time until all the towns in Massachusetts have been covered."

"Oh."

I'd become silent again afterward, too lost in my own grief and thoughts to carry on a conversation with them. I could still smell Bailey's caramel scented skin, still feel his warm body against mine. His broken wails, tear-filled eyes and flushed cheeks haunted me. A sob lodged in my throat as I stared at my clasped hands.

I hoped he didn't think I'd abandoned him, that I had chosen this over him. If it wasn't for my request to make sure they were safe and away from our mother, they would have had to drag me kicking and screaming from that house. Now I knew my brothers would both be taken care of, and I didn't have to traumatize Bailey by causing such a scene. They would be together, and they wouldn't go hungry, and as much as this hurt, that knowledge made it better.

My entire life, I'd known I was different from others, but I'd never expected that difference to rip me away from my family. They would be okay, I kept telling myself. Asante and Lisa would take good care of them until I could return. They would keep my mother away from my brothers. Gage was tough and he'd get Bailey through this. They'd cry, they would miss me, but they'd get through it.

I lifted my head again to stare at the farmland passing by outside the window. "Why don't you send some of these crops and livestock to us?" I inquired.

The colonel glanced at me. "Your community is surviving on its own. These supplies are needed for those residing over the wall, the cities, and other areas where it is difficult to grow crops, fish, or raise livestock. Believe me, no community is better off than another. There is no wealth and plenty, not anymore. We all have to eat to survive." His gray eyes burned into mine when he turned to look at me. "We are all equal in this world."

"Just a regular old utopia of kidnapping people," I quipped bitterly.

His clean-shaven jaw clenched at my words, forming a little dimple in the center of it. "Far from a utopia. Everything we have we've fought for, and in order to keep it, we must all do things we don't want to do. Including you."

"Maybe if I knew what it was I'm supposed to be doing, or why I was taken, I would be more willing to help."

"If you're meant to know, you will," he replied.

The more and less he said, the more I questioned if I'd ever walk away from this alive. I glanced at the door of the truck and the woman sitting by my side. Maybe I could get the door open and shove her out before leaping out myself. I had no problem with knocking her out of my way, seeing that she'd had no problem with tearing my life to shreds.

The woman's gaze was on me; her lips flattened as she seemed to guess at what I contemplated. I smiled sweetly at her in return.

"Why can't I ride in the back with the others?" I asked.

"You know why," she crisply replied.

"If I knew why, I wouldn't be asking."

My statement was met with stony silence. I glanced at the door again. If I could somehow manage to get away from these people, then what? Run into the countryside and walk the hundreds of miles we'd already traversed back home? I would do it if I thought I could make it, but they'd hunt me down, and the first place they'd go to look for me was my brothers. I had to do everything I could to keep them out of this.

"I'm not going to run," I said.

"Not if you want your brothers to be taken care of and for them to stay free of us," she replied.

And there it was, the confirmation they would use my brothers as leverage over me if I didn't play nice. She'd also confirmed my dislike of her. I turned away from her before I opened the door and shoved her out, just because.

My thoughts turned back to what had happened at my house. The idea that Asante had volunteered to take my brothers in as a way for the government to know where Gage and Bailey were at all times crossed my mind. I hastily buried it.

Asante was my friend. He may be a Guard, but there had been true regret in his eyes when he'd stepped through my door. Besides, I didn't think they'd expected me to request my brothers be removed from my mother's house.

I focused on the darkening horizon as the sun slipped behind the land. Reds, yellows, pinks, and oranges lit up the sky as the truck rolled down the highway. I glanced over at the gages on the dash, trying to figure out which each one of them was. Some of them I knew, others I couldn't recall, and some I'd never seen before. It had been so long since I'd been in a vehicle, I'd forgotten what the wheels on the pavement sounded like and the bouncing, almost soothing feel of them spinning on the road.

The sky was almost completely black when we pulled into a gas station and parked next to one of the pumps. Lights filtered onto the pavement from the store to the right of me, illuminating a small patch of the rutted asphalt. A man opened the glass door and hurried out to us. He said something to the driver of the truck in front of us before walking to the side of the truck.

"Gas," I whispered in amazement.

The woman snorted before opening her door, jumping out, and walking around the front of the hood. The colonel turned toward me, draping his arm over the steering wheel to face me.

"You got a raw deal. You shouldn't be here, but your

brothers are safe and working the wall is something this country needs," he told me.

I bit back a 'save me the speech' retort. The woman already didn't like me for some reason, not that I cared; I didn't like her either. This man wouldn't give me any answers, but I felt starting out with both of these senior military members disliking me was a bad idea.

"Colonel..." I strove to recall his name from the volunteering earlier.

"Colonel Ulrich MacIntyre. For now, you can call me Mac."

"Is there a lot of gas out in this area?"

He shook his head and turned back around in his seat. "This station is only for military vehicles. Most things out here are the same as where you're from. Only less seafood."

"And more meat."

"But I bet many of the people out here would really enjoy a lobster or a crab leg once in a while."

"They probably would." I'd grown sick of seafood over the years, but now I realized I may never have it again. Tomorrow, I would not be able to wake up and go fishing. For all I knew, I might not wake tomorrow. I had no idea what these people planned for me.

"You'll be able to write your brothers, and you'll find your compatriots on the wall will become like family to you," Mac said.

"Yeah," I mumbled. At least it sounded like they planned to keep me alive for a while.

He didn't say anymore, and I sat wordlessly as I waited for the vehicles to be filled. I didn't know if I preferred getting back on the road or dragging this out for as long as possible. I was exhausted, but once we arrived at our destination, it would be final. My life as I had known it would be over. At least right now, I could still somehow hold out hope they would come to their senses and take me back where I belonged.

The woman climbed back into the truck, closed the door, and we pulled out onto the road again. The next couple of hours passed in silence. The stars shone in the sky, and the full moon and headlights lit the black ribbon of road before us in a ceaseless pattern that had caused my mind to go numb hours ago.

I was so used to the same old sights out here that at first I assumed I was imagining it when something began to take shape in the gloom in front of us. Leaning forward, I rested my hand on the dash as two red lights blinked into view on the horizon. As we drew closer, I noticed more and more identical lights high in the sky and stretching endlessly onward across the horizon.

"What are those?" I murmured, though I didn't expect an answer.

"The markers of the wall," Mac answered.

I glanced at him, but I couldn't take my eyes off the distant wall for more than a second. Alongside the road that had been mostly barren for a few miles, houses materialized again. Livestock roamed some of the pastures in the distance, and leaves and tall grass swayed in the breeze. The closer we got to the wall, the closer the houses sat toward the road. People emerged from their homes, curious to see the arrival of the newest recruits.

Then, there it was.

My head tilted back as I craned my neck to try and see all the way to the top of the wall. It loomed above us like some kind of monstrous Goliath set to destroy us or save us all. It easily stretched a hundred and fifty feet into the air, blocking out the moon behind it. I'd heard parts of the wall were enormous, but I hadn't been prepared for *this*.

The TV cameras didn't do it justice, and I wondered if they had been avoiding this section of wall just as they avoided the more hastily assembled ones. Whereas the sections made of debris looked weak, this looked like overkill and would have people dreaming of King Kong-sized monsters lurking on the other side. Much like I was doing right now.

As we drove closer, the blinking red lights cast an eerie red glow across the cab of the truck and the people sitting on either side of me. I half expected an alien spaceship to rise over us, to drift down and say hi, or to suck us up and have us for dinner. Instead, it was only lights, which I now realized were set out at certain points and connected by a wire stretching another twenty feet into the air. I'd bet anything no blackouts affected this wall.

I went to sit back in my seat when a low, grinding noise caught my attention. Sitting forward again, I couldn't hold back the startled *puh* I emitted as what I'd believed was a solid section of wall now had a crack spreading across the bottom of it as it began to rise up before us to give us entry to the other side of the wall.

Before the war, I'd seen the movies *Jurassic Park* and *King Kong*; neither one of those movies could have prepared me for the sight of the wall sliding up from the ground before me. I'd expected the truck to pull to the side of the road and park near one of these houses to unload us, and then we would find a doorway through to the other side, or maybe stay in this town for the night. Instead, we drove straight on through the large opening in the wall.

For the first time, I felt more apprehension for myself than I did for the family I'd been torn away from.

CHAPTER EIGHT

Kobal

"Kobal."

I glanced up from the book I'd been absorbed in when my name was spoken. I may not have much use for the human race, but I did enjoy these books they'd created. It had taken me a while to learn how to read them, but over the years, I'd become more adept at doing so. Humans were creative; that was the best I could say about their species.

My gaze focused on Corson in the doorway, staring at me. His orange eyes were brightened by the lanterns flickering within the tent. His black hair, so dark a hue it appeared midnight blue in some lights, stood up in jagged spikes around his narrow face. He must have recently been with one of the human women again as his pointed ears had earrings dangling from the tips of them. Those women enjoyed decorating his ears, and he happily let them do it.

"What is it?" I inquired, trying to ignore the dangling pink butterflies swinging from his ears when he stepped forward. I'd never understand why a demon as powerful as Corson, and nearly as old as me, would wear those ridiculous things. If I stared at them for too long, I'd rip them from his ears, and I'd been working on trying to curb my temper. The humans were apprehensive and timid enough around me on the best of days, never mind witnessing me tearing the earrings from one of their favorite demons.

"They've returned," Corson replied.

"And?"

"There is a possibility with them."

Closing the book, I dropped my legs from where I'd propped them on the table we often used for meetings and my feet hit the floor. "How good of a possibility?" I demanded.

"I don't know. I kept all the demons away from the new volunteers this time. That whole screaming and running thing is a real turn off."

"Don't want a repeat of last time?"

"No."

The last time, some of the new recruits had gotten a look at some of the more obviously demon kind among us before we could keep them penned in, and they had run screaming into the night. We found four of them, but two had been lost to the nightmare of the world the humans had created.

It was often quite a shock for humans to learn of our existence, and our appearances didn't help much, or at least some of our appearances didn't. Some of us, like Corson and myself, were more human in appearance than others, but some of us were what humans would consider nightmarish.

Personally, I considered the humans all pussies, but then I had little use for their species. Except for one, and if we ever located that *one*, I'd do everything in my power to make sure they accomplished what had to be done, even if I had to drag them kicking and screaming into the fray.

"How do you know there is a possibility with them then?" I inquired.

"There is someone riding in the cab with Mac and Bernadette."

A person separated from the other volunteers and riding with the soldiers was a good indication they had not come here willingly. Rising to my feet in the tent that stood over seven feet high to accommodate my size, I strode toward the flap that had been pulled back to allow air to flow through.

"Take those earrings off," I said to Corson before slipping outside.

The cool air brushed over my skin as I surveyed the town nestled into the valley below us. There was far more going on down there than on a normal night at the military compound. The headlights from the newly arrived trucks were still on and facing what I'd been told was a human development.

The dwellings all looked the same and had the same square yards. Apparently, this was what humans had once liked and strived to live in. To me, the development was just like humans, they all looked the same and possessed rather flat personalities.

I watched as the new volunteers climbed from the back of the trucks. They stretched their muscles as their eyes darted around, trying to take everything in.

"So young," Corson murmured from beside me and pulled the last earring from his ear. "They seem too young for this."

"They're not."

I spotted Bernadette standing by the door of a truck. She stared into the cab as she spoke with another. From inside the truck, a slender hand rested on the door before the person moved forward. I caught sight of raven-colored hair as a woman emerged into the night.

"A woman," Bale said. I turned to watch as Bale made her way across the ground toward us with a natural grace I'd become well familiar with over the years. She and Corson were the two demons who had been with me the longest and through the most battles. Bale stopped beside me to stare down the hill toward the new arrivals. "I had bet it would be a woman."

"We don't know if she's the one we've been searching for," I reminded her.

Bale lifted a delicate shoulder. "Go find out."

I shot her a look, but she only smiled back at me, revealing all of her teeth. She didn't have her razor-sharp fangs descended, but then, I'd only seen them when she was in a full-on rage. Her mischievous, lime green eyes shone brightly in the dark surrounding us as she watched me. The fiery color of her hair tumbling to her ass wasn't the only reddish color about her as her skin had a scarlet hue to it that some humans believed to be a sunburn.

"Who's in charge here?" I inquired.

"You know you're as curious as the rest of us about her, and you won't make her run screaming." Her gaze raked me from head to toe as she pursed her lips. "Well, maybe you won't. We should get you some contacts or sunglasses."

"That will never fucking happen." It was bad enough we wore the humans' clothes and tried to adapt their mannerisms and ways in order to keep from scaring the delicate little mortals; I'd be damned if I hid my eyes from them too.

"Don't think contacts would work anyway," she replied.

"You're the one who suggested coming back to this area of the wall. Do you think she's the one we've been searching for?"

Bale's smile slipped away. "I don't know. All I know is something instinctual pulled at me to return here. It could be because there might be an attack on this section of the wall, or maybe it was because of the impending arrival of a possibility. For all I know, it could have been to enjoy the spring weather. We know how my intuition goes."

"You've had no visions about her arrival or anything else?"

"I've had no visions since the one four years ago telling me the progeny lived and could be the key," she said. "You know how those things work for me. I could have visions ten times a day for ten years and then go a century without. I'm only shown what I'm meant to see."

I turned away from her to focus on the people milling about below. Bale and Corson may be two of the oldest and most powerful demons in existence, but Bale's premonitions were often sporadic, and Corson had turned into a pincushion for the humans. They were also my two most trusted advisors. If Bale had suggested coming here, then there was a reason, and I wanted that reason to be the progeny.

I had to see the possibility the humans had brought back with them. Breaking away from the two of them, I strode down the pathway winding toward the human dwellings below. What few humans I encountered on my way stepped quickly aside to let me pass.

The truck engines were turning off when I arrived at the line of vehicles. I strode purposely forward, surveying the group of new recruits as the older soldiers herded them along. The distress of the newest volunteers beat against me, and the acrid stench of their despair filled my nostrils. My nose wrinkled at the disgusting aroma.

Through the crowd, I spotted Bernadette in her dark green uniform standing with what had to be the possibility at her side. Colonel Mac, one of the few humans I could actually tolerate, appeared beside them. He stood on the other side of the possibility, keeping her boxed in between them. She scowled at the two of them before turning her attention to the crowd funneling past her.

Definitely not a willing one. More than a few possibilities had arrived behind the wall against their will, only to discover they weren't who we were searching for after all. If a few human lives were upended and sacrificed to save the many, so be it.

The possibility folded her arms over her chest as the last of the new recruits trudged by her. "Now what?" she asked. "Am I some sort of sacrificial lamb or something?"

"Not at all," Mac replied.

"That remains to be seen," I replied as I stepped before her.

Her black eyebrows shot up at my words. Her gaze remained on my chest for a second before her head slowly tipped back to take all of me in. A muscle in her cheek twitched when her eyes finally reached my face, but I saw the curiosity in her gaze as she took me in.

Her eyes! I clamped back the small thrill that went through me as those amethyst eyes settled on mine.

Looking at her, I realized more than her eyes marked her as different from the other possibilities I'd encountered. Unlike the other unwilling ones, or the new volunteers, I didn't smell her fear. No, anger and resentment simmered beneath her outwardly calm surface. I may not look as different to the humans as some of my brethren, but I certainly didn't look like a typical human male, either. This girl was only the second human to show no fear of me; Mac had been the first.

I studied her more closely. Her black hair hung in waves about her shoulders down to the middle of her back. The tendrils of it emphasized her round face and proud chin. Sweeping black lashes framed the amethyst eyes currently holding mine. Her skin was tanned to a golden hue from the sun. Freckles speckled the bridge of her slender nose and a faint white scar marred her right eyebrow, but otherwise her skin was unblemished. There was no denying she was pretty, for a human.

My gaze slid over her flat stomach, round hips, and long

slender legs. I'd been with human women since arriving on this plane. Being with them had been more the slaking of a need in a willing body, but then that had always been my experience with women both human and demon alike. Pleasurable but not memorable. This one though, I was stunned to find myself actually desiring her as my gaze lingered on her plump breasts and my cock swelled with need. I had a feeling I would remember burying myself within her.

Her shoulders thrust back, emphasizing her breasts in the thin linen shirt she wore. Her eyes burned with fire when I met them again. She may not be the one we were looking for, but she had more spirit to her than most of those we encountered, and I found myself enjoying it immensely.

"And who might you be?" I inquired of her.

Her full lips pressed into a thin line; it was Mac who answered. "Kobal, this is River Dawson."

"River," I greeted.

"Kobal," she replied flatly.

I felt my lips quirk toward a smile; this human was almost amusing, in a way.

"Is it her?" Mac inquired.

My brow furrowed as my attention was drawn to Mac. He knew it would be difficult to know if someone was the progeny until we had worked with them for a while. We were all growing tired of the search, but the normally stoic man had asked a question he never had before.

"I don't know. We will find out," I replied.

"Find out what?" River demanded. She tried to act indifferent, but I saw something like *interest* in her gaze as she surveyed me.

"That will come in time," I told her.

My eyebrows rose when she glowered at me before turning

to Mac. "Where am I staying, or am I expected to sleep on the ground? Or will it be a cell?"

"No need for a cell; the only place you can run is out there." I pointed at the empty night beyond the rows of houses. "And unless you want to die, I would suggest not going that way."

CHAPTER NINE

Kobal

She stared out at the darkness as if she could somehow pierce the veil. From somewhere in the night, the forlorn cry of a creature not of her world echoed through the air. Her face remained impassive, but I caught a flash of uneasiness in her eyes.

"I will escort you to where you'll be staying," Mac told her.

River gave me a scathing glance before following Mac down the street through the row of houses toward the home where he resided. Over the past four years, there had been possibilities from around the world. All of them were housed away from the other humans until either myself, or whatever demon I'd left in charge of the area, cleared them of being a possibility. Afterward, the debunked possibility was moved in with the others to assimilate into their new lives.

I stood and stared after the enticing sway of her hips, unable to believe she had absolutely *no* fear of me. Even if she took my eyes as some kind of deformity, my size alone caused most humans to stumble out of my way or gawk at me. It would be interesting to see how River fit in.

Turning away from the tempting spectacle of her taut ass, I adjusted my erection and walked back up the hill toward the tents set up at the top. It had been a few days since I'd been with a woman, perhaps that was why she affected me so strongly.

Mac would be joining me in my tent soon, so that meant it would be a while before I could attend the fire blazing hotly on the hill behind the tents. The flames leapt high into the night, illuminating the dark sky and the trees surrounding the clearing. Demons and humans alike would be gathered around those flames. Many of the women there would be more than happy to ease my lust after I met with Mac, but as my gaze drifted back to where River walked with Mac, I realized I wasn't interested in any of the women attending the fire tonight.

Get it together. She's a human, and if she's the progeny, then she may be the key to it all.

I turned my attention to the canvas tents on top of the hill where we resided. Mine was the largest tent and the most noticeable with the meeting room at the front and another tent attached to the back for my sleeping quarters.

We could have established ourselves in one of the homes the humans were so fond of, but living in a house wasn't something we understood or wanted. If there had been caves in the area, we would have taken over those, but there weren't any around here.

Bale and Corson were waiting for me at the top of the hill. Behind them, the heavy canvas cloth of my tent flapped in the breeze. The fluttering sound was one I'd become accustomed to over the years.

"Is it her?" Bale demanded.

I quirked an eyebrow at her, she knew as well as Mac that it would take time to know. "Too soon to tell," I replied.

"How long do you think it will be before we know?"

"As long as it takes."

Bale scowled at me and folded her arms over her chest. "I'm tired of waiting."

"We all are."

I ducked under the entrance to the tent and into the main meeting room where my book sat on the table. I released the pinned back flap, allowing it to fall closed over the entrance. The conversation to come with Mac would be held in private, something Corson and Bale knew. Walking over to the sideboard, I lifted a bottle of wine and poured two goblets. I would have much preferred the demon beverage mjéod to the wine, but it was brewed in Hell and I hadn't had it since leaving my home behind.

Returning to the table, I settled into my chair and surveyed the dark wood furniture in the room. All of the furniture within the tent had been collected from the abandoned homes in town. It would be left behind when we eventually moved onto another town bordering the wall.

Leaning over, I placed the other goblet in front of the seat beside me and leaned back to wait. It took a full thirty seconds after I detected the spicy scent of aftershave for a low voice to call out, requesting permission to enter my tent.

"Come in," I said.

The flap pulled back with a rustle, and Mac's boots thudded across the dirt floor as he walked over to join me. I gestured to the empty seat before he pulled out the chair and sat down. "Thank you," he said as he took hold of the goblet. "I needed this."

"She didn't come willingly."

"In the end, she did, but this is not where she wants to be," Mac said before downing half the contents of his goblet.

"This is not where any of us want to be." I rose to my feet and moved to the sideboard. Retrieving the bottle of wine, I returned to the table and topped off Mac's goblet. "How did you find her?"

Mac's gray eyes were haunted when they met mine. "On a door-to-door search; her *mother* turned her in."

I lifted an eyebrow as I leaned back in my chair. I had no offspring, and most likely never would, but demons cared for the children they had with their Chosen and had often perished to keep them safe. I'd been led to believe it was the same for humans. It was one of the few human attributes that I actually respected.

"I thought you humans were so fond of your offspring," I said.

"Not all of us," he muttered and drank down his goblet. He grabbed the bottle and poured himself another glass. I'd never seen him drink so much or so fast before; whatever had happened out there had rattled him completely. "River turned the tables on her though. Her mother will be fed, but she'll get nothing else from us, and her other two children have been removed from her house."

"There were other children and you did not bring them?" I demanded. Bale's vision had said there was only one progeny still alive, but if River had siblings then either Bale's vision had been wrong or River was *not* the one we sought.

"According to her mother, the other two children show no signs of being different and they have different fathers than River."

Then it can still be her.

Mac lifted his head to look at me; his normally steely gaze was clearly disturbed. I'd never seen that look in the unwavering, unyielding colonel's eyes. "Her mother said River sees things, but they weren't close to each other, so she may have been making it up to receive what was being offered to her. Or there may be other things she can do that her mother never knew about."

"We've had other possibilities who could see things. It's not common, but humans can possess extrasensory abilities."

"I know," Mac murmured and drank the rest of his wine. He took hold of the bottle again and refilled his glass.

"What happened out there?"

"We tore that girl away from her family; I'd like for there to have been a reason why we did."

"Doesn't sound like much of a family."

"The mother wasn't, but she had brothers. The youngest, I can still hear his sobs..." Mac's voice trailed off, and he focused on the far wall before finally looking at me again. "Her mother said she has the Devil's eyes."

I took a sip of my wine as I contemplated his words. "They're definitely unusual, but Lucifer's eyes are a completely different color." *Now they are anyway,* but I kept that to myself. River's eyes were the color of another being's though.

"I see," Mac said and ran a hand through his close-cropped, graying hair.

"I will find out if she is the one we've been searching for," I assured him. "Are you going out with the group tomorrow for more volunteers?"

"I was supposed to," he replied, "but I've decided to stay."

"This girl really rattled you."

"They had to pry her baby brother from her arms while he screamed for her."

For some reason, I didn't like the idea of that happening to her. My fingers curled into fists on the table; I took a deep breath to steady the temper I felt rising within me. *Too much time on the mortal plane is making me soft.* I had to return to Hell soon and claim the throne, which was rightfully mine by birth.

Mac finished off his wine and rose to his feet; he rested his fingers on top of the book I'd been reading. "One of my favorites," he said. "It was the best of times." His fingers fell away from the cover.

"It was the worst of times," I said.

He stared at the book before lifting his head to look at me. "That it is," he said. "I'll see you in the morning, Kobal."

I listened to his boots thudding across the ground and the rustle of the canvas settling into place once more as he made his way out. My fingers rested on the binding of the book as I stared at the green canvas wall across from me. The image of pure purple eyes haunted me as I sipped at my wine.

I had to find out what she might be capable of, and soon.

CHAPTER TEN

River

I pushed a loose strand of hair behind my ear as I surveyed the group of a hundred or so volunteers gathered around me. I folded my arms over my chest, feeling as though I stuck out like a sore thumb. I may only be six years older than most of them, but as I stared at their pimpled, youthful faces, I felt decades older.

Maybe it was their enthusiastic expressions, the way they stood with their shoulders thrust back and their eyes riveted on the group of older soldiers gathered before them. They looked like puppies ready for a treat; I felt like a sullen cat looking to claw the eyes out of anyone who tried to touch me.

Mac stood in the center and slightly in front of the soldiers across from us. The soldiers were all dressed in green uniforms, while us newbies had been given drab brown clothes to wear. The only color on my clothes, and on the clothes of the volunteers surrounding me, was the yellow band encircling our right biceps to differentiate us from the other groups of volunteers. Groups I could see training in the distance with other soldiers.

Tilting my head back, I glanced up at the top of the wall. The red lights still flashed, but they weren't as vivid or as noticeable in the morning sun. I could also see men and women walking on top of the wall now. The sunlight glinted off the scopes of the rifles strapped to their backs. Last night, they had blended in with the shadows. Now they were small figures moving back and forth as they surveyed a land far beyond what anyone on this side of the wall could see.

Looking away from the wall, my gaze slid past Mac and the soldiers to the landscape beyond them. Past the houses and trees, the horizon stretched on endlessly. It all looked so peaceful out there, but all night, cries had echoed across the land. The awful sounds had to have been the ones igniting the rumors of monsters beyond the wall. They'd made my skin crawl as I tossed and turned throughout the night, caught between the urge to punch something or cry out my misery and loneliness.

I knew one thing, all of these little sixteen-year-old volunteers may be eager to please and do what was expected of them, but if they expected me to run or do anything else, they'd be in for a rude awakening. They'd forced me to be here, but they couldn't make me follow their rules. I'd come here without a fight because of my brothers; that didn't mean I'd be a compliant captive.

I stifled a yawn as I leaned against the cold concrete of the wall. Amid the exuberant young volunteers, I spotted Carrie with her head bent close to another young girl.

What are we all doing here?

From across the way, the man I briefly met last night strolled across the front of the soldiers. I frowned when he stopped beside Mac and they exchanged a few words. Around me, the others all stopped speaking and straightened up. I felt the current of astonishment that went through the crowd, heard the indrawn breaths, and saw the looks they exchanged when they got a good eyeful of Kobal. They probably didn't know what to think about his strange eyes and imposing size, I sure didn't.

I remained leaning against the wall, my arms folded over my chest as my eyes ran over him again. There were mountains smaller than he was, I decided. He stood a good foot over my five-nine frame, and more than a head above most of the people around him. The width of his shoulders blocked out two of the soldiers standing behind him.

A sheen of sweat coated the thick muscles of his biceps and caused the thin shirt he wore to cleave to his hard pecs and flat stomach in a way that revealed every etched detail of what lay beneath. While the men and women around him were all dressed in green, he wore a thin black tank top and black pants that hugged the powerful muscles of his thighs and ass. I had no idea where he'd found clothes big enough for him, but I couldn't stop myself from admiring the way he looked in them.

In the light, I could see that though his hair had appeared black last night, there were actually deeper shades of brown in it. Strands of his hair fell to the corner of one of his entirely black eyes. There were no whites within his eyes; I had no idea what had caused the odd phenomenon, but what should have been unnerving, I found fascinating and strangely attractive.

Around me, people shifted back and forth uneasily, but I still wasn't scared of him. He was the largest, strangest man I'd ever encountered, yet the only reason my pulse picked up around him was because I found myself wanting to get closer.

I'd never seen eyes as black as his before, and though they were so black that movement was impossible to notice, I felt his gaze the instant it landed on me. His eyes burned into me like hot coal.

Judging by the small lines around his mouth and eyes, he

looked to be in his late twenties or early thirties, but it was difficult to tell for sure. I didn't know if I'd consider him gorgeous, but there was something so striking, feral, and captivating about him, that it made me itch to run my fingers over those carved muscles in a way I'd never longed to touch a man before.

His full lips thinned as he watched me, and his square jaw, which tapered into a pointed chin, clenched. His eyes narrowed over his aquiline nose as we stayed locked in a stare. I didn't know what he was looking for from me, but I didn't think he was going to find it.

Mac said something that drew his attention away from me. Now that I could look away from his stare, my gaze was drawn to the intricate tattoo on his left arm. Black flames started at the tips of his fingers on the back of his hand. They wrapped around his wrist before rising up his arm to encircle two snarling wolves on his bicep. The wolves were so realistic looking they appeared ready to leap from his bronzed skin at any second.

Continuing onward from the wolves, the flames disappeared briefly beneath the strap of his tank top. When they reappeared, the tips of the flames licked against the base of his neck but didn't rise any higher. Hints of black beneath the tank made it seem as if there was more on his chest, but the only way to know was to see him with his shirt off—a prospect that was both scary and mouthwatering.

Unable to see any more of the tattoo, my gaze traveled to the tattoo on his right arm. Like his left arm, this one also started at his fingertips and encompassed his entire arm. It didn't involve wolves but was made up entirely of black flames all the way to the base of his neck, just like his left side. I thought I saw something more within the flames, some strange symbols or something, but I was too far away to make out what they were.

Sensing his eyes upon me again, I lifted my gaze to his and jutted my chin out. His face remained impassive as he stared at me, but I felt his intense scrutiny. I had no idea where this man had come from, but he was unlike anyone I'd ever seen before. Even his name was odd.

My attention shifted to Mac when he cleared his throat and began speaking. "I know you're all wondering why you're here, and before we begin your training, you will be filled in on some of the details." My heart thundered at the possibility of *finally* getting some answers. "As you all know, a war was started in this country thirteen years ago, but what you don't know is that the war still rages on to this day.

Now he had my complete attention.

"We still fight it every day. *You* will be amongst those working with us to take back our once great nation from the ongoing and ever-increasing threat against it."

People shuffled around me; I could feel their distress ratcheting up at the knowledge the war had never ended.

"The war we fight has never been waged against another country, but against an enemy none had ever imagined thirteen years ago."

What does that *mean? Were King Kong or a T. rex running around somewhere out there after all?*

"There are creatures out there you never knew existed, that none of us ever knew existed," Mac continued. Beside him, Kobal shifted. "There are beings out there seeking to destroy us and growing stronger every day. The entire world is facing this growing menace. *You* will be trained to face this enemy head-on and to protect those who must remain innocent to what resides on this side of the wall."

Around me, the crowd murmured with each other. My skin crawled at his words, and despite the warmth of the May day, my bones felt chilled. I'd resolved not to look at Kobal again, but my gaze flicked to him. I wasn't surprised to find his eyes still on me.

"Protected from what?" someone near the front blurted.

The disapproving stare Mac gave the young man caused him to blush and look away. Turning his attention back to the crowd, Mac focused on us once more. "From demons that walk the earth, demons from Hell itself."

I heard a few scoffs from those around me, some murmured "He's insane," and a couple gasped. Nervous laughter moved through the group, some of them having decided Mac must have been kidding. I continued to watch Kobal, standing there with his hands clasped behind his back. Why did he keep staring at me? I could feel him sizing me up, but why? What was he expecting from me?

I didn't know what to make of what Mac had revealed. He looked as if he actually meant what he'd said, but it simply could not be possible. Places like Heaven and Hell didn't exist, and if they did, neither spawned creatures that would attack Earth and blow things up. Did they?

Mac didn't try to calm the crowd again; instead, he turned and gestured toward someone, or something I couldn't see. Then, the soldiers gathered behind him parted to allow others to move forward.

And *others* was the best way I could think to describe them. I somehow managed to keep my mouth shut as people, or not quite people, spread out to stand before us. I remained leaning against the wall, but inwardly my heart plummeted. My mind screamed denials at me, and my feet were ready to run away, but I remained where I was as my eyes scanned over the fifteen or so new arrivals standing beside Kobal.

They were all so different in appearance from us and from each other. Some of them were truly disturbing looking with their tails, razor-sharp teeth, and horns the size of baseball bats.

Others were extremely handsome or, in the case of the woman with the bright red hair and reddish skin, stunning.

Then, my eyes slid back to Kobal. And in his case, I realized, he was fascinating.

~

Kobal

I watched River carefully as she took in Mac's words. Her forehead furrowed, but she still showed no signs of apprehension as Corson, Bale, and the others stepped forward to reveal themselves. Some of the new volunteers gasped loudly, all of them took a step or two back. Soldiers hemmed them in on all sides, making sure none of them ran off as they had in the past. A few screams went through the crowd, and more than a dozen of them began to cry.

After the years I'd spent working around humans, I'd become accustomed to reactions such as these. I didn't usually come to the new arrival greetings anymore, as I'd seen enough of them over the years. Corson was right about the crying and screaming being annoying, but the humans would adapt; they had no choice. By the end of the month, they would be far more comfortable with everything they would learn and see today.

I'd come today to see her. It was *her* reaction intriguing me most. Her gaze flickered over everyone, lingering upon Bale before sliding back to me. I saw the realization in her eyes as they ran over me before meeting and holding my gaze. She was the strangest human I'd ever encountered, and I couldn't stop watching her and trying to gauge her thoughts.

"Silence!" Mac commanded in a loud, clear voice. The crowd quieted, but sniffles still sounded as some of them stifled their sobs. "I know this is difficult for all of you to understand and accept. It's a lot to take in, but you volunteered to be here for this. The demons you see before you will help train you and will teach you some of the dangers you can expect to find out here in the wilds."

River's eyes went past me toward the rolling land beyond my shoulder. She had no way of knowing what was really out there, not yet anyway, but she would learn; they all would. If they were lucky enough, they would survive it, but if she was the one we'd been searching for these last four years, her chances were slim; most wouldn't survive what would have to be done in order to use her.

"Now that you've been better informed, it's time for your training to begin," Mac continued. "First things first, run."

When no one moved, Mac stepped forward and pointed to the right. "Now!" he barked.

The volunteers all jumped, a few burst into tears again. The soldiers who had been fencing them in fell back to give them room to run past them. Some of the volunteers walked forward, others remained mulling around aimlessly, but when Mac yelled at them again and the soldiers stepped forward to push them on, they all broke into a slow jog.

Except for one. She remained where she was, leaning against the wall, her striking eyes watching the volunteers fall into line amid a bunch of yelling soldiers who would lead them on a five mile run. She turned and started walking toward Mac's house.

"Ms. Dawson, where do you think you're going?" Mac called after her.

"To sleep, hopefully," she muttered the last word under her breath, but I heard it.

"Not today."

She turned back to him and lifted her hand to her forehead to shade her eyes from the sun. I tilted my head as I watched her, intrigued by the gleam in her eyes. "And what am I supposed to do today, run?"

"Yes."

"No."

"Ms. Dawson—"

"You took away my freedom, but I'm not about to fall in line like a goddamn—" She winced as her gaze went to the sky and she bit her bottom lip. "Like a child," she finished.

"You will train with the others. You could be an important part of what we are trying to do here."

"When you figure that *important part* out, you let me know. Until then, I'm going back to bed."

Around me, a couple of demons chuckled. Corson and Bale remained unmoving by my side, raptly watching her.

River went to turn away but Bernadette stepped forward and stopped her. "We could arrange for your brothers to be returned to your mother."

River froze; her hand fell back to her side. She glared at the woman before turning to look at Mac. "I willingly left with you to keep them away from her."

"We can do whatever we want. We could even have them brought here," Bernadette continued.

River's mouth parted on a breath. Her eyes dilated as they darted over all of us before she gazed at the wilds beyond the houses. She had to have heard the cries last night, and now that she knew we weren't human, she had to know worse lay beyond the protection of this camp.

"No," River said. "You can't do that. They're all I have... No. You promised they would be safe."

"Then fall in line," Bernadette replied.

River took a step forward, not to follow the others as they ran along the wall, but in a hostile advance toward Bernadette.

I broke away from the others and strode toward them when I realized River was about to launch herself at the woman.

"It's all right," I said to Bernadette as I stepped in between them. "I would like to spend some time with her anyway."

I almost felt a small amount of pity for her as River gazed helplessly at the rest of us. Almost. While I found her fighting spirit to be amusing, she was going to have to accept her new fate and make her peace with it. We all did, or had to do, things we didn't want to.

She'd really hate what she would have to do if she was the one we'd been looking for.

CHAPTER ELEVEN

River

I couldn't tear my eyes away from Kobal as he moved around the inside of the tent he'd brought me into. I should be terrified of this man, this *demon*. Instead, I found myself raptly watching the way his muscles rippled as he moved. Attraction to someone was not something I'd experienced often, but now it swelled within me as I longed to run my fingers over his bronzed skin.

Being torn away from my family had rattled my brain, I decided.

His head nearly brushed against the roof of the tent as he strode around to the chair at the end of the table and pulled it out. "Sit," he said and gestured to the chair.

"I'd prefer to stand."

A hint of a smile quirked his full mouth before he walked over and settled into a different chair. "So, River, do you plan to sullenly refuse to do anything for your entire stay here?"

I scowled at him as I folded my arms over my chest. Sullen wasn't the way I'd gone about my life up to this point, but I had every reason to be more than a little bad-tempered right now. "You mean for the rest of my life? That will be my *entire* stay here, from what I've been led to understand."

Those entirely black eyes glistened in the light of the lanterns behind him. "You are correct."

Inwardly, I flinched at his abrupt confirmation of my fate, but I kept my face impassive. I didn't care what he said, I would figure out a way to see my brothers again.

"I didn't sign up for this. I'm not going to fall into place because I'm told to," I said.

"No, your mother signed you up for this."

I barely managed to stop myself from recoiling as if I'd been slapped. Apparently, Mac had told him what had happened yesterday. Fine, whatever, I was used to how fast word traveled in a small town. I didn't care who knew my own mother had thrown me to the wolves... or more accurately, demons.

I hated the twinge to my heart caused by the reminder, but I couldn't deny it. My mother, the woman who had given birth to me, avoided, berated, and abused me throughout my life, had hated me enough to send me somewhere she'd never have to see me again. Had hated me enough to send me somewhere that she had no idea what would become of me.

Bet you didn't expect this, Mother.

I threw back my shoulders as I held his gaze. "Mac told you."

"He did."

I didn't say anymore as he clasped his hands before him and rested them on the table. My gaze moved to his long, elegant fingers. His fingernails were entirely black, not dirty or painted, but naturally as black as his eyes. It was another difference between us that probably should have disturbed me, but didn't. Had I somehow lost all sense of self-preservation and reason when they had pulled Bailey from my arms, or was it the man himself *—demon, you idiot—* making all my fear vanish?

"Why are you not afraid of me?" he inquired.

I tore my gaze away from his hands and met his eyes once more. "Am I supposed to be?"

"Most humans are."

"I can see why. You're different; they're not used to you."

"You're not used to me either."

"I'm not afraid of different," I replied.

"Because *you* are different."

"I'm no different than anyone else."

"Your mother told Mac you see things."

He could probably hear my teeth grinding at the reminder of how badly she'd betrayed me.

"She also believed I had the Devil's eyes, something I'm sure Mac told you too. My mother wasn't entirely stable."

"He did, and as I told Mac, I know the Devil personally and your eyes are not the same color as Lucifer's."

It took everything I had to keep my mouth shut over that casual comment. He knew the Devil, *personally*? Holy hell in a handbasket, for the first time I truly realized what I was dealing with. They could parade a bunch of horned, fanged, tailed demons in front of us, but to think of them bumping elbows with the Devil himself made my knees go weak.

"Really?" I asked, unable to stop myself.

"Yes. Perhaps you should sit." He gestured to the seat I'd refused to take earlier.

This time, I wasn't stubborn enough to refuse it again. Walking toward him, I settled into the chair across from him, across from a *demon*.

"Due to the events of thirteen years ago, Lucifer can now walk the earth if he chooses," he said.

This time, I couldn't keep my mouth closed. It dropped

open so fast I half believed it might dislocate and bang off the table. "That's possible?" I blurted.

"Anything is possible," he replied with an air I found far too casual considering the topic.

"Even for Lucifer himself to walk the earth?"

Kobal snorted and rose to his feet; walking over to the sideboard, he pulled a bottle of wine and two gold goblets inlaid with rubies from the cabinets underneath. The lanterns and candles flickering in the tent glinted off the goblets and caused the rubies to glisten like blood. He turned toward me and lifted the bottle of wine in an inquiring gesture. I shook my head no and watched as his large hands elegantly filled his goblet. His hand could probably encompass my entire head; I was struck by the certainty he could squish my skull like a bug.

He settled in across from me again. "He hates the name Lucifer."

I did a double take at this odd statement. "Why?"

Kobal actually smiled at me to reveal all of his even white teeth as he leaned back in his chair and stretched his long legs before him. I realized his muscles had muscles as they flexed beneath his tank top. "Lucifer actually means shining one, morning star. It was the name he was given before he was cast from Heaven, the place where he once was the shining one. When he settled in Hell, those who called him by that name again were ruthlessly slaughtered."

"Who would have guessed he'd be so testy about a name."

"We are what we make ourselves. He wanted no reminder of his former life."

If it hadn't been for Gage, Bailey, Lisa, and Asante, I would have completely understood that statement. I loved my small town, but my mother's betrayal would forever be stamped on my soul, would forever taint what had once been a fairly happy place for me. Whenever she wasn't around anyway.

"And what does he prefer to be called?" I asked.

"Satan."

I leaned forward to take hold of the goblet he'd set before me. I'd never had wine before, but this conversation called for it. His hand engulfed the wine bottle before I could take hold of it. "I will pour it for you," he murmured.

Settling back in my seat, I watched him as he poured the wine and set the goblet down again. "Polite, for a demon," I murmured.

"Brave, for a human," he replied. "Or stupid. Which is it?"

I shrugged and lifted the goblet. It was heavier than I had expected and by far the most expensive and exquisite thing I'd ever held in my life. It may be beautiful, but it wouldn't fill my belly, so it had little relevance to my life. Unless I melted it down to make hooks out of it, I thought with a smile.

"Maybe a little of both," I admitted, but I had the insane feeling he wouldn't hurt me, even if he probably could crumple my body and use me as an accordion if he wanted to.

I took a sip of the red liquid inside the goblet. My nose wrinkled when the bitter taste hit my tongue and slid down my throat.

"It's an acquired taste," he informed me.

"Apparently so."

"There's many misconceptions about demons, and some truths."

"Are you going to tell me which is which?" I inquired.

"You'll learn. We'll be spending a lot of time together over the coming weeks."

I didn't know what to make of that statement. The man may not outright frighten me, but his massive size and demonic nature were more than a little overwhelming. "Why?"

"So that you can be trained properly to protect yourself."

"Do you not want to kill humans?"

"Oh, there are a fair number of you I'd like to kill. You're a rather annoying species in all honesty, but you serve your purpose."

"What is that?"

"To help end this war."

I tilted my head to study him. "Why would you want to end it? Aren't demons supposed to want to walk the earth and stamp humans out?"

"No, not all of us," he replied. "We are fighting against those of us who would wish to see you all enslaved and begging for mercy. There are also creatures living in Hell that have been locked away for many millennia and should never be set free. We must make sure they stay that way. Now, River, what else can you do, besides see things?"

"Nothing," I lied straight-faced. But then maybe it wasn't a lie; I wasn't sure about the curtain fire, and static electricity on someone's fingers would be of no interest to a demon. There was also that one dream, but I was certain that had been a fluke too.

"Hmm." His gaze raked me from head to toe and back again. "Would you tell me if there was something else you could do?"

"Will you tell me why I'm here? What is with the fliers looking for people with abilities? What exactly are you all searching for, and what will happen if this person is found, whoever it is?"

"I can't give you those answers."

I hadn't expected anything different from him than I'd gotten from Mac, but frustration still caused my gut to clench. "If I am the person you're looking for, will I still be kept in the dark?"

"No, you will be informed of what you need to know then."

My fingers played with the edge of the goblet as I admired

the rubies and tried to think of questions he might be willing to answer. I may not be able to learn everything, but I would learn as much as I could. "Is Hell as bad as we've been led to believe?"

"Better and worse. Depends on what you're there for."

I lifted my head to meet those seemingly fathomless black eyes. "Were you sent there?"

"I was born there, all demons are in one way or another."

"Was it horrible for you?"

A small smile quirked the edge of his mouth. "What is Hell for one may not be Hell for another. It is my home; I miss it."

"Did you, ah... did you hurt people?"

"People as you think of them are not there, their souls are. Every soul within Hell belongs there."

"But did you hurt them?"

His fingers tapped on the table as he studied me. "They are there to be punished; therefore, they are."

My hand wrapped around the bottom of the goblet. I took another sip of the liquid to wet my parched throat. "I've broken many of the commandments in my lifetime; perhaps we would have met one day anyway."

"It's not all about the commandments," he replied. "The souls of the people who are sent there did far more than covet their neighbor's goods."

I tilted my head to the side as I pondered everything I'd learned so far today. "So there really is a Heaven and a Hell."

"There is," he confirmed and finished off his drink. He poured himself another glass of wine and sat back in his chair.

"Are angels going to come down and help us?" I felt as foolish asking that question as it sounded, but then I was sitting across from a demon, so why couldn't white-winged beings swoop down to beat back the demons looking to enslave us?

"No."

"How can you be so sure?" I demanded.

"Because your idiot human species didn't rip a hole into Heaven. They ripped it into Hell and set almost everything inside free."

I was going to have to start wiring my jaw shut if I kept talking to this guy.

CHAPTER TWELVE

River

"I imagine you would all be floating around on clouds if things had gone the other way," he said.

I blinked at him, managing to close my mouth again, but felt it starting to unhinge once more. How did anyone respond to *that* revelation? Humans had ripped a hole into *Hell*? I didn't like the taste, but I had a feeling I was going to need more wine, so I took a big gulp of it.

"What do you mean humans ripped a hole into Hell? How?"

"Poking around with things they shouldn't have been. I don't understand the science behind it, and most of the people who knew exactly what they did to make it occur, are now dead."

"Did they die in the war?"

"No. They died when they tore open the gateway and a horde of demons slaughtered them."

I didn't ask if he was one of those demons; I preferred not to have that answer. "What do you mean? I saw the planes, and I saw the bombs on TV. Another country attacked us."

"No," Kobal replied. "No nation attacked another one. Your own government released those bombs in an attempt to stifle what they'd set free in your country. The same bombs were dropped by other countries on the other side of the world. Your country wasn't alone in their ignorance. Multiple countries were messing around with things they had no business messing around with. The bombs killed some of us but ultimately they didn't work. Hell absorbed the radiation that didn't have any effect on us anyway."

I propped my chin on my hand to keep my mouth closed; it would be a lot easier than trying to figure out a way to relocate my jaw later. I couldn't comprehend everything he was telling me. My mind spun, and the wine curdled in my stomach.

"Why are you telling me all this?" I whispered.

"You would have learned it all today anyway, if you had agreed to go with the others. It's part of your first day of training."

My stomach still felt sour, but I lifted the goblet and downed the contents in one swallow. I hated the tremor in my hand when I set it back on the table, but I couldn't stop it. "So Luci—ah, Satan is walking the earth right now?"

"Call him Lucifer, I do," he said with a smile that couldn't hide his dislike of said demon.

"You said he hated that."

"He does."

"I'd prefer not to piss off the king of Hell if I can help it right now."

Kobal's fingers tightened on his goblet, and his muscles rippled in such a way that his tattoos appeared to move. "Lucifer is not the king of Hell, so you don't have to worry about that."

"But—"

"No, he is not walking the earth right now," he interrupted brusquely. "He remains in Hell, gathering his troops and trying to figure out a way to free the abominations who have been trapped behind the seals for many millennia. Thankfully, for all of us, he hasn't been successful at it and won't be if we can find a way to defeat him. Demons were not meant to walk freely on this earth; there were strict rules set in place for those who did come to earth in the past. However, this is not where we belong, and our battles against Lucifer and his followers, who we call the Craetons, never should have become a war that the human race fought too. Thanks to the actions of humans, there is no longer a choice in this. They upset an intricate balance, existing since the dawn of time, and are now reaping the consequences of their actions.

"All demons enjoy and thrive on agony and vengeance in our own way, but there are those of us who will punish any human they come across. There's a reason why humans were only able to freely cross the boundaries of Heaven and Hell as souls before. If the Craetons have their way, they will murder or enslave every human they encounter."

"Why wouldn't they kill us all?"

"If all humans were to die, there would be no new babies for souls to be born into. We have no way of knowing what would become of those souls. They may simply vanish, which is something no one can risk."

I blinked at him; my throat was beyond parched as my heart hammered in my chest. "Aren't souls supposed to last forever?" I croaked out.

"Yes, in a way. A soul's sentence in Hell depends on their crime or crimes. When their time is up, they're sent back to Earth to start again, in a new life. The soul would be theirs once again to do what they would with it, a fresh start. They are reborn with no memory of who they had been before. If they were sent back to Hell, they *remembered*."

He said remembered in such a way it caused goose bumps to erupt on my skin. I didn't want to know what they remembered.

"The same for Heaven," he continued. "Souls float around with their harps, or at least that's what I imagine they do, until all of their loved ones arrive. Once they're all reunited, those souls have a happy little reunion. Then the oldest of those souls one day are sent back to Earth. However, all souls must go through this transition of life and death."

"How come souls don't get to stay in Heaven with their loved ones?"

"That's just the cycle of our dimensions; it's the way it has always been. And just because a soul makes it to Heaven once, doesn't mean they won't eventually make it to Hell a time or two also. Humans are able to create new souls—you're the only species who can—but new souls are born into this world every day then make their way to one of our planes. Without this life cycle, we don't know what could happen, but there is a reason things were balanced the way they were before."

"I see." Lifting my necklace, I pulled at the shells lining it, moving them back and forth as I tried to digest his words. I had a feeling that later, I'd probably do a whole lot of banging my head against the wall and maybe some hugging myself, but right now, I felt strangely calm. I must be in shock; that had to be it. Kobal's gaze went to my necklace, and his forehead wrinkled as he stared at it. Releasing it once more, I leaned toward him. "It seems like all of the religions got at least a piece of it right."

"They did, but anything or anyone that is 100 percent certain they're right, is bound to be wrong."

I couldn't help but smile over his words. "Probably. So, if Heaven gets harps—"

"I'm not sure about that, but it's the way I always pictured those bastards."

My eyebrows shot up; apparently, the animosity between Heaven and Hell was real too. "Okay, so maybe no harps, but something with fluffy bunnies. What happens to the souls who go to Hell?"

"Angels and demons feed on souls in different ways, without them we will all starve and die. Demons inflict pain on a soul when they feed on them. I much prefer a fresh soul; there's more vitality in them. They are more satisfying. Other, lower-level demons aren't so picky and are used to having the leftovers from the more powerful demons, such as myself."

Now I had a full-on shiver running through my body. "If you're not in Hell now, how are you feeding?"

"Demons weren't the only things set free from Hell. Some souls have remained in Hell, but though you may not be able to see them, many souls are also free now. They're not being punished in all the ways they should be, but we're still able to feed from them."

"How often do you do that?"

"Once a week."

It was all so strangely different. I'd almost believe I was dreaming if it hadn't been the longest and most realistic dream of all time. "And you breathe our air?" I asked as I watched his chest rise and fall with his breath.

"We do," he replied. "The planes were all an extension of each other until the humans caused this disruption. We are similar to humans in many ways except we are stronger, faster, and our senses are more heightened. We also do not get sick and cannot catch your diseases."

"Why are you helping us with this?"

"I want my life back, we all do, and so do all of you. Lucifer must be destroyed, and as much as I don't like it, your kind may be able to help us with that. We must work together in order to put wrongs to right, no matter how much I'd rather kill most of you myself sometimes."

Wasn't that a delightfully fun thing to learn about the demon sitting across from me? My eyes raked over him again, but despite his words, I still felt no apprehension toward this lethal creature. Folding my arms over my chest, I leaned back in my seat. "What were humans trying to accomplish when they tore into Hell instead?"

"They were working with governments on the other side of the world—"

"You said that before, so those countries weren't bombed either by China and Russia like we were told?"

"No, and the civilians there were told your country is the one that bombed the countries destroyed over there. Whatever they were doing tore open an unnatural gateway into Hell on both sides of the earth. At the time, there were many nations working on the project, which ultimately destroyed everything you've ever known. And no, there is no giant hole going all the way through the center of the earth. Think of it as an open hole to another dimension. One opening is on this side, in what you used to call Kansas, and the other is in Hungary. The gates connect to each other. They opened at the same time and we're counting on them closing simultaneously."

I rubbed at my temples as I tried to assimilate everything he was telling me with everything I'd *known* to be true these past thirteen years.

"Why would they do such a thing?" I mumbled.

"Men trying to play at being God," he replied simply. "Unfortunately, they got far more than they bargained for. Mac has informed me they were trying to do something good by expanding the universe to offer other opportunities to your increasingly overrun planet."

I couldn't help but laugh at his words. At first, it started as a giggle, but then I was holding my stomach before progressing into a full-on, uncontainable body laugh. His head tilted as he studied me like I was some kind of strange creature. Perhaps, I was.

"What is so funny?" he inquired.

"The old saying..." I got out in between bursts of laughter.

"What old saying?"

"The road to Hell is paved with good intentions. Who knew it would ever come true?"

Perhaps it was the wine, but I slapped my hand on the table as I laughed loudly. He continued to study me, but I heard him chuckle too.

CHAPTER THIRTEEN

Kobal

I twirled the goblet in my fingers as I watched her across the way. The lantern and candlelight danced over her raven hair, causing her thick, wavy locks to shimmer in the red and orange hues cast by the flames. Her amethyst eyes sparkled, tears actually escaped them as her musical laughter continued to resonate through the air. I couldn't help but chuckle with her as she wiped the tears from her eyes with the back of her hand.

"Oh," she said with a shake of her head that caused her hair to fall in waves around her pretty face.

My eyes latched onto the scar above her right eyebrow. How had she received it? I dismissed the question. I didn't care what had happened to her before coming here. All that concerned me was the possibility I might be able to use her to get what I wanted. To claim the only thing I'd ever coveted since I was born.

"I don't know why that made me laugh so much. It must be the wine," she said with another giggle.

Leaning forward, I took hold of her goblet and poured her

another glass. I didn't know what it was about this little human, but I found myself actually enjoying her company. Pushing the goblet toward her, I watched as she lifted it and took a sip. Her nose wrinkled again, but she didn't make the same disgusted face she had with her first sip. Her lips, stained by the wine, had become a deep red color, and I found my gaze riveted to them when she pulled the goblet away from her mouth.

I had to fight the impulse to lean over the table and drag her toward me when her pink tongue slid out to lick the wine from her lips. Whatever it was about this human, she affected me in more ways than one.

She stopped laughing and lifted her eyes to mine. They sparkled with the wetness of her tears; the sweeping lashes framing them were spiky with water. She wiped at them again before settling back in her chair and studying me with a frown.

"So if you exist on a different plane that humans couldn't get into, then how did the stories of Heaven and Hell begin?" she asked.

Insightful, inquisitive girl, I realized. "Some mortals can see things they shouldn't be able to," I told her.

"Like me?"

She freely admitted her ability then. "Yes, and it would be interesting to know what you can see."

Her fingers flicked dismissively beside her head. "*Nothing* of any interest to a demon I assure you, and nothing pertaining to me. I wouldn't be sitting here if I saw things about myself."

No, she wouldn't. She would have fled before they ever showed up on her doorstep. "Some humans can see more than others; they can look past the veils of your plane and see what lies beyond to both dimensions. Some could even communicate with others outside your mortal coil. In Hell, we could see what you were doing on this side, not that we watched often; you mortals are mostly boring."

She laughed again and sipped at her wine. "I suppose we would be boring to a bunch of demons and Lucifer himself."

"There were times when I would look through. It helped to give me a better understanding of your world, once demons stopped entering it."

"Wait... *What*?" she sputtered.

I chuckled again at the bewildered look on her face. I couldn't recall ever being this amused by another before. "Demons used to cross into your plane, though the gates were closely guarded and monitored by those of *my* kind. The ones who crossed to Earth were to keep our existence a secret. If they somehow slipped up, they were punished ruthlessly and in the most gruesome ways when they returned."

"Why would they return then?"

"Some didn't. Some chose to stay on Earth and perish rather than return and live. Others believed they could get away with their indiscretion and no one would know. They were always caught. My kind has always ruled the guardians of the gate."

"How many guardians of the gate are there?" she asked.

"I was the only one who could open a gate and allow demons to pass back and forth, before you humans went and fucked *that* all up. There are two other sub-guardians who guard the gate along with me."

I didn't know what was going on behind those beautiful eyes of hers, but I was struck with the realization that I enjoyed the way she assessed me, the way she had no fear of me. Even those humans I'd bedded on this plane had been nervous, but their desire and curiosity had won out and they'd eagerly come to me to have their curiosity quenched.

"So you can no longer open a gate?"

"I can. Anywhere I choose and I can still close it, but there is little reason for me to do so now that your world is wide open for the taking."

"You said the demons who remained on Earth perished as if they had a choice in the matter," she said.

"All demons are immortal—"

"Holy..." She nearly spit out the wine she'd taken a sip of.

Coughing, her hands flew up to her strange necklace again. She ran it through her fingers as she stared at me as if she were trying to figure me out. *Never going to happen, young human.*

"Okay, so they were immortal but died on Earth, why?" she asked.

"When demons enter into the mortal realm, we begin to age. We show no adverse effects from it, if we cross back and forth, but if we stay here we will die."

"So, you are dying now?"

I liked that she sounded displeased by this notion. "No, with a gateway into Hell wide open, we are suffering no ill-consequences from your realm."

"Fascinating," she whispered. "Wouldn't the souls of those demons come back to Hell once they died on Earth?"

"No. Demons don't have souls like you humans do, just another part of the balancing system."

She rubbed at her temples again. "So, the people who glimpsed between the veils and who stumbled across demon-folk on Earth spread the word about them after?" she asked.

"They did. Some were condemned and destroyed because of it, others were believed and the word spread."

"I hate to disappoint you, but I've never glimpsed anything beyond this world. I knew who was going to volunteer yesterday, and I also knew one girl's name. I could often find the hot fishing spots and could see things hidden from me, like my brother under the kitchen sink. I know nothing about other worlds, much less whole other dimensions."

"Doesn't mean you're not who I'm searching for."

"You're the one searching for someone?" Her voice took on a razor edge.

"I am."

All humor vanished from her face; her mouth pursed as her eyes narrowed. Her scar became more visible when her skin paled. "So you're the reason I was torn away from my family?"

"Yes."

A muscle jumped in her cheek, and her eyes deepened to an almost plum color. Her head fell into her hand. When she looked at me again, I couldn't tell if she wanted to leap across the space between us and attack me, or start screaming in frustration. Her hand clamped around her goblet. "Why?"

"I can't tell you that."

She stood up so quickly the chair skidded away from her. Her hands fisted and un-fisted as she stalked toward the flap in the tent before freezing and coming back toward me. Stopping before me, she slammed her hand down on the table. Her lack of fear over me both fascinated and irritated me. No one, not even Corson and Bale, were so free and defiant around me.

When she leaned closer to me, her enticing scent assailed me. She smelled like the earth, of fresh spring rain and flowers in bloom. I had been on this dimension for thirteen years, and the various scents, both good and bad, had become one of my favorite things about it. Since I'd been here, I had almost forgotten the burnt smell of brimstone, and the coppery aroma of blood that permeated Hell.

I inhaled her aroma, taking it into me. Highly attuned to all scents, I knew hers would be one I'd never forget. My fangs pricked as blood rushed into my dick and I swelled against my pants. She looked like she was about to throttle me. All I wanted was to drag her into my lap and tear the clothing from her body so I could sink myself into her and have her scent all over me.

"If it's not me, this person you're searching for, will you allow me to go back?" she demanded, pulling me from images of her body working over mine. "I understand why volunteers are kept here and not allowed to return after what you've told me, but what of me? I would never tell anyone what I've learned here, and my brothers need me."

I found myself unwilling to shatter the glimmer of hope I saw within her pleading, amethyst eyes, but I had no choice but to deny her.

"That cannot be allowed."

She didn't cry, didn't start screaming and carrying on. She simply stood there and stared at me before turning away. I knew she intended to leave here and not look back. Something inside me couldn't allow that. She didn't make it two steps before I loosely seized hold of her wrist and tugged her back around.

"If you tell anyone I said this, it will not happen, but perhaps in the future, there can be a supervised visitation with your brothers," I said to her.

I didn't know if it was an idea I would ever be able to make a reality, but I couldn't stand seeing such misery in her eyes. There were demons I cared for and would try to make happy, but never had I considered trying to please a human.

The callouses on her palm and the nicks on her fingers brushed over my skin when her small hand covered mine and she squeezed. She'd done no training in camp yet, but she already had working hands. What had her life been like before this?

I don't care what it was like; all that matters now is if she is the progeny. I told myself this, but I still found myself intrigued by her.

"On my life, I would never say a word," she vowed. "Why would you do that for me?"

I released her, unwilling to touch her any longer. She rattled my resolve in a way no other had done in all my fifteen hundred and sixty-two years. I didn't entirely trust myself to keep touching her, didn't trust myself to let her leave here without knowing what those plump, reddened lips tasted like.

"Despite popular belief, we are not all evil. We have needs, and we can be incredibly cruel if necessary, but we aren't inherently evil. We are simply a means to an end. No creature, demon or otherwise, is completely evil."

"What about Hitler?" she asked.

"That one is debatable." This time, the smile she gave me caused her eyes to twinkle. She sat back down into her chair. "I'm not promising you anything, you know."

"I know, but something, *any*thing, is better than the solid wall of nothing I've met for the past two days."

"Understandable."

"So, what exactly happened on your side when the humans cut into your world?"

"Hell broke loose."

She gave a small laugh as she drew her feet up onto the chair and hugged her legs to her chest. "So you've said. I know what happened on this side, we watched it unfold on TV, but what about you? Where were you? What did it look like?"

"I was right where the gateway opened," I told her. "At first, it was only this small beam of light piercing through the veil between our worlds. Normally, for us to see into your world, we had to go to the oracle." At her furrowed brow, I expanded on this. "It's a lake of fire deep in the bowels of Hell where we could look upon your world if we wanted to. Few made the journey, as the lake was also the central source of all the heat in Hell."

"Oh," she murmured.

"When the humans tore through the veil, I was with the rest of the higher-level or arch-demons."

"Much cooler where you were?" she quipped.

"It was, but even if I'd been near it, the heat of the lake has no effect on me."

"Why is that?" she asked.

"Maybe one day we will have that conversation." Her eyes burned with annoyance, but I continued before she could speak. "When the first pinhole of light showed through, I was drawn to it. Bale and Corson followed me. They are here with me in this camp and are also my seconds-in-command. Looking through the hole, we could see into your world, but unlike when we looked into the oracle, we couldn't get a full view of different places in your world. All we could see was a street and a building on the other side.

"Then it exploded. The force of the blast threw many of the higher-level demons into the lower-level pits. That was the first war we fought. The lower-level demons mistakenly assumed us weakened by the blast, and though some of us perished in the ensuing battle, more of them did."

"I see," she murmured. "What is the difference between a high-level and a low-level demon?"

"High-levels are all born in Hell, lower-levels are souls who were so hideous they were never allowed to leave Hell again. Hell forged them into twisted monstrosities that fed off our leftovers."

"So they're the vultures of Hell."

"Yes. They also all possess some kind of deformed, animalistic appearance. They are physically strong, and because higher-level demons don't breed often, they outnumber us, but they are weaker than us and they have no powers. All of them are on Lucifer's side."

"But I saw demons with you who had horns and tails like an animal."

"Horns and tails can be a demon trait. If you ever have the misfortune of seeing a lower-level demon, believe me, you will know the difference." *And if she is who I seek, she will most likely see more than one.*

"But Lucifer wasn't born in Hell, wouldn't he be considered lower-level?"

"He is a fallen angel. Heaven works like Hell does; Lucifer was supposed to perish on the mortal plane after being cast out, along with the others who were cast out with him. Instead, he somehow managed to find his way into our world and brought his cohorts with him; there is nothing lower-level about that. Many demons decided to follow him because of that fact alone.

"He didn't try to take over Hell the minute he arrived, or so I was informed by elder demons who passed on our history. He bided his time and grew a following who believed they should be allowed to pass freely between Hell and Earth whenever they chose, and should be able to rule over the weaker and more desirable human plane. Over time, Hell became divided into two factions who have battled each other ever since. The Palitons, my side, who fights against Lucifer, and the Craetons who follow him."

"So God tossed the angels onto Earth to die; what about the humans there at the time? Didn't God have any concern for their safety?"

"Lucifer and the other angels couldn't have killed them all in the time they were here, considering he was as vulnerable to injury as the humans were. There was no concern about the angels being discovered, as humans already spoke of demons and angels, Gods and Goddesses. At the time Lucifer fell, the world was an entirely different place. One of magic and mystery. The angels would not have garnered the same reaction from humans as we did when we were thrust into your world."

"Trying to bomb you into oblivion?" she asked with a smile.

"Exactly."

"How did Lucifer make it into your world?"

I drummed my fingers on the table. "That is something only he knows the answer to, and he's not very forthcoming. Unfortunately, it's an answer we require as we think it may be the key to closing the gateway the humans created. He opened the hole and my ancestor closed it after him. No demon has been allowed to cross into the mortal realm since."

"Why not?"

"No one would risk opening the portal while Lucifer was in Hell. He had discovered a way in, but he couldn't find a way out, and we couldn't risk what he would do if he walked freely back and forth between the two dimensions."

"Is there any way to find out how he got in?"

"If there is, we will find it." That was all I could tell her on the matter. Fortunately, Bale standing outside and requesting entrance saved me from any more of her questions.

CHAPTER FOURTEEN

Kobal

"Enter," I called out.

Bale pulled back the flap and ducked to come inside. Her gaze slid over River before glancing at me. Over her shoulder, I could see the lengthening shadows of the day; I hadn't realized how much time had passed. River's feet hit the floor, and I followed the direction of her gaze to a plate I hadn't noticed in Bale's hands. I kicked myself for not realizing River was probably hungry.

"I assumed she might like some food," Bale said. "The other humans have all returned and are eating."

"Yes, please," River said. Bale strode forward and placed the plate before her. River stretched out her finger and poked it into the chunk of meat on the plate. "Steak?"

"Yes," Bale said.

River smiled at her. "Thank you."

Bale shot me an incredulous look before focusing on River's bent head. It wasn't often the humans thanked us for anything.

River grabbed her fork and knife and happily cut into the

piece of meat on her plate. After shoving a chunk into her mouth, she let out a low groan. Her eyes closed as she enjoyed the bite. "Delicious."

I waved toward the flap. Bale had been right to bring her food, but I wanted more time alone with her. "I will escort her back shortly." Bale's eyebrows shot up, but she bowed her head in deference to me and left the tent. I watched River eat with an enthusiasm I'd never seen before. "Do you not have such food where you are?"

"No," she answered after swallowing. "It's been years since I've had any beef. Some chicken, yes, but as a fishing community, seafood has been our main supply since the war started. I'd forgotten how delicious it is. Is that woman your girlfriend?"

I hadn't expected the abrupt change in subject or the absurd notion she believed I would have a steady relationship with a woman. "Bale? No."

"You sound surprised I would ask. She's stunning."

This little human was the most enthralling and unexpected creature I'd ever encountered, and I'd encountered thousands over my lifespan. She found Bale stunning when many of the human women avoided her, either because of their uneasiness around her or because of how much she outshone them. I'd watched some of the human men trip over themselves to get closer to her.

"We do not have *girl*friends."

She paused in the middle of cutting her food. "I see. Well, are you two together in whatever way demons are together?"

"No. Bale is one of my commanders and that is all."

"Oh."

Finishing off the meat, she turned to the potatoes and vegetables still on her plate. "The fliers only started circulating around my town four years ago," she said when she placed her fork and knife on the empty plate. "Why?"

"It took a couple of years after the gateway was torn open to regroup and to assure the humans we weren't *all* here to kill them. That was one of our main obstacles, but after the first two years, we managed to convince them we were on their side by helping them to fight back the Craetons who were trying to spread further out. Mac had a big hand in getting them to accept us after I encountered him twelve years ago. Over the years, we've spent a lot of time building the wall, training and educating the humans on what they need to know about us, and fighting back the waves of Craetons trying to spread further across the land."

Her mouth parted on a breath as she lifted her foot onto the chair again and draped her arm over her knee. My eyes tracked the way the movement caused her shirt to pull tighter over her breasts. What I wouldn't give to take those breasts in my hands and knead them before bending my head to suck on one of her nipples. To hear her moans—

"The volunteering started eleven years ago," she said.

I tore my gaze away from her breasts and compelled myself to focus on what she said. Getting involved with a possibility would be the worst decision I could possibly make; it could never happen. I told myself this, but it did nothing to ease the raging hard-on I had right now. Shifting uncomfortably in my chair, I lifted the goblet and took a drink of wine.

"Yes," I said when I was finished swallowing. "And four years ago, we learned there was a hope out there for us, we only had to find it."

"How did you find out about this... *hope?*"

"Bale can also sometimes see things."

"And what did she see?"

"That is not for you to know, human."

She placed her chin on her knee. "Can't blame me for trying."

"Not at all. We have made much progress over the years with the humans, but there are still a large number who are distrustful of us."

"I can understand that. It's not every day you learn of a whole other plane of existence and that the plane is actually Hell. It's a tough pill to swallow."

"You seem to be swallowing it quite well."

She drank down some more of her wine. "For tonight. Who knows, maybe I'll be drooling on myself in the morning."

"I doubt that. You've taken this better than any human I've seen before."

"Devil's eyes, remember? Visions, knowing things. I think that makes it a little easier for me to believe there's something more out there. Would I have guessed Heaven and Hell would be that something more, probably not, but it does make it easier for me to take at least some of this. Though, I'm still not at all pleased about being torn from my home."

Her eyes filled with malice when they turned toward me. I was contemplating lifting her onto the table and sinking myself into her, and she looked as if she were contemplating my death. I remained silent, amazed she so relentlessly held my gaze when many others wouldn't.

"That could not have been changed," I told her. "It is extremely important, for everyone, including the entire human race, that we find who we are looking for."

Some of her antagonistic spirit slipped away as she turned to look at the wall of the tent. "I almost hope I am this person," she murmured. "At least then there would have been a reason."

I hoped she wasn't. The realization hit me with the impact of a hellhound barreling into my chest. I barely knew this woman; the person we sought could well be the key to taking back a throne that was supposed to have been mine at birth; a throne Lucifer stripped from my ancestors before I'd had a chance to claim and defend it. I'd spent my entire existence working toward this one goal. Now, all I could think about was how much I hoped this woman was not the one who could help me regain my rightful position in Hell.

"Why sixteen-year-old volunteers?" she asked. "Why so young and why cut the age off at twenty?"

"That was not my decision. The humans believed that younger people would have an easier time accepting what they would see and learn here. Even still, more than a few humans haven't been able to handle this revelation. They've been secluded for their own safety and the safety of those around them. Some have killed themselves and others have fled into the wilds, never to be seen again. The volunteers aren't considered soldiers until they've been through two solid years of training and can pass all stages of the training."

"What happens if they don't?"

"They take care of the animals, make the clothes, the food, and take care of other things requiring maintenance in every camp along the wall."

"I see. How many other people, like me, have you found over the past four years?"

"Throughout all of the establishments and camps in the world, a couple hundred possibilities have been uncovered. Some of them actually could do things, some couldn't, but none of them were the person we're searching for."

"And I am a possibility?"

"Yes."

Her fingers curled into her shin. "Were all those people brought here?"

"No."

"But you're the one looking for them?"

"Demons have been established in many camps throughout the world in order to work with the humans and focus on our goal. They know the requirements we are searching for; the person will be brought to me if they're uncovered."

"How will they get here if they're on the other side of the world?"

"There is still an open airport in Canada and one in London as well."

"Could demons travel through the hole in the dimensions to the other side?"

"We could," I confirmed. "But no human could survive Hell. It has also become too volatile to risk more of our members. We can get in without a problem, getting all the way through without notice is an entirely different matter. Guardians of the gate have been established on both ends to try and stop more demons from exiting Hell and to report to us if Lucifer makes his move out of Hell."

Her foot hit the ground with a thud. "Shouldn't you all be there in case that happens?"

"Right now, our best option is to defend the wall and keep them back from invading the lands beyond. There will be no protecting or controlling the humans anymore if the Craetons get beyond the wall. Demon attacks on top of panicked humans would only result in massacres."

She shuddered; her hands ran up and down her arms as her gaze went beyond me.

"Many of the nightmares of Hell now roam free in the middle of your country as well as Europe," I told her.

"What about Africa, Canada, Australia, and South America, are they still mostly out of it?"

"Australia is; the ocean has kept them secluded from the chaos. Most of Canada still is, but there are some problem areas on the wall along the border. There was a breach in the southern wall and an influx got through into Mexico. South America is still somewhat safe, but it's only a matter of time before it too falls. There are also reports of Africa having been breached."

Her gaze came back to me, and she chewed on her bottom lip as she studied me. "Why did you settle in this area?"

"I travel to all of the encampments on a rotating basis to check on things. I just happened to be here when you were brought in."

"Do you bring all the possibilities you encounter in to talk with them?"

I poured us both some more wine. "No, you are the first."

"Why me?"

"Because you are the first who has refused to go with the others and who didn't turn into a blubbering mess once the secrets were out."

"Have the others all been older than the volunteers, like me?"

"No, some were younger."

"No wonder they started to cry; they were children."

"You're not much older than a child."

"Maybe not, but I was never really able to be a child either."

I folded my fingers together and rested them on the table as I studied her. Her fingers rose to fiddle with her necklace again; her eyes shadowed and distant. "What are those?" I inquired of the pink and white decorations around her neck.

She pulled it forward, her eyes crossing as she smiled down at it. "Seashells. Have you never seen them before?"

"I have never seen the sea."

"Not even through the oracle?"

"I didn't look often or for long."

"You must see it; it's beautiful. It's life," she breathed with a reverence that made my skin tingle. "The smell of it, the sounds, they're all something I could never fully describe, but once you stand on the beach, with the birds soaring in the sky, the breeze blowing over you, and the water crashing on the shore, you'll know."

Her words captivated me, and the serene expression on her face had me mesmerized. Had I considered her simply pretty? She was breathtakingly beautiful with that look on her face. I could never understand her sense of peace; I'd never felt peace in my life. My existence had always been about battles, war, and death.

"What will I know?" I inquired, my voice hoarser than I'd expected.

She blinked, and her head turned toward me. Though her peaceful reverie vanished, she smiled at me. Her smile kicked into my chest, causing my breath to hitch as she watched me.

"That you've come home," she murmured and released her necklace. "If you get the chance, you should see it."

I'd never had the inclination to do so before, but I did now. The smile slid from her face. I despised the melancholy creeping over her features again. The compulsion to draw her into my lap and hold her there seized me. I shook my head to clear it of the notion. Grabbing my goblet, I drank more wine as I realized she had some kind of a strange effect on me that I couldn't understand.

"You have to train with the others," I told her brusquely. "You must know how to protect yourself on this side of the wall. I understand your resentment and frustration, but if you continue to refuse the training, you will get yourself killed. You must learn from us how to survive."

Her jaw clenched, and her hands balled. For a second, I believed she would fight me and I would have to force her into it. Instead, she nodded. "I don't like it." She gave me a pointed look that I returned with a smile. "But you're right. I don't intend to be demon food."

"Only some kinds of demons would eat you."

"Good to know. You're involved in the training?"

"Not normally, but until I know what to make of you, I will work with you personally."

She snorted. "There's not much to make of me, Kobal."

Hearing my name on her lips made more blood pulse into my throbbing cock. What would it be like to hear her scream my name as she moved beneath me, I wondered.

"I think there's more to you than you give yourself credit for."

Her head tilted, and I noticed a slight hitch in her breath as her gaze fell briefly to my lips before darting away again. "You're going to be disappointed."

"Not so far."

Her eyes came back to me, and her fingers fiddled with her necklace again. Her heartbeat increased, but more than that, so did her enticing scent. I wasn't the only one becoming aroused, I realized. If I pulled her into my arms, she wouldn't resist me.

It would be so easy to draw her close—

She's a possibility, I reminded myself sternly. *She could be the key to everything, and you could ruin it because she's the first human you've ever desired to bed.*

To be honest, she was the first woman who had ever wound me up this much and had me walking the fine line between everything I had always sought to be, and something I *craved.* It would be best for me to put some distance between us, to turn her over to Bale and Corson, and let them figure out if she was the progeny, but I knew I wouldn't.

Raising her hand to her mouth, she stifled a yawn. "If you don't mind, I didn't get any sleep last night."

I subtly shifted my erection to keep it hidden from her as I rose to my feet and extended my hand to her. She studied my hand for a minute before taking hold of it. An electric jolt slid through my body when her flesh touched mine. For the briefest of seconds, I thought I'd seen a spark flare to life between us, but it was gone too fast to have been real.

I followed her graceful movements as she rose to her feet before me. If I stepped closer, I could feel her body flush against mine. I could have those breasts pressed to my chest, my hand in her hair, and my mouth on hers in mere seconds. I'd never wanted to kiss a woman as badly as I did her.

Kissing was not something I partook in often. Demons rarely kissed, unless they were each other's Chosen. For the rest of us, there was no need when we were simply coming together to ease a need. Humans tended to want to kiss more, and a few of the human women I'd been with had insisted on kissing, but it was not something I thought about. Now, all I could think about was running my tongue over her lips, feeling her breath mingling with mine as I tasted her in long, slow thrusts of my tongue. Thrusts that would mirror what I wanted to do to her body.

I could possibly be throwing away everything I'd worked for by doing so. If we ever found the progeny, I would drag them kicking and screaming into what needed to be done. However, I knew some humans equated sex with emotions, and if she turned out to be the progeny, I could not take the chance that an entanglement with her would lead her to believe there could be more. A scorned woman was not one I wanted to deal with.

I released her hand and stepped away from her. She watched me as I took hold of her elbow and led her toward the flap. I lifted it for her and followed her into the night descending over the camp. I didn't look back at Corson and Bale, but I sensed them hovering in the shadows, watching us as we walked down the hill.

Keeping her close to my side, I steered her through the

patrols on the streets until we arrived at the main house. Mac answered the door after my firm knock. His eyes widened on the two of us, but he hastily stepped aside when I released her arm.

"Good night, River," I said when she stepped into the candlelit interior of the house.

She smiled at me over her shoulder before vanishing into the shadows.

"You think it's her," Mac said the second she was out of earshot.

"I don't know if it is or not. She's definitely different than any other human I've encountered. I'm going to work with her during training."

Behind his glasses, his eyes sharpened. "If you're not sure it's her, then why would you do that?"

Very good question. "I might be able to find out faster if I do."

I said the words, turned on my heel, and walked away, but as I was making my way up the hill toward my tent, I knew there was more to it than that. River Dawson affected me in a way no other had, and I wasn't going to let anyone else get close enough to touch her.

CHAPTER FIFTEEN

River

By the end of two weeks, the only thing I hated more than being here was Kobal. I'd never had my ass so thoroughly kicked before in my life. The fact he had a good foot or so on me and probably about a hundred and fifty pounds didn't deter him in the least. It was because he was a demon; I was certain of it. He took amusement in continuously knocking me on my butt. My bruises had bruises and sitting had become an uncomfortable ordeal I went out of my way to avoid.

When I'd arrived, I'd sworn I wouldn't fall into line with the others, but as much as I resented it, I'd rather go along with the training then become some demon's meal because I'd refused to learn how to defend myself against them. I was also determined to learn how to take Kobal down, just *once*. It would make my entire freaking year if I did.

Now, trudging my way through the line of young volunteers in the high school cafeteria to get my food, I was so focused on my own unhappiness that I didn't notice those around me had stopped speaking and were exchanging looks. I lifted my head and glanced around tiredly, but I didn't see anything that would cause such a reaction. Then, I noticed that most of their curious stares were directed at me as they whispered behind their hands.

I removed an apple from a basket at the end of the line and placed it on my tray next to my chicken. I walked over to the table I normally shared with a group of teens. They stopped speaking when I neared. I placed my tray on the table, grabbed a chicken wing, and leaned against the wall to eat it. There was no way my tailbone could handle sitting on the wooden bench today.

I studied the crowd of hundreds of volunteers gathered within the cafeteria. I'd been relegated to staying with the new volunteers I'd arrived with and designated official ass-kicking plaything of a demon.

New volunteers arrived each day, sometimes we worked together, but they were on different levels of training than my group was. It wasn't until we were done being divided, whipped into shape, and beaten and battered for the morning or afternoon that we were allowed to mingle together at all with the others. However, there were groups of volunteers still out patrolling and drilling now. I didn't think I'd ever get a chance to see everyone here.

The cramps growing in my calves and thighs had me eyeing the bench with longing, but thinking about sitting on my bruised butt made me want to cry. One of the girls stood up and came back a minute later with a rubber ring. She placed it on the empty seat before my tray.

"It will help," she said when she turned toward me.

I blinked at her; it took me a minute to finally recognize her as Carrie, the girl from my town who I'd seen volunteer in a vision. She'd cut her hair into a bob below her chin. Her brown clothes hung off her slender frame, a frame made thinner by the endless miles we'd run, walls we'd had to climb, and hand-to-hand combat we'd been going through daily. Most of them had been battling against other humans during these drills, whereas I'd been taking on a mountain who went by the name of Kobal.

"Thank you," I murmured as I fought against the tears of gratitude burning my eyes. I hadn't encountered much kindness since arriving here.

Her cat-green colored eyes twinkled when she stepped aside. "No problem."

As I settled carefully onto the soft rubber cushion, my shoulders sagged and my eyes closed. My feet and legs screamed their thanks as my bruised ass finally found some comfort.

"Better?" Carrie asked when she settled in across from me.

"So much," I said eagerly.

I'd never noticed her at the table before, but I'd been so exhausted every day, I probably wouldn't have noticed an angel floating before me and knocking me on the head. I lifted another chicken wing and was about to bite into it when I noticed everyone staring at me. Sitting on a rubber ring probably wasn't the most normal thing, but it didn't warrant all the strange looks. Even if it did, I was contemplating strapping the thing to my ass from now on; I didn't care if they all stared at me and my new padding.

I turned away from them to find Carrie focused on me too. "What is it?" I inquired.

Carrie glanced down the table as their attention shifted to her. I could feel their minds urging her to go on, but I didn't need any extra abilities for that; it showed on their faces. The one good thing about being so exhausted was I'd had absolutely no visions, or knowledge of *anything*, since arriving here.

Carrie glanced around before leaning forward on the table.

"We're all curious as to why they brought you here? You're older than us and it was obvious they made you come."

I shrugged and pulled up the sleeve of my shirt when the motion caused it to slip off my shoulder. Carrie wasn't the only one who had lost weight since coming here. We had more food available to us here than any of us had at home, but it still wasn't enough to keep weight on. Given our training regimen, we were burning calories faster than we could put them back in.

"I am older and they did."

They all exchanged a look before focusing on me again. "So why did they take you? Did it have something to do with the fliers?" Carrie pressed.

I sighed and placed the chicken wing on my plate. "Yes, my mother believed I could be one of the people they were looking for." I saw no reason to deny it; some of them had been there when I'd been escorted from my house.

"Wow," the girl next to me breathed.

I didn't know how to respond, so I returned to eating my chicken.

"Are you able to do anything special?" Carrie asked.

The half-chewed chicken wing dangled from my fingertips as I stared at her. "I'm just me."

More volunteers from other groups edged closer to us. "Then why has Kobal spent so much time with you during training?" a woman with blonde hair and brown eyes demanded of me.

Judging by the forest green uniform she wore, she had completed volunteer training to become a soldier. She looked older than me but not by much. Though the room was filled with volunteers mostly, there were some soldiers mingling throughout the crowd, grabbing their lunch before heading back to whatever job they had or the training fields.

The volunteers saluted the soldiers moving through the room but no one saluted the woman; they were all too focused on me right now, and I refused to salute anyone here. Even if I managed to complete training, I would never be the soldier they were trying to turn me into.

"All of the demons train with us," I said to the blonde woman.

"But he pays far more attention to *you.* He's never done that when he's been in this encampment before; he usually ignores the recruits still in the training stage. So why you?"

"I don't know," I lied.

She scoffed before tossing her shining hair over her shoulder. A hostile gleam radiated in her eyes when they raked me from head to toe. I had no idea why, but dislike was the biggest understatement for what this woman felt for me. More than loathing radiated from her but also some jealousy. How well did she know Kobal?

I hated the guy, he'd made me far more familiar with dirt than I'd ever wanted to be in my life, but my stomach threatened to heave its contents up at the idea of him with another woman. I watched her as she turned and walked over to sit at a table with some other soldiers.

"I'm glad you came with us," Carrie said, drawing my attention back to her.

"Why?" I asked.

Carrie bit into her chicken before answering. "You're another familiar face in a crowd of so many unfamiliar ones. We may not be friends, but it's nice to know I can talk about home with someone and have them understand."

"Me too," I said before finishing off my lunch. "It is good to know someone else who can recall the scent of the ocean."

"It was amazing." A nostalgic smile played at the corners of her mouth.

"It was," I agreed. "I saw you volunteer. Your mother didn't know you were going to do it."

"She would have tried to stop me if she had, but we were sinking and she needed more help than I could give her with my brothers."

"Brave of you, considering you didn't know what you were signing up for."

"I would have been signing up to watch them go hungry more often than not if I'd stayed. Maybe cowardice made me run away from that."

I decided I liked this girl, and without thinking, I reached over and rested my hand on hers. "I have two brothers I took care of before coming here. What you did was brave."

A dull blush slid across her cheeks, but she was saved from having to respond when Mac stepped in the cafeteria and barked, "Yellow Team, fall out!"

Yellow had become my least favorite color since arriving here. As far as I could tell, there were fifteen different groups of colors at the moment, with a new one cropping up every day. Reluctantly, I pulled my butt away from the rubber cushion.

Better than a cloud, I decided as I lifted my tray and stepped away from the bench. Balancing the tray in one hand, I bent and retrieved the cushion.

"Thank you," I said and held the cushion out to Carrie.

She gestured toward a side room. "They're stashed in there."

"That would have been good to know on day two," I muttered.

She giggled. "I discovered it yesterday. I think they purposely kept it hidden from the newcomers."

"Probably," I agreed.

The blonde-headed soldier who had been questioning me moments ago gave me a scathing look when I passed by her. I smiled in return. Carrie followed me to the tray return area and then the storage room on the side before heading for the door. For the first time, I noticed people stopped talking when we walked by. I tried not to pay them any attention as we stepped back into the warmth of the midday sun, but I didn't like being the main topic of their conversation.

My gaze went to the field in the distance and the line of demons standing there, waiting to teach us some more fighting moves. My shoulders sagged in resignation, but I couldn't deny the little flutter in my heart when my eyes fell on Kobal in the center. It was impossible to miss him as he towered over the others surrounding him. I found my body didn't ache quite so much, and my heartbeat quickened as we strode across the field toward them.

I stood in the center of the group of eighty-three volunteers who had arrived with me on the first night. Across from us stood Kobal and five other demons who resided within the tents on the hill. Over the past two weeks, I'd learned who each of them were and that these five were closer to Kobal than any of the other demons in the camp. I'd come to learn they'd all arrived in camp again only a couple of weeks before I had.

Bale was the beautiful red-haired demon. Corson stood at about six-four and was the friendliest of the demons. He had pointed, almost elf-like ears. He usually had sparkly earrings hanging from the tips, but right now, they were free of any jewelry. He had a lean, whipcord build that flowed with easy grace when he moved.

Corson stood next to Shax, the most human looking of them all. The most demon-like part of him was his sunflower-colored eyes and they were beautiful. His blond hair fell around his ears and he flashed a grin that caused some of the girls in the front to smile and wave their hands at their faces. At six-one, he was the shortest of the male demons but looked like he could lift a house and flip it over with one hand tied behind his back.

Morax stood beside Shax and was an inch taller than him. The sun glinted off his leaf-green, lizard-like skin. Pine shades of green color were etched throughout his flesh, giving it the appearance of scales. It looked as if his skin would be rigid to the touch, but I'd brushed up against him before and knew it was actually silken. His tail, resting on the ground behind him, was a good foot in diameter and as long as he was tall. He had orange, snake-like eyes with two sets of eyelids that blinked at the same time. From the top of his bald head, two black horns, at least six inches in length, curved toward each other and nearly touched in the center of his head.

Verin stood beside him, her rounded hip stuck out to the side with one of her hands resting on it. Hair the color of the sun tumbled to her waist; her eyes were the same color as her hair. Sexuality oozed from her pores, and every time I saw her, all I could think of were the sirens who lured sailors to their deaths, or maybe a succubus. I imagined humans who could see between the dimensions had gotten a glimpse of this woman and spun her tale quite successfully.

No matter how beautiful she was, and how all the men tripped over themselves when she walked by, I'd come to realize she and Morax were together. I didn't know exactly how it worked with demons, but they were rarely apart from each other and both of them had bite marks on their necks.

Somehow, I instinctively knew the bites were their way of marking their relationship with each other. Those bites caused something to stir in me, something I didn't understand but craved. I glanced at Kobal before hastily looking away and focusing on all of the demons before us once more.

They all wore loose-fitting linen pants in a variety of earth colors. A hole had been cut into the back of Morax's pants to let his tail through. Their shirts were also made of linen and matched the colors of their pants. They looked perfectly natural in the clothes, but I had a feeling this wasn't their normal attire. They'd simply donned the outfits in order to fit into our world better. I still wasn't sure who made Kobal's clothes, but I didn't envy them the task.

Behind the demons, an assortment of weapons glinted in the sun. Targets had been set up and pads lay on the ground behind the swords, knives, katanas, and other assorted blades within the box. I hadn't believed it possible, but I'd actually become decent with a katana and I enjoyed the weapons part of our training. Unfortunately, thanks to Kobal, I was going to find myself lying on the ground more often than not for the next hour or so before I could get my hands on one again.

"Let's begin," Kobal declared.

His deep, baritone voice caused odd little flutters in my belly that I forced myself to ignore. Getting distracted by the Hell beast would only result in me meeting the ground faster than normal.

We'd been doing this for long enough that we automatically separated into our assigned groups. I stretched my legs, hoping to loosen my muscles a little before we started. Kobal strode purposely over to my group, his black eyes surveying me as he moved.

Despite my dislike of him, my pulse picked up as he approached. The way the sun caressed his muscles and the clothing hung on his massive frame was enough to make my mouth water. I hated being tossed around like a rag doll, but I savored feeling his hands on me and those muscles moving against me when he took me down.

This place, and his presence, were turning me into a masochist.

Four soldiers walked over to join us. I stood, waiting for my turn to go through the moves. They'd been teaching us a combination of karate, krav maga, jujitsu, and something Kobal liked to call demon dirty, which pretty much meant anything goes if your life was on the line.

Kobal stepped in front of me and I silently questioned if my tailbone would still be in one piece after this. "Time to warm up," he said as he held his palms up toward me.

Still wouldn't do me any good, we both knew I'd be staring at the sky often over the next hour. I delivered a series of loose punches and palm-heel strikes to his hands before stretching my calf and thigh muscles by delivering a series of easy kicks to his palms.

My muscles felt looser as I danced away from him. "Ready?" he inquired.

No. "Yes," I replied instead.

He stepped forward, and before I had a chance to move, his leg swept out and knocked me off my feet. One second ago, I'd still been dancing around, getting ready for whatever he would throw at me. The next, I was on my back, watching a puffy white cloud float by and laboring to catch my breath. His shadow fell across me as he stepped alongside my sore body to peer down at me. Thankfully, he didn't smirk, but I saw the amusement dancing in the obsidian pools of his eyes before he thrust his hand out to me.

I waved his hand away and shoved myself back to my feet. I didn't bother to wipe the dirt from my backside. The first time I'd done that, I'd hit the ground again so fast I'd nearly blacked out from it. *Always pay attention*, he'd told me, and I'd learned my lesson.

I danced back and forth, trying to avoid him as he moved around me again. Going at him head-on had never worked for me; I'd learned avoidance was the best way to save my skin, bones, and pride. I'd almost completed a full circle out of his reach when he charged at me suddenly.

Prepared for the move, I darted to the side and swung my leg out in a roundhouse kick that would have leveled a human. He seized hold of my foot and flipped me through the air so fast I was dizzy by the time my chest slammed into the ground.

My breath exploded out of me; an acute pang seared through my side when something gave way in my chest. Stars burst before my eyes, dirt clogged my nostrils, and I struggled not to pass out. I felt him beside me before his fingers rested on the ground next to my head.

Placing my hands beneath me, I wheezed as I pushed myself into a seated position. The motion caused fresh agony to lance through my body, but I refused to give into it. Wiping the dirt from my nostrils didn't help me to breathe much better.

He held his hand out to me again, but I shook my head. "No."

He dropped his hand. "Who's next?" he inquired of the others when he rose to his feet.

"I am," I grated through my teeth before I spit out the dirt I'd inhaled on impact.

"You're bleeding," Kobal said. "Your injuries must be taken care of first."

I wiped away the blood I now felt trickling down my forehead. "Fixed."

The corner of his mouth quirked into a rare smile. I pushed myself to my feet and took a staggering step back as a wave of dizziness assailed me. Bending over, I rested my hands on my knees as I waited for it to pass and labored to get more air into my lungs.

When I was certain I wasn't going to fall over, I righted myself and brushed away the blood trickling into my right eye. I felt like a broken porcelain doll as something literally grated together within my chest, but pride and anger refused to let me back down. If I didn't breathe too deeply, it didn't hurt all that bad, I told myself. It was a lie, but I'd had enough of this.

"I don't know if you're more stubborn or stupid," he said.

"Both," I murmured.

"Ready?" he inquired.

Releasing my wounded side, I nodded to him. My feet weren't anywhere near as fast when we started again. I somehow managed to keep out of his range as I tried to figure out which way this would go.

Then, the sensation of icy fingers running up my spine slid over my skin and enclosed on the base of my skull. The fingers slid toward my brain as the strange feeling that came over me when I would see something or *know* something gripped me. I forgot about my inability to take a deep breath. Images fired through my brain, and before he started moving, I knew what he was going to do.

He danced toward me like liquid mercury, all elegance and supple grace as he moved with a fluidity I wouldn't have believed possible for someone of his size. I threw my forearm up, blocking the first blow coming toward me before slapping aside both hands that swung at me and would have grazed across my skin.

Over the weeks, I'd been on the ground more times than not, but he'd never hit me hard enough with his hands to leave a bruise on my flesh. He'd always moved so fast I'd never been able to stop the glancing taps he delivered. Now, I saw each one of those blows coming at me, seconds before he actually made the move, and they didn't land on me as I deflected them.

The scene continued to play out in advance in my mind, and when he swept his leg toward me next, I jumped over it. He leapt up and came at me again with a roundhouse kick I knocked back. This time, when his hands rapidly came at me, looking to land on me in some way, my forearms flew up to block him.

I felt as if I stood outside of myself, watching this faster and more competent me blocking his moves with an ease I'd never dreamed possible. Was I really moving so fast and keeping up with a *demon*? Was it really me who kept slapping his hands away or breaking his attack plan before he could fully unleash it.

I almost couldn't believe it, but it *was* me. I could feel his hands on my body and see the black pools of his eyes. It was all strangely mesmerizing and astonishing. I'd never felt so powerful before, so competent, so *me*. I didn't know where the sensation came from, but it felt as if I'd finally started to discover who I was and I *loved* it.

I blocked a blow that would have caught me in the stomach. Slapping his arms down, I drove my hand forward in a heel strike that hit him dead center in his chest. The blow didn't cause him to take a step back, but it was the first one I'd ever managed to land on him. Pride filled me as his head tilted down to where my hand still rested against his rock hard chest.

The icy tendrils retreated from my brain as gasps from the crowd who had followed us across the field filled the air. I hadn't realized we'd moved so far from our starting point until now.

CHAPTER SIXTEEN

Kobal

River's shoulders slumped forward, a smile tugged at the corners of her mouth as she stood before me. Looking at her now, I saw her eyes were a lighter shade of violet than the normally deep, amethyst hue I'd come to know so well. The difference in color was so subtle, I didn't think a human would have been able to detect it, but I knew something had just happened to her.

I stared at the hand she'd hit me with as it slid down my chest. My heart accelerated when her fingers brushed over my stomach before falling back to her side. The heat of her touch had burned through my shirt to become a fiery brand on my skin. I barely managed to refrain from grabbing it and flattening it against me once more.

Her eyes slowly returned to their normal hue as she stepped further away from me.

I had to know what had just happened. *No* human had ever landed a hit against me, and only a handful of demons had ever managed to do so. Only one creature had ever landed a blow on me more than once, and I would see him dead by the time all of this was finished.

Granted, I hadn't been going at her full force, but by the end of our skirmish, I'd been near full speed and she'd still been deflecting me. I could easily overpower her, but there were many demons who wouldn't be able to do so, many who were smaller and slower than she just was.

The inhalation of breaths around us alerted me that the others had all been watching and following us. I glanced at Bale and Corson; their eyes were riveted on River as she stood before me unmoving. The three of us had been working together long enough for me to know they were thinking the same thing as me…

If River wasn't the progeny we sought, there was still something different about her. She had an ability of some sort that we may be able to use to our advantage.

I was struck with a brief second of uncertainty as to whether I wanted to use her in any way, before quickly shaking off the ridiculous notion. Of course she would be used. The whole reason she was here to begin with was because there was a possibility she could aid us in this war. I would make sure she did what had to be done if she was the progeny.

River blinked and her gaze slid over the crowd creeping toward us before coming back to me. Before I could say or do anything, her eyes rolled back in her head, all the color drained from her face, and her knees buckled. Leaping forward, I caught her in my arms before she hit the ground.

People surged forward around me. A young girl with short blonde hair hovered at her side before Mac pushed her out of the way to get to River. She felt so small in my arms as she lifelessly slumped against my chest with her eyes closed and her hands dangling at her sides.

Human. Mortal. I had no idea why, but my fangs pricked

and a rumble of discontent slid through my chest at how fragile and precarious her life was compared to mine. The impulse to make it less so caused my hands to tremble against her slender frame.

Mac took hold of River's wrist before resting two of his fingers against her neck. Leaning over her, he pressed his ear to her lips. "We have to get her to the infirmary, now."

"What's wrong with her?" I demanded.

"I think she has a punctured lung."

Not waiting to hear anything more he had to say, I shoved through the crowd gathered around and ran as fast as I could across the field. Wind whipped my hair back, tore at my clothes, and whistled through my ears as the world sped by in a blur. I ignored the startled looks of the people within the town as I bolted past them toward the small medical clinic that had always been a part of this town.

I smashed through the doors and ran across the blindingly bright tile lining the floor. "You!" I barked at the first person I saw. "I need help."

~

Kobal

"What happened?"

Closing my book, I placed it beside the bed and leaned forward at the sound of River's hoarse voice. I didn't think I'd ever heard anything more pleasing in my life. She blinked at me before her fingers flew up to the tubes in her nose.

"Leave them," I told her, taking hold of her hand and gently placing it back at her side.

Her eyes crossed as she tried to take in what was stuck in her nose before her gaze traveled around the room. Her fingers twisted into the sheets beneath her. "Where am I?"

"The infirmary."

Her eyes flew back to me. "Why?"

"You broke a rib during our skirmish; it punctured your right lung."

"But you didn't hit me."

"It broke before our last sparring match, when you hit the ground the second time."

"Oh."

She tried to grab at the tubes again, but I pulled her hand away. "You must leave them in. Relax, you will be fine."

She had better be fine. I had no idea why this woman fascinated me so much, but I'd found myself unable to leave her side since I'd brought her in. The others had tried to pull me away and offered to sit with her, but I'd ordered them all to leave.

Leaning back, she relaxed into the pillows. She looked pale against the white sheets surrounding her, the black of her hair a stark contrast I found myself unable to resist. She watched me as I lifted a strand of her hair and slid the silky length of it between my thumb and index finger.

"You should have told me you were injured. I would have put a stop to it," I told her.

A small smile tugged at her lips. "Apparently, I wasn't hurt too badly. I finally managed to get one in on you."

"Badly enough that you ended up in here, with these tubes coming out of you." Those tubes and the mortality they represented for her made my skin feel too tight. I could recall the panic that had squeezed my chest when the humans had pulled her from my arms and wheeled her away from me. I'd stalked the medical personnel through the halls, refusing to let her out of my sight as they'd worked on her. "Things could have been much worse if I hadn't gotten you here in time."

"I'll be fine."

"Hmm. How *did* you manage to land a blow against me?"

"I'm a fast learner and I've been well trained," she replied flippantly.

My fingers stopped their movement over her hair, but I didn't release it. I found myself unable to part with this small piece of her. "How, River?"

She turned her head away, her eyes focusing on the ceiling. "I just knew. I don't know why it happened, it never has before, maybe it was because I was in pain, maybe because I was sick of being dumped on my ass, but my ability to see things came over me and I saw each move you were going to make *before* you made it."

The breath froze in my lungs when her eyes came back to me. There was a defiance about her I'd never seen before, a look that dared me to doubt her, but I didn't; I couldn't. I'd seen her on that field. It was my chest she'd hit.

"How did you move so fast? You were keeping up with me. I wasn't at full speed, but you shouldn't have been able to stay with me."

Her eyebrows drew together. "I didn't realize I was."

"River—"

"I really didn't realize it, not until you just said so. I knew I was moving faster and was somehow able to deflect you, but I didn't think it was that fast."

Releasing her hair, I leaned back in my chair to study her as I contemplated her words. I never doubted that she'd kept some of what she was capable of from me, but I didn't think she was lying about this. She hadn't known she could move with such speed and see her opponents moves so clearly before they made them until today, which meant there might be far more she didn't know she could do.

Since my creation, I'd known only one thing—I had to defeat Lucifer.

If River was the one we'd been searching for, there was a

good chance she could be the key to accomplishing that, or at least be of some use in closing the unnatural gateway again. In over fifteen hundred years, I'd never been this close to a secret weapon against Lucifer, one he most likely knew we were searching for, but one he may not be able to protect himself against. I'd never been so close, and I found myself wishing I could keep her from the destiny that could be awaiting her.

"Can you at least tell me, this person you're looking for, what is it you expect them to be able to do?" she asked.

I couldn't imagine living in the dark as she did, residing in a world of unknowing, away from her brothers and the home she'd spoken of with such reverence. I wanted to give her some shred of an answer to her question, but I couldn't.

"I cannot tell you," I replied.

She inhaled a deep breath and then winced.

"Are you okay?" I demanded as I leaned closer to her.

She tried to lift her hand to her side but the needle embedded in the top of it stopped her from getting it off the mattress. "Fine," she muttered. "Kobal?"

"Yes."

"Why do all the demons look so different?"

Some of my tension faded away as I relaxed in the chair again. I kept waiting for her to turn on me, to become incensed with my inability to help her and tell me to go away. Instead, she continued to surprise me. She may never be told why she'd been brought here, but she was determined to learn everything she could about her situation.

"There are many different types of demons, and sometimes their Chosen is a different kind of demon. If that is so, they create new breeds and versions of demons."

"What is their Chosen?"

"Every demon has a fated partner, or Chosen, whether they find their Chosen or not is something else entirely, but when they do, they mark their partner, their strength increases, and they are able to reproduce."

"So a demon can't reproduce until they find their Chosen?"

"They cannot."

"It's all so strange yet fascinating," she murmured.

"I suppose it is."

"Have you found your Chosen?"

Had that been distress in her voice or was I looking for something that wasn't there? "No, I have not."

She smiled at me and I found myself irresistibly drawn toward her once more. I inhaled her fresh scent, relishing in it as I brushed a strand of raven hair off her forehead. My fingers slid over her soft skin. Her eyes briefly closed before opening once more.

"Do you want children?" she inquired.

"It is unlikely that will happen," I replied. "If it did, my children would not possess any of my demon traits, only their mother's. They may look like me, but they will not be a varcolac demon such as myself."

With my fingers, I smoothed the lines that appeared on her brow. "Why not?"

"Because unlike other demons who come from a pairing like you humans, my type of demon is only born from the fires of Hell."

CHAPTER SEVENTEEN

Kobal

"Wait... *what*?" River sputtered.

I couldn't help but smile at the confusion in her voice as my finger trailed over the small scar on her eyebrow. Touching her helped to ease some of the burden and wrath that had been a part of me since the moment I'd been born. It was the strangest sensation, to feel freed in such a way by this frail mortal, and I didn't want it to stop.

"There is only one varcolac in existence at any given time. When that one dies, another rises from the Fires of Creation to take their place. I was born from those fires and rose within the chamber as you see me now. The varcolac before me was a woman who lived for sixty years."

"Why is there only one at a time?"

"Because there can only be one ruler of Hell at a time."

"*You* are the rightful ruler of Hell?"

"I am, and I *will* be the one to see Lucifer cast aside and defeated. I am the most powerful of my kind to ever rise. I will not fail in this."

"So you are not born of two demons?"

"I am born of anguish, hate, pride, torment, wrath, envy, lust, greed, and sorrow. I am born of the suffering of the souls and of the necessity to replace a leader who had fallen. Before Lucifer arrived, there had been only six varcolacs born in Hell over a couple hundred thousand years. They were killed during battles with other demons. In the six thousand years Lucifer has been in Hell, there have been over fifty varcolacs. I have survived the longest and am the eldest demon now. I was born with the knowledge of what I am and what I am to carry out. I have none of the memories of my predecessors, but I *know* I am to rule."

"Why are varcolacs the rulers?"

"We have always been the strongest of the demons. Varcolacs are the fastest and by far the most brutal. I fight with the fires of Hell on my side. We are also the only kind who can create and open a natural gateway within Hell, as well as close it. The varcolac also controls the hellhounds."

"Those are real?" she breathed.

"They are, and they're more ferocious than you could imagine. They obey my every command. I have left most of them in Hell, guarding the seals to keep Lucifer from opening them."

As her pulse quickened, I cradled her cheek with my palm, looking to comfort her in some way, though I had no idea how to do so or why I wanted to do it.

"Why do they obey you?" she inquired.

"The first pair of hellhounds was also born of the fires with the first varcolac. Though those firsts have all since died, I still share a kindred spirit with the hounds that is forged through the fires. Unlike me, the hounds are able to breed others like them, but like demons they can only do so with their mate."

"Amazing," she whispered. "If you were born of all those

things, why are you not more evil? Why aren't you cruel and vicious?"

Her words left me speechless. She was the first to believe I wasn't those things. That was exactly what I was, what I had always been and would always be. Except with her, I wasn't that way for some reason.

"I am," I said flatly. "Don't ever doubt I'm not. I will do what must be done in order to survive and put an end to all of this. I've twisted and tortured souls in ways you could never imagine possible, and I thrive on it. There is a reason I was forged in those fires."

She swallowed before nervously licking her lips. My gaze fastened on her mouth; I resisted leaning down to follow her tongue with my own. To taste her. I had a feeling she would taste better than she smelled, and feel even better beneath my hands.

"How are you created from the fires? How is that possible?" she asked.

I shrugged as I dragged my gaze away from her enticingly wet lips. "It is simply the way it has always been."

"The demons who are born, are they born babies who grow?"

"They are and they have the same developmental time frame as humans do."

"Do they stop aging at a certain point and become immortal?"

"It is different for all, but most stop aging between their mid-twenties and mid-thirties when they reach their strongest potential."

"What other kinds of demons are there?" she asked.

"So many," I replied. "There are fire demons, visionary demons, lanavours, adhenes, canaghs, chimera, and many more. Plus, there are demons who are mixes."

"What about the demons who are always with you, what are they?"

"Most of them are a mix. Corson is the only purebred amongst them, and he's an adhene. They're mischievous and what you would know as elf-like demons."

A small smiled curled her mouth. "That makes sense for him."

I didn't tell her Corson may be the most easygoing and fun-loving one of us, but when he unleashed his abilities, he became one of the most savage and brutal bastards I'd ever encountered. It was why he'd risen to his position by my side.

She licked her lips again. "May I have a drink?" she inquired.

Rising to my feet, I lifted the pitcher from the table beside the bed and poured her a glass of water. I helped her to rise and made sure she was comfortable before handing her the glass. She tried to take it, but the needle in the back of one hand and the broken rib on her other side made it difficult for her to move.

"I got it," I told her and held the glass against her lips.

She drank some of the water before pulling away. "Thank you."

I returned the glass to the table and sat again.

"Why do most of you look almost human?" she asked.

"All the beings on the three planes have some of the same features, as you can tell."

"Why is that?" she asked.

"Millions of years ago, when the planet itself was created, the three planes were also forged. In the beginning, the planes were more together, fighting against one another to try to thrive, but as time moved on and the colossal force of energy that created the planet expanded, the dimensions were more clearly divided.

"Hell broke off first, leaving the planet cooler and more inhabitable. The increasing amount of water on the earth made it easier for life of all kinds to flourish. The kinds of life meant to flourish in extreme heat and with less water went with Hell. That life thrived in the underworld and evolved into demons and other creatures who resided within Hell's bowels. As humans evolved, so did demons," I told her.

"And what of Heaven?" she asked.

"The energy that had originally created the three planes broke Heaven away after Hell. It is believed by demons that Heaven was separated to remove the toxic gases remaining on the planet after creation and leave the air more breathable on your plane. Over time, the air within Heaven has filtered itself out."

"How do you know that?"

"Because the fallen angels have been able to survive on Earth and Hell; they wouldn't have done so if their air was drastically different than ours."

"I see. So what about God? How does he or she or it fit into all of this?" she asked.

"The energy that created the planet was powerful enough to also create the force you know as God. However, it has been called many various names over the years and many different Gods and Goddesses. When Heaven went last, that force broke away with it and forged the angels from the image of what man was becoming.

"Over time, the planes became a symbiotic network of different species. Some of us are more different from others, but for the most part, demons and angels are all men and women. The angels all look very similar to each other too, though the fallen ones changed upon plummeting to Earth and entering Hell. They became more demonic in appearance than their cloud-hopping counterparts."

She started to laugh then winced when the movement jarred her ribs. Taking hold of her hand, I squeezed it within mine. I'd tried not to harm her during our sparring sessions, but I had done this to her, and I would have given anything to take her pain away from her. I wouldn't be able to take it easy on her when she was healed either. In battle, no demon would take it easy on her, and she must learn how to kill in order to survive.

"How do you know the fallen angels changed?" she asked.

"Legends passed down through the generations."

"What do the angels who are still in Heaven look like?"

"Like humans, they're all different colors and races. They have their feathery wings and glowing auras. Disappointingly, there is no halo."

"That is disappointing," she agreed. "What else do you know about them?"

"Like us, they're exceptionally powerful, but some of their abilities are different than ours." I held up my hand to fend off her next barrage of questions. "No, I can't tell you what they can do."

I also wasn't going to tell her that *all* non-fallen angels had one distinctive feature in common.

Her face fell, and her mouth twisted to the side as she stared thoughtfully at me. "Can you tell me everything you're capable of?"

"Maybe one day, but not today."

She started to sigh but broke off on a hiss. She waved me away when I rose and reached for her. "I'm fine."

My hands fisted impotently as I sat in the chair again.

"Do Heaven and Hell fight each other?" she asked.

"No. We have no contact with each other, and until they tossed out their garbage, we had no problem with the flying saints. Now, I'd happily pluck the feathers from their wings before cutting their heads off. They may not have known what would happen when they threw those angels from Heaven, but we're the ones who have had to deal with the consequences of their actions."

"That sucks," she mumbled.

I hated the pallor of her skin and the shadows beneath her striking eyes. *Mortal.* The reminder caused my claws to lengthen slightly as they dug into the palms of my hands. I felt the almost overwhelming need to make her immortal...

Then what? Stay with her? That was not my way. That was not the demon way unless it was with their Chosen, and she could not be mine. There had only been two varcolacs in history who had found their Chosen. They had been some of the first leaders, before Lucifer entered Hell, and it had taken both of them tens of thousands of years to discover their Chosen. I did not expect to find mine.

"How old are you?" she inquired.

"Far older than you. I am fifteen hundred and sixty-two years."

Her eyes widened as she gawked at me. "Holy shit that's old!"

I couldn't help but smile as I ran my finger over her brow again. "I suppose, to a human, it is."

"To anyone it is." I wondered if her eyes might actually pop out of her head as she watched me. A smile tugged at my lips as her eyes ran over me again. "Amazing."

"And how old are you?" I inquired.

"I turned twenty-two on March eleventh."

So young, and yet there was such an aura of wisdom and age about her, of knowing things one her age should never know, at least not on this plane. I'd been far younger than her, barely free of the fires, when I'd waged my first battle and killed my first of Lucifer's followers.

"For someone so old, you've really adapted to our world," she said.

"We've made ourselves fit into your world so you humans won't fear us as much, and so our species can aide each other. These clothes aren't our way of dressing; your culture isn't our culture. Your languages are not our languages."

She tilted her head to the side. "But you speak English so well."

"We spoke all languages at least a little before coming here. Over thousands of years of watching, human languages were picked up and spread amongst our kind. We weren't proficient in them before, but we've learned a lot more since arriving here."

"I never would have imagined demons to be so... ah... cultured," she finished.

"There is much you wouldn't expect of us." I couldn't stop my finger from tracing over her scar. "How did you get this?"

"Stupidity," she replied with a smile. "I accidentally hooked myself on one of my first fishing trips. Thankfully, a neighbor helped me to get it out and made sure I caught fish instead of myself the next time."

"And you fished often?"

"Almost every day. It was how I fed my family." Sadness filled her eyes as they fell away from mine and onto the book beside her bed. "You read?"

"I've taught myself over the years."

"What are you reading?"

"*Of Mice and Men*. Have you read it?"

"No. I enjoy reading, but I had little time for it at home. I taught Gage when he was old enough to learn. I hope he teaches Bailey one day..."

Her voice trailed off, and tears shimmered in her eyes as she remained focused on the book. More than her pain, I hated her sorrow. Her physical pain would fade soon enough; this heartache never would.

"Are they your brothers?" I asked.

"They are. Gage is fourteen and Bailey is only two and a half. I miss them so much."

I didn't know how I would do it, but somehow I would find a way for her to see them again.

"I borrowed the book from Mac, but I'm sure he wouldn't mind if you read it while you're in here," I said.

"But you're reading it."

"I can wait to finish it."

"I'd like that." Lifting it from the table beside her, I held it out to her. She went to take it from me but winced when the movement pulled at the needle in her hand. "Maybe when I'm out of here."

"How about I read it to you?" I suggested.

"Aren't you needed somewhere else?"

"They can wait."

When she smiled at me, I knew I would have read her a hundred books to see her smile again. "Thank you," she said.

I stretched my legs before me and opened the book to the beginning.

CHAPTER EIGHTEEN

River

I was released from the infirmary two days later. By then, Kobal had finished reading *Of Mice and Men* to me as well as *All Quiet on the Western Front.* Today he'd intended to start a book called *It.* He swore it would make demons look a lot friendlier by the time we got to the end, but I was cleared to leave before he could start reading it.

He'd told me he could be brutal and cruel, and he was a demon, so he would have to be, wouldn't he? But no matter what he said, I couldn't bring myself to actually believe it.

He'd been nothing but kind to me. Even when he was knocking me into the dirt, he'd never set out to intentionally hurt me. He'd spent hours reading to me in that deep, melodic voice of his. Hours in which I'd been enthralled by listening to him and watching him as he'd read the heartbreaking tales. He'd barely left my side for *two* days. I would often wake to find him watching me from the chair, or once sleeping himself.

How could he possibly be as bad as he said he was when

he'd never purposely done anything wrong to me? Was I really feeling all warm and fuzzy and trying to say a *demon* was good?

I should hate him; he was the reason I was here. He was the reason I would wake crying in the middle of the night with Bailey's screams echoing in my head, and he showed no regret over it. Despite those things, I found myself unable to hate him. My life had been torn apart, but he somehow made it all a little better.

There was nothing I could do to change what was done; harboring fury and resentment would only eat away at me. There was no way I was going to be able to escape past the wall. If I somehow could get to a weaker section, there were still too many guards patrolling for me to slip by unnoticed. If I did somehow get free, I would never be able to get to my brothers before the government found me or got to them first, or both.

The only thing I could do was train and get better at fighting. My only hope was that one day this war would come to an end, and I would be able to return home afterward. I didn't think I was the person they were all searching for, but until they knew for sure, all I could do was play along, and I was okay with playing along if it meant more time with Kobal.

I didn't understand what it was about him that had me so out of sorts. All I knew was I wanted *more* of him. More time, more touches, more smiles and talking.

Ugh, I shoved those thoughts away as I stood on the sidelines and watched the others going through hand-to-hand combat training. I'd been told I'd be on the sidelines for at least two weeks. I resented being forced to be here in the first place, but I didn't like standing on the side and watching either. Especially when Kobal worked with other people, sparring with them like he had with me.

Jealousy slid through me every time another woman got to feel those muscles around her and inhale his entirely masculine scent. Born from the fires of Hell, he smelled faintly like fire, and despite the fact I knew I should stay far away from him, I desperately wanted to play with those flames.

I couldn't help but admire the way he moved and the flow of his muscles beneath his smooth skin as he trained with the others. I watched the tattoos on his arms and the flex and bunch of his biceps as he lifted his shirt to wipe away the sweat beading across his brow from his exertion. My gaze latched onto his tapered waist and chiseled abs as I drank in the sight of his mouthwatering body before he pulled his shirt down again.

His dark hair was slicked with sweat as he pushed it back from his intriguing face and walked away from the man he'd left splayed on the ground behind him. Corson slapped him on the back and stepped forward to take his place in the sparring.

Kobal lifted his head, the black pools of his eyes latching onto me. I should have been embarrassed to have been caught staring at him, but I found I couldn't look away. What I wouldn't give to run my fingers over his face, into his hair, down over his arms, and lower across his abdomen. To sink my teeth into his flesh.

I had no idea where *that* inclination had come from, but it caused wetness to spread between my thighs. I had a difficult time catching my breath, but now it had nothing to do with my punctured lung and everything to do with the desire sliding through my belly.

His nostrils flared as his gaze leisurely traveled over me. I knew it wasn't possible, but it felt as if his hands followed his eyes and caressed every part of me. I could almost feel him touching me, fondling me. My breasts tingled and became heavy in a way they never had before as he lazily perused his way back up my body.

His eyes latched onto mine again as Morax clasped his shoulder, drawing his attention away. Freed from his gaze, my shoulders sagged and I inhaled a ragged breath as I tried to regain control of my body.

"How are you feeling?" Carrie asked as she appeared at my side.

"Good," I told her with a small smile. "I'm sidelined for a little bit, but I already feel better."

"That's great!" She gave me a cheerful smile before squeezing my arm and hurrying forward when she was called.

I glanced back to where Kobal had been standing. Disappointment filled me when I saw he was gone, but I knew it was for the best; I should keep my distance from him. Still, I couldn't help wishing I was well enough to hop back into the fight, if only so I could touch him again.

The next few days passed in a blur, and I saw little of Kobal outside of the hand-to-hand training. At the end of the week, I was told I could return to firearm training. I stood at the target line with my earmuffs on and repeatedly pulled the trigger. When I'd first come here, I hadn't been good with a gun, but I was getting increasingly better with steady practice. When I went to retrieve the target, I was pleased to see only two holes outside of the range of the shadow person on the piece of paper.

Folding it up, I tossed it in the trash and pulled the earmuffs off. Glancing down the hill, I watched the training going on in the field below me. I easily picked Kobal out of the crowd as he weaved his way through the people fighting, kicking, and punching each other.

Lifting my head to the sky, I took in the streaks of pink and orange, but they were mostly overpowered by the red spreading toward me. The sun was a vibrant crimson color as it hung on the horizon.

"Red sky at night," I murmured as I made my way down the hill toward Mac's house.

I'd never asked why I wasn't housed with the other volunteers or why I'd never been treated like any of the rest of them, and I doubted I would get an answer if I did. I was almost to the door when a lonely wail echoed over the hills and through the town. The hair on my nape rose, and I turned away from the door as the wail built in volume. I'd heard it the first night I'd arrived, but the following nights had remained blessedly undisturbed since then.

The soldiers patrolling the streets froze with their guns against their shoulders as more cries echoed through the fading daylight. I stepped off the porch and made my way down the street as the noise intensified until it reverberated off the windows and buildings surrounding us.

"What is that?" I asked one of the soldiers.

"It's some of *them*," he replied. His mouth flattened into a thin line and his skin turned an ashen hue.

"Them who?" I inquired.

"The beasts," another voice answered. I jumped when Kobal's hand slid around my elbow and sent a jolt of something hot and electric through my body. My mouth went dry as I tipped my head back to find his inky eyes upon me. I couldn't tell if he'd felt the jolt too, or if I was simply imagining this magnetic connection between the two of us, but I welcomed his touch. I'd been starved for it this past week. "Come with me."

"The beasts?" I inquired as I turned to follow him down the road.

"Not everything from Hell is a demon such as the ones you've met so far; some of them are what you might consider an animal. They are volatile creations that evolved to punish souls and were relegated to the lower-levels of Hell. Now they are taking advantage of their freedom."

My gaze turned toward the darkening horizon as I searched for the creatures he described. "And they come here?"

"Sometimes," he murmured.

"Where are you taking me?"

As I asked the question, we arrived at the steps of the home I'd just walked away from. He opened the door and walked me inside. "Stay inside."

"Aren't I supposed to learn how to fight them?" I demanded.

"Yes, but right now there is nothing for you to fight and your injuries will only hinder you."

"I'm feeling better," I protested instantly.

Turning me toward him, he grabbed both of my arms as he held me before him. Despite my irritation with him, I swore even the cells of my body flooded toward his hands, craving more of a connection to him.

"Stay inside tonight," he commanded.

Before I could reply, he turned and walked out the door. I stared at his back as he descended the stairs and strode into the street. He stopped at the young man I'd been talking to before, said something, and pointed at the house. The young soldier hurried toward me while more wails resonated through the night and caused the glass in the windows to rattle.

The man climbed the porch steps and grasped the knob of the still-open door. "You should probably lock this, miss," he told me before he closed it.

I stood and stared at the door for a minute before walking forward and turning the lock into place. I tiredly climbed the stairs and entered my room. Drawn to the window, I rested my fingers against the glass as I stared out at the night. The wails continued to resound throughout the town. On the hill with the tents, a fire blazed to life, its flames leaping into the air to illuminate the night.

I spotted Kobal with the demons on the hill. They lined up together, facing over the top of the hill to look out at the nothingness beyond. I wondered what they saw out there. My gaze traveled to the wall. I wasn't surprised to see more troops than usual patrolling the top of it.

Feeling eyes on me, I turned my attention back to the hillside. An ache spread through my belly and deep within me when I found Kobal's hungry gaze riveted on me. The glow of the flames danced over his striking face and those intricate tattoos as he watched me. I'd never seen his emotions so clearly before, never seen him look so stark and ravenous, for *me*.

Wetness spread between my legs, and I was unable to stop myself from swaying toward the window, a motion that caused him to take a step toward me. The temptation to stroke my breasts, to slip my hand down my pants and ease the growing need between my thighs while he watched hit me.

What would he do if I did? My heart hammered so loudly the noise of it drowned out the wails.

Unable to resist the aching, heaviness of my breasts, I slid my hand leisurely up over my belly and brushed it against the bottom of my breast. His eyes fastened on me; I didn't have to be near him to know he stopped breathing as he watched me. An overwhelming sense of power made me braver as I slid my hand further up and brushed my thumb over my sensitive nipple. My need for him made me forget all about the creatures stalking the night outside of this town.

I swayed toward the window again when his hands fisted and the muscles in his corded arms vibrated. His gaze remained locked on my hand as he watched my every move. I'd never experienced anything like this before, never felt so out of control. I'd explored my body before, when the yearnings of it had awoken me in the night and I'd sought some release, but never had it felt this erotic and sensual before, and it was all because of *him*.

I couldn't move away from the window as I slid my hand across to knead my other breast.

Bale stepped before Kobal, pointing toward something beyond the hill. His eyes remained on me until she grabbed his arm. The look that crossed his face caused Bale to take a step back from him.

With his eyes drawn away from me, and the strange spell between us broken, I retreated swiftly from the window. My cheeks burned with the realization of what I'd just done, but his gaze had been an erotic spell I'd been helpless to resist.

My body ached with need when I stripped and crawled into bed. With the hungry look on his face emblazoned in my mind, I ran my hand down my stomach and slipped it between my legs to ease some of my sexual tension. I knew it wouldn't be enough, nothing less than Kobal himself would ever be enough.

Kobal

As soon as Bale moved away from me, I looked back to River's window. My lips curled back in frustration when I realized she was gone. I took one step toward the house before I froze. I could go get her right now, and she wouldn't put up a fight, not after her little display at the window.

However, I could not throw everything away for sex, even if that sex was with the most unusual mortal I'd ever encountered who now had me harder than I'd ever been in my life. I could still picture her at the window, her hands sliding over her belly and breast. The image caused my dick to strain so forcefully against my pants that I worried for my button.

My fangs tingled, but this time it was not from rage over being interrupted. Now, I hungered to run them over her flesh while she moaned and writhed beneath me. I knew she was up there now, running her hands over herself, easing her longing for me without letting me play a part in it.

Instead of going to her, like we both wanted, I turned away and stalked toward my tent. Ignoring the startled looks I received, I flung open the flap of the tent and stalked inside. I could go to the fire, someone would be there who could ease this throbbing tension from my cock, but none of them would be good enough. None of them would be *her*.

I tore my pants from my body to release the pressure against my erection. The need for release was so intense that I knew I wasn't going to make it to my bed. Wrapping my hand around my shaft, I groaned as images of River touching her breast pummeled my mind. Jerking off was not something I did often; I'd never needed to as I'd always sought my sexual release with another when I required it.

Now I had a feeling my hand and I were going to become well acquainted with each other before I was able to either free myself from thoughts of River or bury myself in her delectable body. The only problem was I didn't want to be free of her, so that left only one other option. As I continued to stroke myself to images of her, I knew it was only a matter of time before I went against what I knew was best and brought her into my bed.

CHAPTER NINETEEN

RIVER

I got little sleep that night, or any other night over the following week, neither did anyone else within the town as those endless cries tormented us. For the first few days, the sound had me wanting to tear out my hair. Now they were a distant, annoying noise I'd somehow managed to shove into the back of my mind.

When I did sleep, I dreamed of Kobal and would wake filled with a yearning so fierce I couldn't ease it no matter what I did. I'd never been like this before. I wanted *him* so badly it had become a hollow pit in my stomach.

At least I was finally able to go back to training on the field today, where I could try to work out some of my increased sexual frustration. If I was exhausted from training, I wouldn't dream of him, or at least that's the lie I told myself.

Kobal had been scarce in my waking life since the day he'd sent me inside the house, but he was the one who stepped across from me on the training field now. I tried not to blush as I recalled his gaze on me in the window and the way I'd touched myself in front of him.

I should be mortified, but I wasn't. Instead, I found myself wanting to step closer to slide my fingers inside his shirt, then over those chiseled abs as I'd imagined doing last night.

"Are you ready for this?" he inquired in his deep voice.

His eyes raked over me in a way that caused my nipples to harden. I had to fight not to lick my lips. What was freaking wrong with me?

I thrust my chin out as I tried to retain my composure. "More than ready."

"Do you think you can see my moves before they come again?"

"We're about to find out. If I can, hopefully, it will be with my ribs and lungs still intact."

A smile tugged at the corners of his full mouth. "That would be preferable. You've been out of it for a bit, so we'll take it easy at first."

"I'm fine," I insisted, not in the mood to be babied. No, I had to be so tired by the end of today that I could barely walk; otherwise, I would never rest without visions of this man playing in my head.

Lifting my hands, I got into a fighter's stance, staying on the balls of my feet as we danced around each other. He took a couple of swats at me that I deflected with ease. I tried to relax, tried to let my mind go free in order to tap into the visions that could roll so easily through me sometimes, but I felt nothing as we continued to move around each other.

I took a few swipes at him, nearly connecting with his chin, but he dodged me. He honed in on me, his movements becoming more aggressive and demanding. It wasn't some mystical power or whatever flowing through me that helped me deflect his hands, it was the training I'd endured before I'd been injured.

I could feel the heat of his body against mine and smell the fiery scent of him. The sensation of his skin brushing over mine became overwhelming. All I wanted was to touch him, to run my tongue over his sweat-dampened skin as I tasted him.

My head spun as he filled my entire world until there was nothing but his skin against mine and his scent in my nostrils. I felt dizzy with the sensation; my breath came in rapid pants. Then I realized that though I could see him, everyone else on the field had faded away; the wails were finally silenced as I stood alone with him on the field.

Bewilderment filled his eyes as he stopped coming at me to stare around the strangely empty landscape. The green grass blew in the warm June breeze beneath my feet and the hills rolled endlessly onward around us, but there was no longer a wall, or people, or homes; there was only *us*.

Confusion swirled through me. I had no idea what I'd done, but somehow I knew I had pulled him into this alternate reality with me.

Slowly, his gaze came back to me, but I didn't meet it. My attention was focused on the hill behind him as what I could only describe as monsters burst over the top of it from the direction of the wilds. They barreled toward us, their four stubby legs carrying their plump bodies faster than I would have assumed possible given their awkward build.

There was something about them that reminded me of a boar, maybe it was their shape or maybe it was the giant tusk sticking out the center of their foreheads, but they were far more hideous than any boar I'd ever seen a picture of. Their skin, a mottled red and black, shone in the sunlight beating down on them. Plumes of smoke or something like it shot from the blowhole in the top of their extended, rounded skulls.

Cloven hooves left dents in the ground and beat out a pounding rhythm as they carried the monsters over the earth.

"What are those?" I whispered.

"Madagans," Kobal replied. "The beasts."

"They're coming."

The minute the words left my mouth, the almost dream-like world I'd created slipped away, and I found myself standing face to face with Kobal. He blinked and shook his head as his gaze drifted over the people and noises surrounding us once more. The sounds of flesh hitting flesh, steel clashing against steel, and grunts filled the air. They all continued as if nothing had happened, completely oblivious to Kobal and me standing there.

Beyond the sounds of training and fighting was the noticeable lack of the wails.

Kobal's focus came back to me; he seemed to be trying to assess me and figure out what had just happened. Maybe if he figured it out, he would let me know. His head turned toward the hill, his nostrils flaring as he scented the air.

"They're coming," I said again.

He gave a brisk nod that caused a lock of hair to fall into his eye. "Yes. Everyone be prepared!" he bellowed. Those closest to us jumped away from him, and others glanced around in confusion. Lifting his hands, he cupped them around his mouth as he looked toward the wall. "Arm the wall!"

Through the town, the streets exploded with commotion. The shine of the sun reflecting on rifle scopes could be seen as people on the wall lifted their guns. Kobal spun back toward me as the first of the creatures I'd seen in my vision burst over the horizon. Frightened shouts came from some of the volunteers surrounding us. They were used to beating on each other and shooting at targets; they weren't prepared for something like what was coming at them.

And, truthfully, neither was I. My pulse picked up at the sight of them, and my stomach plummeted. We didn't have any guns with us, but as soon as I realized it, shots rang out from the wall. Dirt exploded in front of the monsters barreling toward us. One of them squealed as it tumbled forward and slid to the ground. Plumes of dirt skidded up in front of it as its heavy body slid down the hill.

"Stay close to me." Kobal pushed me behind him. "Get in line behind us!" he shouted at the others as more gunfire echoed over the land.

Soldiers from the town were running up the hill to help, but the first wave of beasts had already reached us. More screams resonated as the creatures launched themselves into the air. I cried out when the first one slammed into Kobal, knocking him back a step. I leapt forward to try to help him, but he seized the four-foot-long creature and held it dangling in front of him. The stubby legs kicked in the air as awful, high-pitched squeals rang from it. The screams and gunshots filling the air echoed in my eardrums.

Still holding the madagan within his grasp, I watched as Kobal drove his hands inward, crushing the sides of the hideous creation. More of the monsters leapt forward, but the demons managed to keep them away from us.

Kobal tossed aside the crushed body of the madagan and turned to take on the next one. At least fifty of them had come over the top of the hill; it was only a matter of time before the demons fighting with us were outnumbered.

Morax fell back with a shout as one of the madagans drove its tusk through his leg and lifted him up. Verin grabbed hold of him, jerking upward and pulling him free of the tusk, but it had already become the first break in the line. Shax fell back next when one of the madagans lowered its head and barreled through him. His body flew upward, and he flipped head over heels through the air before crashing into the ground.

Some of the volunteers turned and raced down the hill. Others fell back but didn't retreat entirely. I tried to see where the swords and other weapons were, but I couldn't find the box of supplies through the chaos surrounding me. I didn't know how much good a sword would do against one of these things, but it would be a lot more helpful than only my bare hands.

Kobal seized another one and flung away the two-hundred-pound monster as if it weighed no more than ten pounds. More creatures leapt forward, knocking back Corson and Bale. They stayed on their feet but more of the madagans broke through the line. I tried to remain close to Kobal, but I found myself being separated from him by people and madagans.

"Fall back!" Kobal shouted.

I took a stumbling step away as one of the monsters sprinted around Bale and raced toward me. The ground quaked beneath my feet; the vibrations rattled my teeth as large plumes of smoke burst from the top of its head.

"River, run!" Kobal bellowed.

All I wanted was to sprint away from here, but there would be no outrunning this thing. Adrenaline rushed through me, and my heart leapt into my throat as those beady red eyes latched onto me like I was waving a red flag at it. Screams resonated around me as the beast reeled back on its hind legs and flung itself into the air. I raised my hands to do I don't know what, grab it, punch it, I had no idea, but the gesture had been instinctive.

The monster was almost on top of me when I felt a crackle of something surge through my body. Heat pooled into my hands, and before I realized what was happening, fire burst from my palms. A hideous squeal erupted from the madagan when it landed head first, ten feet back in the direction it had come from. Its stubby feet kicked in the air as flames licked over its body; its skin popped and its body blackened as the fire consumed its flesh.

Around me, I felt a current of shock, but it was nothing compared to the disbelief that went through me. Even knowing the odd things I was able to do, I had never truly believed that I'd been the one to set those curtains on fire all those years ago. I had thought it was a fluke. Apparently, I'd been completely wrong.

Turning my hands toward me, I gawked at the unmarred flesh of my palms. Where moments ago there had been flames, now there was nothing but smooth hands. I felt no heat coming from my skin and saw no signs they'd just set fire to that hideous monster, but the smoking pile of bones across from me proved they had.

"River, watch out!"

Kobal's shout drew my attention away from my hands and back toward the chaos of the day. I spotted two more madagans coming at me. I didn't have time to react before a pair of arms wrapped around my waist. The impact of Kobal's body crashing into mine knocked us both backward. He turned as we fell to the ground, taking most of the impact with his shoulder as we bounced across the unyielding earth. The air was knocked out of my lungs and I gasped before taking a ragged breath.

I lay still, trying to catch my breath and staring up at the clear blue sky as the ground shook beneath me. I didn't have time to get my bearings before he was rolling us rapidly over the grass, further away from the beasts. My head spun and my stomach lurched. I closed my eyes against the spinning to try to calm my growing nausea.

Finally, he stopped rolling across the earth. I was on the bottom now, pinned beneath his body. I'd often imagined this position with him over the past couple of weeks, but it had been a lot more fun then, and not a life-or-death situation while my stomach threatened to reveal what I'd eaten for breakfast.

Kobal loomed over me as he hastily brushed aside the strands of hair sticking to my face. The black fingernails that had extended into three-inch-long claws retracted as he touched me. I blinked at him, my heart lurching when I saw his eyes. They were no longer the color of night, but a vibrant, amber gold with a black pupil in the center of the golden iris. They were more like human eyes now with the pupil and whites surrounding the iris, but they reminded me more of a *wolf's* eyes as they burned into mine.

"Are you injured?" he demanded.

I was so focused on those startling eyes and the four fangs I could now see when he spoke that I didn't answer. Two long fangs had extended from his upper canines and another set had risen from his bottom canines. They were so extremely wolf-like that I found my gaze going to the intricate tattoo on his left arm.

"River!" he yelled, his voice harsher than I'd ever heard it before.

"Fine," I finally muttered. "I'm fine."

His hands stilled on my face as he stared at me. His fingers gently grasped hold of my chin. Those impossibly golden eyes were turbulent as they flickered over my face and his grip on my chin squeezed subtly.

Climbing off me, he took hold of my hand and helped me to my feet. I looked toward where the creatures had come from, but the ones who weren't already dead were turning and running back up the hill. Bullets pummeled the earth behind them, kicking up grass and dirt.

Kobal stepped closer to my side, his chest pressing against my arm when Mac arrived, panting beside us. Mac's gaze ran over me before going to the still smoldering body of the one I'd barbequed.

"It's her, isn't it?" Mac demanded.

The way he spoke about me, as if I wasn't there, rankled, and I found myself glaring at the man I'd come to like during my time here.

Kobal's hand folded possessively around my elbow. "She'll be staying with us from now on."

My head shot toward him. "What? Why?"

Kobal ignored my questions and instead turned toward Bale as she jogged over to us. Her green eyes focused on me when she arrived. "Make sure everything is taken care of here," Kobal commanded.

She barely glanced at him before responding. "I will."

Corson and Shax walked over to stand beside Kobal, their eyes darting from him to me and back again. I thrust back my shoulders as I met their inquisitive stares. They said something to him in some language I couldn't understand; it sounded guttural, foreign, and ancient. It made my head spin more.

It's their language.

Kobal snapped something at them and they bowed their heads before hurrying away. "Come with me," he ordered and tugged on my elbow.

"It doesn't sound like you're giving me much of a choice," I muttered as he propelled me across the ground toward the cluster of tents on the hill.

"I'm not," he retorted.

I shot him a fierce look as I struggled to keep pace with his relentless strides. The color of his eyes had faded back to their midnight color. I could still see the outline of his fangs against the inside of his mouth though. Reaching the tent, he threw back the flap and gestured for me to enter first. The rustle of the flap sliding into place caused a strange sense of finality to descend over me.

I turned toward him as he loomed in front of the exit, his arms folded over his chest while his gaze surveyed me from head to toe. I swallowed heavily, uncertain of what to expect or what had happened. One minute, I'd been going about my training, trying not to throw myself against him and lick him, and the next, I'd been in some strangely hushed world before it had shattered and flames had erupted from my palms.

Turning my hands over, I once again stared at my palms. *Not normal.* I'd always known I wasn't normal, but now I was beginning to question exactly *what* I was. These demons were looking for someone, I would be staying with them now, and I'd shot *fire* from my freaking hands.

Lowering my hands, I took a deep breath before focusing on Kobal. His jaw clenched, and a muscle jumped in his cheek when his eyes raked over me again. I didn't think this visit was going to be as pleasant as our last one.

CHAPTER TWENTY

Kobal

River's violet eyes were guarded when they met mine. She folded her arms over her chest and stuck her chin out as she stared at me. My gaze slid over her slender frame, rounded hips, and long legs. She appeared far too fragile and human to be the one we were searching for, but there was no denying what she'd just done.

I'd been hunting for her for years, and she may be the key to ending all of this. I may finally be on the verge of putting everything to right again, but I would have given anything for it to be someone other than her.

She may not survive this.

At the thought of losing her, wrath slithered through me like a serpent. *She will survive,* I decided. No matter what it took, I would make sure she survived, but in order for her to do so, she was going to have to start telling me the truth.

"Why didn't you tell me about the fire?" I demanded.

Her eyes flashed over me. "I wasn't aware I had to tell you *every*thing about me."

I took a step toward her, hoping to intimidate her in some way, but she merely tilted her head back and narrowed her eyes. I didn't think she had an ounce of knowledge as to what she might be capable of, yet she was still brazenly courageous.

"I asked you once what else you could do."

"And I told you what I was aware of, mostly," she added the last word as an aside.

I stepped so close that my chest brushed over her folded arms, but she didn't relent in anyway. "Mostly?" I growled. "What else can you do, River?"

"I don't know," she replied and her eyes fell away from me.

Taking hold of her chin, I tilted it up so she had to look at me. "How did you bring me into your world on the hill?"

"My world?" she asked in confusion.

"Your vision, world, whatever you call it. How did you draw me in?"

"I... uh... I don't know."

"Tell me, River."

I moved closer as I struggled not to shake the infuriatingly stubborn woman standing before me. She had me so on edge that I couldn't get my fangs to retract. They throbbed to rip into something and tear it to shreds. To destroy anything that ever dared to endanger her again.

"I don't know!" she cried in exasperation. "I don't know what brings on the visions. They just come to me sometimes! And today you were on that field with me and you were all I could see, smell, and feel before it happened. You were so..."

"So what?" I demanded when her voice trailed off.

"So *there!* So overwhelming!"

Her arms fell away from her chest, and she pushed back a strand of hair that had fallen into her eye. The musky aroma of her sweat mingled with the lingering scent of her lemon-scented soap, and dirt streaked her golden skin.

"And then we were alone and they were coming." Her gaze went past me to the wall of the tent, but I had the impression she was looking beyond it. "I have no idea how it happened today, but once before, I shared the same dream with my brother, Gage."

Without meaning to, my thumb stroked over her chin before I released it. "So you can enter other's dreams?"

She frowned at me. "No... I mean, maybe. We had the same dream *one* night."

"What else?"

This time, she did take a step back from me when I moved further into her personal space. "There's nothing else!" she snapped and placed her hands on my chest to push me away.

I didn't budge in the slightest. Taking hold of her chin again, I loomed over her as the backs of her thighs and ass pressed against the table. She leaned back over the table, her eyes shimmering with anger. Before I could speak, the rustle of the tent flap silenced my next question. My head turned as Corson and Bale stepped into the tent.

"Kobal—" Bale started.

"Leave us," I commanded brusquely. Bale's eyes shot to River before coming back to me. "*Now.*"

She hesitated before ducking out of the tent. Corson followed swiftly behind her. I turned back to River when the flap settled into place once more.

"I don't appreciate you trying to intimidate me!" she snapped.

"I don't appreciate you lying to me."

"You forced me here!" she spat. "For some reason no one will tell me, I was torn away from my home and thrust into this madness. All I've ever gotten is a runaround instead of answers, so why would I tell you everything about me? I have to protect myself, and I'm not going to reveal everything when everyone is hiding things from me!"

She pushed against my chest again and this time I relented to her hands. I walked away from her and over to the sideboard and the wine.

"You're right," I said as I poured two goblets. "Sit."

"No."

I glanced at her over my shoulder before re-corking the wine and walking over to the table. I placed one goblet in front of my chair and the other before the chair next to it. I grabbed the back of the chair and pulled it out for her. "You'll get your answers; now sit."

She stubbornly stared at me for a minute more before finally settling into the chair. Her eyes followed my every move as I walked over to my chair and sat down.

"What does it matter what I can do?" she demanded.

"It matters a lot," I told her. I took a sip of my wine, watching her as she stared at me. Then she looked at the wine and lifted it to her mouth. The liquid slid down her throat, putting some color back into her pale face. "Tell me what you know."

"I lit the curtains in our house on fire once, by accident," she murmured. "When I was a teen. I was never entirely certain if it was me who did it, or if it was some other fluke thing that had occurred. I guess I know now."

"And what else can you do?"

She stared at her hands before lifting her head to me. "And that's it."

I didn't know if she was telling me the truth or not, but staring at her now, I became aware of a sickening emotion so unfamiliar to me that at first I had no name for it. It made my hands sweat and my belly twist in a new and stomach-turning way. My fingers traced over the delicate designs etched into the goblet as I finally put a name to the emotion, fear.

I'd never known fear before. Power had always been mine for the taking. There had only ever been one as powerful as me, and Lucifer and I had each walked away from our battles more broken and beaten than before, but alive. Unlike my ancestors, he had not been able to defeat me.

Now though, I felt fear for this woman, which was something I had never believed myself capable of. There was no denying whom she was now, and it meant she was going to have to do things no other mortal or demon would, or could, and I would be the one who would lead her to Hell.

"Are you sure?" I inquired. "Have you ever been able to move things with your mind?"

"No."

I frowned at her as I tapped my fingers on the table. "Can you harvest power from things?"

She released a small snort and shook her head. "Nope, I've never had that happen before."

I pondered her words as I studied her. She appeared to be telling me the truth, but there could be something she was keeping from me or maybe even something she didn't know she could do. "I'm going to teach you how to use your power and increase it," I said.

"Why?"

"Because you may be the only one who can close the gateway the humans created again."

Her mouth dropped open before a burst of laughter escaped her. "You've lost your mind."

"No, I haven't."

"How could *I* be able to do such a thing?"

"Because you are the only living progeny of Lucifer." *My*

mortal enemy and the bane of my existence, I kept those words back as she looked tempted to bolt.

The increased smell of her sweat drifted to me along with the accelerated thump of her heart. She'd yet to run screaming from anything she'd encountered so far, but this may be what finally pushed her over the edge. Instead, she remained sitting, outwardly calm while I sensed the changes in her body.

"Are you going to explain or is this going to be another one of those, if I need to know things?" she inquired in a steady voice.

"This is something you need to know." Her pulse increased further as excitement radiated in her eyes. She would finally have her answers, answers I wished I didn't have to give her.

CHAPTER TWENTY-ONE

Kobal

"When Lucifer was cast out of Heaven, he spent some time on Earth. I'm not sure how much, some say months, others say years, some say only days," I told her. "Only Lucifer and his angels know the truth, and they keep it to themselves. During this time, he and his followers sheared off their wings to fit in with the humans. They also started to become something different from the angels they had been."

"A demon?"

"We believe it was a mixture of human, demon, and angel."

"Why were they changing?"

"I don't know if it was the removal of their wings that caused the first changes to take place or if it was because they were shut off from their world, forced to live in a plane not their own, and one that would eventually destroy them all."

Her fingers drummed on the table as she contemplated my words. "How many angels fell?"

"I don't know. They say a third were tossed from Heaven, but only fifty survived their time on Earth to enter Hell. I have no idea how many angels there were before Lucifer was cast out."

"So Lucifer lived amongst humans?"

"Yes and he procreated with them."

"You mean to tell me an angel, who never saw Earth, and knew he wouldn't be capable of living eternally on it, spent his time on our plane looking to get laid?"

I smiled at her as I leaned back in my seat and folded my hands before me. "Fucking doesn't sound like such a bad way to pass the time to me, especially since he'd never had the pleasure before. It's not an act angels get to enjoy."

She blinked at my words, and color blossomed high in her cheeks. I shifted as blood flooded my groin and my gaze fell to the breasts I'd watched her caressing. I knew she was recalling that night too when her breathing picked up and her nipples strained against her shirt.

She lifted her goblet and took a sip before lowering it and wiping the wine away from her lips. My gaze fell on her full mouth, stained a deeper red by the wine now. What I wouldn't give to run my tongue over those exquisite, pouty lips and to taste her as she panted beneath me.

"But demons get to enjoy it," she said in a husky voice that set my blood on fire.

I tore my gaze from her lips and looked her in the eyes once more. The lanterns flickering over her cast her in a sensual light that had me digging my nails into the table to keep from reaching for her.

Mine. I had no idea where the possessive instinct came from, but the certainty behind it made me realize it was right. This woman, with her raven hair, violet eyes, and proud features was *mine,* and I couldn't have her.

"Yes, we enjoy it often and thoroughly." The increasing pressure in my chest and my growing erection made speaking difficult. All I could think about was pulling her from her chair, taking her into my bed, and burying myself inside of her. To sink my fangs into her neck...

I broke the thought off. To sink my fangs into her would be a claiming act, one I had never committed before. What was she to me? I studied her as impulses I'd never experienced shot through my body and a new possibility started to dawn on me.

The color in her cheeks heightened as her fingers fidgeted on the table. The scent of her arousal tickled my nostrils; I had to sate her need. I bit back a snarl as the fangs I'd finally gotten to retract, extended once more.

She is the one you've been seeking. Do not get involved. Use her as she is supposed to be used. Fix what was broken six thousand years ago and claim your *throne.*

I kept telling myself these things, but I wasn't nearly as excited about finally having Lucifer's child in my grasp as I would have been a month ago. Now the only thing exciting me about having her was the possibility of actually *having* her.

"So what happened after the angels spent their time on Earth?" she asked.

"That is the question we would all like the answer to. Somehow, Lucifer figured out how to open a gateway and slip into Hell."

"Maybe it was one of the other angels who did it?" she suggested.

"No, it was Lucifer. Believe me, that is something he made clear when he arrived. I'm not sure his followers know how he did it, or if it's perhaps an ability only he possesses."

I gazed pointedly at her with those last words and she sat up straighter in her chair.

"I've told you what I know of myself," she replied defensively.

"But there may be more. We will find out."

A muscle in her cheek jumped. "Okay, fine, Lucifer magically opened the door. Still not sure what that has to do with me."

"Before he figured out a way into our world, he left a child behind, growing in the belly of one of the women he'd lain with. Perhaps he left more than one child behind, but we know there was at least one. That child grew up capable of surviving in your world, and producing offspring of their own. A line that would continue for over six thousand years. Once Lucifer entered our realm, he never produced another offspring. I believe he became constrained by our laws once he became Hell-bound and could only procreate with a Chosen, which he has not found."

"And you believe I'm a descendent of that child?"

"I do."

"Why?"

"Many reasons. The visions and the ability to dream connect are all powers that angels, and some demons possess. Your eyes are another sign—"

"The Devil's eyes!" Her hand flew up to the corner of her right eye. The color drained from her face and a look of dread came over her. "My mother wasn't crazy; she was right."

The distress in her voice touched something deep within me. Without thinking, I leaned across the table and rested my hand on top of hers in a foreign attempt to try to offer comfort. I ran my fingers over her supple skin as she gazed at me.

"Your mother was completely wrong," I said. "Lucifer's eyes are now as black as mine. Lucifer's eyes *were* your color; *all* angels have violet eyes. They are not the Devil's eyes; they are the eyes of the angels."

Unexpected tears bloomed in her eyes, and she ducked her head away before rising to her feet and pacing away from the table. The first chink in her armor, I realized, and it was because of her mother. Whatever she'd experienced with her mother over the years had left her wounded and vulnerable in a way I'd never imagined possible from her. If the woman had been standing before me, I would have torn her to shreds for inflicting such hurt upon her child, upon *River*.

I watched her rigid back as she stalked over to the flap of the tent and stood there for a minute. When she turned back to me, her eyes were dry. "So you're telling me I'm part angel?" she demanded.

I couldn't help but smile at the challenging, brazen tone of her voice. "I am. You're also part human and part demon."

"So there is evil within me?"

I settled back in my seat. "We are not evil; we are simply a means to an end. We are a natural process met by those who deserve it. Humans have such a limited concept of good and evil, expand your mind a little."

She waved her hand at me as if she were brushing aside my words. "Okay, demons are not inherently evil, I can get that, but *Lucifer* is, right?"

"River—"

"God threw him out of Heaven. He tore your world apart—"

"Humans tore our world apart too." Her hand fell back to her side. "Lucifer is an abomination that should never have been thrown to Earth. He should have been taken care of by his own kind instead of foisted off onto humans and later demons. You have always had a concept of the angels being the good guys; yet they are the ones who started this whole mess six thousand years ago, and now you humans have brought our war into your realm by opening the gateway. There is no good and evil as you think of it; there are only different realms, each with its own purpose and balance, and now those balances have been tipped."

Rising to my feet, I almost went to her to draw her into my arms and give her the comfort I knew she needed. Instead, I compelled myself to walk over and retrieve another bottle of wine.

My hand clenched around the bottle. She was mine, and I could not have her. It was not only my life or hers hanging in the balance, but the millions of humans and demons who still lived and would perish if Lucifer continued to grow his army and made a move to conquer the humans.

Turning back to her, I walked over to the table and poured another glass of wine before settling into my seat. "I have known much of what you humans would consider evil in my lifetime. You are as far from that as anyone I've ever known before," I told her.

Her head tilted to the side and her mouth parted as she studied me with a look of partial longing and gratitude. I'd require vats of wine to stay away from this woman. "How can I be part demon if Lucifer was still on Earth when this child was created?" she inquired.

"Because he was already changing, warping into something more. That's where your ability for fire comes in. It is a solely demonic trait, not an angelic one. You may have other demonic traits as well, but we will discover that as we train. Premonitions and visions are possessed by demons and angels; that is a trait shared between our species."

Walking over, she remained standing as she lifted her goblet and finished off her wine. "Did the other angels leave offspring behind before they entered Hell?"

"They did, but their lines have all perished over the years. Many historic figures sprang from their lines and yours."

"Like who?" she inquired.

"Like Jesus, Moses, Job, Abraham, Joan of Arc, Noah, Rasputin, Hitler, Nero, Caligula, Ivan the Terrible, Ghengis

Khan, Vlad Dracula, and many others. Their lineage is how some of them were able to communicate with God, walk on water, part seas, get millions to follow them, and so on. Of course, not all of the children of the angels had such strong displays of abilities. Many of them had more latent abilities or they kept them hidden."

She gawked at me before speaking again. "Jesus was the son of God."

I shrugged. "More like grandson."

"Jesus Chr... ah... shit," she finished and glanced nervously at the roof of the tent.

"You will not be struck dead," I assured her.

"Yeah," she muttered, but her eyes went to the roof again. "How can you be so sure all of those angel lines are gone too?"

"Demons kept track of them for a long time or tried to, but eventually they were unable to do so anymore. We believed *all* the angel lines had perished, until four years ago when Bale received a vision that Lucifer's line continued. We had no idea what to expect. If you would be male or female, young or old, we only knew you still existed and that you would possess at least some of the abilities of your father."

"I have no idea what abilities my father could be capable of. He left my mother when he learned she was pregnant with me and hasn't been heard from since."

"Your father is Lucifer."

CHAPTER TWENTY-TWO

Kobal

She shot me a look, her mouth pursing at my words. "If you're right, there are six thousand years in between me and his actual child that disagree with you," she retorted.

"He is the creator of your line; he is your father."

"A line that never should have existed," she murmured.

There had been many times over my life I had cursed the existence of Lucifer, of the chaos and death he'd wrought upon our world, a world that was supposed to be *mine* to lead. He'd twisted what was supposed to have been a thing of function and necessity and turned it into a perversion of what it was meant to be. He'd slaughtered countless demons over his lengthy time there, and he sought to disrupt the balance between Hell and Earth. If he could figure out a way to get back into Heaven, I knew he would seek to destroy it too.

He'd tried for many millennia to get free of Hell in order to bring death and destruction to the mortal realm, but through bloodshed and sacrifice, the Palitons had fought and succeeded in keeping him suppressed. I'd often cursed the day Lucifer had been tossed through those pearly gates. However, looking at River now, I would have thrown him through those gates myself to have her here.

The realization rattled me so much I nearly crushed the goblet within my hand. My breath rattled out between my teeth.

Mine.

Fuck. I took another drink of wine as I grappled to keep demonic instincts, which I'd never experienced before, buried. She simply couldn't be what I was beginning to suspect she might be.

"What is it you want from me exactly? Why were you looking for me?" she asked.

I was grateful for the distraction her question gave me from my musings. "Lucifer somehow figured out how to get into our world; he didn't shut the gates behind him, my ancestor did, but there is hope an heir of Lucifer's would be able to close the gate as he once opened it. And according to Bale's vision you, River, are his only living relative."

"Oh, you believe my actual father is dead," she breathed as realization settled over her.

"I do. When Mac said you had siblings I'd thought there was a chance, no matter how small, Bale's vision could have been wrong about you being the last of Lucifer's line, or that you were not who we sought, but I don't believe so now."

"You will leave my brothers out of this!" she spat at me. "They have never shown any differences."

I lifted a hand to calm her as her fury beat against me. "They will remain safely where they are. This has come from your father's line if they show no differences."

She gazed at me for a minute, her expression unreadable as she tried to process this information. "I never knew my father, but I always believed he was out there, somewhere." She dropped her head into her hand. Finally, she shook her head and focused on me once more. "If you can open and close gateways to Hell why can't you close this gate?"

"The gateway the humans tore into our world is unnatural. The gateway Lucifer opened into our world wasn't natural either, but it was much smaller and my ancestor was able to control it. I have managed to close the gateway the humans created more than it was originally, but I cannot shut it completely."

"But Lucifer only opened the gate before; maybe he can't close it, which means I couldn't either."

"Maybe not," I replied. "But you may be one of the most powerful beings on this planet. Our main focus is for you to develop your powers before we take you to the gate and see if it can be closed."

"And if it can't?"

My teeth ground together so forcefully my jaw ached from the pressure. Part of the plan had always been to take on Lucifer, if it became necessary, but I would find a way to keep her protected. "Then you may be capable of destroying Lucifer."

She looked as if I'd slapped her. The color drained from her face so fast I thought she might pass out. She inhaled sharply and her hands flattened on the table. Wordlessly, she slid into the chair. Her gaze focused on the tent wall behind me, before shifting to me. "How is that possible?"

"It's the combination. You *do* possess the abilities of all three species."

"I seem to be leaning more toward the demon side," she murmured. "Nothing I can do is truly angelic."

"As far as we know, but we could discover more, and you *will* become more powerful and better able to handle those powers. It is possible you could walk in all three worlds, but we won't know until we are at the gateway. If you are capable of entering and withstanding Hell, then you could take Lucifer on, if you become proficient enough with your abilities. The main focus, after we develop your powers further, will be trying to close the unnatural gateway."

Her fingers drummed on the table. "What abilities does a human have?"

"They have the ability to one day enter the other realms as a soul. The ability to let love and hate fuel their actions and drive them to feats they never believed possible. There is more power in a human than they realize. You do not possess all the abilities of angels or demons, but your combination is rare, and it may be what we need to defeat Lucifer."

Her fingers slid to her neck and she fiddled with her necklace. "What more can *you* do?"

"You haven't scratched the surface of the things demons are capable of, or yourself, I'm guessing. With time, you will learn more."

"How do you *know* I'm the only offspring left? There could be dozens, maybe even a hundred or so, fallen angel kids running around out there."

"Humans are known for many things, including being afraid of things they don't understand, especially people who are different from them. Not all of the offspring would have had your eye color, but all of them would have been different in some way, even if it was only in a small way. Think of the witches who were slaughtered, the people who were burned at the stake over the centuries for being different. Some of them actually *were*. Most of the angel lines were lost in this way over the years."

She rubbed at her temples as she bowed her head. When she looked at me again, shadows marred underneath her eyes. "What do you expect me to do to close the gate?"

"I do not know. Perhaps your instinct will take over and you will *know* what must be done when we get there."

I didn't know what kind of reaction I'd expected out of her, but her eyes remained unwavering on mine. She didn't say a word, yet I could almost see the thoughts tumbling through her mind. I listened as the seconds ticked into minutes on the clock in the corner.

"And what if it doesn't?" she finally inquired.

"We will figure that out when we get there, but this is the closest we've ever come to having a possible way to shut the gate down and saving the human species."

"But if the gate is shut down, and you haven't been able to defeat Lucifer before, how will you do so now? I'm thinking he's not going to give up even if the gate is closed."

"If we can draw him out beforehand, then with you, the weapons the humans possess, and the demons who will join us at the gateway, we have a chance of being able to defeat him. We've never had the human weapons on our side before; they won't kill him, but they will slow him down, and we've never had your abilities before. This battle will be different. If he doesn't come out, and you can enter Hell, we can go after him."

She looked as if I'd just dropped a bomb on *her* as she blinked at me, opened her mouth to say something, but then closed it again. More minutes ticked by before she said, "So, you plan to fight Lucifer on Earth?"

"Yes, if we can."

"Nothing could possibly go wrong with that," she muttered.

"We've never had this kind of opportunity before. Out of it all, even if we cannot defeat him, the gateway *must* be closed."

"What if it's not me?"

One could hope, but I knew that most likely wasn't true. We'd never encountered another human like her; she could do too much for her not to be the one we sought. "I'm almost certain it *is* you, and we will work together until you are ready for the journey."

"The journey?"

"It will be a long road to get us to the gateway, and it will not be an easy one. However, we will worry about that when the time comes."

Much like her father, her stare was unrelenting and unfathomable. I had no idea what was going on in that head of hers. "I know you said I'd be staying here, but I think I should go back to town."

"You'll be staying with us from now on. I don't trust humans around things they don't understand and fear."

She winced at my words. "I can guarantee they don't understand you and they fear *you*, but you're doing fine," she retorted.

I folded my hands on the table before me as I leaned toward her. "They know what *we* are; they have an idea of what to make of us even if they fear us. You look completely human, you came from one of their towns, and you just became a flamethrower in front of them. They have *no* idea what to make of you, and that makes them volatile where you're concerned. I'm not going to have our greatest asset injured or possibly even killed by a bunch of idiots."

A muscle in the corner of her right eye twitched when I said the word asset. "*Possible* asset," she replied.

I couldn't deny she was fiery. I wondered what it would be like to have that fire beneath me as I took possession of her body. My eyes slid to her breasts again under the thin brown shirt she wore. I'd told her she couldn't go back to town because of the humans, but her biggest danger may be staying in this tent with me.

"Possible asset," I replied. "Something we will begin to dig deeper into tomorrow."

"Where will I stay?" she asked.

"You can have my room."

Her hand clamped on the base of the goblet. "Your room?"

"Yes. I will stay in here."

Rising, I walked to the back of the tent, undid some buttons, and pulled up another flap to reveal the room beyond. I heard her rise and pad over to stand behind me. Her warm breath heated my skin when it blew against my arm.

Stepping aside, I gestured for her to go into the tent beyond. It was as large as the main meeting area, but it was more elaborately appointed with a king-sized bed and an armoire holding my human clothes.

"Make yourself comfortable," I told her. "I'll have Mac arrange for someone to bring your things here."

Her hand fell on my arm before I could leave her. I gazed down at her tanned, calloused hand resting against me. Beneath her touch, my skin rippled and I felt a stirring within the markings covering my arms. What would happen if she were to run her fingers over them, to trace every intricate design? Would she be able to feel the power within them?

And what would it do to *me*?

"What about a bathroom?" she inquired. "I don't know what you demons have to do, but we humans do have some other needs."

I grit my teeth against the scorching passion her touch provoked in me. "I'd forgotten about that. Our bodies may be the same as a human's in most ways, but feasting on souls makes us different in other ways."

Her eyes ran over me. I could see the questions running through her mind as her gaze briefly rested on my waist before darting upward. The shirt hanging over my waist was the only thing covering the evidence of my erection; otherwise, she would have had a clear view of exactly what I wanted from her.

"So, bathroom?" she prompted.

"I know of one you can use."

"Not outside would be preferable."

I walked through the room to the back of the tent. I undid the buttons holding the flap closed and pushed it upward before gesturing for her to exit. Holding the flap back for her, I inhaled her enticing scent as she slipped by me to go outside. I emerged beside her into the large, grassy clearing with at least forty tents encircling it.

The tents were all smaller in size than mine as they didn't have the main meeting room attached, but they all looked similar with their heavy, green canvas siding. The breeze blew against them, causing the canvas to flutter in the currents of air. Most demons were still on the training fields with the volunteers and soldiers, but some milled around the clearing and by the tents playing games.

I pointed to the small house at the bottom of the hill where we stored food for the livestock in camp. "Because the house is on the outskirts of the other homes, no one has moved into it. It's too far away from the others for the humans to feel secure staying inside it at night. You can use the bathroom in there," I told her.

She stared at it for a minute before responding. "Okay."

"There is a shower over there." I turned and pointed to the shower at the edge of our camp. A simple hose hung over a wood wall that did little to shield the demon within from view. On the wall was a bar of soap and a bottle of shampoo, two things I actually preferred about this world to our own. As a whole, demons were exceptionally clean, but in Hell we used rocks to scrub our flesh clean in the warm, red waters; the soap and shampoo was a nice bonus.

"I'll use the shower in the house. I prefer walls to open air and exposure," she said.

"You humans and your modesty." Then I realized I much preferred her to shower in private. *No* one else would see what belonged to me.

"I guess we really can blame Eve for that," she muttered.

"Perhaps."

"Perhaps? Isn't that the story? Eve ate the apple, kicked from the garden, yada, yada."

"There are many stories, some are true, others are questionable. If you think there were only ever two humans on this earth to begin with, you'd be wrong. There were others already here, but Adam and Eve were the favored ones, and the only ones granted entrance to Eden. Eve did pluck the apple, and she did get them booted from the garden, but your ancestors were already running around with loin clothes covering them when Adam and Eve emerged from paradise."

"I guess nobody wanted bug bites on their privates."

A short burst of laughter unexpectedly erupted from me; her eyes widened at the sound, and a smile curved her luscious mouth as her eyes twinkled in amusement. Sitting in the center of the clearing, Shax, Bale, Verin, and Morax stopped in the middle of their game of cards to look at us in surprise. It had been a long time since I'd laughed around them. Corson had been flirting with a pretty girl from town; he had her blonde hair twined around his finger when he looked at us. The girl pouted at him, but he didn't pay her any attention.

Ignoring them all, I took hold of River's elbow and led her back into the tent. "I suppose that would explain it," I said to her as I closed the flap and slid the buttons back into place. "You're probably hungry."

"I am," she admitted.

She followed me into the main tent where a meal already waited for her. Sitting in the seat across from her, I watched the candlelight playing over her features as she dove into her meal.

"Do you think you could pull me into one of your visions again, like you did today?" I inquired when she finished the last of her chicken.

She pushed her plate away and wiped delicately at her mouth. "I don't know, but if I did it once, I don't see why I wouldn't be able to do it again."

I tapped my fingers on the table. "It will be interesting to find out."

Her eyes went to the tent wall as laughter echoed outside. The scent of smoke and the crackling of a fire drifted to me. They must have already started the bonfire on the hill. A bonfire I would make sure River stayed far away from.

"It would be best if you stayed inside at night," I told her. "Things can get a little wild out there. If you have to go somewhere, come and get me and I will take you."

Her mouth pursed but she nodded her agreement.

CHAPTER TWENTY-THREE

River

Over the next couple of weeks, I didn't really know what was expected of me as I continued to train with Kobal and the others. The volunteers I'd come here with avoided me now. The demons all watched me like I was the mouse and they were the hawk circling above. I didn't think they planned on picking my remains, but they were definitely intent upon my every action.

I'd also noticed a growing tension and withdrawal from Kobal as time slipped by. He still trained with me every day, but he seemed to be holding something of himself back. Yet sometimes I would catch him looking at me with such hunger in his gaze that it would cause my entire body to quicken with longing.

My dreams of him had ebbed since moving into his tent. I blamed that more on my exhaustion when I finally did fall asleep than a waning in my yearning for him. No, that grew every day his distance did.

Even Mac stayed away from me now, but his eyes were

always on me whenever I was on the field. Unlike the others who watched me with rapt curiosity and animosity, the sadness in Mac's eyes troubled me.

I didn't understand any of it; the humans accepted the demons more readily then they accepted me. Kobal had been right, they had no idea what to make of me, and they were afraid. That fear had made them distant and wary. The demons didn't know what to make of me, and I wondered if perhaps some of them disliked me for my supposed heritage or at least because of who had possibly created me.

I didn't know what it was, and by now I was so exhausted from the nonstop training, stress, and uncertainty, that I was getting to the point I wanted to hit every single human and demon who gave me a sidelong glance. Or if I could figure out how to make that handy-dandy frying things ability work, maybe I'd burn all their pants off them and watch them run around with their asses on fire.

However, I hadn't been able to set anything on fire since that day with the madagans. Kobal had to be wrong about who or what I was; I kept telling myself this, but the certainty he was right had taken hold of me. I hadn't admitted it to him, but when he'd told me what he believed I was, a part of me had lit up in an *aha* moment, and it had all made sense. A part of me, deep inside, could not shrug away his words no matter how badly denial kept screaming through my head.

Perhaps they were all right to distance themselves from me. I was the only living ancestor of Lucifer himself, of evil incarnate. I tried not to think of things in terms of good and evil as Kobal had told me to, but I couldn't shake the feeling there could be something inherently evil within me.

Then again, maybe there wasn't, but could I be easily turned to evil? Lucifer had been an angel, the morning star, and now he was looking to destroy and enslave the human race.

Was there something in me that could make me become like him too?

I didn't care what I had to do, I would never let something like that happen to me. I would *never* become like him. Still, I couldn't rid myself of the idea that my mother had been right, and I really was an abomination who never should have existed.

I lay awake at night torn between fantasies of the man sleeping in the room next to mine and plagued by the idea I could become a monster.

I didn't dread traveling to the gate or trying to close it; that was easy-peasy compared to the idea my DNA shared the same code as Lucifer's. I could face what would come with the journey to the gate; I could prepare and fight any threat. I couldn't fight genetics.

Moving through the food line, I could feel the hostility and dread radiating around the people who moved hastily away from me. I was worse than the smelly kid in class, as I had a five-foot-wide space around me. Demons lingered nearby and I had no doubt they were there to watch over and protect me if it became necessary. Grabbing an apple, I placed it on my tray and turned to face the crowd.

The heads around me bent down and shoulders hunched up. The tops of their tables became extremely fascinating as people pretended not to see me. I took a deep breath before winding my way through the tables to sit at an empty one in the back. My gaze slid over the people at the tables around me; it settled on Carrie who focused intently on her sandwich.

A pang of betrayal and longing speared through me. I should be used to this shunning and loneliness by now, but I wasn't. The apple I bit into felt like lead in my mouth; it took all I had to swallow it down as tears burned in my chest. I missed my brothers, my home, and Lisa; I missed not being an oddity. I missed companionship and people who cared for me. I missed Gage's smile and Bailey's giggles. I even missed his atrociously stinky diapers.

I placed the apple on my tray and poked at the sandwich on my plate. The more curious and distrustful stares came my way, the less of an appetite I had. The shifting of the table alerted me someone had sat down across from me; I knew it was Kobal without having to look at him.

Lifting my head, I found his pure black eyes staring back at me. I'd become acutely attuned to his presence over the past few weeks. Around us, the talk died down and I saw the startled expressions of those closest to us as they gawked at Kobal. He didn't notice any of them, or at least he paid them no mind as his attention centered on me. The way he looked at me made my insides turn to goo.

"Aren't you going to eat?" he inquired. I glanced at my plate before pushing it away. "You're going to need your energy for training later."

"I'm not hungry."

His gaze slid over the people surrounding us before he leaned back on the bench and stretched his legs out before him. "Humans are such strange creatures."

"Is that supposed to be an insult or a compliment?"

His eyes glimmered like obsidian in the light of the room when he looked at me again. I'd never seen him in here before; his massive size and aura of power was completely out of place in this world built for teens but taken over by volunteers and soldiers.

"You're not entirely an average person, River," he said with a tight smile, as if the reminder somehow displeased him.

"So you suspect." *And so I* feel *deep in my gut.*

"No matter what you say, or what I suspect, you're the only mortal here who can throw flames with her hands."

"I haven't done it since that day on the field. It may have been a fluke."

"No fluke. We just haven't figured out what to do to get you to do it."

"Hmm," I murmured.

"You should eat."

"I should be doing a lot of things I'm not."

"Like what?" he inquired.

"Like being with my family, like sitting with my friends." I glanced around the room and shook my head. "Never mind, you wouldn't understand."

"I told you people would be apprehensive."

"You did," I agreed.

"Come."

He rose to his full height, towering over me as he stood with his hands resting on the table. I frowned at him before rising and walking around the table to join him. His hand clasped my elbow, and he started to lead me out of the cafeteria. The heat of his body enveloped me, and I instinctively moved closer to him, needing to feel more of his strength as whispers and murmurs ratcheted up to swirl around us. My stomach turned, but I thrust out my chin and kept my gaze focused ahead of me.

"Where are we going?" I inquired.

"Somewhere you can have some peace."

"I have nothing but peace in here," I replied with a bitter laugh.

"Kobal." We were brought up short when the pretty blonde woman who had inquired about my relationship with Kobal weeks ago stepped in front of us. Her shameless gaze swept over his body. The knowing gleam in her eyes caused me to stiffen. I glanced at Kobal to gauge his reaction, his forehead was creased as he impassively stared at her. "We haven't had a chance to catch up much since you returned to camp."

"Been busy," he replied in a clipped tone.

The woman's eyes ran over me before she dismissively looked away. My hands fisted when her gaze fixed raptly on Kobal once more. Beating the shit out of her would *not* win me any new friends, but it was a very appealing idea.

"Maybe I'll see you tonight. We can spend some time together, *again*." She gave me a pointed look with her last word.

The air in the cafeteria became increasingly difficult to breathe, and clamminess slid over my skin. I wanted to jerk my arm away from Kobal's and storm out of there, but I couldn't give any of them the satisfaction of doing such a thing. Instead, I stood there and endured the humiliation of his lover and him making plans to meet.

"No," Kobal replied crisply.

She gave him a sulky look that some would have found cute; I found it simpering and annoying. He went to step around her, but her hand fluttered out and rested against his arm.

"Don't touch me."

The low, gravelly tone of his voice caused the hair on my nape to rise as I sensed within it an undercurrent of menace. The woman's hand fell away, and the pouty smile left her face as she straightened away from him. Her gaze was far more hostile than dismissive when it came back to me again. Kobal released a sound that would have made a wolf cower and run as he tugged me a step closer to his side. The woman remained standing where she was.

The more I was immersed in it, the more I realized I didn't understand this world I'd been forced into. I felt like a square peg trying to fit into a round hole, and everyone here knew I was an imposter. I didn't belong in any of the worlds. Least of all here.

“I’ll let you two talk,” I murmured. I had to get away from all of this.

CHAPTER TWENTY-FOUR

River

I went to step away, but his hand tightened on my elbow and he nestled me closer against his side. "There's nothing to talk about," he said.

Unwilling to cause a scene, I remained where I was, feeling like every eye in the building burned into my back. The people closest to us were focused on their meals, but I knew they were hanging on every word. I was going to kill him for making me stand here for this.

"Come." Kobal nudged my elbow, drawing me forward a step.

I could feel the woman's gaze boring into my back with every step we took. "I'm not a dog," I told him when we finally stepped outside and into the fresh air. I inhaled it eagerly, but I couldn't shake the lingering tension in my body. "I don't obey commands," I expounded when he gave me a questioning look.

"Would you like to stay and talk with her?"

"No, I don't want to talk to your girlfriend."

"I don't have girlfriends."

"Your fling or whatever she is."

"I don't have flings. Our world is not so boxed as your human one; it is more flowing."

"What does *that* mean?"

He stopped walking, and releasing my elbow, he turned to face me. "It means we don't place the constraints on ourselves like your species does by having to define and label everything we do. When demons meet the one they are Chosen to be with, they mate for life such as Verin and Morax, but the rest of us do what we please until then, and for many, finding their Chosen doesn't happen."

"I don't think she realized that when she got involved with you; maybe you should have made it clearer to her."

"I'm not in the habit of having to explain anything I do to anyone. I'm not about to start now with some silly human who should know better to begin with."

"And why should she know better?" I demanded.

You should know better! I screamed at myself in my head. *Listen to what he's saying and keep your distance. Women and sex mean nothing to him; remember that, and keep your libido in check, dumb ass.*

"I do not make promises of relationships to anyone, especially not a human."

I managed to keep myself from recoiling at his words. With the sun behind his back, an aura surrounded him that should have warmed him. All I felt was coldness and indifference wafting from him.

My hands rubbed at my arms as I took a step away from him. Many times he'd been almost caring toward me, more so than my own mother had been over the years, but was it a pretense to get what he sought from me, a trip back to Hell?

"What is that woman's name?" I asked.

"I don't recall."

I blinked at this statement; it was the only reaction I could have to it. "You hurt her feelings, that much was obvious, but so is the fact you don't care."

His head tilted to the side, and his forehead furrowed as he studied me. I understood him about as much as he seemed to understand me, which was not at all. "Why would I care?"

I threw my arms in the air and turned away from him. "There are walls with more understanding than you!" I shot over my shoulder at him as I made my way up the hill toward the tents.

I didn't realize he'd followed me until he reached around me to pull the flap on his tent back for me. "I have understanding," he said as soon as we entered. "It's why we have adapted to your ways more than I would have liked."

Turning on him, I placed my hands on my hips as I met his gaze. "Yet, you still don't understand you hurt her feelings."

"The women and men who look to satisfy their curiosity about what it is like to be with a demon, or are simply looking for a good fuck, should know better than to become attached to any of us. We have made no secret we will return home; the woman is a fool for believing there could have been more between us."

My hands fell back to my sides as his blunt words sank in. He was right. I understood the woman's unhappiness, but he had a point. Most of the people here may not know what the demons were searching for, what they believed the key to closing Hell was, but they did know the main goal here was to defend the wall, close the gate, defeat Lucifer and for the demons to one day return to where they'd come from.

So why did I feel so upset and betrayed?

Because of *him*. I hated thinking about him with other women or of him returning to the fiery depths where he had come from originally. I certainly didn't want to be the one who sent him there. He'd knocked me on my ass more times than I could recall, he infuriated me, he was the main reason I was here, yet all I craved was to feel those powerful arms around me. To know what his body would feel like moving against mine, to have those lips and hands sliding over my skin.

I kicked myself in the ass for allowing the fantasy to enter my mind. It could *never* be, and I wouldn't be another non-fling to him. "You're right," I murmured.

Before I could flee to my section of the tent, his hand snaked out and he took hold of my wrist. An electrical current flowed over my flesh, and my breath caught as I struggled not to step closer to him and rest my hands against his chest.

"You haven't eaten," he said.

"I don't feel well. I'm going to lie down."

It wasn't entirely a lie; my head was pounding, but I was aware that I was acting like a coward as I tugged my wrist free of his grasp.

"Do you need me to get you anything?" he asked.

"No."

I didn't look back as I slipped into my section of the tent, kicked off my shoes, tugged my bra off from under my shirt, and crawled into the bed with its soft mattress and tempting pillows. I could hear the thump of punches and the clashing of swords and knives as instruction resumed on the training field, but I didn't crawl from the bed.

As the day progressed, I found it increasingly difficult to open my eyes, and it hurt almost as much to keep them closed. I didn't dare move; every time I did, I was certain I'd throw up. Instead, I lay unmoving on the bed as the migraine took hold of me.

It had been years since I'd had one; I'd believed it was something left behind with my childhood, but the stress and misery of these past six weeks had finally caught up to me.

Eventually, I fell into a fitful sleep. When I woke again, I knew it was night only because of the dimly lit lantern on the table next to the bed. Beside the lantern sat a plate of food.

My stomach rumbled with hunger. The lingering throb of the migraine pulsed in my head when I swung my feet out of the bed, but I knew the worst of it had passed. Washing my face, drinking some water, and eating some food would help to rid me of the rest of it. I greedily ate the chicken on the plate before diving into the potatoes. I was full by the time I was done.

I licked the juices from my fingers before lifting the handle on the lantern and walking silently toward the flap leading outside. Kobal had told me to get him whenever I had to go somewhere at night, but I'd prefer not to wake him if he was sleeping, and I didn't want to wait around for him to get dressed. Besides, I didn't need a bodyguard.

Undoing the flap, I pushed it back and stepped into the night. I inhaled deeply as I savored the warm air blowing against my skin. My gaze went to the flames of the bonfire leaping on the hill about a hundred yards away. Tents and trees blocked my view of the fire, but the orange glow lit the night, and I could see the tips of the flames dancing in the air. Laughter and music floated down the hill toward me.

My head tilted to the side as I pondered for the thousandth time what went on up there. I took a step toward the fire, but the pressure in my bladder had me turning and walking down the hill toward the small house at the bottom. I'd only planned to use the toilet, but once inside, I couldn't resist the lure of a shower. I undressed and stepped beneath the spray, letting the warm water wash away the rest of my lingering migraine as I shampooed my hair and used the straight edged razor on the shelf.

My step was much lighter when I emerged from the shower

feeling a hundred times better. I hummed to myself as I dressed and reclaimed my lantern. Walking up the hill, my gaze returned to the fire. Kobal had told me to stay away from it, but it sounded like a good time. Besides, what could one little peek *really* hurt?

Turning, I strode toward the fire crackling high into the sky. More laughter trailed down the hill, and I picked out the sounds of a guitar as I slipped past two of the tents while making my way closer to the flames. The heat of the fire in the air warmed me before I arrived to stand behind a large oak tree. I lowered the flame on my lantern and placed it on the ground beside the tree.

Pieces of bark broke away beneath my fingers when I rested my palms against the tree and poked my head around the side of it. My breath froze in my chest as I gawked at the scene before me. Most of the demons were gathered there, their hair alight in the flames playing over their bare skin. Amongst the demons, there were a couple dozen humans gathered in the clearing around the fire. Not all of the humans were naked too, but almost half of them were. They all appeared my age or older, and I realized they were all soldiers.

Bale sat on a fallen tree trunk, playing what looked like a guitar. Her red hair shone in the fire that lit her bare flesh. Two naked women danced before her, leaping and jumping as their laughter trailed from them. Drinks were passed around, and a loud cheer arose from the group circling the flames.

Shax leaned back in a chair, his arm draped around the back of it as he stretched his legs before him. There was a naked woman kneeling between his legs with her head moving enthusiastically up and down.

What is she doing?

Heat blazed up my neck and burned into my cheeks when I realized her mouth was encircling his shaft. I ducked back to rest my forehead against the tree as I inhaled a tremulous breath. I should leave. I should run back to the tent and forget all about this night, but I found my feet wouldn't move.

Where is Kobal?

I wasn't sure I could handle it if I saw him with another woman. However, I found my head sliding out from behind the tree again. My gaze ran over the demons once more. There was Morax leaning against a tree with Verin; both of them were still fully clothed. They didn't appear to notice anyone else around them as they remained close together. Not for the first time, I found my gaze riveted on the bite marks on their necks.

Another demon I didn't really know stood in the shadows of a tree with a human. He lifted her from the ground and, turning on his heel, walked over to the nearest tent. Corson sat on the ground next to a couple of women. They all touched and kissed each other, their hands traveling over each other's bodies as moans of excitement emanated from them.

I made myself look over the clearing once more, but I still didn't see Kobal anywhere. That didn't mean he couldn't be in one of the tents, like the other demon who had just left. The idea of him with another woman caused my teeth to grind together as my chest constricted. My fingers dug deeper into the tree bark. I had zero experience with anything like what was going on in the clearing. However, I knew he would participate in this, and it would be something he enjoyed.

Probably something he'd enjoyed with countless others. I couldn't bring myself to look for him again as I listened to the carnal sounds emanating from the clearing. I would give anything to be the one to ease him in such a way, but this was not my life, not who I was.

Walk away.

It was the best advice I could give myself, and finally, I managed to turn on my heel. I didn't get one step before I almost smacked into Kobal. His arms were folded over his chest; the firelight played over his chiseled features. My heart plummeted into my sneakers when I realized I'd been caught spying. Well, not completely spying as I'd really been looking for him, but I'd still been lurking in the shadows like some kind of creeper.

Which I guess I was.

CHAPTER TWENTY-FIVE

River

The flames from the fire reflected and leapt in his eyes when he looked over my shoulder. I was going to need a fire extinguisher if my cheeks burned any hotter. I had no idea what to say or do as he remained focused on what was going on behind me before looking at me again. Had he been on his way to join them?

Before I could decide between sprinting all the way back to the tent or melting into the ground, he clasped hold of my shoulder and turned away from the fire. For the first time, I realized he was wearing clothes. Did that mean he hadn't been a part of what I could only consider some kind of orgy?

The profound relief filling me caused my knees to shake. He wasn't mine, never could be, but I didn't want him to be anyone else's either. Then I recalled the woman from the cafeteria earlier; he already had been someone else's, most likely *thousands* of someone else's given his lifespan.

"I told you not to leave the tent alone at night." His tone was far gruffer than normal.

His body vibrated with a different energy as he moved me down the hill toward the tent. Daring to glance up at him from under my lashes, I noticed the sweat beading across his brow and the firm set of his jaw. His head turned toward me, and a black eyebrow rose when he found my eyes on him.

I looked away hastily before responding, "I had to go to the bathroom."

"The house is in the complete opposite direction."

I couldn't deny the truth.

His hand squeezed my shoulder. "It's not safe for you to wander outside alone. You shouldn't have disobeyed me, and you shouldn't have gone near the fire."

Yep, bring on the fire extinguisher. Maybe, just *maybe*, I could have gotten over him catching me gawking like an idiot if he had *never* mentioned it, but I should have known better. "I was curious," I muttered.

He released a derisive snort. Stopping abruptly, he drew me back with him. Over his shoulder, I saw the distant flames leaping into the sky. I was still curious about what was going on there, about what it would be like... with *him*. My pulse raced as a throbbing ache spread between my legs.

"And did you have your curiosity answered?" he inquired.

"I, uh... I, ah... I guess," I managed to stammer out.

"You guess? What did you expect to find?"

"I don't know. What they were, ah... doing, do they do it often?"

"Every night." My jaw fell faster than an apple from a tree. He folded his arms over his chest as he leaned back on his heels to survey me from head to toe. "Why is that so shocking to you?"

"I've never seen anything like it before," I murmured. "I didn't know..."

"Didn't know what?" he inquired when I couldn't get the words out of my mouth.

I couldn't stop my gaze from running over him. It lingered on his full mouth before traveling over his broad shoulders, tapered waist, and finally settling on the enticing bulge in the front of his pants. I bit my bottom lip and tore my attention away from it to look at anything other than him.

"Didn't know *what*, River?"

The gravelly tone of his voice did funny things to my insides. "They looked like they were enjoying themselves."

"Oh, they were." The purr of his voice drew my attention back to him. "It is *extremely* pleasurable with a demon. We're known for our stamina and... size."

A shiver raced down my spine. The goose bumps breaking out on my flesh had nothing to do with the air blowing over my dampened hair and skin. I rubbed my arms, but found the sensation only made my body feel more alive.

When I looked at him again, I found his gaze latched onto the front of my shirt. Glancing down, I realized my nipples stood out against the thin material. I hadn't bothered to put a bra on before going to use the bathroom, so they were now clearly visible for him to see.

I folded my arms hastily over my chest to cover them. When his eyes lifted to mine again, they were that striking gold color I'd seen only once before. My heart felt like it would explode out of my chest. It might actually latch itself onto him if it did, I realized in disgust—everything in me wanted to latch onto him.

"They do that willingly?" I croaked out.

"Didn't they look willing?"

"Well, yeah," I hedged, "I've never seen humans act like that before."

A smile curved his mouth; it was anything but kind. "There

are many things you've never seen humans do that they do often. You expected it of my kind though."

"I don't know what to expect of your kind," I admitted.

"We take pleasure where we can find it, much like humans, except we have none of the reservations about it your species does. And we have *many* needs we satisfy as often as we can and with whomever is willing."

"Why aren't you at the fire with them?" I managed to get out past the lump in my throat.

"Because I don't wish to be."

"But you have been?"

"Many times."

"And with many women."

It wasn't a question, but he replied anyway, "Yes."

I couldn't stop myself from wincing when the image of that woman from earlier, with her head in between *his* legs, blazed into my mind. A red-hot poker of jealousy pierced my chest. Just once it would be nice if he pulled some punches, but the only thing he ever held back on were things concerning and affecting *my* life.

Ugh, I hated them all, I decided.

"And now I have to watch over you," he continued.

Nope, I simply hated *him*.

"I don't need *any*one to watch over me," I grated out. "In case you haven't noticed, I'm able to defend myself better than any other human here. So don't use me as your excuse. Go, have fun."

I spun on my heel to return to the tent, but his hand snaked out and his fingers enclosed around my wrist, jerking me back around to face him. I didn't have time to protest before he pulled my body flush against his. My breath rushed out of me; my body reacted as if it were hit by an electrical bolt.

A blast of power rushed from him and into me. I moaned, and my head tilted back as I instinctively sought to get closer. I didn't know if it was his desire causing such a rush, or if he'd let some of his defenses against me down, but I'd never felt this flood of energy from him before.

Rising onto my toes, I gasped when the movement brought the bulge between his legs into contact with the yearning, sensitive area between my thighs. I didn't know what possessed me to do it, but I rubbed against him, crying out when the motion caused pleasure to scorch through my body.

I felt crazed and out of control for him as I ground against him again and again. The whole time, he watched me from those amber eyes, his body unmoving as his erection swelled further.

Breath heaving, I gradually regained control of myself as the initial rush ebbed. The pulse of his power continued to beat against me, but I could handle it now without feeling as if I were going to crawl all over him and tear his clothes off. However, my fingers still itched to shred his shirt from him, to run my tongue over his body, and taste his fire-scented flesh.

He leaned over me, inhaling deeply and causing a fresh firestorm to go through my body when his eyes blazed brighter than the sun on an August afternoon. His head turned into mine, his nose pressing against my ear as he inhaled again. I was afraid if I moved even a centimeter, I would somehow ruin the moment or break the spell.

Then his fingers released my wrist and slid up my arm. I barely perceived his touch on me, yet my skin felt seared by his caress. His hand cupped my cheek within his palm and lifted my head toward his. My eyes fell to those enticing lips I'd craved to feel against me for so long now. I held my breath as I waited for something, anything.

He remained unmoving, seemingly torn as he stood against me. Just when I was about to yell at him to end my torment, he bent his head and his mouth claimed mine. I'd thought the original wash of power had been jolting, now I nearly screamed as his mouth slid hotly over mine and something surged up between us.

A dim crackling noise barely penetrated the haze of passion consuming me. When his tongue traced against my lips, my knees gave out. His hands on my waist kept me standing when his tongue brushed over my mouth once more. On a sigh, I parted my lips to his.

His tongue slid into my mouth, tasting me in deep, penetrating waves that stoked the fire within me higher. I'd never been kissed with such hunger and reverence before. He branded me with every thrust of his tongue against mine. I couldn't breathe, but it didn't matter as our breath mingled together until I couldn't tell if it was his air or mine I inhaled.

He easily plucked me off the ground. I could sometimes set things on fire and see my opponent's future moves, but when he held me, I felt incredibly small and fragile. I wrapped my arms around his neck and my legs around his waist. Some of the pressure in my chest eased when I rubbed my aching breasts against his solid pecs and broad chest.

The low rumble he emitted vibrated his chest and caused my nails to dig into his nape. The heat of his body and the thrusting motions of his tongue made the wetness between my legs spread. Lifting myself, I slid my aching center back down over the bulge pressing against me. My body bucked in reaction to the delicious sensation the movement caused.

His hands clenched on my waist. "Fuck," he groaned against my lips when he lifted me up and slid me down him again.

Feeling as if I was rapidly spiraling out of control, my tongue slid over his lengthening, bottom two fangs before running over the top two. Like the hard length of him I could feel swelling in his pants, his fangs grew longer the more aroused he became. They didn't scare me as they probably should have; instead, they fascinated me as they grew against my questing tongue.

His grip became almost bruising as his body shuddered. I was so awash in the overwhelming sensation the friction of my body sliding over his caused that I didn't realize he was striding across the earth while carrying me until I heard the flap on the tent pulling back.

Too fast, this is happening too fast. Remember his attitude about sex.

However, my damn traitorous body told that sane, still somewhat logical part of my brain to *shut up*. I had to admit I much preferred my body's instincts on this one. Kobal never broke our kiss when he ducked beneath the flap.

His hands slid under my shirt, burning into my skin when they flattened against the small of my back. I was lost to the sensation of his strong, calloused palms running over my flesh to settle against my ribcage before he lifted me off his waist. My eyes opened to find his startling amber ones burning down at me.

The image of that woman in the cafeteria blazed back across my mind. Had he looked at her like this too? A cry escaped me, but it had nothing to do with the fervor shooting through my system and everything to do with the idea of him with someone else. I jerked my hands away from him and stepped out of his hold.

Now that the contact with him had been broken, reality returned, and reality told me nothing good could ever come of the two of us. I would only end up with a broken heart, and he would end up with different and numerous women sometime in the near future.

"I can't." I took another step away from him.

"River," he growled, coming toward me.

"No, I can't. I'm not enough for you. I can't be. I'm not one of those women at the fire. What you need isn't what I can give you."

I took another step away and held up my hands to ward him off. He wasn't at all deterred by my words or my next step away from him as he took another one toward me. "You can give me exactly what I need."

"Oh, God," I panted and moved further away.

A sardonic smile curved his mouth. "God most certainly isn't here. Something you should be grateful for, considering what I anticipate doing to you. And all of it will be wickedly sinful."

My eyes widened at his words. I wanted to scream at him that I wouldn't be used for sex, that I wouldn't be willing to share him with anyone else, but I bit the words back. I would only be leaving myself vulnerable if I said those words to him.

He would leave if I told him to. He may be a demon, he may be horny and rock hard, but he wouldn't force me. I knew that and I couldn't reveal to him how much I was coming to care for him. Not when he was willing to ease his needs whenever and with *who*ever he could.

He snatched hold of my palms and held them before him. Whatever argument I'd been about to unleash died away when golden-white sparks flickered over the tips of my fingers. The sparks crackled between us, firing like the sparklers I'd played with once as a child, before all Hell literally broke loose.

I'd seen the strange electrical currents dance over my fingers briefly before, but never this vividly or strongly, and I'd never experienced the surge of power that I felt from them now.

He stared at the sparks for a minute before lifting his head to look at me with narrowed eyes. "You didn't tell me you felt the pulse of life," he accused.

CHAPTER TWENTY-SIX

River

"I didn't tell you I felt the what of what?" I stammered, too astonished by those sparks, the twitching muscle in his cheek, and the angry tone of his voice to fully comprehend what he'd said. A spark shot between my index and middle fingers, looking almost like a mini-lightning bolt. My jaw went slack as I watched the small lightning bolt zip all the way through to my pinky finger before fading away. "That's beautiful."

His hands tightened around mine. "You didn't know."

I shook my head, trying to clear it of the awe and confusion before focusing on him again. "Didn't know what?"

"How could you not know you can harvest power from things?"

"What are you talking about?"

"You feel the pulse of life in the things around you."

He kept a firm hold on my hands when I tried to tug them away from him. I gave up fighting to get my hands back, so I could glower at him. "Of course I do, everyone does."

He lifted both of my hands so they were almost dead center between us. "*No* one else on this plane can do this. No one else can harvest from the life forces around them and use it as a weapon. You should have told me. We would have focused on working on this instead of the fire."

I blinked at him and tried one more time to free my hands from his grasp. My teeth grated together when he refused to relinquish them. "Some weapon, it's not getting you off of me!" I retorted. "And I can assure you, I've never turned into a mini-lightbulb before!"

"Of course it's not affecting me; you don't know how to use it. If you did, it would be an entirely different story."

"Then mark it down as number one on my list of things to learn from here on out. Give me my hands back!"

Finally, he released me. When I lifted my hands before my face again, they remained still, no golden-white light leapt from my fingertips. Disappointment filled me as I willed it to come back to me. There had been something so comforting and familiar about it. So *right.* I grabbed Kobal's arm out of curiosity. A single spark leapt to life before fading away.

My fingers dug into his arm, but nothing more came out of me. "I don't understand," I murmured.

I glanced at him, but his face was shuttered and his eyes had returned to their pure black depths. *He's shut himself off from me again,* I realized.

He'd been open to me moments ago in a way he'd never been before. Now that was gone, and I was left with the remorseless demon I was becoming more accustomed to. Straightening my shoulders, I released his arm and tilted my chin up.

"You should have told me," he said again.

"Told you what?" I demanded. "Yes, I feel life around me,

all the time. However, unlike strange visions of who's going to volunteer, or where my brother is hiding, and that one time where I *maybe* could have set the curtains on fire, it's something I assumed everyone felt. And if I suspected they might not feel life all around them like I do, I never mentioned it to anyone because it was something I could keep hidden, something I actually enjoyed! The life flowing around me doesn't hit me out of nowhere; it's a constant soothing presence to me. So how was I supposed to know it wasn't something everyone else experienced and never spoke about? How was I supposed to know *every* human on the planet didn't feel the exact same way as me?"

I wasn't about to tell him I'd had strange little sparks before. He would only assume I really had been keeping this from him on purpose and would never understand I'd written it off as simple static electricity.

"Maybe," he replied in a tone that screamed *liar* at me.

"There is no maybe!"

This time, I was frustrated enough to stomp my foot. It had been a horrible day. I'd met his sort-of ex, had a migraine, stumbled across an orgy, nearly mauled a demon out of lust, and shot sparks from my fingers like a broken robot. All in all, in the list of bad days, it was in the top five, and I'd had enough of it.

"You don't know me! *I* don't know me anymore! Six weeks ago, I was a somewhat odd human, with my brothers to take care of and fish to catch. Now I've been torn from my home, I have no idea what I am, what I'm capable of, how I feel, or if I'll still be alive in another year since you're all determined to drag me to Hell, but no one has ever said anything about me coming back!

"Not to mention, you're telling me Lucifer himself is my ancestor. You're telling me there could be something evil in my genetics, and I'm just supposed to be all *la-di-da* about it because you say there is no such thing as pure good and evil, but he was an angel once and now he's a monster. I'm not supposed to question if I could somehow become twisted and broken in that way too! I don't know what or who I am anymore, but I'm leaning toward the demonic side with the fire throwing thing, and even if demons aren't evil, it terrifies me!"

The tears of frustration and anger burning my eyes only infuriated me further. I wiped them away before folding my arms defensively over my chest. He stared at me as if he didn't know me; it made me want to hit him.

"River—"

"Please leave now."

"We must talk about this."

"We can do it tomorrow. I would like to be alone right now."

I found I couldn't meet his eyes when he ran a hand through his disheveled hair and gave a brief nod. "Fine, but we will be working on trying to harvest this power tomorrow."

"I never had a doubt. It is all about getting me ready after all; it is all about the power."

He'd stayed a couple feet away since I'd become the human equivalent of a lightning rod, but now he stepped so close I had to press my back against the canvas wall to keep from touching him again. His hands rested on either side of my head as he lowered himself until he was eye level with me.

"Let's get this straight between us right now. It's not all about the power. You may be the key to saving both our species and righting the wrongs that have been done. I am going to make sure you are prepared for that, as well as any other threat, but I will do everything I can to make sure you come back *alive*."

My breath froze in my throat as his eyes shifted back to

amber. He lowered one hand and brushed his fingers over my cheek before stepping hastily away. He turned toward the flap dividing my new room from the rest of the tent. I stood, unsettled and uncertain what to do as my gaze fell to the floor.

"River." I lifted my head to look at him standing in the small doorway. "What you just did, what you feel and assumed everyone felt, that's an *entirely* angelic power."

What was I supposed to say to that? I believed he was trying to be comforting, but I couldn't be sure. "Oh."

"If you leave this tent again without me by your side, I'm going to start tying you to the bed at night."

He was enough to give me whiplash as he went from being almost nice to domineering again in the space of a heartbeat. My teeth clamped together and my hands fisted, but no sparks shot from the tips. Oh yes, I'd definitely figure out how to get that little ability to work again, if it was the last thing I did.

I didn't get a chance to respond before he disappeared into the other side. I stared at the flap, still swaying between us, and tried to digest his words. Up until now, he'd said he believed I could be the one, but there had always been at least a little doubt, in him, in me, and I'm certain everyone else in the encampment.

With those sparks, it had vanished. There it was now, a little bit of every species in *me*. I could fling fire like a demon, die and love like a human, and feel the pulse of life like an angel, which somehow turned my fingers into their own Fourth of July celebration when around him.

Exhaustion clung to me as I shuffled over to the bed and pulled back the red blanket and sheets. I'd forgotten the lantern on the hill, but the dim glow of the ones in Kobal's tent filtered around the edges of the flap dividing us. All I wanted was to go to sleep, but I knew I wouldn't.

Not only had this night gone to complete shit, but my body

still throbbed with its need for him. I tried to ignore it, but it was impossible as I curled into a ball beneath sheets smelling far too much like him to give me any relief from him.

Nothing could be worse than this, I decided. I was already in Hell.

CHAPTER TWENTY-SEVEN

Kobal

"Try harder."

If she figured out how to harvest the life around her, I was fairly certain I'd be lying in the middle of the field a hundred feet from here. She couldn't know her fire wouldn't have an effect on me, but if she learned how to turn that pulse of life into a weapon, she'd have me on my ass, and with the look on her face right now, she may keep me there.

"I *am* trying!" she snapped. "Maybe you could show me a better way to do it instead of barking at me to feel the pulse and try harder! I'm not Luke Skywalker; I can't just feel the force like he did."

A stab of jealousy tore through me at the mention of another man. I'd never felt jealousy before, never expected to experience the searing heat tearing through my chest and making my blood boil. My claws extended and if he'd been standing before me, I would have killed him.

"Who is this Luke?" I demanded.

She rolled her eyes. "He was a character in movie I saw once, years ago."

"You humans and your infatuation with fictional characters."

Her eyes narrowed on me. The shadows rimming them made their color a deeper almost midnight purple. "You demons and your dickhead comments."

My eyebrows rose at her statement. She continued to glower at me, looking as exhausted and stressed as I felt. Dirt streaked her cheeks and the tip of her nose. Her black hair, pulled onto the top of her head when we started, now hung against her nape. Strands of it stuck to her flushed forehead and cheeks.

She was sweaty and disheveled, yet blood flooded into my cock at the thought of running my hands over her. I could still feel and taste her on me from last night. Could easily recall the suppleness of her flesh, the fullness of her breasts against my chest. Breasts that would fill my hand as I rubbed and kneaded them before running my tongue over her puckered nipple. I had never craved a woman the way I craved her. Never been so stimulated and frustrated by the inability to be with one before.

I kept telling myself I was this on edge because I hadn't been with a woman since she'd arrived here and had never gone so long without one before. There was no need to deny myself for so long; there had always been plenty of willing women in Hell. There had been men too, but unlike some of the others, my tastes only ran to the women. I enjoyed the feel of them, the sound of them, the way their bodies moved and flowed with such easy grace. Their breasts, their breath, and the softness of their skin. Even in Hell, they had smelled sweeter and been more inviting.

But none so much as her. My fangs, having extended of their own accord, pressed against the inside of my mouth as she walked away from me, her firm ass swaying in the shorts she wore. The curve of her upper thigh had been revealed during her last fall, which had shoved her shorts up her legs.

I'd been keeping away from the fire and the women to make sure she stayed protected, but I couldn't take one more night of relieving myself with my hand while images of *her* ran through my mind.

River had completely thrown me off, but I could end that easily enough tonight by returning to the fire. I'd be able to get her out of my mind after a few hours of rutting on top of one of the other willing humans. Bale could watch over her; she would make sure River stayed safe. I'd far prefer to have River in my bed, but entangling myself deeper with her would only create more problems. I was supposed to be training her, making her stronger, and preparing her for the fight ahead. Not fucking her senseless.

The only problem was, just thinking of trying to screw another woman caused something within me to recoil. My suspicions about what she might be to me grew every day, but there would be no way to know for sure if she was my Chosen or not without being inside of her. If it turned out she wasn't my Chosen, sex would complicate our already complicated relationship.

I'd never had to consider such things before, but I did with her. Even if she wasn't my Chosen, I didn't want her to be hurt, and I would one day claim my throne and return to where I belonged. If she was my Chosen, I still intended for those things to happen. There was a chance she wouldn't be able to live within Hell, and if she could, there was a bigger chance she wouldn't want to.

I had been so close to knowing if she was my Chosen or not last night. If I'd kept kissing her, she wouldn't have had any time to come to her senses. I also wouldn't have noticed the sparks that had brought us to this empty patch of land, away from human and demon eyes alike. For now, I preferred it that no one else knew what she could be capable of.

My cock jumped when she bent over to reveal more of her tantalizing legs to the curve of her round, firm ass. I wiped at my mouth when saliva filled it. *Take her, she's yours!* I thought as I watched her grab a bottle of water from the ground, open it, and greedily gulp down the contents. *Her mouth around me in such a way, sliding up my shaft as her hands— No!*

No matter how badly I wanted her, no matter how badly everything in me screamed she was mine, I could never take her in such a way. I couldn't take her then abandon her. My body recoiled against the idea of leaving her at all. If I took her, I would never let her go, but as a mortal, I could never keep her.

Turn her. I immediately shut the startling impulse down. That couldn't be a possibility, not with my River.

Adjusting my erection, I took a deep breath and slowly regained control of myself enough to resume her training.

"Try again," I said quietly.

She shot a look at me over her shoulder before dropping the bottle and resting her right palm against the trunk of a tree. Her back remained to me as her attention focused on the valley I knew lay beyond this hill. Walking over, I stood beside her to stare down at the ruined town nestled below. The blackened remains of the homes and the giant crater in the middle were all I needed to see to know it had been a victim of the war. Most of the residents probably hadn't survived the devastation unleashed there.

"Have you ever gone down there?" she inquired.

"No."

"Why not?"

"Why would I?" I demanded impatiently. "They're dead, and it's a wasteland. Come, we must practice."

The look she gave me was one of pure exhaustion. Her lids hung heavily over her shadowed eyes; her shoulders were slouched and her face strained. It was good to know I hadn't been the only one tossing and turning for the rest of last night. The only difference was I'd been kept awake with fantasies of her plaguing me and a stiff dick that refused to be eased by my hand. She'd probably been contemplating my murder.

Throwing her shoulders back, her chin jutted out. "It's not getting me anywhere. You have to be able to tell me something that will help me do it."

I ran a hand through my hair, tugging at the ends of it. "I know only the rumors about the ability. Angels are able to harvest energy from other living things and use it against their enemies."

"Well, if they're not fighting you, like popularly believed, then who are they fighting?"

"Each other. Satan didn't throw himself out of Heaven."

"Why are they fighting each other?"

"What else is there to do in Heaven? Hanging out on clouds and playing harpsichords gets tiring for everyone after a century. Just as hanging out in Hell does."

She frowned at me before her gaze slid back to the town. "The demons did a lot of infighting?"

"There was some before Lucifer arrived and turned it into an all-out war. Mostly the lower-level demons would try to launch an uprising that was quickly squashed. Now battling is an everyday part of our existence."

"Why wouldn't God put a stop to the angels fighting?"

"I have no idea. Perhaps God likes a good fight too."

"It all sounds so silly."

"You humans enjoy your battles too. Look at all the wars, fights, and murders of which your species has taken part. It is the way of all of our worlds."

"I suppose," she murmured. "It's all so sad."

"Come." My hand fell on her arm. When my cock jumped again, I realized immediately I never should have touched her. Gritting my teeth against the urge to place her hand on my erection and have her ease from me what I could no longer do on my own, I turned her away from the town. "You must concentrate."

"It would probably help if you told me more than concentrate and focus. What did Lucifer do to get this ability to come to life?"

"I don't know; he was unable to use it once he became more of a demon. It's the only ability he was never able to channel again."

She looked tempted to punch me when her head tilted back to look at me. "You're yelling at me to use a power you've only ever heard about being wielded!" she accused. "And you have no idea if I'll be able to do what you've only *heard* of."

"You can use it."

She slammed her hands on her hips. "And how do you know that?"

"Because you are the strongest, most capable human I've ever met. This ability has been brought forth in you already; it will come forth again."

Her mouth had dropped open when I'd called her strong and capable; now confusion shimmered in her eyes as she stared at me. "I'll try."

"You have to do more than try. We will be leaving in a month."

"A month?" she croaked.

"Yes. They are working now to split off some of the best soldiers, who are willing to go, into a group of about two hundred; from there we will be culling the numbers lower and taking only the best of the best with us."

I had given Bale and Corson the order this morning to start the process, but we had been watching the humans for a long time now and preparing for this moment. It would not take them long to get the soldiers organized.

"You expect me to be ready in a month?" she asked in disbelief.

"I don't expect it; I know you will be. I will not fail you."

She gaped at me before closing her mouth and folding her arms over her chest. "A month," she whispered.

"Other demon camps around the country are doing the same and preparing to go to battle. Many will not survive the journey."

"Do they know they might not survive the journey?" she inquired tremulously.

"They are soldiers. They were informed this mission would have a high mortality rate when they agreed to try for it. They also know this mission may bring an end to what has happened."

"No pressure though," she said with a small smile.

She was so young, so mortal, and she had the weight of the world on her shoulders. My fingers itched to enfold her in my arms and shelter her against my chest. She deserved happiness; I was handing her death.

Before I could stop myself, I placed my hand around her nape and pulled her close to kiss her forehead. Her natural fresh rain and earthy scent assailed me, but I didn't become aroused by it this time. Instead, I found it pacifying the anguish I felt for her. I'd never been one to comfort someone before, yet the gesture felt natural with her.

"No pressure," I said against her silken flesh.

Her eyes looked dazed when I reluctantly released her and took a step back. She couldn't feel anymore dazed than I did right now.

"How many will go with us from here?" she asked.

"Around fifty."

Her eyes shifted in the other direction, and her attention focused on the wall. "I'd hoped to be able to see my brothers again," she murmured before shaking her head. "Pipe dreams."

"As I said before, I'll see what I can do to make it happen."

"Really?"

I had no idea why I'd ever promised her such a thing the first time, and now I'd said it again. It certainly wasn't something that was *ever* done. No one on the other side of the wall could know what was over here. The humans had already panicked enough to release nukes. The truth would drive some of them mad and others to bloodlust.

Small groups of humans at a time, willing to be trained and who were never allowed to see their families again, were all that could be trusted with the knowledge of our existence. I still didn't fully trust those, but at least we could monitor them here and put down any revolts that might form.

"I'm not making any promises, but yes," I said.

"Why?"

I folded my hands behind my back as I pondered her question. I had no answers for her, other than the smile on her face, but I couldn't tell her that. "You have to practice."

She bowed her head and walked away from me. I watched as she knelt down and dug her hands into the thick green grass with her back to me.

"Maybe we should find you something with more of a life force," I suggested.

"The last time I got any kind of reaction is while touching you, and that's not working anymore." I strode over to stand beside her, and her head tilted back so she could look at me. "Besides, the earth is a giant conductor of life. Not to mention all of the insects teeming inside of it. There's *loads* of life beneath my hand right now."

Closing her eyes, she inhaled deeply and turned her face toward the sun. The rays spilling over her illuminated her golden skin and freckles, making her glow with vitality. Clenching my hands, I kept them by my side instead of caressing her cheek like I wanted to do. I couldn't get over the lust and tenderness she stirred in me.

Lifting her left hand, she held it before her and stared at it as if willing it to explode, or at least fire to life. "Traitor," she said to it.

I quirked an eyebrow at the word but refrained from telling her to try harder again. I could feel the disappointment in her eyes, see it in the set of her shoulders. The fingers of her right hand dug deeper into the earth, trying to tap into something I couldn't comprehend.

Much like her.

CHAPTER TWENTY-EIGHT

Kobal

"You've become more of a watchdog than your hounds." Bale tossed back her flame-red hair as she stepped beside me.

"Of course I am," I grated through my teeth. "She must be protected."

Bale's mouth pursed as her eyes ran over me before she lifted one slender shoulder in a delicate shrug. "I know that, but we are all capable of protecting her. You must take a break once in a while."

I knew they were all almost as capable as I was, but I was the strongest of them, their leader. I had helped to train them for battle; I trusted any one of them with my life. Then why didn't I trust any of them with River's? No, I trusted them with her; I just didn't like the idea of not being there to see her.

She had managed to slip out on me last night after all. She would definitely get past one of them if she chose to do so.

"Are you screwing her?" Bale inquired.

"No, she's vital to the mission."

Bale snorted. "So, you haven't tried then?"

I didn't bother to respond to her as I focused on the mass of humans swarming to get into line. I refused to leave River alone in this mess after the way they'd started to treat her. A frightened human was a dangerous thing, and they were definitely afraid of her. They were also jealous of her. It was a combination I worried would get her hurt.

Not to mention, I saw the way some of the men still watched her. Despite their fear of her, she was alluring and they would bed her if given the chance. I may not be able to have her, but I'd kill any one of them before I allowed them to take her.

"I thought so," Bale continued. "It's in our nature. We take what we want, but for once, deny yourself. Humans tend to put more value into sex than we do. It will only cause complications if you get mixed up with her."

"It is none of your concern, and we will *not* be discussing it."

She lifted an eyebrow and her jaw clenched, but she didn't say another word. It was rare I didn't want to hear what she or Corson had to say, but I would not discuss River with either of them right now.

River emerged from the crowd. She didn't bother to glance at the tables around her. She kept her head held high as she wound through the people who hastily stepped away from her. Her step hesitated when she spotted us and her brow furrowed, but she continued forward.

"What are you doing here?" she demanded when she stopped before me.

"Hello to you too," I greeted dryly while Bale grinned annoyingly.

River glanced between the two of us before brushing by me to walk out the door. I turned to follow her, glowering at any man who turned to watch her passing. A young solider blanched and turned quickly away when my lips skimmed back and I bared my teeth at him.

"What are you doing?" she hissed.

"Making sure you stay safe," I replied.

She shot me a look over her shoulder. "I don't need a guard dog, and part of the reason they don't like me is because of what they consider your excessive attention to me."

"And the fire shooting from your hands," Bale pointed out. "They didn't really like that much either."

"And the fire," River agreed with a roll of her eyes.

She walked over to a large tree and settled beneath it. Her back rested against the trunk as she unwrapped her sandwich. I found myself fascinated by the mundane movements she somehow managed to pull off with an easy grace most of her species lacked.

Is she more demon or angel?

She seemed to be such a perfect combination of the two species that I didn't know which part could be stronger. Add in her humanity, which was something both demons and angels sorely lacked, and she was an enchanting combination I found irresistible. The angels were nearly as ruthless as we were from what I'd been told. They simply treated souls better than we did, but then they didn't get the souls we received either. I'm sure they would have been more than happy to make Stalin's eternity as excruciating as we had.

Are we simply the same as the angels, in different locations, and different surroundings?

The concept had never occurred to me before, but perhaps it was true. Neither side coveted what the other had. I couldn't care less about ever seeing the fluffy clouds of Heaven, if there were clouds up there, just as I was sure they wouldn't give a shit about the fiery pits that had given birth to me.

Though I was sure the new situation the humans had

thrust upon Hell and Earth had all the angels in a fit. The planes had been upended, and the existence of all our species hung in the balance after all. If we lost, the balance would be forever altered, the flow of souls changed. Demons and angels alike would die as angels thrived on the purity of a soul as much as we thrived on its impurity. The flow had to remain consistent to sustain us all. We needed the human race.

How our fates became hinged on the shoulders of the dumbest and greediest of all our species was beyond me, but it was.

I stared at River as she ate her sandwich and watched the sunset over my shoulder. No, our species could hinge on *her*. And I believed she was someone who could do anything she set her mind to. I believed she was capable of far more than she realized.

One thing was for sure, no matter what she feared, she was nothing like her father. She never could be. I could sense the purity of her soul, the warmth she radiated from her. Lucifer was none of those things. I couldn't imagine going back to a life without her. The prospect was so barren and bleak that for the first time in my life, I actually felt hollow inside.

Turning, I glanced at Bale who was watching us both from under her bright red lashes. Her gaze slid from River to me and back again. "Will I see you tonight?" Bale asked me.

River froze with her apple halfway to her mouth. "Perhaps," I replied.

Bale bowed her head before turning and walking away. River bit into her apple before focusing on the sunset again. She didn't speak, but a line marred her forehead.

"We'll work on having you draw on the pulse of life again tomorrow," I told her as I settled beside her on the grass.

"I had no doubt," she muttered. "But if you don't know how to bring it out and neither do I, it could prove to be useless."

"We'll return to your regular training tomorrow too, just in case, and we'll add this in at another time."

Her eyes flashed when they slid to me. "Where will we add it in?"

"In the morning, before you eat."

"Who needs sleep?"

Sensing she didn't expect an answer to her question, I didn't respond. I stared down at her hand in the grass; it was so much smaller than mine and tanned a golden hue on the back with the delicate bones visible. I could easily recall the feel of them when they had run over my shoulders and back.

I'd never be able to forget the vision of those beautiful sparks shooting from them, illuminating her eyes with an inner glow. I'd been nearly certain she was Lucifer's daughter before then, but I hadn't expected this depth of power from her. Nor had I expected the gut reaction I'd had to the beauty of those sparks and the look of joy that had suffused her face.

I wanted that light, even if it could blast me onto my ass and possibly kill me, if she ever learned to use it well.

Placing my hand on the ground to push myself to my feet, my fingers brushed over hers. A single spark shot from her, seeking me out. It had always been rumored the life force was the most lethal weapon an angel had, but I felt no pain from it as warmth flashed over my hand and through me.

I looked at her, but she was so focused on the sunset she hadn't noticed the small spark between us. Rising to my feet, I walked away from her and toward the hill overlooking the wall and town below as I tried to gather my scattered thoughts.

I couldn't have her, but I couldn't stay away from her either. A return to the fire tonight was exactly what I needed to get my mind off of her.

CHAPTER TWENTY-NINE

River

My eyes fluttered open before closing again. Grabbing my pillow, I dragged it over my head and rolled to the side to try to block out the noise. After barely getting any sleep last night, and the demanding day of dealing with Kobal and his endless training, I'd passed out as soon as my head hit the pillow, and now he was doing something over there...

What is *he doing?*

I lifted the corner of the pillow off my ear to hear what was going on. Was that a moan? No, it was definitely a groan, maybe? I buried my head under my pillow again, determined not to care what was going on over there, but I found myself pulling the pillow back again.

I had never heard anything from the main part of the tent before at night. My hands clamped around the pillow as something clattered against the table. I listened to it rolling across the solid surface before the sound ended abruptly. It must have fallen off, or maybe he'd caught whatever it was. It had sounded like one of his goblets. Was he over there getting drunk?

Fan-freaking-tastic, I'd have a hungover, dissatisfied demon to deal with tomorrow. Could things get any worse?

They could, I knew they could, but I still didn't want to have to deal with it. Something knocked against something else. With a sigh, I threw the sheets and blanket aside and sat up on the edge of the bed. I didn't know what I was thinking, the last thing I needed to contend with was a drunken demon, but I would never get back to sleep with him staggering around over there doing whatever he was doing.

Rising to my feet, I walked over to the flap, pulled the buttons apart, and stepped into the main tent. At first I didn't see him as my eyes immediately went to the lantern burning on the table beside the large cot he'd set up in the tent. Then a flash of motion to my right caught my attention. I took a step forward and froze when I spotted him.

He sat in one of the chairs, his chest bare and his head thrown back. The look of rapture on his face robbed me of my breath. His long legs were bared and a deeply tanned hue that had not been acquired from the depths of Hell but more the fires themselves had bronzed his skin. His feet were planted into the ground, his knees bent.

The muscles of his neck stood out starkly as he emitted a guttural sound that made my pulse skyrocket. The tattoos running over his arms and shoulders appeared to come to life in the flickering lanterns. I swore the fangs of the hounds glimmered in the light playing over him. For the first time, I was able to see all of those markings on his front as more flames circled around his rock hard pecs but didn't move beyond them.

I was so fixated on seeing him so bared to me, and entrenched in the throes of ecstasy, that it took me a minute to notice the woman in his lap. I don't know how I hadn't immediately seen her; she simply hadn't existed when his stark beauty held me so completely captivated.

Now, the curve of her bare back, the spill of her dark hair cascading over her and him was all I could see. Unreasonable hurt filled me; my hand flew to my mouth to stifle the startled cry rushing up my throat at the sight of the naked woman rising and falling in his lap. She rode him with abandon and clearly enjoyed it if her cries and the increasing pace of her body were any indication. His hands ran down to grasp her ass to guide her movements.

I took a staggering step back. I never should have come here. I never should have been witness to this, but no matter how badly I wanted to flee, I found myself still standing there as my shock steadily built toward anger. Only last night he'd been holding me in an intimate way, his tongue and hands had been caressing me. Except I hadn't gotten the chance to feel all of his bare flesh against mine like this woman was, to experience the pleasure he could give me.

And now I never would. I was nothing special to him as a part of me had almost started to believe. I was the mission, the goal. The one to use and protect. No matter what happened, I wouldn't allow myself to ever be used in this way by him. *Ever.*

All I wanted was to get as far from him as possible, but I was stuck with him, my life tied to his in this hideous way until all of this was over. I knew he would never hand my care over to another demon, knew he wouldn't release me until he'd gotten what he sought from me. I took another step back as I struggled not to release the tears burning my eyes or the scream of rage burning my throat.

"Kobal," the woman panted in a husky voice resonating with sensuality.

Stretching out my hand, I went to grab the flap in order to get away, but my eyes were drawn inexplicably to him once more. His mouth was against the woman's shoulder now; his eyes open and blazing that enthralling amber color. My breath caught when I found him watching me with a look of astonishment and hunger.

I'd been caught creeping *again.* Instead of fleeing as any sane, somewhat human would do, I remained frozen, unable to make a single move. Those eyes continued to hold mine as his lips skimmed back to reveal his glistening fangs. The sight of those lengthening fangs caused warmth to spread between my legs.

His gaze never left mine as he raked them against the sensitive flesh of the woman's neck. She cried out; her hands clasped more desperately at his shoulders, drawing him closer as his tongue swirled out to lick over her skin. I swore I felt his breath and tongue against my own shoulder as he tasted her flesh.

My breasts tingled, my nipples puckered. He seemed to know this as his eyes fastened on my chest in such a way that my thighs trembled.

How could he be staring at me with such desire while he was inside of *her*? What was I still doing in here? Why hadn't I fled? How could I be standing here watching him with another woman, while *he* watched *me*?

Was I stuck in freaking quicksand? I wondered as my feet remained frozen to the ground.

The sheen of sweat on his body caused my tongue to lick over my lips with the urge to taste him. I'd lost my mind, I decided right then and there. He was having sex with another woman and I found myself longing for it to be *me*.

I finally managed to take a step back.

"Do you like this?" His words froze me before I could bolt out of here faster than a rabbit from a coyote.

His hands slid higher on the woman's back when she panted, "Yes."

He turned his head into her hair and, still holding my eyes, said into her ear, "Then come for me."

My body reacted as if he'd said this to me. Unable to bite it back, a moan escaped me when he sank his fangs into her shoulder, something I would have believed excruciating, but the woman threw her head back and cried out in ecstasy.

I took another step back, torn between unanswered yearning and wanting to scream over my irrational reaction to him. A sane woman would have stormed out of here as soon as she'd entered.

She most certainly wouldn't be watching him as he lowered his mouth to take one of the woman's nipples into his mouth, nipping at it in such a way that the woman bucked and screamed as her fingers tore scratches into his shoulders. My need grew deeper as she marked him in this way, and I scented his blood on the air.

He lifted his head from her breast and, for the first time since he'd noticed me standing there, he looked away from me to focus on the woman. I tried not to, but I found myself helplessly following his gaze. My eyes landed on the woman as she arched against him and threw her head back again.

The world lurched out from under me as I gazed at her face while I started questioning my sanity all over again. I was looking at my *own* face. I couldn't move while I watched her... me... her...

I couldn't figure it out as the room spun around me. On wobbly legs, I took a step to the side and placed my hand against the thick canvas of the tent.

Movement drew my attention back to him. She... me... whoever had vanished and now it was only the two of us. His amber eyes burned into mine when he leaned forward and clasped his hands between his legs.

"Welcome to my dreams, River," he murmured.

~

River

I jolted awake. My heart beat so forcefully, I could hear each pulse of it in my eardrums and feel it bashing against my ribs. I remained frozen, unable to move as the dream replayed over in my head. Not a dream, at least not *mine*.

Sliding up in the bed to lean against the headboard, I pressed my hand against my mouth when the movement caused the sheets to rub against me. Cloth that had felt so soft and inviting when I'd first crawled into this bed now felt abrasive against my hypersensitive skin.

I was *aching*; it was the only word I could think of to describe what I felt. I ached everywhere, for *him*. My hand skimmed over my breasts and a whimper sounded in my throat, but as the need of my body increased, I knew my hand wasn't enough. It couldn't be, not anymore, not without him.

He was dreaming of *me* and somehow the dream had been strong enough for me to latch onto him, just as I'd dragged him into my vision that day on the hill. Maybe I'd opened a connection between us that day and it was still open. It didn't matter; I'd seen his dream, knew what he wanted, and I wanted it too, *so* badly.

My gaze fell on the flap dividing us. I could feel him over there, waiting. If my hand so much as fell on those buttons, he would be in here in a heartbeat, kissing me, on me, *in* me. Another whimper slid through me.

Go, a voice in me advised, but the small sliver of sanity still within me kept me on the bed, my hand resting on my lower belly. My body throbbed for release, but I held back. Before it had always been enjoyable to bring myself to orgasm, but I knew it wouldn't be enough anymore. I would never get any real release from this torment if it didn't involve him.

A sound, half moan and half sob came from me. I kept my hand flat against my stomach as I stared at the flap. He wouldn't come to me, not after last night; he would wait to see what I would do.

I lay there until the sun came up, staring at the flap, knowing that the same need wracking through me was also keeping him awake.

CHAPTER THIRTY

River

Over the next week, I became personally familiar with, and increasingly resentful of, the term sexual frustration. The only one more short-tempered than me, was Kobal. Every day we would wake up and go to the field to try to draw some sparks from me, and fail. Then we would go about our regular training. He would demand I try harder; I'd tell him to stuff it, often with the middle finger included. We would snipe at each other in ways we never had before.

Then we would go to sleep, and he would dream, and no matter how much I tried to resist it, I always found myself irresistibly lured forward to watch.

Because of those dreams, I now knew the tattoos encircling his pecs had an identical circular pattern on his back and both sides were a continuation of the patterns on his arms.

The things he did to me in those dreams left me quivering and desperate for more every time I woke from them. I hadn't known some of those things could be done until he showed them to me, and he showed me with an enthusiasm that made me think some of them were done to shock me, and they did, but they also left me wishing it actually was me he was doing them to and not dream me.

Last night, he'd held my gaze while taking dream me—as I now referred to her—against the table. Dream me's elbows had rested on the table as she lifted her hips to him while he stood behind her. Eager cries had resonated from dream me as he'd driven in and out of her before pulling away.

The cry of disappointment she released when he stepped away from her echoed inside of me. Lifting her up, he'd placed her on the table and leaned closer to whisper in her ear that he wanted to watch her make herself come. Though his words shouldn't have carried beyond her, I heard them as clearly as if they'd been whispered in my own ear. I tore my gaze away, unsettled by his words.

"Watch, it's more pleasurable that way," he commanded gruffly.

Since that first night, he'd never directly spoken to me again, only watching me while I watched us, but I somehow knew those words were meant for me. I found I couldn't refuse him as my head turned back toward the two of them. I watched as dream me's hands slid over her body in a way that no longer satisfied me. Her face relaxed as she kneaded her breasts and her hand slid between her thighs to delve inside herself.

"Do you like it?" he inquired, focused on me.

"Oh yes," dream me replied.

"As much as you enjoy me inside of you?"

"Never."

My eyes narrowed on him. I didn't know how he knew, but I became certain he was well aware I lay awake every night after this, yearning to be touched, desperate for release, yet finding none.

I'd awoken from the dream after.

Now, I stood on the training field with all of the humans who avoided me as if I not only had the plague, but also as if I stunk like I had been rolling around in garbage. Admittedly, I didn't smell great. I was dirty and sweaty, yet I didn't smell any worse than any of them.

I was a lot angrier than everyone else, testy as I battered at the straw dummy before me with a katana. All of the finesse moves I'd learned were gone out the window as I hacked the straw man into pieces so thin a mouse wouldn't use them for a nest. Wrapping both hands around the handle, I lunged forward, driving the blade through the straw man's heart, all the way to the hilt.

Someone chuckled from nearby. Bale stepped forward and pulled the katana free. "Not much in the way of skill, but it got the job done."

"That's what I do," I muttered and wiped away the trickling sweat streaking down my face.

I was doing better than the other humans in the sweltering July sun; many had to take breaks to avoid heatstroke and a few had been admitted to the infirmary with it, but I rarely took a break. The heat was not helping my temper though.

I hated the surveying look in Bale's striking, lime-colored eyes. I found myself scowling back at the demon who could probably rip my head off as a party trick. She smiled back at me. "Let anger fuel a battle, but don't let it rule you in one."

She handed the katana back to me and walked away with a sway of her hips that had the men nearby leaning back to watch her go. I envied her the ability to be so free with her sexuality, and if I didn't believe my heart would become entangled in the whole mess, I would have jumped Kobal by now, consequences be damned.

However, I couldn't put a Band-Aid on a broken heart. Not to mention the kick in the nuts my pride would take when he turned to another soon after. That would always make for a great first time experience—me wanting more of him, and him sleeping with another woman the next day.

I sliced the head off the straw man and kicked it across the ground. Humans jumped out of the way and glared at me. I glared back at them. I wasn't in the mood for their shit today, or anyone else's, especially not the giant mountain of a douche canoe who stepped forward to stand across from me. He glowered at me as intensely as I glowered at him.

The straw man's head settled against his feet, appropriate as far as I was concerned. If he told me one more time I wasn't concentrating enough during our special training time, I was going to make it impossible for him to even dream about having a hard-on.

"All right, everyone, let's get back to work on some hand-to-hand combat!" Mac shouted from the top of the hill.

I smiled at Kobal as I drove the katana into the straw man's groin. A few of the closest humans winced and scurried to get away from me. He simply lifted an eyebrow and maintained a bored expression that made my fingers curve with the urge to claw his eyes out of his head. That seemed like a more demonic instinct to me, or perhaps it was entirely *human*.

Kobal stepped forward to be my sparring partner, again. My skin came alive; I wanted to touch him, but at the same time, I dreaded having to touch him. The confusing impulses only made it all worse.

He feigned a punch at my head; I ducked back and blocked at the same time. Something went through his eyes when he launched another jab at me that I dodged. As he moved closer against me, I could feel the heat of his body as his jabs and swats came at me faster than they normally did, but I still fended him off, barely.

"Dick," I hissed through my teeth when his speed picked up more.

"From what I've seen, you crave mine," he said so low I knew no one else heard him.

I certainly hadn't been expecting *that* from him. Excitement and resentment shot through me in equal measure. We'd never mentioned the dreams to each other; they'd remained this unspoken thing festering between us. We were both acutely aware of them, but neither of us knew how to deal with them.

Now, I felt an unraveling, a push and shove against the imaginary line we'd divided between us. He was looking to cross that line, to see how far he could push me before the line broke, and I was more than ready to push back. I'd had enough of this hideous standstill myself.

The only problem was, I didn't know how I wanted it to end. My pride continued to war with my body. He was a demon, and I'd never be enough for him, never satisfy him, and I could *never* allow myself to be one of the many.

My mother had always been one of the many. I'd sworn my entire life I'd never be like her. I'd never let a man use me and toss me aside as she had over and over again through the years. She'd never stood up for herself. It would have been one thing if she'd been the one to decide the course of her relationships, but she'd always been the doormat for the new guy passing through our lives.

I wouldn't be anyone's doormat, not even a fifteen-hundred-year-old demon with the body of a Greek god and the personality of a crocodile. My hands moved faster as his jabs and swipes sped up. My breathing and his filled my ears as the world slid away and my vision became centered on him.

My body jerked as once again his moves unfolded in my mind before they came. This time, I didn't block and dodge, but jabbed and punched myself. He jumped back, his stomach sucking in as he barely managed to avoid a roundhouse kick I swung at him. I leapt off the ground, knowing what was coming next before he released a kick that would have otherwise taken me off my feet.

I landed again and went at him in a one-two combo that had him dodging back before coming at me again. Knowing what was coming was barely enough to keep me ahead of him as exhaustion beat at me, but I refused to throw in the towel as he relentlessly pushed me backward.

My footing remained sure as we moved, not because I knew where I was going, but because I could see the path behind me through *his* eyes. All I saw was him and his punches before they came at me. All I heard were his breaths and grunts of exertion. His flesh was smooth beneath my hands, the muscles etched as they flexed and bunched.

I stepped to the side to avoid the large maple he'd been intentionally steering me toward in the hope of trapping me. The slap of our flesh against each other filled the air as we continued steadily across the field. I lost ground to him, but he didn't take me down.

The battle didn't relent as we headed toward the burnt out homes of the abandoned town beyond the training fields near where we practiced in the morning. We'd traveled almost two miles.

My legs wobbled and sweat stuck my clothes to me and slid down my face. He showed no sign of exhaustion or slowing as he continued to come at me. Down over the hill, we moved across the blackened grass and into the burnt out village of the damned as I'd come to think of it. My back stayed to the few houses that remained standing in the way, but through his eyes I was able to avoid walking into one of them.

He leapt to the side when I kicked out at him, my foot grazing his testicles. His head snapped toward me, his nostrils flared, but something had changed in him when he came at me again. Before he'd been trying to prove a point, to exert his dominance and bend me to his will. Now, I felt something sexual in the hands brushing over my flesh, sensed excitement building in his thrumming body.

I'd assumed nearly kicking him in the nuts would have incensed him; instead, it had brought everything to a whole new level. My own body reacted to it, and I edged closer even as I threw more punches and kicks his way. I thrilled in the feel of his hands against mine and relished the fiery scent of him filling my nostrils as my hands brushed over his sweat-slickened body.

He grunted when I finally managed to land a solid punch into his stomach. I dodged the sweeping kick he threw at me next. However, exhaustion made it almost impossible for me to avoid his following jab. I twisted to the side, but it still landed on my shoulder, knocking me back.

I'd anticipated darting to the side in order to avoid the wall of a charred house behind me. I managed to turn awkwardly in an attempt to do so, but before I could get completely out of his way, his hands crashed against the wall beside my head. The wall trembled behind me; dust and soot fell on my shoulders from the holes he'd punched through it.

He pinned me between his body and the crumbling remains of the building. His shoulders blocked out the sun behind him as he towered over me. My breath heaved in and out as I tried to catch it; every inhalation caused my breasts to brush against his solid chest. I half expected him to move away from me, yet he stepped closer.

My fingers curved into the wall behind me as I fought against grabbing him. There was a savage look on his face that had me desperate to feel more of him. His knee bent forward so it brushed against the outside of my right thigh in another move to keep me against the wall, but I found I didn't care as long as he stayed there with me. The black of his eyes faded away to become molten gold once more. The beauty and wildness within those eyes caused my breath to catch when they blazed down at me.

The change of color was more a sign of his passion than the rigid evidence of his arousal against my thigh. His own chest heaved with his breaths, rubbing enticingly over my taut nipples as they strained against my shirt. A small sound, partially of desire and partially a plea to put me out of my misery either by kissing me again or walking away, slipped past my lips.

Please don't walk away.

He didn't do either of those things. His head bowed closer until I could feel his breath tickling over my face. Goose bumps erupted over my flesh when his lips brushed my ear while he spoke.

"Real life will be *far* better than any dream, River. I promise you, I'll make you come harder than you ever have before."

His ragged voice and the confidence of those words caused me to inhale sharply. My teeth bit my bottom lip, drawing his attention to it. A sound of hunger reverberated through him, and my breaths came more rapidly, driving my breasts more firmly against the unrelenting flesh of his chiseled chest.

I didn't have a chance to respond before his hands fell to his sides. He gave me a look full of promise and turned away from me. He froze when he spotted the large crowd who had followed our battle since the start. His upper lip curved into a sneer at everyone gawking at us.

The demons stood at the front of the large group filling the burnt-out town. Their expressions were a mixture of amusement and intrigue. Our fight must have gathered soldiers from the town too, as the number of people around us was nearly triple that of the volunteers who had been on the hill training with me.

Most of them were slacked-jaw, some looked irritated by what they'd witnessed, and a few were staring at me as if I were the lowest life form in existence. I noticed those stares were mostly from the women, but there were a couple of men staring at me as if I repulsed them too.

Apparently, some people didn't approve of interspecies relations, even if there weren't any relations between us. *Yet*, I had to admit to myself. *Weakling*, I scolded afterward.

Turning back, Kobal took hold of my elbow and propelled me forward. I tried to pull my arm from his grasp, but he only clamped his hand more firmly around it. "It's better if they know you're under my protection."

"I can protect myself," I finally managed to protest as my exhausted legs strove to keep up with his lengthy strides.

His eyes had returned to black when they latched onto me. "You're *mine* to protect now."

"I'm not *any*one's. I am not a possession. I'm a person, sort of, and I'm not here for you to order about or for them to judge!"

The arrogant oaf didn't bother to respond as he continued unrelentingly through the wasteland of the town surrounding us. I tried jerking my arm away from him again, but he held on. I could feel my blood pressure rising as my temples pounded with the beats of my heart.

In an instant, he faded away and all I saw were the burned out homes and landscape surrounding us. The blackened trees still standing amid the rubble stretched into the cloudless sky. A single crow sat on the branches of the only other living thing, a large maple tree near the edge of town. Some green grass peaked through the rubble here and there, but most of it was buried beneath the remaining wreckage of the leveled town.

After thirteen years, the smell of fire and death still permeated the area. Layers of blackened walls from the homes were stacked where they had fallen on the ground. Charred beams rose into the sky, and more than a handful of brick chimneys still stood as testament to the homes and people who had once loved, laughed, and died here.

Died. The breeze blowing over my skin dried the sweat on it and sent a shiver down my spine. Death, so much of it here and somehow I knew there was more coming.

Then I saw the eyes, or not eyes, as there was nothing within the shrunken, weathered eye sockets facing me from underneath the remains of a roof. Even if there was nothing left to stare from, I could feel its gaze on me. Around those empty eye sockets was a glistening rim of white bone. Shrunken and discolored skin stuck to its skull.

A hand slid out, the skin of it was grayed and flaking with decay. Bones poked out from the ends of its fingers. No clothing covered its withered chest and arms as it pulled itself from beneath the roof. My throat went dry as a strange combination of mummy and skeleton emerged from the wreckage.

It looked like it would fall apart at the same time fresh, slimy flesh adhered to its bony remains in some areas. It dragged its right foot behind it on the ground; the bones of its knees were clearly visible but green clumps of skin clung to its broken foot. The clumps fell off the creature as it moved forward. It may not have any lips, but I was certain it was smiling at me as its teeth chattered together.

So focused on that one, I didn't see the others until more hands slid out from beneath other toppled homes.

"River. *River.*"

The abrupt tug on my arm caused me to blink. I shook my head to clear it of the images still filling my vision.

"*River.*"

I looked up at Kobal. He gazed at me with concern; the fine lines around his eyes and mouth were more visible as he stared at me. I had no idea why I hadn't pulled him into this vision with me, maybe because I was so tired, but he hadn't witnessed the insanity I had. What I'd seen simply couldn't be true. Bones didn't come to life and drag themselves from rubble.

And demons didn't exist either.

"What did you see?" he demanded.

"Death," I answered as the gleaming eye sockets of the first one emerged from beneath the house. "Death is here."

CHAPTER THIRTY-ONE

Kobal

River's feet planted so firmly into the ground I almost lost my grip on her arm when she abruptly stopped walking. Turning toward her, I was prepared for whatever tirade she was about to unleash on me. Instead, I found her eyes glazed over. They had become the pale violet color they turned when she was in the grip of something beyond this world. They'd been the same way when we'd been fighting, but the color had flooded back into them as soon as she'd hit the wall of the house.

I pulled on her arm, hating the terror growing in her eyes and that she became so vulnerable when these visions took her over. I tugged on her arm again, stepping closer in the hopes of pulling her free from whatever held her.

"River." She finally blinked, and her eyes returned to their normal amethyst hue when she came back to this world and herself. "What did you see?"

"Death. Death is here."

My head shot up as I surveyed the horizon in search of

more madagans or some other new threat. I saw nothing, but she'd seen something, and it was coming.

"Let's go," I commanded brusquely.

"It's too late; they're already here."

I instinctively pulled her closer to me, determined to protect her from whatever she had seen. I didn't care what happened to the humans surrounding us, *nothing* was going to harm her. My fangs lengthened, and my fingers curled into her arm as the possessive instinct hit me with far more force than it ever had before.

Mine! This time there was no brushing off the thought, no denying the strength with which it rocked me. My gaze fell to her shoulder, the one I'd often sank my fangs into in our shared dreams. I'd never marked a woman in such a way, never had the compulsion before, but I would mark her. I would claim her because she was *mine*, and now something was after her.

"Where?" I demanded.

Her hand pointed past me as something slithered free from the remains of a downed house. "Shit!" I hissed from between my teeth when the revenir rose to its feet and shuffled toward us.

Grabbing hold of her arms, I lifted her up and thrust her behind me. I steadied her when she wobbled for a second. "You stay behind me!" I commanded her.

"I'm supposed to fight these things, aren't I?" she protested.

She was, but everything in me screamed against her going anywhere near abominations such as these. I knew what their presence here meant, but that was something I was going to have to deal with later. Right now, all that mattered was keeping River alive.

"Stay behind me!" Her chin tilted up at my harsh command, but I turned away from her before she could protest. "Revenirs!" I bellowed at the others.

Bale and Verin did a double take before leaping forward. The others moved toward the approaching revenir as my eyes scanned the large group of humans who had followed us here. Half of them had been on the training field and didn't have guns; the other half had followed from the town and had weapons slung over their shoulders. I didn't know if bullets would do anything against the revenirs. We were about to find out.

"Get your guns ready!" I shouted at the humans still unaware of the danger. "Mac, get them ready! And cover your ears!"

I turned toward River to make sure she was still behind me when an ear-piercing shriek rent the air. The humans recoiled; they screamed as they slapped their hands over their ears. A few of them hit their knees as the relentless shriek continued. I winced against the noise, but having heard it before, I was prepared for the revenirs' cry.

River's hands already covered her ears and I enclosed mine over hers for extra protection before pulling her against my chest. Her body quaked as the lenses of the glasses on three of the soldiers near us shattered. The humans' screams couldn't be heard over the continuous shriek of the dead rising around us.

More humans fell to their knees; River's nose scrunched up, and her eyes squinted closed. I would have given anything to take her away from this, to keep her from hearing it, but I couldn't get her away from here in time and these things would only follow us. Now that they knew there was life nearby, they would be ruthless in their pursuit to feed from it.

I would rend every one of these walking sacks of bone limb from limb for causing her this pain.

Then, as suddenly as it had started, the revenirs' scream

broke off. The shriek had done what it was intended to do, distracted their prey and left them weaker.

River blinked up at me when I released her hands. "Whatever you do, don't let them kiss you." I commanded. "River, do you hear me?"

"Yes, yes," she managed to stammer out then winced at the sound of her own voice.

"None of you let them kiss you!" I shouted to be heard over the sobs and mewls from the humans surrounding us.

"That's not something you had to tell me," a man with an AK-47 muttered.

I spun to face the horde now coming at us as revenirs rose from beneath the remains of the homes. Around me, Bale, Verin, Morax, Shax, and Corson fanned out. Bale pulled two swords free from where she had them sheathed against her back.

"You know the best way to deal with them," Corson said from beside me.

"I do." The problem was there were some secrets I preferred to keep from the humans. They couldn't know all that we were capable of, and if River had scared them with her burst of fire, I'd have them pissing themselves. "Keep yourself leashed unless it becomes necessary."

"And you?"

I glanced back at River. With her hair stuck to her face and her eyes wide, she looked young and vulnerable. There wasn't anything I wouldn't do to keep her safe. She had nothing other than her hands and her fire with which to defend herself. The fire would be her best option against the revenirs, but there was no way to know how long she would be able to use it. Her shoulders continued to heave as she struggled to catch her breath. I never should have pushed her so far when we'd been fighting.

I never could have expected revenirs to arrive in this world though. The first seal of Hell had been broken. The dead now walked the earth.

River's violet eyes were searching as more and more revenirs poured from beneath the homes, pushing the humans closer against us as they tried to avoid the dead.

"I'll do what has to be done," I told Corson.

His orange eyes flicked toward River. "I hate these fuckers."

"So do I." I focused on River once more. "Fire is your best weapon against them."

She didn't get a chance to respond before the revenirs rushed forward as quickly as their hideously rotten bodies would allow them to. A low squeal of excitement emanated from them as one; the squeal rose toward their ear-splitting pitch once more.

Before they could reach their full, paralyzing screech, I shouted, "Fire your weapons!"

Bullets exploded from the guns, shredding through the remaining skin and bones of the revenirs. Some of them jerked and lurched from the impact of the bullets, others toppled to the ground like broken sticks. The ones hitting the ground continued onward, dragging themselves forward with their bony, malformed hands. Bullets pierced through skulls, shattering them and finally ceasing the movements of some.

On the other side of the close circle, humans fell back, toppling beneath the weight of the revenirs clawing at their bodies. The shrieks had ceased now that they were so focused on achieving their meal.

One of them leapt at me, its mouth open and its bony fingers hooked into claws. My hand shot out, and I seized hold of its throat and snapped its head from its neck with a thrust of my thumb against the bottom of its chin. Releasing it, I stomped on its skull before turning to grab hold of two more charging forward.

They had no eyes, but I knew their attention focused on River when their cries of excitement increased. My stomach did an odd somersault when I realized they had recognized what she was. Either they sensed in her something I hadn't, or they believed Lucifer's offspring would be the only one I'd defend to the death, but even if she hadn't been the possible key, I would have laid down my life in order to protect hers.

Lucifer may have sent them in search of her, and if any of these revenirs managed to get away, they would report to him where she was.

"None of them can be allowed to survive. Kill them all!" I bellowed.

Bale and Corson carved through the ones leaping at them with swords, while the other demons beat and pummeled the revenirs into a pulp.

CHAPTER THIRTY-TWO

River

Kobal kept his body in front of me, moving with the lethal speed I'd seen when the madagans had attacked us. His eyes blazed with their golden fire as he tore the head off one of the oozing skeletons leaping and rushing at us. My head spun as I tried to take it all in while still trying to rid myself of the lingering pain their hideous screaming had caused to explode in my head and ears.

My bones felt like they were quaking as gunshots continued to pelt the malformed, twisted bodies of those things coming at us. Screams resonated from the humans falling beneath the onslaught of the dead.

I kept my hands up in a defensive position, but I felt my muscles go slack when one of those things pounced on the chest of a man ten feet away from me. Its mouth opened as it pushed the man further into the ground. Its head twisted to the side as it pressed its rotten, scaly lips against the man's mouth.

People ran back and forth between me and the man, but I couldn't tear my gaze away as I helplessly watched the man's hands beat against the creature's chest, shoving at its bony shoulders. His feet kicked against the ground, but no sounds came from him as the hideous creature continued its macabre kiss. The man's flesh shriveled as the life drained from his body and into the monster on his chest. I had to help, but it all happened so fast that I only made it one step toward them.

The mummified skin of the revenir filled out; the grayish yellow color faded away to be replaced by a healthier white hue. Skin slid over the bones at the tips of its fingers as the man looked increasingly like a worm left out on the sidewalk in August. Around me, screams, gun shots, and the slicing sound of steel filled the air, but I couldn't take my eyes off the monstrosity before me.

The kiss of death. It now had a completely new meaning, and I couldn't help but wonder if it didn't get its origin from just this sort of scene. Some poor human had witnessed this through the veil and spread the word amongst those who would listen to him.

The man's hands slid away from the creature, falling to his sides as his feet stopped kicking on the ground. A dried husk was all that remained of him when the thing lifted its head. My breath froze, and my blood ran cold when the creature looked at me. Its eye sockets were still blackened holes but now a red light burned from within those pitch-black depths.

Flakes of its skin fell off when its dried lips pulled back to reveal the empty maw of its mouth. The pointed tip of its blackened tongue flickered out before it launched itself off the withered corpse of its victim. It raced across the ground at me with far more speed than it had displayed before draining the man of his life.

I shook off the stupor clinging to me and braced my legs apart when the creature leapt at me. I spun, throwing out an elbow, catching it in the cheek, and sending it spiraling to the ground. It released one of those hideous shrieks before rising to its feet again. I resisted clamping my hands over my ears like it wanted me to do.

I would have given anything for a gun or sword right now as it came at me again. *Fire*, Kobal had told me. Lifting my hands, I winced against the hideous sound the revenir continued to emit. I tried to will the fire from my palms when it leapt at me again, but nothing happened.

Spinning to the side at the last second, I ducked to let it soar over my head. Its hands dug at my back, shredding my shirt with its skeletal fingers. I threw myself to the side, scrambling to avoid it as it came at me again. Something crashed into my back, knocking me to my knees, and I realized the thing had pounced on me like a cat on a mouse.

Swinging back, I drove my elbow into its jaw. Despite the hard blow, it stubbornly hung on to me. Through the ruined material of my shirt, its fingers clawed at my back. Its excited chattering increased when it succeeded in spilling my blood. I shoved myself up and flipped onto my back, smashing it into the dirt and finally knocking its grip free.

I rolled over to my side and off of the monster. My fingers tore at the blackened earth as I scrambled to evade the bony fingers clutching at my legs. Spinning around, I pulled my foot back and slammed it into the creature's face before pulling back and kicking it again. I continued to bash it with my foot repeatedly until its face caved, and its fingers finally released me.

My chest heaved as I pulled myself backward with my elbows until I fell against the body of the man who had been sucked dry. The sounds of the battle poured into my ears as my eardrums finally heard something other than the hideous shriek of the one who had attacked me.

My gaze fell on Kobal's bare back as he fought four of them off. They'd ripped his shirt from him; his back bore the marks of their bony fingers across the intricate tattoos circling his shoulder blades. He didn't appear to feel any of the damage they'd inflicted on his body as he continued to slash at them with his claws.

Putting my hands under me, I shoved myself up to go back and try to help the others. A hand caught my wrist, jerking me back before I could get to my feet. My heart plummeted into my stomach when I turned to stare into the empty eyes of the man who had been killed.

"It's you." The tone of his voice reminded me of the doors on dusty tombs pulled open for the first time. I half expected flecks of dust to fall from his arid mouth onto me. "I see you."

Panic like I'd never known before seared through me. I felt like I was falling into the empty pits of his eyes, being pulled away to something more, something that was watching me from the other side. Something I had to resist, or I would be lost.

Screaming, I threw myself backward before I could be sucked further into the abyss. I knew whatever was on the other side would latch onto me; what it would do to me afterward was something I didn't want to contemplate. Fire burst from my palms, smashing into the man so brutally that I launched him five feet straight into the air. I rolled out of the way before his roasting body could plummet back down onto mine.

Panting, I lay on the ground, staring at the empty eye sockets across from me as the fire consumed the man's flesh. My arms trembled when I got them underneath me and managed to push myself to my feet. I took a stumbling step forward before something leapt onto my back. Bony fingers encircled my throat and dug into my flesh.

I grabbed hold of the hands, trying to pull them away before it could crush my windpipe. Stars burst before my eyes as I labored to draw breath. I choked, gagging when the fingers dug in deeper. Dizziness assailed me, and the world lurched beneath my feet as I staggered to the side.

Fire flashed from my palms, sizzling into the creature's hands around my neck. Its shriek caused my legs to buckle when it released me. My knees hit the ground as air rushed into my lungs. I'd knocked the thing off my throat, but now its bony fingers clawed at my back. The feel of its hands scrambling over my flesh caused a shudder of revulsion to wrack me.

A maddened bellow rent the air. I'd just managed to get my head up when Kobal arrived at my side. His arm swung down and he backhanded the thing on my back so hard he knocked its skull from its spine. Its body flew off my back; its head fell at my side. I gawked at the skull until Kobal lifted his foot and crushed it, splattering bone and bits of flesh across the ground.

I didn't have time to react before Kobal wrapped an arm around my waist and plucked me off the ground. My head fell back against his shoulder as my lungs still labored to draw air into my deoxygenated brain. I hung limply in his grasp as he braced his legs apart.

The revenirs surrounded us on all sides. No matter how many were cut down, more arose from the remains of the soldiers and volunteers who fell beneath the monsters. No more gunshots filled the air. As I watched, some of the soldiers used their empty guns to beat back the death hoard closing in on them.

"Kobal!" Bale shouted as Shax fell beneath a pack of those creatures.

Kobal placed my feet down, but he kept his left arm around my waist, pinning me to him. "Stay against me, no matter what," he commanded in a hoarse voice.

I didn't think I had the energy to move anywhere right now anyway. As he raised his right arm, disbelief filled me when the strange symbols and flames tattooed on him began to move and twist across his skin. I had the strangest compulsion to touch those symbols, to know what they would feel like as flames leapt to life across his flesh.

I didn't recoil from him as the fire spread over his arm and up toward his shoulder; instead, I burrowed closer to the warmth of those beautiful flames crackling over his flesh. Keeping me against him, he turned to the side and released a stream of fire that shot from his palm and across the air toward the creatures clawing at the other demons. Shrieks erupted from the monsters as they were flung away.

The fire slid over the demons, illuminating their flesh and burning their clothes away from them, but they remained otherwise unaffected by the flames as the fire sputtered out around them.

He turned in a circle, releasing more waves of fire upon those creatures, careful not to hit the humans though some of them lost a few articles of clothing too. I couldn't imagine having that much control over my ability; it must have taken him hundreds of years of wielding it to become so adept at it.

Around us, fire blazed to life to eat away the remains of the already charred town. Any of the creatures trying to scramble away were hit with a ball of flame that sent them spiraling to the ground with screams of agony.

The heat of the fire coming from him didn't burn my skin or char my clothing. Instead, it enveloped me in its warmth as he continued to emit a punishing wall of flames. Adjusting me, the hand of the arm around my waist slid beneath my ruined shirt. His thumb brushed over my flesh soothingly as he held me closer.

When only a few of the creatures remained and the rest of the demons were ruthlessly slaughtering them, he withdrew his stream of fire. The symbols and flames of his tattoos readjusted over his deeply tanned flesh, looking the same as they had before.

I was tempted to burrow against the heat still radiating from him and lose myself in the security of his arms, but I couldn't. Exhaustion beat against me, and my head still felt murky from the lack of oxygen, but even feeling as if I was wading through mud, I saw the confused, terrified, and angry stares of the humans swinging in our direction.

CHAPTER THIRTY-THREE

RIVER

Mac took a step toward us, his mouth opened and closed, but no words came out. His gaze shot between the two of us before settling on Kobal's arm around my waist. Kobal's hold tightened on me; a growl reverberated through his chest. The tension in him ratcheted up to a whole new level. A chill raced down my spine, but I didn't try to slip free of his arms; there was no taking back what they had all witnessed, and I wasn't ready to lose contact with his body yet.

The rest of the demons, finished with dispatching the remaining skeletons and any humans who might rise again, walked toward us. They barely acknowledged the humans as they strode by on their way to stand behind Kobal. The flames still crackling in the town found no ground to spread across the scorched earth and dilapidated buildings; they began to sputter out around us.

"What were those things?" Mac inquired, finally seeming to find his voice again.

"I'll meet with you in an hour to speak," Kobal said to him.

Kobal turned away before Mac could reply. With a jerk of his head toward the demons, he strode purposely away from the survivors. "They didn't know you could do that, did they?" I whispered.

"No," he answered in a clipped tone.

I glanced over my shoulder at the people still gawking at the carnage surrounding them. Many of their gazes still slid between Kobal and me as he carried me across the ground.

"You should put me down," I said. His jaw clenched and a muscle twitched in his cheek when he looked at me. The amber had faded from his eyes to leave them the liquid pools of obsidian I'd once found a little unsettling; now they caused a strange flutter in my heart. "I have to walk out of here on my own. They didn't trust me before; they'll distrust you more now. They have to think I'm stronger than this."

Reluctantly, he released me from against his chest and moved me to stand beside him. I'd assumed he would release me completely, but he kept his arm locked around my waist as we started walking again.

"What were those things?" I inquired.

"Revenirs," he replied.

"Some of the lowest forms of life in Hell," Bale said.

"That means there's more spilling out of Hell than we realized," Morax said.

"I know," Kobal grated from between his teeth. "The first seal has been broken."

"Which is?" I inquired.

"The dead will walk the earth, or revenirs will anyway," Corson sneered.

I swallowed heavily at those words.

"What of the hounds, Kobal?" Verin asked.

"I don't know," he tersely replied. "If some had fallen, I would know; something else has happened to them."

"How do you know that?" I inquired.

"If Lucifer has broken a seal, that means not only has he figured out how to, but something has happened to the hounds defending it," he replied. "I will find out what and get them free of whatever it is."

I recalled his words about his kind of demon rising with the first hounds from the fires of Hell. His bond to the creatures must run deep if he would somehow know if one or more had fallen. "How many seals are there?" I inquired.

"A couple hundred, and each one holds back an abomination no one wanted to see loose in Hell, never mind Earth."

I tried not to concentrate too hard on all the possibilities. "Why would Lucifer set them free then?"

"Those things he sets free will be loyal to him. They will help him fight his war and they will search out what he is seeking. You."

I stumbled but Kobal's arm around me kept me briskly walking forward. "How would he know about me?" I demanded.

"The same way we did." His words were brusque; he didn't look at me, but his thumb slid over my skin again in a motion I found comforting despite everything that had happened. "Someone had a vision."

"Why would he want me?"

"No one knows what you may be capable of, River. Just as you could be a big asset to our side, you could also be one to his."

"Or, if he feels you're a threat to him, to kill you," Morax said.

Kobal's lips skimmed back. The sound he emitted caused Morax to take a hasty step to the side.

"Great," I murmured. "I may have become number one on Lucifer's hit list."

"Not going to happen," Kobal vowed.

The hair all over my body stood up as I recalled what the dead man had said to me. "I felt something watching me," I told him. "Through the eye sockets of the man who was killed. He... he spoke to me."

Amber flooded his eyes when they met mine. The corded muscles of his arm swelled against my back. "What did he say?"

"It's you. I see you." I shivered at the memory. "And it felt as if something were trying to draw me in."

"Lucifer," he snarled.

"Or one of his flunkies," Shax said.

"Did you connect with him?" Kobal asked.

"No," I said tremulously.

"Good."

"He can connect with me through one of those *things*?" I was unable to keep the higher pitch from my voice when I asked the question.

"You have connected with me at times," Kobal replied. "He's more skillful at using his ability and a lot older than you."

Bale's eyebrows shot up and Corson nearly tripped over his own feet when Kobal revealed I'd connected with him. Morax and Verin exchanged pointed looks before she smiled in an 'I told you so' way. Shax looked as if someone had punched him in the stomach as his gaze shot back and forth between us. I could feel the questions burning in all of them, but they remained quiet, probably waiting until I wasn't around before interrogating Kobal further.

"They'll know where she is," Verin said.

"No, not if there was no connection between them," Kobal replied.

"But if they sent the revenirs—"

"The revenirs could be anywhere in the world; it only takes one to infect others. Lucifer most likely split them up and one of them got lucky enough to stumble across that town. They can rise up from any dead who remain above the earth, but Lucifer will have no way of knowing the exact location of this rising," Kobal interrupted Verin.

"What exactly *are* they?" I croaked out.

"They're a perversion of some of the souls who were never allowed to leave Hell because of their actions on Earth. They drain the life from their victims and turn them to their side. They can also infect the dead, which is most likely part of the reason you humans burn or bury your dead. Someone at some point in time must have glimpsed a revenir through the veil. They get no life from the dead, but their kiss can turn the bones into one of them. My first ancestor locked them behind the first seal over two hundred thousand years ago to protect against every demon in Hell becoming like them. It has been the duty of the hounds and the gate keepers to make sure the seals stay in place ever since."

"So they're kind of like zombies?" I asked.

"They're leeches," Corson said.

"They're worse than that, and we can't allow them to spread past the wall," Kobal said.

Corson ran a hand through his dark hair. "We should leave soon."

"We're staying with the plan," Kobal replied brusquely. "We're not ready to leave yet, and after what the humans witnessed from me today, I'm not sure what to expect from them. I'm probably going to have to work on regaining their trust."

"You saved their lives; they'll get over it," Bale snorted and looked toward me questioningly.

I shrugged and held my hands up before me. "I only shoot small fireballs, and they don't like me; he just torched a hundred of those things. Why didn't you tell them what you could do before today?" I asked Kobal.

"They know what they need to know. We have to ensure we keep ourselves protected. We may be far stronger than humans, but they still outnumber us," Kobal replied.

I refrained from asking what else they could all do; I knew they wouldn't tell me. I was a full-blown one-of-a-kind oddity no one trusted. I had a feeling I'd get the same treatment from the angels, if I ever encountered one of them in my newly formed, messed up life.

"That's not going to help you with gaining their trust," I said.

His eyes were still amber in color when they landed on me. "*You're* still walking with us."

A bitter laugh escaped me. "I'm more of an oddity than any of you. I'm not exactly welcome anywhere."

His fingers dug into my waist before rubbing over my flesh in a way that made all of my exhaustion fade away. More heat than the flames he'd shot from his hands spread through me. I couldn't stop myself from resting my hand against his chiseled abs. The carved muscles bunched and flexed beneath my palm as he moved. His skin was completely smooth; his body hairless other than his eyebrows and head. From my dreams, I knew he was hairless below too.

A blush colored my cheeks at the memory of those dreams and the feel of him against my body now. *Totally not the time, River!*

Yet, I could not stop the volatile response of my body to his. Seeming to sense my growing desire, his hand flattened against my side before slipping up to stroke over my ribcage. I nearly jumped out of my skin and ducked my head before I could see if anyone else had noticed my reaction to him.

Relief filled me when the tents came into view. A shower and bed sounded like a little bit of heaven to me right now.

CHAPTER THIRTY-FOUR

Kobal

I stood in the bedroom of the house where River showered, listening to the water beating down from the shower in the adjoining bathroom. Beating down on *her*. Earlier, I'd left Bale outside of her room while I'd showered in the small bathroom downstairs. Stepping into the shower stall had instantly reminded me of why I hated the human bathrooms. I'd nearly broken the showerhead off when I'd banged my head against it. I'd barely been able to turn sideways within the tiled walls.

Despite my dislike of the small space, I couldn't be far from River right now, and I'd needed to wash the filth of battle from me. I did have to admit the warm water had felt good beating down on the healing wounds the revenirs had inflicted. Wounds that were already completely closed.

Now, I'd sent Bale from this house while I remained in the room, listening as River stood naked beneath the spray of warm water. I lifted the ruined shirt she'd tossed onto the bed before going into the bathroom. My hands fisted at the sight of the jagged tears shredding the back of it. I'd come so close to losing her today.

There was a good possibility I would lose her in the future. I planned to drag her into the middle of a war, possibly into Hell itself after all, and Lucifer knew she existed. He didn't know where she was or who she was with; we'd be facing the full might of his army right now, if he knew her location.

My entire existence had been about regaining the throne I'd never even sat upon, but I would lay down my life and let the next varcolac rise before I let something happen to her.

As the water turned off, I listened to her moving about for a few seconds before the door opened. Steam and the smell of lemon soap wafted out the door behind her, enshrouding her in a misty haze. She froze when she spotted me in the room. Her black hair hung in tumbled, wet strands around her pretty face and over her shoulders.

Taking a deep breath, her hand clasped the towel wrapped around her closer to her body. My gaze was drawn to the black and blue bruises marring her delicate throat. The perfect imprint of fingers on her flesh stood starkly out against the white towel and caused an involuntary snarl to tear from me.

Her breath caught at the sound, and she took a startled step back, but didn't get far before I descended on her. Seizing her arms, I dragged her against me. I'd spent far too much time dreaming about being inside of her, denying myself, and staying away from her. However, she'd almost died today, almost been torn away from me. I wouldn't be denied anymore.

My hand entangled in her wet hair, pulling her head back as my mouth claimed hers in a possessive kiss that caused her to squeak. Her fingers dug into the flesh of my chest. I hadn't bothered with putting a shirt on again after showering; I'd barely bothered with pants in my haste to get back to watching over her.

Wrapping my hand around her, I grabbed hold of her ass through the towel and pushed her more firmly against the erection straining against my pants. She moaned low in her throat, a sexy sound that only drove me crazier with my need to possess her. Lifting her up by her ass, I held her against me until her legs circled my waist and clung to me.

"Let me inside you, River," I murmured as I ran my tongue across her luscious lips. I may not have kissed many women in my life, but I couldn't get enough of it with her. She tasted of fresh rain mingled with a sweetness that I would never forget.

She quaked when I lifted her and rubbed her against the throbbing length of my hard-on once more. Lowering my other hand, I slid it beneath the edge of the towel and up across her silken thighs. Her bare flesh beneath my hand was the most exquisite thing I had ever experienced, and I wanted *all* of it.

Her breath came in pants; her heart beat rapidly in my ears, but it was the strong aroma of her arousal that held me most enthralled. Musky with need, sweet like her lemon soap and extremely potent. I'd never experienced anything like it in all of the many demons and humans I'd been with. I wanted to bury myself in it, in *her;* to lick her from head to toe, taking the taste of her into me as that scent enveloped me.

She became still against me; her body trembling with anticipation as my fingers dipped between her thighs. I'd planned to tease her, to hear her beg for more as she did in my dreams, but real life was far better and more consuming than any fantasy. I had to feel her, *now*.

Slowly, I slid my hand forward, my palm brushing against her center. I groaned when I found her already slick with want for me. My fingers stroked over her, causing her to buck in my arms as she whimpered. My head spun, the world was spiraling out of control. I'd planned to savor my first time with her, yet I was on the verge of tearing my pants off, shoving her against the wall, and fucking her until she screamed my name and collapsed from exhaustion.

Somehow managing to maintain my restraint, I leisurely slid my finger into her heat. A shudder wracked me at how deliciously tight she was. Her muscles clenched around me, drawing me deeper into her. She released a harsh breath against my neck and pressed closer to me.

"It will be better than any dream," I promised.

I slid my finger in and out of her in a rhythm her hips surged forward to meet. Her mouth pressed against my neck and her teeth scraped over my skin. The crackle of her sparks sounded in my ears as her hands slid over my shoulders.

Spinning, I turned her toward the bed in the room and walked the three steps to it. I refused to let her go, refused to let her have a chance to change her mind as I placed her on the bed. Leaning over her, I took hold of the towel and pulled it open to reveal her breathtaking body. She tried to grab the towel and cover herself up again, but I wouldn't relinquish it to her. Not when I was finally getting to take her all in.

She was stunning with her flushed skin and luscious curves. Training had turned her muscles and body into something more honed than when she had arrived, but her hips were still rounded and her gorgeous breasts were full. Trimmed, black curls shaded her sex from my view but my mouth still watered at the sight of them. I even found her tan lines entrancing as my gaze raked over her.

She went to pull the towel over herself again, but I held it away from her. "Let me look." Her midnight lashes fell to shadow her striking eyes. "You're beautiful."

I saw the awe and uncertainty shimmering in her eyes when they came back to mine. As I watched, her dusky nipples puckered beneath my gaze. Nudging her thighs apart, I kept my right thigh between hers when I knelt on the bed over her. I slid my hand over one of her breasts, letting it fill my palm as I cupped it and ran my thumb over her nipple. When I bent to take it into my mouth, sparks shot from her fingertips and her back arched off the bed.

She tasted better than any dream ever could have, I realized as I swirled my tongue around her nipple. Drawing it gently between my teeth, I nipped at it before lavishing it again. Her hands entangled in my hair, pulling me closer as her hips rose to rub against my thigh. Her head thrashed to the side as she eagerly rode my leg.

"That's it, River," I murmured. I leaned my thigh into her as she spiraled farther out of control beneath me. "Let go."

My entire body screamed for release, but I was fascinated with her wild abandonment. She had always kept a part of herself guarded, but now she was completely uninhibited beneath me. Releasing her nipple, I left a trail of kisses over her skin, tasting the shower water on her flesh before taking her other breast into my mouth.

All I'd thought of for weeks was being inside of her, feeling her straining against me and her legs around my hips as I relentlessly drove into her, but I found myself relishing every inch of her silken body. I didn't savor or linger with others before her; it was not my way. I made sure my partner found satisfaction, but learning their body had never been part of the process.

I couldn't get enough of learning her.

"Kobal!" she gasped, tugging at my hair. Her body went rigid against mine as I slid my hand over her flat stomach and toward the enticing juncture between her thighs once more. Her mouth turned into my ear. "Kobal, someone is in the house."

I jerked away from her as I leapt to my feet and spun to face the door. I had no idea who would have dared to interrupt us, but right then I could have killed them. River jerked the towel around her and sat up as Bale appeared at the top of the stairs. When Bale looked to River, I stepped protectively in front of her to block her from view.

"What is it?" I barked.

She rested her hand on her hip. "Mac is waiting for you at the tent. If you are to repair our relations with the humans, I'd suggest you don't keep him waiting."

I ground my teeth together, resentment and disappointment crashing through me. "I'll be right there."

She nodded before retreating down the stairs. I took a deep breath to regain my control before turning to River. She sat on the bed, her hand clasping the towel against her chest. Color crept high into her cheeks as she kept her gaze focused on the floor.

"You have to go now," she murmured.

"I'm not leaving you here." She still wouldn't look at me as she rose to her feet and grabbed the fresh set of clothes she'd gathered from my tent before coming here. I moved to block her when she hurried toward the bathroom with them. "Let me watch you."

She clutched the towel tighter against her body. "Kobal, I don't do this kind of stuff; I'm not sure how to. I've never..." her voice trailed off, and her face turned redder than the fire she could wield.

My fangs pricked as a new possibility dawned on me. But it couldn't be; she was far too desirable and alluring to have remained untouched for this long. However, perhaps it *was* possible no other had taken her before; she'd spent most of her life raising her brothers from what she'd told me.

"Never what?" I inquired.

"Never done anything like this with anyone. It's all *so* much and so overwhelming. No one has ever made me feel the way you do, or touched me the way you do. I don't know what to make of it, and I can't escape you, not even when I'm sleeping."

The desperation of her words and the tone of her voice tugged at my heart in a way it had never been tugged at before. I could feel the confusion and anguish swirling out of her. "Have you never been with a man?" I asked.

Her nostrils flared as her vulnerability slid away to be replaced with exasperation. "I have no way to protect myself from you, and you keep coming at me!"

"I don't want you to protect yourself from me. I want *all* of you."

"Then what will be left of me when you're done?" she cried in frustration.

"Have you ever been with a man?" I asked again instead of answering her question.

"That's none of your business!"

"No, then." If she had figured out how to wield her life force power, I had no doubt I'd have been blown through a wall as she glowered at me.

"And if I'd been with dozens or thousands upon thousands of others like I'm sure you have, would it make a difference? Would you still want me?"

"Yes," I answered honestly. "It would not matter to me, because I will be your last." I thought her eyes might pop from her head. "It is not the same amongst demons; we don't judge in the way humans do. You could have been with more men than I've been with women, and it would not matter, not to me. And I have not been with thousands upon thousands."

My words to her had been true, demons didn't judge sex in the same way. The only time it meant anything more than satisfying an itch was when it was with one's Chosen. If she wasn't my Chosen, it would be different between us simply because I *liked* her more than any other woman I'd ever been with.

I respected her determination and steadfast way of approaching things. I admired the way she kept forging forward even after losing everything she'd ever known, having her new heritage and powers thrown at her, and a whole new life and possible death sentence tossed into her lap.

My words had been true, but I was still inordinately pleased by the realization she'd never known another man. I'd never been with a virgin; I preferred a more experienced partner, but with her, she would be only *mine*.

Her chin tilted up. "So not thousands upon thousands," she muttered. "Woo-hoo for you."

"You will judge me then?"

She nibbled on her bottom lip in such an enticing way that fresh blood flooded my groin. "No," she finally said. "I won't. How do I know you're not trying to get in my pants because the man who stole your throne from your ancestor is *my* ancestor? Maybe you're looking to punish him or spite him in some way by trying to have sex with the person you consider his daughter?"

My lips skimmed back at her words as uncontrollable anger surged through me. Swiftly moving toward her, I slammed my hands into the wall beside her head before she had a chance to move. She jumped when the plaster gave way beneath my fists.

"Don't *ever* say something like that again!" I snarled.

Her gaze remained on mine; I saw no fear there as her eyes narrowed minutely. I caged her in when she tried to duck my arm, pinning her against the wall with my body and hands. She pulled back and pressed herself against the wall again. Unlike so many others who would have cowered before me, her chin rose and her lips compressed.

Despite her defiant front, I could hear her heart hammering in her chest. I knew I was overwhelming her, knew she was frightened of everything she was feeling, but I couldn't get myself to move away from her.

"You're here because of your heritage, I will give you that, but I do *not* desire you because of it. I desire you because of *you*. I am not one for spite; I am one for death. Never forget that, River. I don't do ulterior motives, play games, or use sex as a weapon. Besides, Lucifer wouldn't give two shits about me throwing his daughter one. He only cares about the power you may be able to bring him or the damage you could possibly inflict on him."

"I don't know what to do!" she cried in frustration. "I'm not sure I could satisfy *your* needs. I know they are far more than human, you said so. How do I handle that? And when you return to the fire and other women..."

Pulling my hand from the wall, I brushed my knuckles over her silken cheek when her words trailed off and hurt flashed through her eyes. "All you have to do is be you. That is all I want from you. I'll only take what you're willing to give me, but know I want it all. There will be no other women for me, solely you."

"You can't know that."

"I haven't been with another woman since you stepped foot in this camp." I'd never intended to admit that to her, but the stress and unhappiness radiating from her tore at me. I couldn't keep her from what lay ahead of us, but I would do everything I could to make her happy now. "I've never gone so long before."

"And after you've had me, then what? You'll toss me aside like all the other humans and demons you've used!"

I buried my annoyance at her words. I had to remind myself that humans saw things so differently than demons did. "No. You are *nothing* like any other woman I've ever encountered. Once I've had you, I'll have you again, repeatedly."

Stepping closer, I pulled my other fist from the wall. Plaster dust trickled around her, and some of it stuck in her damp hair as I rested my hands on an unbroken section of wall by her head. I gazed at those tempting lips, swollen from my kiss. I lowered my head until my lips were against her ear and I breathed in the scent of her. Her body tensed, but she seemed to lose the battle with herself when she turned her head into my cheek.

"You're beautiful, River, and I'd like to watch you dress. Let me."

I grasped the edge of her towel, giving her time to tell me no, but she remained silent and watchful as I gradually pulled it open. The sight of her full breasts with their pert, dusky nipples standing out as they begged for attention caused me to groan.

Lean muscle ran through her flat stomach. I couldn't stop my hand from running over it before sweeping over the curve of her rounded hips and down toward the mouthwatering black triangle.

She inhaled sharply, her body pushing closer to mine when I cupped her mound in my hand and slid my fingers over her silken, wet warmth. "I've found no release since the dreams started, not even with my own hand. Have you?" I grated against her ear.

Her hands fell onto my shoulders, and her fingers dug into my flesh as her hips moved with my finger once more.

"Have you found your own release?" I demanded, stilling my hand against her. She impatiently thrust her hips against me, but I remained unmoving. "Answer me, River."

"No!" she admitted on a gasp.

Her head fell to my shoulder when I stroked her anew, my fingers sliding deep within her while my thumb rubbed over her clit. Tremors rocked her; her teeth pressed against my neck to stifle her cries.

"Before the dreams, did you slide your hand between your legs and come while imagining it was me inside of you?" I asked.

Her head lifted; her striking eyes flew open to meet mine. I held my breath as I waited for her to respond, finally she gave a brief nod. "I did. I'd imagined it was you often before."

I was unable to tear my gaze away from her darkening eyes as those words unleashed something primitive within me. I'd never felt undone before; I did now. This woman could somehow strip me down to my basest demon instincts and set free something within me I'd never known existed. It felt powerful in a way I'd never known before her.

"Why didn't you after the dreams started?" I asked as I watched her body grinding against my fingers.

"Because I knew I'd find no fulfillment, not unless it was you."

I growled at the admission before bending my head to reclaim her mouth once more. The feel of the cloth of my pants between us was becoming unbearable; I almost tore them from me, threw her on the bed, and took her right then. I held myself back because I didn't want this to be quick, not with her. I would savor her for hours before it was over.

She tore her mouth away from mine; her breathing ragged as she struggled to catch her breath. "Kobal, you have to stop. We have to go. You must meet with Mac."

Something savage built within me. I couldn't bring myself to let her go. I may not be able to find my release right now, but she would find hers. I would not leave her in need when I could bring her fulfillment. Unfortunately, she had other plans as she pressed closer against the wall, pulling away from me with a look of regret and longing. I reached for her again, but she grasped my wrist before I could touch her.

Her eyes searched my face as her fingers stroked over my

wrist, somehow managing to soothe my need to grab her. Her legs trembled and her nipples were hard buds begging to be stroked, but she still refused to let me ease the desire I could smell on her.

"You cannot jeopardize your relationship with the humans further; we *must* go," she whispered.

Reluctantly, I stepped away from her. My dick jerked with disappointment, but it had waited this long, it could wait longer for her.

I stopped her hands before she could pull the towel back over her. "Kobal—"

"I want to watch."

Torture myself further more like it, but I couldn't tear my gaze away from her lithe body. Ever so slowly, I tugged the towel away from her and tossed it on the bed. Red tinged her neck and cheeks but she didn't argue with me when I bent to pick up the clothes she'd dropped on the floor. Grabbing her simple white underwear, I dangled it from the tip of my finger as I held it out to her. She stared at it for a minute before snatching it away from me.

Her necklace fell forward, my eyes drank her in as she bent and tugged her underwear on over one foot then the other. They didn't look so simple when they were sliding over her flesh. I admired the curve of her rounded ass and the way her breasts swayed with her movements. Disappointment filled me when she tugged her bra on and clasped it behind her back.

"You're the only one who will satisfy me, too." I didn't know where the words had come from, but I knew they were true, just as I knew she belonged to me.

She froze in the middle of pulling her shirt on. Through the thin material of her white bra I watched as her nipples puckered. She hastily pulled her shirt the rest of the way over her head and tugged it into place before slipping on her shorts.

I took hold of her arm, pulling her against my chest and brushing back strands of her damp black hair. I wiped the plaster away, hating to tarnish the beauty of her raven locks. "Let me into your room tonight, River." She blinked up at me. "Let me finally satisfy us both."

I didn't give her a chance to respond before I bent and kissed her. I pulled her lip into my mouth, sucking on it briefly before forcing myself away from her. Adjusting my erection, I tucked it into my waistband to keep it hidden from others. When I lifted my head, I found her gaze raptly fixed on my cock with a ravenous look in her eyes that had me rethinking my meeting with Mac.

Tugging on her hand, I started to lead her from the room, but froze when my eyes latched onto the dusty mirror of the bureau in the room. My teeth clamped together as I willed the gold hue of my eyes to return to normal. The gold was a symbol of aggression, a loss of control. This loss of control was something I knew had never occurred when I'd been with other women. This was because of River.

"What is it?" she asked.

"Nothing," I replied when they finally shifted back to their black color.

"I like the amber. It's so... feral."

I smiled as I bent to place a kiss against her damp hair. "You'll see it often then when I'm inside of you." Her breath caught, and her fingers flew to her lips. "Regretting that we stopped?"

"Yes. I mean, no. We must go."

I couldn't help but smile at her as I tucked a strand of hair behind her ear. "Just say yes next time."

Her breath exploded from her. I tugged on her elbow, leading her from the room and down the stairs before I could change my mind about not taking her now. My erection made walking difficult, but it didn't matter, it would be eased later tonight. I kept her close to my side as I walked with her up the hill toward the tents. Bale and the others were standing outside of my tent when we arrived.

"Is Mac in there?" I inquired.

"Yes," Bale answered and pulled back the flap.

I squeezed River's hand before releasing it. I didn't like the idea of leaving her, but I had to deal with Mac alone. "Make sure she stays safe," I commanded gruffly.

"We will," Corson vowed.

The flap of the tent rippled as it fell into place behind me. Mac sat at the table, a goblet of wine before him already and his arm draped over the back of his chair as he stared at me. "What were those things?" he demanded.

"Revenirs," I answered as I walked over to pour myself a goblet of wine. I explained what they were to him while I settled into the chair beside him. "Lucifer's faction is becoming more aggressive and they've succeeded in opening at least the first seal, something I'd planned to keep them from doing. They're looking for her."

"Was she injured?"

"She'll heal."

Mac's steely gaze ran over me. "You've kept your ability to wield fire hidden from me for twelve years."

"I have." *And others.*

"Why?"

"I'm sure you haven't revealed all to me either."

"Maybe not, but no human can do what you did today."

"Except for River."

"Is she human though?"

"She's more human than not."

Mac took a sip of his wine. "What else have you kept hidden from me?"

"I'm sure you will understand when I don't tell you everything. Humans outnumber us after all, your kind tore into our world, and some of your weapons are capable of killing us. We've worked side by side all these years. We saved countless lives today, and we are closer than we've ever been to possibly having a way to close the gate. I think that should be enough for you to trust me."

He folded his arms over his chest as he held my stare. Most humans wouldn't look at me so directly, or for so long, but Mac never backed away. "You frightened a lot of the others today."

"I frighten all of them every day."

"True," he agreed. "But I'm not sure they're going to be able to get over this."

"They're alive because of what I'm capable of. They should feel secure in the knowledge I saved their lives and never so much as singed a hair on their heads."

Mac lifted his goblet and took another sip of his wine. "Was it their lives you were looking to save or was it *hers*?"

I kept myself immobile and my face impassive while inside a riot of emotions tore through me. I had kept my abilities secret from them as a defense mechanism, but I realized now my biggest weakness was walking around outside of me. Given her mortality, she was far more vulnerable than I. There had been no way to hide my need to keep her safe from them today; there would be no way to keep it from my more menacing enemies either.

"Her life is the most valuable and you know it," I replied with a calmness I didn't feel.

Mac took another sip of his wine while he watched me. "Yes, I do. You're going to have to do some damage control tomorrow."

"Play nice with the humans?"

"Are you capable of it?"

I ran my fingers through my hair. "I'll see."

The wry smile slipped away from Mac's lips as he leaned back in his chair. "Would you like to move up the date of the mission?"

"No. We still have more to cut from the group who will be coming with us and River isn't ready to go yet. Lucifer may be searching for her, but he doesn't know she's here. We still have some time."

"Understandable."

Mac leaned back in his chair and folded his arms over his chest. We spent another two hours talking about training, who he considered the best recruits out of the hundred and fifty who still remained separated for special training for the mission, and we discussed the upcoming journey into the interior wasteland of this country. A journey he would not be a part of as he would remain here to supervise the soldiers and demons left to guard the wall.

Finally, Mac rose to his feet and stretched his back. "I never thanked you for what you did earlier," he said as he thrust his hand out to me. "It was a sight to behold, but one that kept many of us alive."

I shook his hand briskly before releasing it. Excitement pulsed through me as thoughts of River filled my head while I walked with him toward the exit. "You're welcome."

I held the flap back for him and stepped into the night behind him. The crackle of the fire on the hill drew my attention to the flames leaping high into the air.

"How did it go?" Corson demanded from where he stood next to Bale beside the tent.

"There will be some damage control to be done, but he understands."

"He's a leader, of course he does," Bale replied.

"Where is she?" I inquired, unwilling to wait any longer.

"She went to bed about an hour ago," Bale answered.

I bit back a curse, gave a brief bow of my head to them, and ducked into the tent. I impatiently closed and buttoned the flap before stalking over to the thin material blocking me from her. I stood there, listening for any sounds of movement on the other side. It remained quiet, but I knew she was awake; I could smell the increasingly sweet scent of her arousal.

My shaft lengthened against my thigh as I waited to see if she would finally allow me to ease her body.

CHAPTER THIRTY-FIVE

River

I sat cross-legged on the bed, my fingers fidgeting with the edge of the white T-shirt I'd donned to sleep in. It was all I wore, yet it felt too cumbersome against my hypersensitive skin. The soothing sounds of Mac and Kobal's voices drifted away and I realized they'd left the tent. My heartbeat picked up and excitement slithered over my skin when I heard the flap on the front of the tent lifting and falling into place again.

I didn't hear Kobal's footfalls, but he was out there; I could feel him. I stared at the flap dividing the two rooms, knowing he wouldn't come to me. This was my decision to make; I would have to get up and go to him. Could I do that? Could I open myself up to him in such a way?

He could destroy my heart, shred it within his hands, but I wanted those hands running over me. If I opened that flap, I would be leaving myself open to heartbreak and misery, but I'd finally get the chance to ease this unending torment that had taken up residence in my body since meeting him.

Turning, I set my feet on the floor; my hands gripped the edge of the bed.

I should be strong enough to turn my back to the flap and shut him out. I should be strong enough to keep my distance from him and my heart protected. This man wasn't human. He could wield fire with his hands, and I knew there was more I didn't know about him, but I found myself not caring about any of it. Didn't care he was the rightful king of Hell or that the man who'd had a hand in creating me, thousands of years ago, was his mortal enemy.

None of it mattered; I had believed him earlier when he said he desired me because of *me* and not because he was looking to stick it to Lucifer in some way. Kobal was many things, manipulative and spiteful were not among them. He didn't play games. If he was going after someone, he went after them directly.

Climbing unsteadily to my feet, I stood in the center of the room and stared at the flap dividing us. Such a small thing, yet it felt larger than the wall dividing what remained of my old world from the unknown horrors beyond. Horrors we might not survive. Could I really take the chance of dying without knowing what it felt like to be possessed by him?

The answer to that was a resounding *no.* I took one step, then another toward the flap. I couldn't stop my trembling fingers from stretching out and taking hold of one of the buttons. It felt like I watched someone else's hand pulling those buttons from their holes and I was helpless to stop it. I thought my heart might burst out of my chest as I released the last button and the flap fell back.

He stood beyond, his hands resting against the tent wall over the top of the flap. His chiseled, bare chest remained exposed to me. The pants he wore hung enticingly low on his tapered waist and did nothing to cover the obvious bulge straining against the front of them.

Saliva rushed into my mouth; any doubts about what I'd done vanished. His hands fell away from the tent, and his eyes burned with amber fire. He moved so fast into the room I barely saw him before his arm wrapped around my waist, and my feet left the ground.

My hands fell onto his amazingly broad shoulders. His skin was soft beneath my palms, but the carved muscles were hard as stone. It was a contradicting sensation I couldn't get enough of as I ran my hands over him.

His hand slid into my hair, cupping the back of my head and tugging it back to take possession of my mouth in a blistering kiss that set my body on fire. I squirmed against him in an attempt to get closer. My legs encircled his waist, and I whimpered again when I felt his erection rubbing against my aching center. I ground against him, seeking some release from this undeniable need.

He laid me down on the bed, pressing me back as he climbed between my thighs. He clutched the bottom of my shirt, tugging it upward. "Have to see," he grated out when the material slid up to expose my stomach.

Giving up on the time it took to remove my shirt the right way, he tore it open. I gasped at the rending sound filling the air before the shirt fell away to leave me exposed to him once more. His nostrils flared as he drank in the sight of me with the enthusiasm of a man in the desert consuming water. The warm July air brushed over my skin as he slid his hands over my stomach before cupping one of my breasts.

"*Mine*," he growled.

My heart leapt at the word and my body arched into his touch. I could feel the barely leashed ardor thrumming through him; feel the razor line he walked as he fought to keep himself restrained from taking me now. His rapidly fading control was only making me want him even *more.*

He lowered his head and took my nipple into his mouth. My fingers entwined in his hair, holding him closer against me as his hot tongue ran leisurely over my sensitive flesh. I relished watching his dark head bent to my chest and his mouth latched onto my breast as he tasted me in greedy pulls. His calloused palm slid over my stomach before dipping between my thighs. I cried out and my hips bucked against him as he rubbed his palm over me before slipping a finger deep inside.

It all felt too good, too overwhelming, too *much.* His finger moved within me as his teeth nipped at my breast. The scrape of his fangs against my flesh startled me. I'd yet to feel them in real life, and they were better than I'd ever dreamed. They didn't dim my need; they escalated it. I had to know what they would feel like sinking into my flesh.

Stretching me further, he slid another finger into me as he turned his mouth to my other breast. "Please!" I panted when the tension within me built higher. I tried to pull back at the same time my body ground more demandingly against his greedy fingers and palm.

He moved his mouth away from my breasts, leveling himself over me. His solid, heavy body pushed me into the mattress. My hands gripped his biceps, clutching at him as his fingers continued their possession of my body.

Sparks shot from my fingertips; they licked over his skin, but I paid them no attention, and he didn't seem to notice either as those beautiful amber eyes burned into mine. His eyes turned golden when he was in battle or enraged, and I now knew they also burned with amber when he was consumed by desire.

Lowering his head, his ragged breaths warmed my ear and

neck when his lips rested against my ear. "Please what?" he demanded.

I didn't know what; this was unlike anything I'd ever experienced before. All I knew was one thing. "I need you."

He sat back from me, allowing air to flow over my heated skin once more. I squirmed beneath him as he pulled the remains of my shirt from me before grabbing for the button on his pants. He grunted in frustration before rending the material open. I barely saw him yank the pants off before he was settling himself between my thighs again.

He'd worn no underwear, something I didn't find at all surprising. What was surprising was the size of his shaft. I'd seen it in my dreams, but it was far larger in real life as it swelled further beneath my gaze. Fear caused my heart to lurch. He'd tear me in two. His fingers slid over my cheeks, brushing aside my hair. I tore my eyes away from his massive length resting against my thigh to focus on his eyes once more.

"I don't think you'll fit in me," I croaked.

"It will hurt in the beginning," he replied in a strained voice. "But I will make sure you are ready for me, and I will let you find your way. I'm meant to be inside of *you*."

A thrill shot down my spine at his words. Reaching between us, his fingers stroked over my aching center again; his thumb slid over my clit. The thighs I'd clamped against his sides at the sight of his heavy erection, eased open to grant him better access.

He dipped two fingers into me again, his shoulders heaving with his ragged breaths. I lifted my hips to him as the heady anticipation of something more to come assailed me once more and his fingers stretched me further. A coiling tension built within me as he thrust and caressed, pushing me closer and closer to edge of release.

His fingers slid away from me once more, but I couldn't be

disappointed. Not when I knew I was about to find out what it was like to have *him* inside of me. Wrapping his hand around his shaft, he directed it forward until it pushed against my entrance. I could feel myself stretching to accommodate the head he partially slipped within me.

"Raise your hips," he grated through his teeth.

Lifting my hips, I gasped when the motion of him only partially within me sent a firestorm of delicious sensations through me. His hands bunched in the sheet, but he didn't move, didn't plunge into me as I experimentally rose and fell on the head of him once more.

More sparks erupted from my fingers and sizzled over his skin. His claws extended, digging into the bed as he tore the sheets from it and his head fell into my shoulder. The restraint he exhibited caused his muscles to quake beneath my touch. I longed to ease his strain, and instinctively I knew how to do it. Lifting my hips again, I pushed against him, taking him deeper within me. I nearly screamed in joy when he slipped in further, stretching and filling me in a way I'd never dreamed possible.

"*Fuck*," he groaned against my ear, but he remained still, allowing me to take him into my body at my own pace. Allowing me to discover his body inch by deliciously slow inch.

I grabbed hold of his taut ass and lifted my hips to him, drawing him deeper into me. He continued to hold back, his body becoming sweat slicked as his muscles bulged.

"Kobal," I breathed, needing more of him, but unable to take him any further. "I can't... get enough."

His eyes burned a brighter gold when he lifted his head to look at me. "Hold onto me."

Wrapping my arms around his neck, I turned my face into him and inhaled his fiery scent. He released the shredded sheets. I watched in amazement as his claws retracted before he seized my hips and plunged the rest of the way into me. I cried out, and my nails dug into his neck as my teeth sank into his shoulder. His body rocked against mine when he felt my teeth; his fingers dug into the flesh of my hips.

There was pain as he stretched and filled me, but having him inside of me also felt so right that tears burned my eyes, and I couldn't move away from him. I had come home; I'd found where I would always belong, in his arms, with *him*. I'd never experienced anything like the overwhelming emotions stealing through me.

The sparks shooting from my fingers slid down to my wrist and spread out across his bronzed skin. The golden-white fire of those sparks spread over his slick, thickly muscled back and lit his tattoos in a way that made them seem to come to life and move over his flesh.

His breath was heavy against my shoulder, and his body quaked as he pushed forward against me again. "I have to," he groaned in my ear as he withdrew from me before plunging in again. "I can't hold back, not anymore, River."

"Don't," I moaned even as my body tried to recoil from the feeling of physical discomfort within it. I grabbed his ass again, kneading his flesh as I drew him deeper into me. "I want all of you, more."

His hands clasped my face when he withdrew and thrust into me again.

CHAPTER THIRTY-SIX

Kobal

Easy, easy, I kept telling myself as the urge to possess her, to drive relentlessly into her warm, willing body swelled within me. The tight, wet muscles of her sheath clenching me were nearly my undoing as her hips began to rise and fall beneath me once more. She looked radiant and angelic as the sparks firing from her hands bathed her face in a golden glow.

So amazing. I'd never felt anything like her, never experienced such control and yet an utter lack of it. She could be my undoing and I'd welcome every second of it.

Her eyes were dazed with passion when they fluttered open to meet mine; her fingers dug into my ass as her hips rocked against me. My fangs extended when I slid my hands over her face and bent my head to kiss her. I had no restraint over them right now, which was something that had never happened to me before, at least not during sex. I always kept them carefully leashed when I was with another, but there was no keeping anything leashed with River. Her tongue swirled over them in an erotic way that nearly caused me to come right then.

Don't hurt her.

Bite her! Claim her!

The opposing needs to keep from hurting her and to sink my fangs into her and mark her as mine battled within me. I tried to ease back, but she wouldn't let me slow down and savor her. My restraint unraveling further, I drove more vigorously into her body. A body made for sin, a body made for *me.*

Her head fell back, and excited pants escaped her as her back arched. My eyes latched onto her perfect breasts and pert, dusky nipples. Bending my head, I took one of them into my mouth, swirling my tongue around the bud and sucking upon it —an action that drove her wild as she writhed beneath me.

One of her hands slid up my back, and her fingers threaded through my hair. She cried out when my fangs scraped over her flesh, drawing blood that I tenderly licked away. The taste of her blood and the sensation of breaking her skin caused my body to shudder. A possessive growl tore from me as that primitive instinct stirred again and the last of my control started to shred.

Mine!

Releasing her breasts, I scraped my fangs over her skin toward her neck.

"More!" she begged.

That plea was my complete downfall. Grasping her hips, I drove into her with a frenzy bordering on insanity. I found myself doing the one thing I'd never been tempted to do in my lengthy existence. My fangs sank into her shoulder, and I clamped down. I expected her to scream or beat at me when they pierced her flesh. Instead, she became more unrestrained as she met each one of my thrusts.

I kept her pinned beneath me. Her fingers entangled in my

hair, holding me close against her as I forever marked her as mine to any demon who saw her.

I released my hold on her shoulder before sinking my fangs into her neck. Out of control, all I tasted and felt was her blood on my tongue and her muscles gripping my cock. I moved to her other shoulder, biting down and pinning her again.

Her fingers raked the skin of my back, drawing blood. Her head turned into my shoulder as her lips skimmed back so I could feel her small teeth against my flesh before they bit down on me until my skin broke.

Such a little demon, marking her territory.

I was more than happy to be marked by her as the scream she released was muffled by my flesh. I felt a growing, heavy sensation in my sac as semen flooded forth. I'd suspected she might be my Chosen, but with the claiming mark and the pressure-filled feeling of semen rising up my shaft, I knew it was true.

I'd never experienced this sensation before; it was overwhelming in its newness as I held back from spilling within her. I desperately needed release from this pressure, but I would make sure she found hers first.

Lifting her hips, I slid my thumb between our bodies to rub her clit as I drove her up and down on me. Her cry of ecstasy was muffled against my flesh as her nails dug into my back and she bit deeper. The muscles of her sheath constricted so forcefully around me from her orgasm that they wrenched my semen from me.

Throwing my head back, I bellowed in possession as I came into her in a stream that seemed to go endlessly on as my body was wracked by the new sensations of this deeper, more potent release. I didn't care if the whole town heard me; they would all know she was mine. Her climaxing muscles continued to grasp me within her delectable body, milking more semen from my body until she collapsed beneath me.

Gathering her within my arms, I pulled her against my chest and withdrew from her as I rolled to the side with her. She sprawled limply across my chest, her fingers trailing over my shoulder toward her bite mark. I felt her smile against my flesh. Holding her close against me, I inhaled the scent of me all over her mingled with our sex and blood on the air.

"I'm sorry I hurt you," I said gruffly as I tried to regain control of my racing heart.

"It was worth it," she murmured, her fingers trailing lazily over my chest.

My dick jumped again and started to lengthen when her hand slipped down my stomach toward it. I'd taken her with a savagery I'd never shown with anyone before, not even a demon. I'd found more satisfaction in her body than with anyone else's, and already I wanted *more.* It was too soon for her. I'd hurt her, and marked her repeatedly; I couldn't hurt her anymore by taking her again now.

I brushed her hair aside, contentment filling me when I saw the bites marking her golden skin and declaring to everyone who she belonged to. Who she would *always* belong to. The newest queen of Hell was Lucifer's offspring. The irony was not lost on me, but it didn't matter. All that mattered was she was mine.

Glancing down, I spotted the blood marring her inner thigh. I'd done that, I'd claimed her and taken from her what no other man had. Something protective stirred within me as I gently eased her back and rose to my feet. I felt her eyes on me as I walked across the room, grabbed the pitcher of water and retrieved a towel from the armoire. I wet the towel before returning to her and gently cleaning the blood from her.

Her hands curled into the bed, her cheeks turned crimson

in color as she watched me. I'd never experienced the impulse to be tender with another, to care for them, but with her it was as instinctive as breathing. Tossing the towel aside, I bent to kiss her before crawling into bed with her once more and pulling her into my arms.

I rested my palm gently against my marks; she smiled as her fingers slid over my chest. "You're mine, River." She lifted her head and propped her chin on my chest. Her eyes were smoky when they met mine. "These marks, they're my brand. You will never spend another day of your life without them on you. No one else will *ever* know the curve of your hip, the heaviness of your breasts, or the wonder of being inside of you."

I cupped her mound at my last words, pleased to feel her wetness against my hand. Her lips parted as she watched me.

Too soon.

"You belong to *me*," I grated.

Her fingers slid over my cheek, trailing down to my lips and touching against one of my fangs. A strange sadness filled her eyes before she lifted her gaze to mine once more. I would do anything to ease that sadness, but I had no idea what had caused it. Was the idea of being my Chosen so bad for her?

"And how many others have you marked as yours?" she inquired with a hitch in her voice.

"None."

Her fingers froze. "None?"

"No. You are my only, River. I can't tell you the amount of times I've had sex over my many years."

I kicked myself when she winced and tried to pull away from me. I'd have to be more careful of the way I worded things, I realized, as I pulled her closer against me, refusing to let her withdraw. I wasn't used to having to deal with a human, but she was more sensitive about these things than I, and I didn't want to upset her. Her jaw jutted out, but before she could begin to fight me, I continued on.

"My life never felt lonely before, but I realize now it was without you in it. You're the only woman who has ever mattered to me, the only one who has ever completely satisfied me. I feel stronger with you in my arms. I *am* stronger with you."

Her rising annoyance faded at my words, and her head tilted to the side. "Is this a demon thing?"

"Yes, demons mark those we bind our lives to. My bite is my mark upon you."

"You want to bind your life to me?" she squeaked.

"I already have."

"And what if I didn't want to do that? Shouldn't we have discussed that step first or something?"

A snarl curved my upper lip; I somehow stayed restrained at the idea of losing her. She may be part demon, but she wasn't full. She wouldn't feel the pull of the Chosen bond as strongly as I did. I couldn't force her stay with me if it would make her unhappy.

"If you don't want this, it will be your choice," I told her.

"I still have a choice?"

"Yes," I grated through my teeth.

Her fingers slid to the set of four fang marks on her shoulder. Looking at her, I was amazed to realize I'd bitten her five times, most of them I barely recalled through the haze of lust and possession filling me while claiming her.

"And what of you?" Her fingers didn't touch when she wrapped her hand around my growing erection. I hissed in a breath when she ran her hand up the swelling length of it. Her thumb slid over the slit at the top, rubbing the bead of precum forming there over the sensitive skin before sliding down me again. "If I belong to you, will you belong to me?"

"Yes." My head fell back when I took hold of her hand and guided it up my shaft before sliding it down again, showing her the way I liked to be stroked. She was hesitant at first, but it quickly faded as her touch became more confident.

"So no one else will know what it feels like to have you inside of them again? You'll never touch another woman again or kiss another?"

"No." I enveloped her neck with my hand and dragged her down to claim her luscious mouth. "You're the only woman for me from now on and the only one I've ever desired kissing."

Sparks flickered from the tips of her fingers again. "Really?"

"Yes." I grabbed her hand, holding it against my stomach to stop her stroking as I resisted rolling her over and sinking my fangs into her shoulder to pin her as I took her again. "It's too soon for you. Tomorrow."

She sighed in disappointment, but she dropped her chin to my chest again and rested her hand there. "How can you be so sure I'm your only?"

I traced the marks on her neck, unable to suppress a smug smile of possession as I gazed at them. "This is one way. Demons do not bite another without staking a claim on them. Their instincts are against doing such a thing unless it is with their Chosen. This is another." I took her hand and brushed her thumb over the fresh bead of semen forming on the head of my cock. She frowned in confusion as she stared at it before looking at me again. "Male demons don't produce sperm until the first time they are with their Chosen. Then they produce it every time thereafter. There is no denying what you are, not to me anyway."

I brushed my hand over the bite she'd left on my neck. "And you have also marked me."

Her gaze fell on where she'd punctured my skin. "It had felt so... I just had to," she finished.

"The demon in you did. It was instinctual. You also recognize me as yours."

Her eyes flew to mine. "Yes," she whispered. "I'm surprised they're not healing on you already. The revenirs marks on you healed so quickly."

"The marks of a Chosen take longer to heal. They do eventually fade, but a demon marks their Chosen on a near daily basis. It is believed a combination of our saliva mixing with our Chosen's flesh keeps the marks open for longer."

"Why do they take longer to heal?"

"So they can be seen by all," I replied.

"So there is something demonic in my saliva too?"

I couldn't help but grin at her. "I'd say when it comes to your Chosen, you are very demonic." I pulled her forward to kiss her. She looked dazed, but smiled seductively when I released her.

"So if male demons don't produce sperm, what about female demons? What happens with them when they find their Chosen?" she asked.

"Both sexes can enjoy sex with another before finding their Chosen."

Her eyes darkened, and her fingers dug into my chest. Perhaps there was far more demon within her than I'd realized as I recognized the possessiveness burning in her eyes.

"Not as much as they do with their Chosen. *No*where near as much." I'd never experienced anything like what had just transpired between us, and it had altered me in some way I didn't fully understand. As soon as I thought she was ready, I would be inside her again. "I'd heard sex was more pleasurable with one's Chosen, but I'd never imagined how *much* more until you."

"You don't have to say that," she murmured.

"I'm saying it because I mean it." Drawing her mouth close

for another kiss, I ran my tongue over her swollen lips before tearing myself away. "I've never experienced anything like what just transpired between us."

"Neither have I," she said in a breathy whisper that had me shooting rock hard again. "Back to female demons."

"The females do not produce eggs until they meet their Chosen. Their cycles are far different from humans as they only produce an egg once every ten to fifteen years. It is rare for a female to conceive. However, a male demon can always scent when his mate is fertile, and they often stay cloistered for the entire month of her fertile cycle."

She released a harsh breath. "A whole month?"

I felt the increased beat of her heart as her fingers traced over my chest, and her gaze fell onto my lips. Her growing excitement beat against me. She was going to test the boundaries of my self-restraint to its very limits before this night was over.

"Yes."

"So, Lucifer must have been in some kind of mortal stage when he conceived a child," she said.

"Yes. As far as I know, there is no sex or reproduction for angels."

"I see. Well, I can say I have been perfectly normal for a human when it comes to reproduction, as far as I know. I got my period when I was thirteen and get it every month like clockwork. I had it last week." I ran my fingers through her hair as she spoke. "Can I get pregnant by you?"

My hand stilled on her as I realized what I could have done by spilling within her. I'd never considered having a child before. With the rare times my ancestors had found their Chosen, I had never expected to find mine. All I'd sought was to claim my throne.

Now, the idea of having a child was before me and the idea

of it being with River caused a strange longing in my chest. However, such a thing at this time could prove disastrous to all of us.

"Yes, you can," I told her.

"Some of those demons who chose to stay on Earth and die all those thousands of years ago, they did so because they had found their Chosen with a human, didn't they?" she asked.

"Yes," I confirmed.

"So demon children also roamed the earth?"

"A few, but like most of your line, they are all gone. Some of them were never able to reproduce as they acquired a demon's necessity for their Chosen in order to reproduce with a mortal's lifespan at birth."

"How sad." Her eyes closed and her head turned on my chest. "I can't get pregnant, Kobal. I'm too young, it's too risky right now, and I believe Lucifer would come after our child with everything he has."

My body stiffened beneath her, and my hand stilled on her hair. It would be the biggest mistake of all for River to get pregnant now, but I wanted that offspring.

"We will take care to prevent pregnancy from now on," I said. "But you must know, I will protect our offspring with everything I am. *No* one will ever harm our children, or you."

"I know," she murmured and stifled a yawn. "But I'd still prefer him dead first."

"So would I."

Her lashes brushed over my skin when her eyes closed. I kept her cradled against my chest as I felt her slip into sleep. I couldn't help but smile as I watched her. She would also be the first woman I would ever fall asleep beside.

CHAPTER THIRTY-SEVEN

River

Kobal's leg was draped over mine with his foot hooked possessively around my calf when my eyes fluttered open the next morning. His arms were securely enfolded around me with his chin tucked on top of my head.

Shadows still enshrouded the tent, but I could see the early glow of the sun filtering beneath the flap and around the edges of it. The growing warmth of the rising sun didn't bother me, nor did the heat of the powerful man lying next to me.

I remained unmoving against him as I took stock of my body. My throat and body were sore from the battle with those things yesterday, and there was a tenderness between my legs that wasn't entirely unpleasant. I couldn't stop myself from smiling at the memory of what had transpired between us.

The smile slid away when doubts descended over me. Did he really believe I was his Chosen, or in the light of day would he change his mind and realize he'd been mistaken?

A shiver of delight ran through my body when I rested my hand against his bite mark on my neck. He had sounded so sure of himself last night, and I could never forget the primal compulsion that had driven me to sink my own teeth into him. At the time, I hadn't understood why I'd been compelled to do such a thing, but now I knew it had been something primal inside of me.

I'd been unable to resist marking him in the same way as he'd marked me. I could feel the urge growing within me once more.

This large, powerful, magnificent man was mine. I felt the rightness of it all the way to the center of my soul. I somehow knew this possessiveness would not abate, that it would not change, and the strength of it was anything but human. Perhaps I'd known it since the first time I'd seen him.

My fingers slid over the flame tattoos on his arm, the flames that had fired to life yesterday and leapt from him to destroy those creatures. I traced over the strange symbols intricately wrought within the flames.

Contentment stole through me as I nestled closer against him, seeking out his strength. "What are these symbols in your tattoo?" I asked, knowing when he woke by the rumble of pleasure reverberating through his chest.

"Part of our ancient language," he replied, fisting his hand so his arm flexed against me. My mouth went dry as the chiseled muscles of his forearm bulged and moved before me.

"Really?" I slipped out of his embrace and sat up in the bed. I tucked the sheet against my chest before grabbing his arm and drawing it closer.

A smile tugged at his mouth when he reached up to pull the sheet away from me. The playful look on his face robbed me of my breath, and for a minute, I forgot all about my fascination over the tattoos on his arms. I'd never known he could look so relaxed and youthful, never imagined the unrelenting demon could look *joyful*.

His hair fell boyishly across his forehead and into one black eye as his finger trailed over my breast before circling my nipple. I was bombarded by memories of the night and the feelings he'd ceaselessly awakened and set free in me. My heart swelled with emotion, and it clogged my throat as I realized I was well on my way to falling helplessly in love with this demon.

"Really," he murmured.

"Why did you have them tattooed onto you?" I inquired in a strangled voice as my body arched into his touch.

"They aren't tattoos. I emerged from the fires with these markings upon me."

His fingers slipped toward my stomach. Grasping his hand before it could dip any lower, I held his arm in front of me. As badly as I wanted him right now, I was also eager to learn more about him.

"What exactly is a varcolac demon? I know you can control the gateways and hounds, but I want to know more."

The blankets fell away from his muscular chest to reveal the markings on it. The sheet covered his waist as he sat up beside me, but it was rising with his growing erection. Grabbing my waist, he pulled me into his lap and held me so my back was against his chest. The rigid evidence of his arousal pressed against the curve of my ass. I melted against him, but he didn't do anything sexual when he wrapped his arms around me.

"In a very loose way, you know of me." His warm breath tickled my neck as he spoke, his lips brushing against the bite marks he'd left upon me. "Humans eventually distorted my kind into the legend of the werewolf."

My mouth dropped, and I twisted in his arms to look at him. His grin revealed the four lengthening fangs that had pierced my skin, marking me as his. As I watched, they retracted so that they were only slightly longer, sharper points than a human's canines would be.

"However, I do not turn into a wolf, I do not howl at the moon, and everything you know about werewolves is everything I'm not," he continued.

My fingers fell to the wolves marking his other arm. "Are these wolves?"

"To you they would be; to me and the other demons they are hellhounds. Three times the size of your wolves, they are more vicious, protective, loyal, and far more lethal than the animals you know. Like me. They also mate for life like demons do when they find their Chosen."

His arms tightened around me. "*My* Chosen. I should have known it when all other women failed to entice me once meeting you, should have known it when you walked into my dreams, but I was too consumed with my desire for you to look past it to what was driving it. And truth be told, I never believed I would find my Chosen. Only two varcolacs before me have, and it took them far longer than it has taken me.

"Things would have been different between us if I had recognized and claimed you sooner, instead of trying to deny it and telling myself to stay away from you. I would have been better able to control myself when taking you, would have expected such an intense reaction to being inside of you. However, I didn't really begin to suspect what you might be to me until recently. By then, my hunger for you had grown to nearly uncontrollable levels. Because of that, I hurt you."

"Not too badly." I rested my palm against his cheek. I stroked the contour of his jaw, dipping down to his pointed chin. His black eyes watched me intently, but I'd sensed the self-reproach in his tone. "And I was told it's always painful for women the first time."

"I would have been gentler with you, taking you with the care you should have been taken with."

Leaning forward, I kissed his firm lips and rubbed my tongue over the tip of one of his sensitive fangs. I couldn't help but smile when he growled. "I wouldn't have changed a thing and I'm fine," I whispered against his mouth.

His eyes searched over me before he gave a small grunt, but I didn't think he believed me. His gaze slid to my neck and fastened on the bruises the revenir had left on me. They'd probably darkened over night. Amber light lit his wolf-like eyes. Though I knew it was death on his mind now, I couldn't help but recall the passion that had blazed from them last night as he'd thrust within me. I withdrew my hand from him before I started licking him all over.

Turning back around, I skimmed my fingers over a symbol resembling a backwards E with what looked like a sword piercing through the center of it. "What do the symbols mean?" I asked.

"That one is Sowa. The best way to translate it into your language would be the blade of fire."

"And this one?" I pointed at one that was two V's with a line connecting the tops of the V's. They could almost be fangs.

"Ziwa, the guardian of the hellhounds. His mark is considered a gift of strength, endurance, and virility. It's also considered a curse as it marks me as having a piece of the hellhound's soul within me. The hounds are known for their bursts of violence, ruthlessness, and territoriality."

"Sounds fitting for you," I murmured.

He chuckled as he kissed my neck. I was really enjoying this more relaxed, easygoing Kobal. I doubted I would see it outside of this tent, but I loved that he felt comfortable enough around me to let it show now.

"The hounds calm when they find their mate," he said.

"However, there is nothing more dangerous than a hound when their mate is in peril."

My breasts tingled from the purring tone of his voice. "What of this one?" I inquired and pointed at a straight line with a triangle attached to the middle of it.

"Risaz, it's a force of destruction."

I moved through the flames before coming to another symbol. This one was three wavy lines amid the flames. "And this?"

"Zenak, the mark of eternal fire and life."

Immortal, I recalled with a pang. Something I most certainly was not, and after seeing those things yesterday, I didn't think I'd live long once we traveled out of this camp and toward the open gateway of Hell. If somehow the two of us managed to survive all of this, I'd think about the implications of being in a relationship with an immortal demon for the rest of my days. Until then, I was going to enjoy the time I had left with him.

"This one?" I asked, pointing to another symbol on his flesh. It looked like a tilted Z.

"Eiaz. A symbol of speed, heightened senses, and protection."

"Amazing," I murmured.

"Humans took some of them and turned them into what became known as the Elder Futhark, also known as runes."

"I don't know what that is," I admitted.

"It's a thing of the past," he said as he brushed the hair back from my face.

"So why did humans create the legend of the werewolf if you don't turn into some kind of a wolf?"

"My ancestors didn't turn into them, but they controlled the hounds." He grinned at me and turned his left arm over to reveal the detailed etchings of the hellhounds on it. "And then I came along. Like the fire, the hounds come to life when I release them. Until then, they reside within me, an ever constant, feral soul looking to be set free. I am the first varcolac to be able to control the hounds, and to have them etched onto my body and housed within me."

"A blessing and a curse," I murmured as I recalled what he'd said about the mark of Ziwa.

"Yes, there is power in these symbols. Ziwa and some of the others are also the reason Lucifer has been unable to defeat me as he has my ancestors. I am stronger and more powerful than they were."

Thank God for that, or perhaps I should thank Hell for forging him in such a way. Who knew? I stared down at those glistening fangs as my hands traced over the beasts trapped within him. I couldn't imagine the strength and control it took to keep them contained; only he would be able to do so.

"Do the humans here know you can release the hounds?" I asked.

"No, and they can't know. This must be kept between us. Just as you have to keep your ability to draw life from the earth from the humans as much as possible. Don't ever let anyone, beside me, know what you are fully capable of."

I kissed his shoulder, nuzzling his smooth skin. "I won't tell anyone," I vowed. There were other symbols on him I was curious about, but there was something I had to tell him first. "There's something you should know."

He stiffened against me, and his obsidian eyes burned into mine when I tilted my head to look at him. "What is it?"

I had no idea how he was going to react to what I had to tell him, but he was opening up to me and it was time I did the same. "I had experienced the sparks a few times before. Nothing like what happens between us," I gushed out. "But smaller sparks that lasted for only a second. I wrote them off as static electricity, or I tried to."

"What were you doing when they happened before?"

I shrugged. "The first time it happened was the first time I held Gage after he was first born." My heart swelled at the memory. "He was so precious with his chubby cheeks and tiny fingers. When one of them gripped mine, I felt and saw a small spark, but he didn't notice as he continued to sleep in his swaddle of blankets. It was the first time I ever truly knew what it was to love another.

"The second time was when the man who taught me how to fish died. He was the closest thing I'd ever had to a father and it... it broke my heart when he passed." His hands slid over me in a soothing gesture when my voice broke. "After he was buried, I returned to his garage, where I'd spent many hours with him learning everything he was willing to teach me. I was crying as I ran my fingers over the poles he'd carved by hand when it happened again. It was only a couple of sparks before they vanished. The third time I saw them was the first time I ever held Bailey. I never told anyone about them, not even Gage."

"Why not?"

"Because it's tough enough to already have a few people knowing about your oddities without adding a whole new item to the freaky list. Plus, Gage already worried about me no matter how much I tried to keep things hidden from him. I tried to give him more of a childhood than I'd had; he deserved better, but he still grew up too fast."

My gaze slid away from him and to the sheets. He brushed back my hair before bending to kiss my shoulder. "You deserved better then as you do now, and I will make sure you have it one day. Listen to me and know this, you are not an oddity or a freak."

I smiled at his words, though we both knew there was a good chance that one day would not come. "Maybe not to you," I said. "But we both know I fit in nowhere."

"You fit perfectly against me," he said and hugged me closer against his chest.

My heart melted as I trailed my fingers over his bare legs. If I'd been well on my way to falling in love with him, those words pushed me over the edge. I'd slammed head first into this, but I had no idea what he felt for me, or if demons were even capable of love.

Looking for a way to distract myself from my turbulent emotions, I focused on something else. "Why do you have no hair on you, like other men do? Like I do?"

"This is the way I rose from the fire. However, most other demons are hairless on their bodies, though some do have facial hair along with the hair on their heads."

"An adaption to the heat of Hell," I guessed.

"Probably."

"Will I ever get to see the hounds come to life?" The prospect of such a thing was both thrilling and frightening.

"Most likely, once we leave here. What we'll face out there will be far worse than anything encountered here."

I couldn't imagine anything worse than those strange, pig-like madagans or those bony, mummy-zombie-like revenirs. My heart clenched in my chest at the prospect of worse things.

"Death waits out there," I murmured.

"Is that a vision?" he inquired.

"No, I simply know it. There's a lot of death out there, possibly ours."

"Nothing will harm you while I live. Do not doubt that."

His skin rippled beneath my hand, and his breath warmed my neck when he nuzzled me. He was the most powerful creature I'd ever encountered, a mountain of strength and ferocity that was enticing and sometimes overwhelming.

And he'd claimed me as his.

"I can be myself around you, I never could with any other men," I murmured and he growled. "I always had to be guarded, I always feared I'd be discovered. I want to be yours."

"You *are* mine, Mah Kush-la."

My head tilted at his odd words. They sounded so old and beautiful. "What does that mean?"

"It means *my heart* in my language."

My eyes widened at the sweet endearment. There he went again, digging his way deeper into *my* heart. This time I didn't stop his fingers when they slid over my skin and dipped between my thighs. I whimpered when he stroked around my center before slipping one inside of me.

"Does this hurt?" he inquired.

I was still a little sore but he eased the discomfort with his stimulating touch. "No."

"Tell me if it does," he commanded, and I somehow managed to nod.

His mouth slid over my neck; the scrape of his fangs against my flesh caused my breath to catch and my fingers to dig into his arms. "Do it," I breathed, needing to feel him again.

His four fangs pierced through my skin, causing my entire body to jerk against his. The pain was sharp and fleeting, replaced with a flood of pleasure that caused wetness to spread between my legs as my body readied for him. I felt his claiming of me in the center of my soul. Sparks erupted at the ends of my fingers, licking over the detailed muscles of his thighs and swirling up to encircle my wrists. His free hand slid over mine, pressing it flat against his legs.

"Why does it only do that with you?" I gasped when his

tongue licked over my skin. "It's never been this strong or consistent before."

He released his hold on my shoulder. "Because even the angel part of you knows you belong with me."

"Is that true?"

I groaned when his hand fell away from its intimate caress between my legs. He lifted me in his lap, turning me to face him and adjusting me so the throbbing length of him slipped slowly inside of me when he lowered me onto him again.

"So fucking tight," he bit out, his lips brushing against mine as his fingers curled into my waist. "I believe it's true."

I had no argument for him, not when I believed it was true, too.

CHAPTER THIRTY-EIGHT

Kobal

"What did you do, Kobal?" Bale said in our native language when she stepped beside me.

Corson and Shax stood on the other side of her. I knew immediately what she was talking about as she stared at me before looking to River.

"My relationship with her is off limits for discussion," I replied in our language. We didn't often speak it around humans, they didn't like it when they didn't know what we were talking about, but few of them were paying attention to us right now and this was not a conversation they should overhear.

"How did she manage to survive that?" Corson tilted his head, causing the earrings in the tops of his ears to spin around.

I resisted ripping those hideous things from his ears as he surveyed the marks on River's neck. Three of my bites were clearly visible on her golden skin, but I knew there were more on her, so many more. Just the thought of it made me shift uncomfortably as blood flooded my cock.

I'd mark her over and over again tonight too.

"She's stronger than she looks," I replied blandly.

"She must be as I'm assuming there are more beneath her shirt."

My fangs burst free as I turned on him. "It's none of your concern what's under her shirt!"

Corson took a startled step back, holding his hands up as he moved away. "Easy," he said. "I have no interest at all in it."

I continued to glower at him, but my fangs retracted before I turned my attention back to River. A girl giggled and brushed one of Corson's dangling, unicorn earrings with her fingertips as she walked by him.

"You could always bring me a set of yours if you came to the fire tonight, love," he told her in English and winked at her.

She giggled again, blushing prettily as her eyes fluttered. "Maybe," she replied and hurried away with one of her friends.

He turned toward me, the smile instantly slipping from his face when I scowled at him.

"We know what those marks mean, but the humans don't," Shax said, slipping back into our native tongue. "There's already been talk among them that the two of you are screwing; this will confirm it in their minds. They'll have no idea what to make of this."

"Am I supposed to care?"

"After yesterday, yes. They're already more wary of us," Bale said.

"The humans barely go near her as it is. They don't know what those marks stand for, but they'll recognize she's under my protection and leave her be," I said. "The men will know to stop looking at her too." *They had better know.*

"She's the key we've been searching for; you risk everything if things go badly between you two."

"*Nothing* will go badly between us!" I snapped. "She is my Chosen; I cannot stay away from her."

My gaze instantly returned to River in the crowd of humans. All I wanted was to pull her from here and shelter her from the glances and whispers swirling around her. She didn't pay them any attention, but I knew she felt betrayed by her own kind. A kind she may save from becoming extinct. I'd like to tear every one of the ungrateful pricks to pieces with my bare hands.

"There *is* no staying away from one's Chosen," Shax murmured. "And judging by the bite I see on your neck, there is more demon in her than I think any of us believed there to be."

I hadn't tried to cover her mark on me; I wouldn't. River may not feel the Chosen bond as strongly as I did and may be uncertain about what it really was between us, but a part of her recognized me as hers also, and I would wear her brand for the rest of my days. Or hers. I loathed the reminder of her mortality.

"Such an interesting change of events," Bale murmured.

Beside her, Corson laughed. "Yes, it is."

"Taken down by a human and Lucifer's daughter to boot," Shax snorted. "I never saw that one coming."

"I could have a vision every day, and still not have seen that one coming," Bale laughed.

"She's not a human," I reminded them, trying not to let my irritation show. Around us, humans glanced questioningly our way when the others continued to chuckle and elbow each other.

"She's not," Corson agreed, the first to regain complete control of himself. "And that's what makes this riskier. You know what she is, know she may be the only hope we have of ending this with Lucifer. The only hope we have of surviving. If the others get their hands on her—"

"That's *not* going to happen!" I interrupted brusquely.

"Then they would also control you," Corson continued as if I hadn't spoken. "There is no denying you've claimed her as your Chosen. She has also claimed *you,* though I'm sure she doesn't quite comprehend the strength of the bond or the power that will start to come with it. But with more power comes new weakness."

"More checks and balances," I muttered. "I have explained to her what has happened between us, what those marks mean. She may not grasp it in the same way as a demon, but she understands."

"And the mission?" Corson pressed.

I raked him from head to toe with a scathing glare. Shax took a step away, but Corson held his ground. "I understand the mission comes before she does."

No matter how much I would prefer not to have River involved in this, I had no choice. The lives of thousands of demons depended on me; they had since the moment I'd been forged as a weapon against Lucifer. There had never been any doubt that the fires had created me specifically to defeat Lucifer.

There was a reason many of my ancestors since Lucifer arrived in Hell barely made it a century while I had lived fifteen hundred years. There was a reason I bore the mark of Ziwa and the hounds when no other had before me. Those fires had forged me to reclaim Hell from Lucifer, and I could not turn my back on the many who depended on me to do so. The humans depended on us too; however, I cared less for them than my demon brethren. I didn't want River involved, but I would keep her safe and do what must be done.

“You say that now, but if something were to happen where she fell into the wrong hands, then what?” Shax inquired.

“It won’t happen,” I replied brusquely and focused on River in the line again.

She grabbed a sandwich and placed it on her tray as a blonde woman stepped into line behind her. The woman looked oddly familiar to me, but I couldn’t quite place her. More filed into the line behind River; they maintained their distance from her but also blocked my view. I knew she was there, could feel her as clearly as if she were still against me.

“Kobal—”

“Enough!” I interrupted Shax harshly. “I understand your concerns, but I will keep her safe and do what must be done. It is *my* throne; I cannot forget that. The need to claim it has been with me since the second I arose from those fires, just as it was inbred into all the varcolacs before me.”

Shax wisely remained silent.

“What of her mortality?” Bale inquired. “You can’t try to change her until all of this is over.”

“She would be stronger as an immortal demon,” Corson argued. “Maybe it would be best if he attempted it before we left here.”

“And if she doesn’t survive it?” Bale demanded.

“There *is* demon in her; she will survive it,” Corson insisted.

“I cannot take the chance,” I murmured as I folded my arms over my chest and studied the crowd of humans. “Not only can I not take the risk of her not surviving it, but there is no way to know what it would do to her. It could amplify her powers beyond her control, or it could douse all of her angel abilities and make her entirely demon.”

“Are you going to be able to tolerate her mortality?” Shax inquired.

"I have no choice."

They exchanged looks that I purposely ignored as I studied the crowd. I would do whatever it took to keep River safe, defeat Lucifer, and claim my throne. Even deny the demon instincts screaming at me to take her mortality from her.

"She is not to know it is possible for her to be able to do such a thing, at least not until I'm ready to tell her," I commanded. "Make sure the others know that too."

"We will," Bale replied.

"Our queen," Corson murmured when River briefly reappeared.

"She is," Bale said. "It is an odd pairing, but it is also a good one. With what she is, she is a powerful ally."

"If she becomes immortal and bears your children, even without your abilities, they will grow to be formidable," Shax said.

My heart swelled at the possibility of children and an eternity with River. She'd somehow managed to bring out more emotions in me and surprise me more than anyone I'd ever known in such a short time. I couldn't wait to discover what else she could do over our lifetimes together.

I only had to make sure she survived her mortality first.

River

"Whore."

Too focused on retrieving food from the line, I didn't realize the word had been hissed at *me* until I felt an elbow in my ribs. I grunted and glanced at the offending elbow before looking into the eyes of the woman who had delivered the blow. I sighed when I recognized the same woman who had stepped in front of Kobal and me to hit on him all those days ago.

Great, now I got to have a fun run-in with Kobal's ex. Jealousy coiled within me as I took in her pretty, almost elfin features and blonde hair. Her brown eyes burned with hatred as they raked over the bite marks on my neck. I couldn't have covered them if I'd tried, and I hadn't bothered to try.

They were *his* marks on me and I didn't care who saw them. They would know he was mine as much as I was his. Women, especially this one, would realize he was off limits, and if they didn't realize it by the marks alone, I had no problem with setting their asses on fire.

"Dirty, filthy, whore," the woman continued.

"I don't think we've had the chance to meet," I said and turned toward her. I extended my hand as I smiled at her. "I'm River, the whore, and you are?"

She stared at my hand like it was covered in slime and had an eyeball in the palm. "Demon slut."

I lowered my hand and pushed my tray down the line again. "And I thought my mom had odd taste in names. Do your parents call you D.S. for short?"

I may be able to start fires, but I was fairly certain her head might explode. I braced myself, ready to smash my tray off her face if she made one hostile move toward me. She didn't like me and the feeling was mutual. The idea of her knowing what Kobal felt like made my hands clamp around the tray so violently the plastic cracked beneath my grasp.

Yep, I would love any excuse to bash her pretty little face into something unrecognizable.

"Bitch," she spat.

At least she was coming up with something new. I turned my attention away from her. I wouldn't be gaining anyone's trust by kicking the crap out of her right now.

"I had him first," she taunted.

Despite my every intention not to acknowledge her again,

my eyes flew back to her. My teeth grated together and something crackled. Glancing down, I jerked my hand back and shoved it in my pocket when a golden-white spark shot across my fingertips.

Emotion, I realized, *strong* emotion was what caused that ability to burst forth.

Finally, I had some knowledge of this inner ability. The only problem was I could feel the sparks crackling between my fingers now and I had no idea how to stop them.

These people had been afraid enough of my ability to emit fire; they would run screaming if I threw this at them too. They could see the demons weren't like them, but I'd blended in. I'd been one of them, even if older than a normal volunteer, but still completely human looking in every possible way, until I'd lit a monster on fire. If I turned into a life-force conductor that shot sparks, I'd have no shot of ever having one of them trust me again.

What does it matter? What do you care what they think of you? You're not one of them, not really.

I didn't know why, but for some reason it did matter. Maybe it was because even with all of my oddities, I still felt like one of them. I'd been human for all but two months of my life. Those two months had completely changed the way I saw everything and upended what had been a mostly normal life. I wanted some normalcy again, and people represented that to me.

I had to get away from this woman before I lost complete control. Grabbing a sandwich, I didn't bother to look at what it was before I slapped it on my tray and turned away.

"You'll get what you deserve, bitch," she spat at me.

I stopped, my eyes narrowing on her. "I already did get him."

Keeping my chin lifted, I strode through the crowd toward

where Kobal stood with Bale, Shax, and Corson. He took my tray from me and carried it outside with the others flanking behind us. I refused to look at her again, but I couldn't shake the sick feeling in the pit of my stomach as I felt the woman's eyes burning into my back.

CHAPTER THIRTY-NINE

RIVER

Over the next week, I spent what little spare time I had alone concentrating on drawing out and controlling the pull of life. I didn't tell Kobal that I'd discovered intense emotion was the key to getting it to work. I was looking forward to surprising him with my ability to control it and use it as a weapon.

On the field, when it was only the two of us, I didn't hide I was getting better with it from him, I just didn't reveal to him *how* much better I'd gotten. I'd reveal it to him before we left, in five days. It was all going by so fast, but the fact we were leaving soon was the only reason I had as much alone time as I did. Kobal's attention had become focused on working with Mac on selecting the soldiers who would be leaving with us.

Now, I sat and watched the rigorous training those soldiers endured on the hill, wincing when they were repeatedly taken down by the demons who held nothing back from them as they did with the volunteers. The soldiers weren't allowed to use guns, not now, but they wielded swords, katanas, knives, and any other weapon they could against the demons.

They were allowed to go after anything except for heads when they attacked the demons. Apparently, demon heads were the only things that didn't grow back when lopped off. The discovery was both a little disconcerting and fascinating. It took a demon anywhere from a few hours to a couple of days to regenerate the lost piece of themselves, depending on the size of the missing body part and the strength of the demon.

Few of the humans managed to succeed in freeing a demon of their hand, arm, foot, or leg. The ones who did were instantly separated into another group. I believed it meant they'd gotten an upgrade on their chances of getting a trip to Hell. I wasn't so sure it was a good thing, but then, they knew what they were signing up for. It had not been kept from them.

The last thing Kobal wanted were humans who preferred not to be on the mission. I thought he'd had enough of that with my start here, and they didn't have the time to work with these soldiers that he'd spent with me. I still missed my brothers dearly, but I'd come to accept my place here and what I was. I may not have liked it in the beginning, but was being able to throw fire and draw on the life of things around me really so bad?

It would have actually been pretty freaking fantastic, if it hadn't made me the spawn of Lucifer and the main hope for demons and humans to somehow right the wrongs the angels had started six thousand years ago, and the humans had escalated thirteen years ago.

I tried not to let my anxiety show, but the closer it came to the day when we would be leaving, the more doubt and terror ate at me. What if I wasn't able to do anything with the gate? What if I failed? What then? What was Lucifer, the fallen angel who had created my line, like?

I hated that I was curious about him, but I couldn't help it. If I failed to close the gateway, would I be expected to enter

Hell and take Lucifer himself on? The idea made my pulse race and my mouth go dry.

I would do anything I could to keep my brothers safe from the horrors lurking on this side of the wall, but I wasn't ready to die. However, I didn't think there was any way I *could* survive a fight with Lucifer when millennia plus, regenerating, immortal demons hadn't been able to take him out in six thousand years.

I shut the thought down; giving into the uncertainty trying to swamp me would do *no* one any good, least of all me. We still had to make it to the gateway before anything else could be a concern. That had to be my main focus, getting strong enough to travel through areas devastated by demons and nukes. It should be a piece of cake.

As the day for departure drew closer, messages were sent to the other demons at the other bases around the country. They were also preparing themselves and gathering humans to head into the deadened interior of our country.

So many would die if I failed. I had to get back to practicing. Rising to my feet, I wiped my ass off as I watched a pretty soldier with black hair, almond-shaped eyes, and a creamy complexion being led toward another soldier who had recently been separated from the main group. The woman nodded to the man with close-cropped black hair and a deep olive complexion.

Earlier, I'd watched the man succeed in slicing an ear from one of the demons. Now, a demon walked past the two human soldiers, holding his stumpy wrist. I couldn't help but smile when the woman with almond-shaped eyes and black hair smiled with pride at the scowling demon. Her blue eyes twinkled in the sunlight shining down on her as she exchanged a high-five with the man with a swarthy complexion, black hair, and brown eyes.

Longing spread through me as I watched the easy

comradery they shared. I'd had that with Gage and Lisa; I'd been accepted and loved. I had Kobal now. It wasn't the same, but my love for him was growing every day, and I'd discovered a happiness with him that I hadn't expected to find when I'd first arrived here. I belonged with him, but I still missed the simplicity and acceptance of those lost days with my family and friends.

I shook my head to clear it of the melancholy reflections and turned away from the training. Most of the volunteers were in class, learning more about the demons. I already knew far more about the demons than they did. Besides, I had my own learning and training to do.

I didn't glance back at Bale and Verin as they followed me toward the tents. They must hate being stuck on guard duty, but this close to leaving, Kobal had no choice but to hand some of my care over to the others. No matter how much I told him I didn't require a guard dog, he wouldn't listen.

I'd resigned myself to being under constant watch until all of this was over. I refused to think about the possibility it might never end; I'd go nuts if I did.

Slipping into the tent, I let the flap fall behind me before hurrying to the room I shared with Kobal. Peace stole through me when I entered and inhaled the lingering aroma of him within it. Taking some time to steady myself, I allowed his scent to fill me and fuel my emotions as I moved about the space.

When I felt more centered, I knelt to rest my hand on the ground. My fingers slipped through the loose dirt to feel the pulse of life in the earth beneath my fingers. I shut off all thoughts of anything else and focused on picturing Kobal. I felt the searing heat of his body moving over mine, possessing me.

My breathing sped up, but not from my blooming passion; instead, it was from the increase of the pulse beneath my fingertips. Warmth slid up my fingertips, into my arm, and across my chest until it was pulsing through my body with every beat of my heart.

Lifting my other hand, I held it before me as the sparks flickered to life and increased. It felt as if the cells of my body were spreading out, flowing down into the dirt to gather more power and drawing it into me like the roots of a tree feeding from the earth. Like those roots, the cells sought to stabilize and strengthen me against the hazards the world would throw at me.

The warmth faded away to be replaced with the fiery heat of life. The sparks at the ends of my fingers increased until they were a glowing energy swelling before me. The energy spun, rising up until it became a ball of golden-white light hovering above my palm. The power of those crackling sparks danced across my cheeks and caused my hair to wave about my face.

Awe slid through me. I didn't think I'd ever get used to this feeling. There was something so freeing yet so connecting about this. It made me feel like I was a part of every living thing on this earth and beyond it.

Small sparks shot off the sides of the ball, but for the most part, I kept the flow of life confined within my grasp. Kobal had seen me get to this part. What I hadn't let him see was the ball spinning before me when I moved my fingers of the palm it hovered above. He'd yet to see me pull my other hand away from the earth and still manage to keep the ball formed before me.

Lifting my hands, the ball rose up then fell back down when I lowered them again. Digging my fingers into the earth once more, I pulled the ball of energy back into myself, flooding it down into the fingers of my other hand and back into the earth before dragging it forth once more to form another ball.

Rising, I held the ball before me, bouncing it as a child

would bounce a ball within their grasp. Lifting it higher, I switched my grasp on it and drove it straight into the ground, returning it to its rightful place in the earth. Joy and disbelief went through me when I spotted the charred spot it had left on the ground; I'd never done *that* before.

A dangerous weapon indeed. I stared at the charred spot before kicking dirt over it to cover it before Kobal returned. He'd definitely be astonished when I showed him what I could do with it now. It would be better if I could get outside and really see what it could do. I had a feeling leaving charred marks in the earth was only the tip of the iceberg. I'd have to tell Kobal soon if I was going to get any real practice in with it before we left the protection of the wall.

The rustle of the buttons on the outer tent pulling apart drew my attention away from the freshly kicked dirt. My heart sped up as I listened to the flap settle into place again. Walking forward, I stepped into the main part of the tent. The light of the lanterns danced over Kobal's face, illuminating his chiseled features and bringing to life the shades of mahogany brown and black in his hair. Had I really not considered him gorgeous at one time? Now I found him the most stunning man on the planet.

His eyes raked over me as I tugged my shirt over my head. It had been hours since I'd last seen him, far too much time as far as I was concerned. We could talk later; right now, all I wanted was to be in his arms.

I stripped off my shorts as I walked toward him. Over the past week, I'd realized if I wanted to continue to have clothes to wear, it would be wiser if I took them off before he could get his hands on me as he had a habit of tearing them from me. I was already wet for him by the time I reached him.

His eyes were the color of golden amber when he swept me into his arms and lifted me off the ground. Sparks shot to life at the tips of my fingers when he set me on the table and pulled my ass toward the end of it.

His large hands were tender when they pushed my thighs apart. His hungry gaze latched onto me. I became wetter at the ravenous gleam in his eyes as he stared at my sex. He hastily tore at the button of his pants, jerking them open and shoving them over his hips. Longing spread through my body when his erection sprang free.

"Mine," I whispered as I brushed my fingers over the pulsing head and smoothed the bead of liquid forming there. I licked my lips with the urge to taste him.

"Always, Mah Kush-la," he breathed hoarsely in my ear before driving himself into me with a low groan.

My legs wrapped around his waist, and I lost all reason when his body took possession of mine.

CHAPTER FORTY

River

"Well, aren't you an interesting little tidbit."

I frowned at the voice whispering at me from the darkness. Turning, I tried to find the source of that voice, but the cavern I stood in held only shadows and secrets. I sniffed the air as the scent of rocks and something more, fire perhaps, drifted to me. Where was I?

Certainly not in camp anymore. Was this another dream? It had to be, but it was unlike any I'd ever experienced before. I sensed it was a dream built on a connection, but those had always involved someone I knew or at least a place I knew. I had no idea who had spoken and I'd certainly never been here before.

Despite the shadows, heat pressed against me. Sweat trickled down my temples and cleaved my shirt to my body. It wasn't unbearable, but it was still hotter than anything I'd ever encountered before.

Hotter than Hades. And then it hit me. I tried to show no reaction to my realization, but my fingers twitched involuntarily. I knew whose voice it had been, who was standing in the darkness. I could feel his eyes on me, burning into my flesh.

"I can't say the same about you, since I can't see you," I said with far more bravado than I felt for someone standing within the Devil's dream.

A chuckle emanated from my right. Turning, I watched as the shadows coalesced around the being stepping from them. The gloom hugged him within its grasp before reluctantly releasing him. I couldn't stop my eyes from widening on the man who emerged.

He was nearly as tall as Kobal as his head almost brushed against the rocks above him. Black hair fell in waves to the collar of his shirt and about his face. Features chiseled into perfection kept me riveted upon a face so flawless it could only be the face of an angel.

I'd never seen anything as beautiful as this man, or so distantly cold. He robbed the breath from my chest as the heat encompassing the room faded away to become filled with the iciness radiating from him.

His black eyes surveyed me from head to toe and back again. "Daughter," he greeted.

"Lucifer."

A muscle twitched in his cheek, and his eyes narrowed subtly; apparently he really didn't like his angelic name. Go figure the Devil would be pissy about a name when he had so many of them.

Something rippled behind him, drawing my gaze to the coal black wings I hadn't noticed amongst the darkness embracing him. Sensing my attention to them, a smile curved his mouth before he unfurled his wings. I gasped when they spread around him, nearly brushing the walls on either side of him. Each of them had to span six feet off of his towering frame.

There was nothing angelic about these wings, from their black color to their almost bat-like form. Where were the feathers? These were more like scales. No, not scales; if there had ever been feathers on them, they were gone. Now all that remained was a leathery blackness, which I realized wasn't solid as my gaze fell on the veins running beneath the flesh. Those veins pulsed black blood through them as I watched.

At the center of the top of each wing was a spiked, almost foot-long silver point, one I knew he could drive straight through my eye and out the other side of my head without so much as blinking. The bottom tip of each wing had another long point. When he took a step closer to me, those points clicked off the rock floor in a way that made the world lurch threateningly.

How could someone be so beautiful yet so twisted?

"What is your name, child?"

I didn't respond; I far preferred it if he never knew my name. Thankfully, his attention was distracted when his gaze fell to my neck; an eyebrow rose as his head tilted to the side. "Who has marked you, child?" he inquired. "Who thinks to claim you without asking for your hand first?"

I took a step away from him as he drew closer. I didn't know if I could die in these dreams, and I didn't want to find out. "Demons are beneath us, daughter. You would do far better with one of *my* men than with one of *them*."

"I'll choose my own man, but thanks for the concern," I replied.

I took a startled step back, turning to the side when one of those wings shot out. I felt the air of it against my skin as my hair blew in the breeze it had created. The rock beneath my feet cracked when the bottom tip embedded itself into the ground with a solid thud, effectively cutting me off from going that way. I didn't think there was any chance of me going anywhere with him in this room with me.

"*Who* has marked you?" he hissed.

Everything in me screamed to keep it a secret, one I would take to my grave if it turned out he could kill me in these strange dreams. Kobal had said every demon would know I was his, but Lucifer wasn't entirely a demon. Or maybe he did know and was just toying with me.

Leaning closer to me, I heard his sharp intake of breath as he inhaled deeply. I could feel the evil emanating from him in waves that beat against my skin and rattled my bones. Maybe Kobal didn't think of good and evil as I'd always thought of them, but this man was evil incarnate. I had no idea if he'd been this way before he'd been thrown from Heaven, or if he'd become twisted and broken by his fall, but he was definitely evil now.

When he pulled away from me, a malicious smile curved his lips. His eyes sparkled in a way I hadn't believed possible for one such as him. "Interesting," he murmured and licked his lips. "I could not have *chosen* a finer daughter than you."

I resisted the impulse to rub my hands over my chilled flesh. *He knows.* Perhaps there was more demon in him than any of us realized if he'd been able to sense it was Kobal's mark on me. *This is bad, very, very bad.*

He yanked the pointed tip from the earth and retreated a few steps. The wings folded behind his back once more so all that showed were those lethal, silver tips above his broad shoulders. Those icy black eyes surveyed me from head to toe again before he turned to retreat into the shadows.

"Wait!" I cried.

His head turned, and his gaze found me over his shoulder. "Yes, daughter."

I shuddered at the realization this man saw me as his child

as much as the demons did. I didn't kid myself into thinking he wouldn't kill me because of it; he may kill me just *because* of it.

"Why did you bring me here?" I demanded.

There was that smile again. "Oh, *my* child, in this it was *you* who finally sought to meet your creator." He turned back to me and took a step forward. "Every child is curious about their father after all."

Sickness twisted in my gut. *I* had brought *him* to me! I wanted to deny his words, but I couldn't shake the certainty they were true. "You are not my father."

"Am I not? You would not be standing here if not for me. The powers you possess were given to you through me. You are *my* offspring and, therefore, part of me resides in you. The more those powers grow, the more they will eat at you until one day it will be you standing within these cavern walls."

"I will *never* be anything like you."

"Will you not? You're only beginning to tap the potential of your power."

One wing flowed forward. The deadly point tapped against his temple much like a person would do with a finger. I realized those wings were as much an extension of him as my own hands were of me.

"The stronger your powers get, the more they will consume you, and when they do, they will take *him* too. There is finally one who can bring Kobal down, and it is *you*. I've seen glimpses of your future, child, and it is *interesting*."

"You're lying!" I accused.

"Like your powers, the stronger your bond becomes with him, the more it will threaten him. When those powers twist you, and they will, he will be dragged down with you. Angels and demons do not see the world in good and evil. I was born to set them free, and I will set them all free. I will show them they were wrong and you will be standing at my side when they learn of pure *evil*. What is inside of me is also inside of you."

"No," I choked out through the constriction in my chest. His words so closely echoed my own doubts and fears that no matter how much I tried to shake them off, they dug deeper into me. "No."

"You will help me to take down the only one who has managed to elude me."

"Lies, it's all lies. You're wrong. We're stronger together."

His smile grew, and the points of his wings tapped together when he ruffled them. "Are they lies? And are you stronger? Maybe if you were a demon, but you're not. You are *my* child and the creatures from this abysmal place have no idea what to make of us, but they will. The apple does not fall from the tree, River, ask Eve. I will be sending you a gift, child, look for it."

Before I could respond, the shadows enveloped him once more and he vanished from view.

Kobal

River bolted upright so fast in bed that she wrenched herself from my arms when she leapt to her feet. I shot up, tossing the covers aside while she spun in a circle around the tent. Her eyes frantically searched for something as sparks shot from her fingertips.

"What is it?" I demanded.

"Lucifer."

Seizing her shoulders, I drew her flush against my chest as my fangs burst free and my claws extended. "Where?" I snarled. She trembled against me before shaking her head. "Where, River?"

"Dream, it was a dream," she murmured as her head fell forward and she rubbed at her temples.

Keeping hold of her shoulders, I pulled her away from me a little to take her in. She looked hollower somehow as her freckles stood starkly out against her ashen complexion and shadows encircled her eyes.

"You dreamt of him?" I asked.

"Nearly as tall as you, black hair, black eyes, beautiful. Has black wings with spiked points in the middle and two more at the bottom tips. Thinks I'm his child too. If that's him, then yes, I dreamt of him."

My blood ran cold as she spoke, and my fingers dug deeper into her bare shoulders. I forced my claws to retract before I pierced her flesh. Brushing the hair back from her cheeks, I clasped them in my hands and lifted her face. Her lower lip quivered when her gaze met mine. The panic in her violet eyes unnerved me.

"What happened?" I asked as calmly as I could, sensing she required my composure more than anything right now. "Tell me everything."

"He *knew* it was you who marked me!" she gushed out.

"Most likely," I replied casually.

Inside, I felt anything but casual. The hounds stalked within me, demanding to be set free, to kill, rend, and tear apart any risk to her. They couldn't know the threat had been her dream and there was nothing here for them to fight. If I set them free, they would rip through this town, shredding anyone who stepped in their path, much like I yearned to do. I didn't care who it was, I had to feel their blood on my hands, had to kill something in order to unleash some of this savagery building within me.

Her hand on my cheek drew my attention to her. I didn't realize my fangs and claws had extended again until her finger brushed over the tip of one of my upper fangs. My lips skimmed back, not in anger but with need. I could kill, or I could take *her* and ease what was inside of me.

"He'll use me against you," she whispered as she pressed her naked body closer to mine.

As my Chosen, she would sense what I needed most now, though there would be no denying it as my hardened shaft pressed against her belly.

"He'll never get the chance to try," I assured her as I guided her toward the bed.

"He saw evil in my future, and I don't care what you say Kobal, that man is *evil*. He is everything humans ever believed him to be."

"He lied."

"But what if he didn't?" she asked.

I froze before I could nudge her thighs apart. Her terror beat against me. River had *never* been scared of anything, not even when she should have been. She'd never feared me, but then she may have sensed from the beginning she was to be mine.

"Do not fear him." It came out as more of a command than I'd intended.

"I'm not afraid of him," she whispered. "I'm afraid he's right. I am his offspring. You all claim he's my father. He was once an angel, and now he's a monster. I am no angel, Kobal. I'm no saint. What if my future is what he predicted? He said the more my powers grow, the more they'll eat at me until I'm twisted like him, and then I would bring you down with me! He said the stronger the bond becomes between us, the more it will endanger you. Angels and demons don't see the world in good and evil, and because of that, he said he was born to set you all free, and *I* will be standing at his side when it happens."

"River—"

"He told me what is inside of him is also inside of *me*. He expects me to help him take down the only one who has managed to elude him, *you*!" she cried as her eyes became more turbulent.

My breath froze in my chest, and my body stiffened against hers as her words sank in. I didn't believe for one second anything he'd told her, but his words had taken root within her mind. She had asked before if she could be evil, but I'd believed it to be a concern of the past; I knew now I was wrong. Lucifer had been able to detect her worries and turn them against her.

"He's a master manipulator, River. None of what he said is true."

"You can't know that," she whispered, "not for sure. He said I am *his* child and that the apple doesn't fall far from the tree. You all consider me his child too. He also said he'd be sending me a gift and to look for it."

Tears! The sight of them shimmering in her eyes tore at my heart. What had that prick done to her?

I had always known I would one day kill him, but now I would make Lucifer's death an excruciating experience that would make all the tortures of Hell look like a day in Heaven in comparison. Unlucky for him, I had over a millennia of torture and suffering to draw on once I had him in my grasp.

"He's lying to try and keep you from growing stronger, to keep you from learning more of your powers, and to get between us. He knows demons become stronger when they find their Chosen."

Corson's words from earlier drifted through my head, *'But with more power comes new weakness.'* I shoved them aside. They may be true, but in no way or in any dimension could River ever become like Lucifer. She would strengthen me more than she weakened me. I would not lose her.

"He knows both of our powers will only increase because

of our bond," I told her. "It was a ploy. He pulled you in to implant these doubts in your head. He can't find you, so he found another way to attack you. Discovering you were my Chosen only made things easier for him to manipulate."

"I'm the one who drew *him* into my dream. I didn't mean to; it's certainly not something I planned to have happen. But I did it somehow and for some *reason*."

I brushed the tears from her cheeks as I leveled my body over hers. I used my thigh to nudge hers apart as I contemplated her words. She bit her lip as her hips instinctively rose toward mine.

"You're about to start a journey that's going to take you toward him; of course you're curious about what you will face. Unlike the humans, you have the ability to ease some of your curiosity. We'll have to try and shut that down from happening again," I said.

"It *will* be shut down."

I smiled at her as I brushed a kiss over the tip of her nose. Her legs lifted so her knees pressed against my sides. Her distress continued to beat against me, but her body instinctively sought to ease it. Her eyes remained latched on mine as I slid into her wet sheath.

"Do you feel me?" I inquired as her muscles gripped my aching cock.

"Always," she whispered.

"What this is between us is stronger than him," I told her as I nuzzled her neck. "Stronger than *any* powers."

"He'll come for you," she whispered, "or for me. What becomes of you if something were to happen to me?"

"That won't happen," I told her as I moved deliberately out and then back into her, allowing her body to ease the burning need to kill something her words had awoken in me. She was everything I had ever needed or wanted in the world. She was my heart and I would not let her go.

"But if it did, what would happen to you, Kobal?"

I smoothed the hair back from her pale face before bending to kiss her lips. I refused to entertain the possibility of anything happening to her. I was strong enough to keep us both alive. "A Chosen is left broken and hollow without their other half," I told her. "But that will never be us."

She paled further as her hands rested against my cheeks and her gaze latched onto mine. "I can't be used against you; I won't allow it."

I smiled at her as I drove into her, causing her to cry out in pleasure. "Neither will I, Mah Kush-la, but you have no reason to worry about any of this." Taking hold of her wrists, I gripped them in my hand before dragging them over her head. "Now, I'm going to make sure you're too tired to dream again."

A small smile curved her lips, but sadness remained in her eyes. I couldn't help but feel like something had changed, as if she were pulling away from me even as she gave herself over to me.

CHAPTER FORTY-ONE

RIVER

Standing on the hill with all the humans who had been training to become a part of the mission to leave, I watched as Kobal, the demons, Mac, and a handful of older soldiers moved to stand before us. They were grouped together, talking between themselves as they scanned the humans gathered before them.

Kobal's eyes latched onto me, and my toes curled at the ravenous gleam in his gaze. I loved him more than I'd ever believed possible, but after last night, I was beginning to question if what I'd thought was so right may actually be the worst thing to ever happen to him. If he wouldn't end up hating me as much as he hated my ancestor.

The possibility caused something inside of me to shrivel. I'd rather be dead than ever have that happen, but if we continued to get closer it might. I just didn't know how I could ever let him go. The idea tore at my insides, shredding them to pieces and leaving me as raw and exposed as I'd felt when I'd first awoken last night.

Because of my curiosity about my ancestor, I'd reached out to him in my dream and now Lucifer knew what I was to Kobal, what he was to me. He would do everything he could to exploit that knowledge. And what if he'd been right? What if one day I became like him and clung to Hell. What if what I could do turned me into a twisted version of what he'd become?

Kobal might be right and Lucifer had been lying to keep me from getting better with my powers, I definitely wouldn't put it past the bastard, but he also could have been telling the truth. I had no idea what had caused him to become the way he was; there may be something that could do the same thing to me.

It was all so confusing, and I found myself unable to breathe as the bodies pressed closer against me and a sense of impending doom weighed heavily on my chest.

Mac stepped forward and approached the soldiers fanned out before him. Only one hundred of the original two hundred remained, the others had already been cut. They all stood rigidly, their shoulders thrust back and their chins tilted up. I tried to assume their proud postures, but I felt like a wilting weed in a field of tall stalks. I'd never been a good soldier; there was no point in trying to pretend to be now.

"We've made our decision about who will be joining this vital mission," Mac announced. "A mission that will present horrors and dangers we have yet to come across, but these horrors will become a daily part of all of humanity's existence if something is not done to end it now. We have an opportunity to do that, and we are going to take it."

A ripple went through the crowd as some murmured in excitement about what was to come. These people may not have known what they were getting into when they'd originally volunteered to come to the wall, but over the course of my time here, I'd come to learn more than a few of them excelled at being a soldier.

"Due to the necessity of trying to keep a low profile, there will only be fifty men and women joining the demon faction on this journey. If I call your name, please remain where you are until you are told to do otherwise." Mac paced before the group, calling out names as he strode back and forth before us.

Eyes swung toward me when my name was called. Questions traveled through some of the people gathered. I was a volunteer; I wasn't supposed to be considered for this journey. I hadn't gone through the special training with them, but then none of them knew I was the whole reason this mission was taking place.

They knew where they were going, what they might face, but they hadn't been told it was me who had set it all into motion to begin with. Kobal had decided to keep that from them until the end.

"Whore slept her way into this."

My gaze didn't waver, but my jaw clenched at the familiar, hated voice. Over the past week, I'd heard the terms whore and slut more times than I'd ever thought possible. I'd also learned the name of the woman who threw those words at me with such spiteful glee. It was Eileen. I'd come to despise that name as much as her.

"They're only taking the best," someone else murmured. "They wouldn't take someone because she's sleeping with one of them."

"She's screwing the leader," Eileen hissed back.

"And so did you, once."

I resisted the urge to tear every blonde hair from Eileen's head. Kobal wouldn't have cared if I'd had a thousand lovers before him, but I despised the reminder he'd had many before me. I really hated that one of them had been *her*.

Jealousy wasn't something I was accustomed to, but she brought it forth so easily in me. I really hoped her name wasn't called for this. I may end up throwing her into the pit of Hell myself if it was.

"I don't see him taking you with him though," the man who had been speaking with Eileen continued. "And from what I've heard of her, she's more lethal than you are."

I bit back a laugh, and my gaze darted to the side to see who it was that had caused Eileen's face to turn redder than the lobsters from back home. The man who had uttered the words wasn't looking at Eileen; his eyes remained focused ahead.

He was handsome with his brunet hair cropped short against his skull. He stood proudly with his broad shoulders thrust back and his hands folded behind him. His indigo eyes followed Mac's every move, but his head never wavered from its forward position.

Eileen glared at him before turning to focus on me with the hate-filled look I'd become so accustomed to since my relationship with Kobal had intensified. She stood in the row behind me and three people to my right. I smiled back at her and gave a little wave of my fingers, something *none* of the other soldiers who would be chosen for this mission would do, which made it more fun.

Turning back around, I focused on Kobal as Mac recited the last of the names and returned to the center of the group.

"If your name was called, please come forward now!" Mac announced.

People moved forward amongst the crowd, walking proudly toward Mac and the others. I was happy to see the man who had been speaking with Eileen heading toward the front while she remained unmoving, her face turning redder and her mouth hanging open. She must have hoped to get accepted for this mission with the goal of getting Kobal all to herself.

Suck it.

I'd taken five steps forward when the world faded away from me, and the image of Eileen lunging at my back with a knife filled my head.

I gasped when I was thrust back into my body. I twisted to the side as a foot-long blade slid past my stomach. It was so close it sliced open the front of my shirt and nicked my skin. If I hadn't seen her coming, she would have stabbed me clean through with it.

Her startled brown eyes met mine before she swung the knife at me again. Keeping my stomach sucked in, I jumped back, barely managing to avoid being gutted by the blade. The movement caused me to crash into the side of someone.

"Get off me!" they snapped.

I lunged to the side to avoid the next lethal arc of the blade. I could release a ball of fire at her, but I was nowhere near as good at controlling it as Kobal was and I didn't want to take the chance of setting someone else on fire. Plus, I really would prefer not to torch a human, even if it was *her*.

I wasn't supposed to let anyone know about my ability to draw on life, and after what it had done to the earth the other day, it might be more dangerous than my fire. My only choice was to stay back from her, until I had a chance to take her down.

Eileen grunted as she swung violently back and forth in a desperate attempt to make my intestines visible for everyone to see. Finally realizing what was going on, the crowd fell away from us to avoid the lethal arc of the blade. I jumped back, tripping over a young man who wasn't fast enough to get out of the way.

With a scream of frustration, Eileen lunged at me again. I wasn't fast enough to get completely out of the way this time and the blade sliced across my arm. Twisting to the side, I brought my other arm down on hers and knocked the blade free. I grabbed the back of her head and drove it down at the same time I lifted my knee and slammed it into her nose.

She howled and clutched at her broken nose as blood burst free. I smiled in satisfaction when I realized I'd pancaked it, much like I'd pictured doing days ago in the cafeteria. Swinging my hand out, I backhanded her across the face, knocking her to the side and causing her to sprawl on the ground.

Inhaling rapidly to calm my racing heart and the rush of adrenaline coursing through my body, I took a few steps away. My body pulsed with the need to do more, to go at her again. I longed to make her pay for every snide comment and for ever having known what it felt like to be with Kobal.

I'd never felt this out of control and so close to brutal violence before. It rattled me almost as much as her attack had.

Not like Lucifer, I will not *be like him.* If I went back after her, it would be the first step to going over the edge, to becoming more like him. He would have walked over to Eileen and finished her off without a second's hesitation; I couldn't.

The crowd had formed a circle around us, but I could see them being shoved apart as Kobal thrust his way through the group. The thunderous expression on his face caused my knees to go weak.

Almost at the small circle Eileen and I stood in, he shoved aside a young man so remorselessly, he sent him sprawling to the ground. His eyes burned with amber fire when they latched onto the blood spilling from my arm and then the slice in my shirt. People scrambled away from him when a snarl tore from him.

The earth shook beneath my feet as he stalked toward me. If I hadn't known him better, I would have scrambled to get out of his way too as fury emanated from him in waves I could feel pulsating against my skin.

Despite the color of his eyes and his lethal air, his hands were tender when he took hold of my wrist and elbow. He inspected my arm before releasing my elbow. His fingers fondled the slice through my shirt as his eyes latched onto my belly. Beads of blood had formed along the scratch there; one slid down my flesh.

His eyes burned so hot I thought they might set my clothes on fire. Lifting his head, his gaze slid past me toward where I'd last seen Eileen. I couldn't bring myself to look at her again yet; I needed a few minutes to regain control of my rocketing emotions over what had occurred. I was afraid I might kill her if I didn't.

"Why would you do this?" Kobal demanded of her.

"Kobal," I whispered, "don't."

I clutched his arm when he took a step toward her. Bracing myself, I turned to find Eileen back on her feet and two men holding her arms. One of them was the man who had been defending me to her. Mac stood to the side, turning the knife over in his hand as he studied the blade.

"Attacking another soldier is absolutely not permitted," Mac said. "Take her to the cells where she will be held until we can try her for her crime."

"She is to be put to death," Kobal grated.

"If that is what a judge decides," Mac replied before handing the knife over to another soldier.

"*I* am deciding," Kobal declared.

The color drained from Eileen's face so fast her knees gave out on her. The two men had to brace their legs in order to keep her up. "Let them take her," I said quietly.

His gaze barely flickered toward me before he pulled his arm from my grasp and closed the five feet separating her from us. No one had a chance to react before he grabbed hold of her head and twisted it harshly to the side.

The crack of bone caused everyone around me to wince, some cried out as they fell back from him. Kobal didn't stop with the breaking of her neck but kept twisting until the rending of cartilage, muscle, and flesh could be heard in a sickening wet, crunching sound that caused my stomach to lurch.

The two men holding Eileen's arms dropped them as if they'd caught on fire and stepped briskly to the side as Kobal tore the head from her body. My hand flew to my mouth as a spurt of blood shot out, spraying over the men who had been holding her and Kobal. Some of the hot wash hit me in the face, staggering me back a step as the beads of it slid down my cheeks to drip off my chin.

Turning to the crowd, Kobal raised Eileen's head in the air as her body collapsed onto the ground. Bile surged into my mouth, and by sheer strength of will, I managed to swallow it back before I could spew it onto the ground. Others weren't so lucky as they retched onto the grass surrounding us.

In Kobal's grasp, Eileen's mouth hung ajar and her eyes were open in unseeing, endless horror. The last thing she'd seen was the man she'd been so obsessed with ripping her head from her body. That realization made me almost vomit again.

Blood dripped from Kobal's hair, slid down his face, and splattered his clothes, but he didn't appear to notice any of it as he continued to hold Eileen's head high in the air. Part of her spine and muscles dangled from the bottom of her head. Some of those around me swayed unsteadily.

"Anyone who dares to attack her again will have their arms and legs ripped from their bodies before I tear their heads from them!" Kobal declared.

Mac stood beside him, his face abnormally pale, but he didn't say a word as Kobal thrust the head at Corson. The demon started when the head hit his stomach, but he took hold of Eileen's hair.

"Have it placed on a stake, along with her body," Kobal commanded.

Before anyone could reply, Kobal strolled across the blood-drenched ground toward me. I forced myself not to recoil from him, though everything in me wanted to get as far from him as possible right then. What he'd just done never should have happened. It didn't matter if he was a demon.

I somehow managed to keep myself from screaming when he slid his hand around my elbow; it felt as if ice slid through my veins. I'd encountered pure evil in my dream last night, and while I didn't think Kobal was evil, his actions certainly hadn't been *good*.

My knees quivered, and my feet felt like lead weights beneath me as I tried to keep up with him when he propelled me across the ground. Blood dripped from my hair, making nausea churn more insistently within my stomach.

"You shouldn't have done that," I managed to croak out before we reached the tent.

"Yes, I should have," he replied brusquely. "No one is going to harm you and get away with it, *ever*."

He'd done it to protect me, but the ruthlessness with which it had been done, the reason she'd attacked in the first place, were all *wrong*.

"She was wrong, but so were you!" I gasped when we arrived at the tent and he pulled the flap up.

His eyes were remorseless when they met mine, and he gestured for me to go inside. I shook my head no.

"Get in," he commanded.

"Kobal—"

"Get inside, River!" he didn't shout at me, but something in his tone of voice made it seem as if he'd bellowed the words for all the world to hear.

He'd never hurt me, but I sensed an unraveling within him

I'd never expected to see or had experienced before. The simmering explosion waiting for release had me ducking into the tent. He followed behind. Before I could open my mouth to speak, he spun me around, clasped my cheeks, and seized hold of my mouth in a kiss that stole my breath from me.

I tried to keep myself held back from him. I had just witnessed a decapitation by his hand, but when his tongue swept in to taste me and his arm locked around my waist to lift me against him, I also wanted to pretend it hadn't happened. His hand cupped hold of my breast, kneading my flesh through my shirt and bra.

His other hand slid over my shirt, brushing briefly against the torn fabric and the scratch beneath. The reminder of what had caused that slice caused reality to crash over me with the effect of water being dumped on my head. I twisted in his grasp, tearing my mouth away from his and shoving my hands against his blood-soaked chest.

"Stop!" I yelled and pushed at him again.

"I need you."

"No, not like this, not in her blood."

"What does it matter?"

I shuddered at the stark reminder of how different we were from each other. I'd been living in this fantasy world where the demon was tamed and he was more like me than not. I'd been an idiot. Her life had meant nothing to him. Though she would have killed me, she hadn't deserved what he'd done. *None* of it would have happened to begin with if he hadn't slept with her and completely forgotten about her after.

I didn't fit into this world of death and Hell and the Devil's offspring. I'd lived in a fishing community with my brothers and had a simple life of work and survival.

I couldn't deny what I was, would not turn my back on

what I had to do, but Lucifer's words rang in my head. There had been no love in that man, no caring; I couldn't let myself become like him, and I felt as if I were slipping down the slope toward it if I condoned *this* in any way.

CHAPTER FORTY-TWO

River

"Let go of me!" I shoved angrily at his massive chest again.

He remained standing before me, not at all fazed by my pushing. "River—"

"I'm covered in her blood, and it matters to *me*!" I practically screeched at him.

He finally released me and took a step away. "I'll take you to shower."

"Her life meant more than the little regard you showed her." I sounded insane for defending the woman who had called me every nasty name in the book and tried to fillet me like a fish, but he had to understand it wasn't *right* to rip people's heads off. That I found myself trying to explain this to him seemed as completely ridiculous to me as defending Eileen's actions did. "You can't do that to people."

He pivoted to follow me as I edged further away from him. I wasn't entirely sure I could resist him if he kissed me again. "I'll do whatever the fuck I want when it comes to keeping you safe."

"Your actions are what put me in danger with her to begin with!" I accused.

His forehead furrowed, and I threw up my hands to ward him off when he took a step toward me. A rumble of frustration emitted from him, but he stayed where he was. "What are you talking about?" he demanded.

"The only reason she hated me, called me a whore and every other thing she could think to call me, and attacked me today is because you had sex with her and *forgot* her!"

"You should have told me she was saying these things to you."

"Why? What would you have done then?" His face remained stony. "Forget it. I don't want to know."

"I would have taken care of it."

"*You* were the reason for it! The woman whose head you just *tore* off was the same one from the cafeteria a couple of weeks ago who you could not remember. I think she believed herself in love with you, and you tossed her aside."

He folded his arms over his chest. "Then she was a fool. If she had come to me, I'd have told her so."

I went to wrap my arms around myself in a sad attempt at comfort. I stopped when I recalled Eileen's blood on me. My hands fell limply back to my sides. "How can you be so callous about a life?"

"Because it's not yours, Mah Kush-la."

The endearment caused my heart to twist with anguish. I wanted to melt into his arms so badly, but I couldn't. "Mine is not the most important—"

"But it *is*, especially compared to all of *theirs*. They mean nothing, and I meant what I said about ripping every one of their limbs off the next time one of them so much as breathes on you the wrong way."

"You can't do that. Our world doesn't work like that."

"It's the way it works now. Humans brought us here, they thrust us into this world, and now they have no choice but to deal with us. I don't see the problem."

I threw my arms up and stalked away from him. "The problem is your actions caused today's events to unfold, yet you killed her as if she were no more than an ant."

"She wasn't worth more than that."

I blinked back the tears filling my eyes and folded my arms around my middle. I stopped caring about the blood on me. I felt barren inside. He was so cold, so unfeeling that I barely recognized him. "You had sex with her."

"I've had sex with many. None of them have reacted in such a way."

My heart wrenched in my chest. "There was no caring in Lucifer either."

"Do *not* compare me to him!" he spat.

"I'm not. I know you're different, but you're also very similar. I can't let myself become like him. There are too many in this world I care about for that to happen. All life is precious to me. I could feel the pulse of it before I knew what I was. It has always been a comforting thing to me. To lose that would be like losing my soul."

"You will not lose it."

A realization settled over me. "I will if I become like him. I would bet part of the reason Lucifer is the way he is now, is because he lost that connection to life. You yourself said he can no longer wield life. Maybe he didn't lose the ability in Hell; maybe he somehow lost it beforehand by standing by while something wrong was committed. Maybe he lost it another way, but I cannot take the chance of it happening to me."

"She *fucking* deserved to die!"

This time, he did bellow the words at me. His eyes burned hotter as his claws extended.

"Whatever this thing is between us, or was, is over," I whispered. "You have no care for humans, no care for life—"

"I care for yours more than my own."

"I can't be with someone who thinks so little of my kind."

"They aren't your kind."

"They are to me!" I cried.

He took a deep breath before speaking again. "You are only saying these things because of your dream last night. I understand you fear becoming evil like him, but you never will."

"You can't know that."

"You can't let him get into your head."

"I can't stand by and tolerate this either, Kobal. I can't take the chance I could be twisted as a weapon against you and others I love."

"You are *my* Chosen; there is no denying that. Even if my marks upon your body fade away, demons will still recognize my claim on you, still sense it and know who you belong to."

I tilted my chin up. "I belong to me. I am not a possession."

"You are *mine*."

"Not anymore!"

Turning on my heel, I stormed away from him and flung open the flap dividing the sleeping area from the main tent. Before the flap fell back into place, he was coming in behind me and filling the room with his overwhelming presence. When he reached for my arms, I dodged his grasping hands.

"River," he growled. He loomed over me as he backed me toward the corner of the tent.

His fingers stretched out to touch my cheek, but I slapped his hand away. "Don't touch me."

"I'll do whatever I want to you."

"If you force me to do anything with you, I will *never* forgive you!"

He rested the palms of his hands on either side of my head

against the canvas wall. "I don't have to force you; your body craves mine even now."

Perhaps it was true, but I refused to acknowledge his words, or how stimulated I was by his nearness. I tilted my chin further up. "And it will crave another."

Gold erupted in his eyes as his fangs burst free of his mouth.

Too far, you pushed too far.

Beside my head, his claws punctured the heavy canvas of the tent. I didn't know if he was aware of it or not, but circles of fire erupted to ring his thick wrists. I held my breath. I'd always been so certain he would never hurt me, but I'd never seen him completely lose control before. He may not turn into a wolf, but I felt as if a wild beast stood across from me, one who was being denied its mate and would not stand for it.

"If you ever turn to another, I will wear his balls as a necklace!" he spat.

"You're acting like a possessive, commanding, overbearing monster!"

His nostrils flared and a muscle in his jaw twitched as a vein in his forehead throbbed. Somehow he managed to keep himself restrained from grabbing me. "You knew what I was when this started, yet you still eagerly welcomed me between your thighs and screamed my name."

I felt as if I'd been slapped. He was right, about everything, but things would be different now; they had to be. "It doesn't change that I want you to leave."

He lowered himself so we were eye level with each other. "You should think long and hard about this. I know what you saw was upsetting to you, but it had to be done in order to make a point and keep you safe. I know what happened with Lucifer last night has confused you, but that was what he intended to do. Right now, you're reacting hysterically to both of those things. Once you calm down you will realize that. However, if you tell me again to leave here, I will not come back."

Maybe he might have had a bit of a point. However, the minute he said I was acting hysterically, my hackles rose, and I had to fight not to kick his nuts into his throat while laughing *hysterically*.

Instead, I gritted my teeth and held his eyes as I uttered two words. "Get. Out."

He stared at me for a minute, so still he didn't even breathe. Then his muscles began to vibrate, and he slapped his hands against the side of the tent. The unexpected motion caused me to jump, but I didn't break his gaze. Turning on his heel, he threw up the flap dividing the rooms and departed.

I stood, my knees shaking and my heart shattering as tears spilled from my eyes. My legs finally gave out on me, and I crumpled to the floor as sorrow tore through my heart. *What have I done?* I rested my forehead against the dirt floor when my muscles began to cramp. *What had to be done.*

Maybe it had, maybe it was best to break this off before it could go any further, but I didn't think I'd ever be able to walk again as a spasm wracked my muscles.

I couldn't give up my humanity and who I essentially was for him, or for Lucifer. It would turn me into Lucifer if I did, and I was determined to be the apple that fell far *far* from his tree!

CHAPTER FORTY-THREE

Kobal

"Stay with her!" I snapped at Bale when I stormed out of the tent.

"Wait, Kobal, we have to talk about what just happened!"

I rounded on her. "What about it?"

She took an abrupt step back and folded her hands demurely before her. I'd rarely seen such a position from her. She treated me like her king when it was required, but she'd always been free to say what she had to around me, as had the others. I valued their opinions. Now she looked like she was trying to handle a live bomb. Perhaps she was; I certainly felt as if I was ticking steadily toward a large explosion.

"You have to admit you handled that poorly," she said.

"No human will attempt to harm her again," I grated.

"They barely trusted us before—"

"I don't care if they trust us or not; they will do what has to be done if they want their species to continue."

Bale looked toward the others as if seeking help.

I turned to face all of them. "What do you have to say about it?"

"Nothing," Morax said. "If it had been Verin that woman tried to kill, I would have eaten her head after to make an even bigger point. She deserved to die."

"I would have done the same if it had been Morax," Verin replied. "And I'm not one for head eating."

At least someone could see reason. My fingernails dug into my flesh as I recalled what had transpired with River. She'd calm down; she'd come to her senses once she realized I'd done what had to be done. She was human, and they were overly sensitive creatures.

Since arriving here, she'd been far more resolute and composed than most of the humans thrust into this new existence of knowledge, probably because of her demon and angel side, but she was now showing her more irrational, human side.

She'd been through a lot, and Lucifer had rattled her last night. I knew he was the main source of her irrationality now, but I wasn't used to dealing with humans in a fit of emotion. They cried far more often than we did, and also showed affection and friendship with far more ease than us. Perhaps, I'd handled it poorly, but I wasn't going to apologize for it.

I couldn't have stopped my course of action anyway, not once I smelled River's blood on the air, not once I *saw* it on her pristine flesh. There had been no control after that. I hadn't been able to protect her from Lucifer last night, but I could protect her from that woman and from any possible future attacks from a human.

We were different, but she would understand, and then she would ask me to return to her. She had to; I wasn't going to give her up. There was no separating the two of us. I'd marked her as my Chosen, and she'd done the same to me.

However, she was not fully demon; she didn't feel the bond

as deeply as I did. If she did, she would have had no problem with what had happened today, and she wouldn't be trying to push me away. She would have done the same thing if the roles were reversed.

If she didn't feel the bond as acutely as me, if she didn't feel this twisting, wrenching disconnect from her as deeply as I did, she may not return to me.

No! I refused to consider the possibility. She would come back. There had been enough demon in her to mark me repeatedly and to wield fire. There would be enough to drive her into my arms once more. I couldn't consider the consequences of it being any other way; I would go mad with the loss if I did.

"Did you stake up the remains of that woman?" I inquired of Corson as I tried to keep my riot of emotions under control.

"That is taking it a step too far," Shax replied, ever the voice of reason. "They all know what you did. Talk is flying around the camp already, but to stake her out somewhere will only upset them and make them believe we're monsters."

There was that word again. River had told me I was acting like one, and perhaps I was. It was time to regain control, to react to this situation as I would have before River had become central to my life. As badly as I wanted that woman's body splayed out for all of the humans to see, I had to admit Shax was right.

"I've already ordered it to be done; I can't back down from that now," I said.

"Then have her remains put somewhere they won't see them much," Shax replied.

I rubbed at my chin as I considered his words. "Have her placed in the field above the burned out town where the revenirs attacked. Few people will see her there, but there will be enough of them to know my command was upheld."

Shax's shoulders sagged as he heaved a breath. "Now to

convince the fifty humans you've chosen for this mission they won't be slaughtered."

"There's a good possibility they will be along the way," I muttered.

"True, and they know this, but I think they'd far prefer to know *you're* not the one who is going to do it. We have to make sure they don't tuck tail and run from this mission, Kobal."

I folded my arms over my chest. "I hate catering to this species."

"It's what must be done if we're going to get them to leave here. And you might think about catering to at least one of them a little more, given your Chosen is more human than not."

My lip curled back and Shax backed cautiously away from me. "Fine," I snarled. "I'm going to speak with Mac. She needs a shower; take her over there," I commanded Bale.

"I will," she said.

"Shax, Corson, come with me. The humans like you best."

"That's what comes of leaving them in one piece," Corson muttered.

I glowered at him, but turned on my heel and led the way down the hill toward the town. I didn't bother with trying to clean myself up. I was tired of pretending to be more human than we were. If this species was going to survive, they had to trust and work with us; they had no other options.

Humans scurried to get out of my way when we arrived at the main road and I strode toward the house at the end. Mac answered the door before we arrived there. His gaze raked over my bloodstained clothes before he stepped aside to let me enter.

RIVER

The man who had been working on hand-to-hand combat with a lanky tall woman took a step back and accidentally hit my foot, knocking me off balance. "Sorry!" he yelped and jumped away from me.

He had to easily be two hundred pounds of solid muscle, yet he backed away from me and shot a look at Kobal like he weighed no more than a five-pound Chihuahua. I scowled at him before shooting an infuriated look at Kobal, who merely smiled blandly at me in return. He held his palms up toward me in offering to be my sparring partner.

Instead of going at him and finally releasing some of my pent-up misery by beating at those palms and his infuriatingly enticing physique, I turned away from my newly assigned sparring partner, Corson, and stalked across the clearing to the cooler of water on the side.

I poured myself a cup from the tap as I listened to the grunts, heavy breathing, and thwacks of flesh on flesh while the group of fifty handpicked soldiers worked together. We would be leaving in two days, and I could feel the sand running through the hourglass of my life. None of the soldiers had done any training with me. They either avoided me like I had the plague or treated me as if I were more fragile than glass.

Either way, I'd officially become an outsider all the way around. I didn't fit in with the humans; they were petrified to brush against me. The demons were mostly protective of me, but distant. Bale and Corson had started to have more interaction with me as they'd been assigned to replace Kobal and work with me in private on my ability to wield life.

I didn't comment on the fact Kobal had told me to keep it a secret. We may not be speaking, but I knew he wouldn't do anything to endanger me. He trusted them, and I was beginning to trust them more too, though I kept how good I was really getting at it from all of them.

Kobal and I continued to avoid each other like the mature adults we were. Well, I wasn't sure if being over fifteen hundred years old qualified him as an adult, maybe an ancient would be a better term for him. Me, I had mastered the art of ignoring him when all I wanted was to throw myself into his arms. The marks on my neck were fading, and the more they did, the more freaked I became over the knowledge they would one day be gone for good.

The realization robbed my breath from me and caused my chest to clench so fiercely I couldn't draw a new breath. I needed those marks *back*.

I wanted to feel loved and cherished, even if it was in the demon way that could result in human head removal.

I shuddered at the reminder of Eileen's warm blood splattering over my face. I wanted to know I would *never* become like Lucifer, or that I couldn't be used as the one weapon he'd never had against Kobal. Kobal had said a demon would still recognize me as his if the marks faded from me, but perhaps without them they wouldn't think of me as a weapon. They would think of me as the Chosen who wasn't. I could hope anyway. I'd rather die than be the one who brought him down.

And then there was Lucifer's gift. Every night I lay away thinking about it, quaking in dread and yearning for the security of Kobal's arms. What could the gift possibly be? Nothing good, of that much I was certain, but how awful would it be? And when would it come? I had no doubt I'd recognize it for what it was the second I saw it.

I didn't look at Kobal when I felt the heat of him against my back. My body tensed as longing and suffering tore through me, shaking my muscles and burning my eyes. *It's for the best,* I reminded myself for the thousandth time.

It did little good.

"You have to get back on the field," he said gruffly.

Finishing off my water, I placed my cup down next to the cooler and turned away. I walked across the field toward Corson. He'd always been the most approachable of the demons with his easygoing smile, handsome face, and the shiny earrings dangling from the tips of his ears. He smiled at me now before glancing at Kobal.

I didn't follow Corson's gaze; Kobal's face had been emblazoned in my mind in the three days since our fight. I couldn't look at him right now without crying, and I couldn't think about the fact Bale had stayed in the main tent last night instead of him. My heart had been sliced open and shredded by the possibility he may have returned to the fire last night while I'd cried myself into a fitful sleep.

You're the one who told him to get out.

And he's the one who told you you were acting hysterically after tearing the head off of someone.

The same someone who tried to kill *you.*

Sometimes I really hated my inner voice.

I thrust my shoulders back and stopped before Corson. I despised the pity in his eyes and the way he glanced at Kobal again, as if asking for permission. I would guarantee he was. He raised his hands before him and took up a fighter's stance.

"Don't pity me," I grated through my teeth at him.

His citrine-colored eyes flickered over me, and his head tilted to the side, causing one of the stars in his ears to twinkle as it spun around. "No pity from me," he replied as he moved around me.

"It sure seems that way," I said as I jabbed at his hands.

Corson moved to the left to avoid a kick I launched at him. "Maybe some, but not for the reasons you think."

"Then why?" I demanded.

"Because there is enough demon in you to have driven you to mark him too. I have never met my Chosen, but I know how much my parents cherished each other. When my father was killed by Lucifer, it destroyed my mother. She threw herself into the fires afterward."

Tears sprang into my eyes at the thought of such loss and pain as I stopped moving. Freaking tears, *again.* I wiped them hastily from my eyes. "I'm sorry," I whispered and started moving again when Kobal stepped toward us.

"It was centuries ago, but I know how strong the Chosen bond is. If you're feeling a fraction of the grief they did, then I do feel sorry for you."

I glanced away from him and focused on the sun dipping toward the horizon. Pinks, oranges, and reds streaked over the clouds floating across the sky. "But you feel I'm an idiot or selfish for resisting the bond that destroyed your mother."

"Kobal told Bale and me about your dream with Lucifer. Fearing for the life of the one you love, and you do love him...?"

I gave a brisk nod when Corson's voice trailed off questioningly. I may not have told Kobal that I did, but there was no denying it. "Yes."

"Fearing for his life, and for what you might become, and suffering unimaginable sorrow to protect the one you love is neither selfish nor idiotic."

My eyes slid back to him. I was half tempted to throw my arms around him and hug him. However, I had a feeling it might end up in his limbs being tossed around if I did. They'd grow back, but I seriously doubted he'd talk to me again after. "Thank you," I whispered.

His head tilted to the side as he studied me. "You stood up to him, which means you can more than hold your own against any of us, including Lucifer."

With those words, Corson had just become the closest thing to a friend, outside of Kobal, I'd had since arriving here, and I so desperately needed someone to listen.

"One thing though," he said quietly.

"What's that?"

"He's not going to be able to let you go. It's not possible for us. You're going to have to decide, when you're not so angry and frightened." I shot him an irritated look, but he merely smiled in return. "Your feelings for him terrify you. They're far deeper than anything a human would feel and you know it. Lucifer has unnerved you, and what Kobal did to the woman was disturbing, but you must realize by now it was an instinctive reaction for him to protect you and not meant as one of maliciousness."

I recalled Kobal's words about the mark Ziwa being a blessing and a curse, and how there was nothing more dangerous than a hound when its mate was threatened. He'd warned me many times he was capable of being vicious, but I still had never expected to see that from him.

"I do," I admitted.

"You reacted out of panic and shock."

"Yeah," I muttered.

"You are going to have to decide if you really *can* live without him, or if you just need some time to come to grips with who and what you are now. Because if you can live without him, you are going to have to get far away from him after all of this is settled. Your presence will only bring him more hurt."

My head canted to the side as I stared at him. The easygoing, earring-wearing demon was far more perceptive than I'd believed him to be. If Kobal knew he was discussing this so openly with me, he may kill him.

"I know." Though I couldn't picture my life without Kobal in it. We may not be speaking or touching right now, but I was still able to see him every day. The idea of not being able to do so nearly drove me to my knees.

"Will he survive without me?" I whispered in a strangled voice.

"Will you survive without him?"

No.

He grinned at me and sidestepped to avoid the leg I kicked at him. "I can understand keeping your distance if you think it really will help protect him; you have to figure that out on your own also. Your instincts are strong, maybe a little frazzled right now, but they're there, so listen to them. The sooner the better would be good too. Kobal was never a ball of laughs before; now I'd rather play keep away with a madagan than deal with him."

I couldn't stop the burst of laughter his words caused to escape from me. I chanced a glance at Kobal to find him glaring at us across the clearing. "I'll figure it out soon," I promised.

"Thank you."

I stayed focused on Corson as we moved around the clearing. Everything had been moving so quickly and become entrenched so fast it had overwhelmed me. What mattered most was stopping the looming threat to the humans and demons and possibly even the angels.

What mattered was in two days' time, we would be leaving here, and we would be exposed to things I'd never dreamed of before. Things that would make my worst nightmares seem like pleasant daydreams in comparison. I couldn't allow the hole in my heart to drag me down and distract me. I couldn't let anything stand in the way of what was to come.

I would survive this. I would do what had to be done to keep Bailey and Gage alive, and one day, I would return to them.

My entire life my mother had told me I was evil, that I was the spawn of Satan. I wondered if maybe somehow she'd known my heritage, or if her rotten mind had accidentally latched onto those vicious words and repeated them often. My ancestor, the one I refused to call my father, believed I would also become evil, but I would prove them both wrong. I simply had to.

Kobal didn't believe in pure evil, but after meeting Lucifer, I knew he was wrong. I'd endured years of my mother telling me I was a monster, and now Satan himself had told me it would one day come to pass. I didn't entirely believe him, but I did believe something had made him the way he was and that there was a possibility it could happen to me too.

Kobal would never believe I could become like Lucifer, and because of that, I worried I could be his downfall. I wouldn't be used as a way to destroy the man I loved. I would figure out some way for that not to happen. Even if it meant I had to put distance between us, and I could never be with him again.

I kept that thought firmly in mind as I continued to do a fighting dance with Corson. I'd been weak and lost when I'd been forced to come here. I'd had no idea why I was different from others or what I could be capable of. Now I was a trained fighter with a better understanding and growing control over the powers that had once ruled me.

I may not have liked the revelation of my heritage, but I now knew why I had these abilities. Instead of being frightened of them, and what would happen if someone else found about them, I'd come to enjoy the fact they were a part of me and I no longer feared discovery.

My world had been completely turned upside down these past couple of months, but in two days, a new journey would begin, and I was ready to face whatever awaited us out there.

Read on for an excerpt from *Carved* Book 2 in the

series, or download now and continue reading:
brendakdavies.com/Cvdwb

Stay in touch on updates and new releases by joining the mailing list:
brendakdavies.com/ESBKDNews

Visit the Erica Stevens/Brenda K. Davies Book Club on Facebook for exclusive giveaways and all things book related. Come join the fun:
brendakdavies.com/ESBKDBookClub

SNEAK PEEK

CARVED, THE ROAD TO HELL SERIES, BOOK 2

River,

As the perilous journey across a country I'd long thought destroyed begins, I don't know who I am anymore or what I'm becoming. My abilities grow stronger with each passing day, as does the fear of what comes next. All I know is that I will do anything to avoid becoming like Lucifer, and to protect those I love, even if that means protecting them from me.

Kobal,

No matter what it takes, I will keep River safe, even if my actions end up driving a wedge between us. River is mine to protect, no matter how hard that might be to do now that our journey has begun. I won't stop until Lucifer is destroyed, won't stop until I claim my throne, and she will be by my side when I do. It's all just a matter of keeping her alive until then.

~

Doors closed around me as the humans exited their trucks and moved in closer. In the stillness following, I could hear something flapping in the breeze and spotted the tattered remains of a curtain hitting the side of the building as it blew out of one of the windows.

Corson and Bale moved to flank River. The seconds turned into a full minute before a single ticking sound drew my attention to a broken window higher up. A single, gray claw had appeared to curve around the edge of the steel frame of the window. My gaze fixated on it as the claw tapped against the frame. It was impossible to tell exactly what kind of demon or Hell creature we were facing without seeing its whole body.

Then a head poked over the top of the window. My lips skimmed back, and my fangs lengthened as flames erupted from my fingers and licked toward my shoulders.

"Gargoyles," Corson growled.

"Are you serious?" a human blurted.

"Yes," Corson replied.

I watched the creature crawl out from over the top of the broken window. It's scaled, slate-colored skin cracked and flaked off as it leisurely climbed down the building on all fours. The sticky, glue-like substance on its palms gave it traction as it moved. Its three-foot-long tail flicked back and forth like a bored cat on the hunt, and there was no doubt this monstrosity was on the hunt.

There were few things in life I found truly ugly, gargoyles were one of them. They had pushed in snouts, mustard-colored eyes, and razor-sharp teeth that clacked together as they closed in on their prey. That clacking sound increased in intensity as it continued its descent and its tail twitched faster.

Slate-colored wings unfurled from its back and flapped once. They crashed against a remaining pane of glass, causing jagged fissures across the surface. Startled cries escaped a few of the humans. They had to keep it together, or they would all be slaughtered, and we couldn't afford to lose them so early in the journey. I needed their extra protection for River.

"Guns ready!" I commanded. "And whatever you do, don't let them scratch you with their claws!"

"Them?" a soldier asked.

As if on cue, at least fifteen more gargoyles emerged from inside to perch on the broken edges of the building. They sat as still as their stone counterparts in the human realm. Humans had come so close to recreating things they'd glimpsed through the veil that had once separated our worlds; gargoyles may have been one of the closest.

The gargoyle's stillness and their ability to remain unmoving for years on end was well known by the demon world as they often entered a hibernation state when they were unable to kill and feed. Kept separate from all demons in Hell, behind the second seal, gargoyles were often reserved to punish demons who tried to launch an uprising and failed, or for the worst souls who entered Hell.

They were a special form of punishment as their claws contained a paralyzing agent they used on their prey. When their victim was paralyzed, the gargoyles would peel the skin from their victims, one strip at a time, and leisurely eat it in front of them.

Once there was nothing but muscle and bone left, the creatures would wait until the skin regenerated before starting the whole process all over again. I'd witnessed it once, and though I'd appreciated the brutality and torment of the act, I'd never gone back to watch it again.

They all fluttered their three-foot-wide wings at once, causing a breeze to blow down the building and over all those gathered below. A wailing cry escaped them before they launched simultaneously into the air. Gunfire exploded in the air as they swooped down on us.

~

Download *Carved* and continue reading now:
brendakdavies.com/Cvdwb

~

Stay in touch on updates, sales, and new releases by joining to the mailing list:
brendakdavies.com/ESBKDNews

Visit the Erica Stevens/Brenda K. Davies Book Club on Facebook for exclusive giveaways and all things book related. Come join the fun:
brendakdavies.com/ESBKDBookClub

FIND THE AUTHOR

Erica Stevens/Brenda K. Davies Mailing List:
brendakdavies.com/ESBKDNews

Facebook: brendakdavies.com/BKDfb

Erica Stevens/Brenda K. Davies Book Club:
brendakdavies.com/ESBKDBookClub

Instagram: brendakdavies.com/BKDInsta
Twitter: brendakdavies.com/BKDTweet
Website: www.brendakdavies.com

ALSO FROM THE AUTHOR

Books written under the pen name

Brenda K. Davies

The Vampire Awakenings Series

Awakened (Book 1)

Destined (Book 2)

Untamed (Book 3)

Enraptured (Book 4)

Undone (Book 5)

Fractured (Book 6)

Ravaged (Book 7)

Consumed (Book 8)

Unforeseen (Book 9)

Forsaken (Book 10)

Relentless (Book 11)

Legacy (Book 12)

The Alliance Series

Eternally Bound (Book 1)

Bound by Vengeance (Book 2)

Bound by Darkness (Book 3)

Bound by Passion (Book 4)

Bound by Torment (Book 5)

Bound by Danger (Book 6)

Bound by Deception (Book 7)

Bound by Fate (Book 8)

Bound by Blood (Book 9)

Bound by Love (Book 10)

The Road to Hell Series

Good Intentions (Book 1)

Carved (Book 2)

The Road (Book 3)

Into Hell (Book 4)

Hell on Earth (Book 5)

Into the Abyss (Book 6)

Kiss of Death (Book 7)

Edge of the Darkness (Book 8)

The Shadow Realms

Shadows of Fire (Book 1)

Shadows of Discovery (Book 2)

Shadows of Betrayal (Book 3)

Shadows of Fury (Book 4)

Shadows of Destiny (Book 5)

Shadows of Light (Book 6)

Wicked Curses (Book 7)

Sinful Curses (Book 8)

Gilded Curses (Book 9)

Whispers of Ruin (Book 10)

Secrets of Ruin (Book 11)

Tempest of Shadows

A Tempest of Shadows (Book 1)

A Tempest of Thieves (Book 2)

A Tempest of Revelations (Book 3)

A Tempest of Intrigue (Book 4)

A Tempest of Chaos (Book 5)

Historical Romance

A Stolen Heart

Books written under the pen name

Erica Stevens

The Coven Series

Nightmares (Book 1)

The Maze (Book 2)

Dream Walker (Book 3)

The Captive Series

Captured (Book 1)

Renegade (Book 2)

Refugee (Book 3)

Salvation (Book 4)

Redemption (Book 5)

Vengeance (Book 6)

Unbound (Book 7)

Broken (Book 8 - Prequel)

The Kindred Series

Kindred (Book 1)

Ashes (Book 2)

Kindled (Book 3)

Inferno (Book 4)

Phoenix Rising (Book 5)

The Fire & Ice Series

Frost Burn (Book 1)

Arctic Fire (Book 2)

Scorched Ice (Book 3)

The Ravening Series

The Ravening (Book 1)

Taken Over (Book 2)

Reclamation (Book 3)

The Survivor Chronicles

The Upheaval (Book 1)

The Divide (Book 2)

The Forsaken (Book 3)

The Risen (Book 4)

ABOUT THE AUTHOR

Brenda K. Davies is the USA Today Bestselling author of the Vampire Awakening Series, Alliance Series, Road to Hell Series, Hell on Earth Series, The Shadow Realms Series, and historical romantic fiction. She also writes under the pen name, Erica Stevens. When not out with friends and family, she can be found at home with her husband, son, and pets.

Made in the USA
Monee, IL
17 February 2025

12485499R00233